CONTENT WARNING

The book you're about to read contains sexually explicit content, profanity, depictions of death (youth included), gore and trauma, and other topics that may be distressing to some readers.
Please proceed with caution.

To Zuko and Mackenzie,
My real-life Daeanimus'.

I love you both more than anything in this world, and any other world.

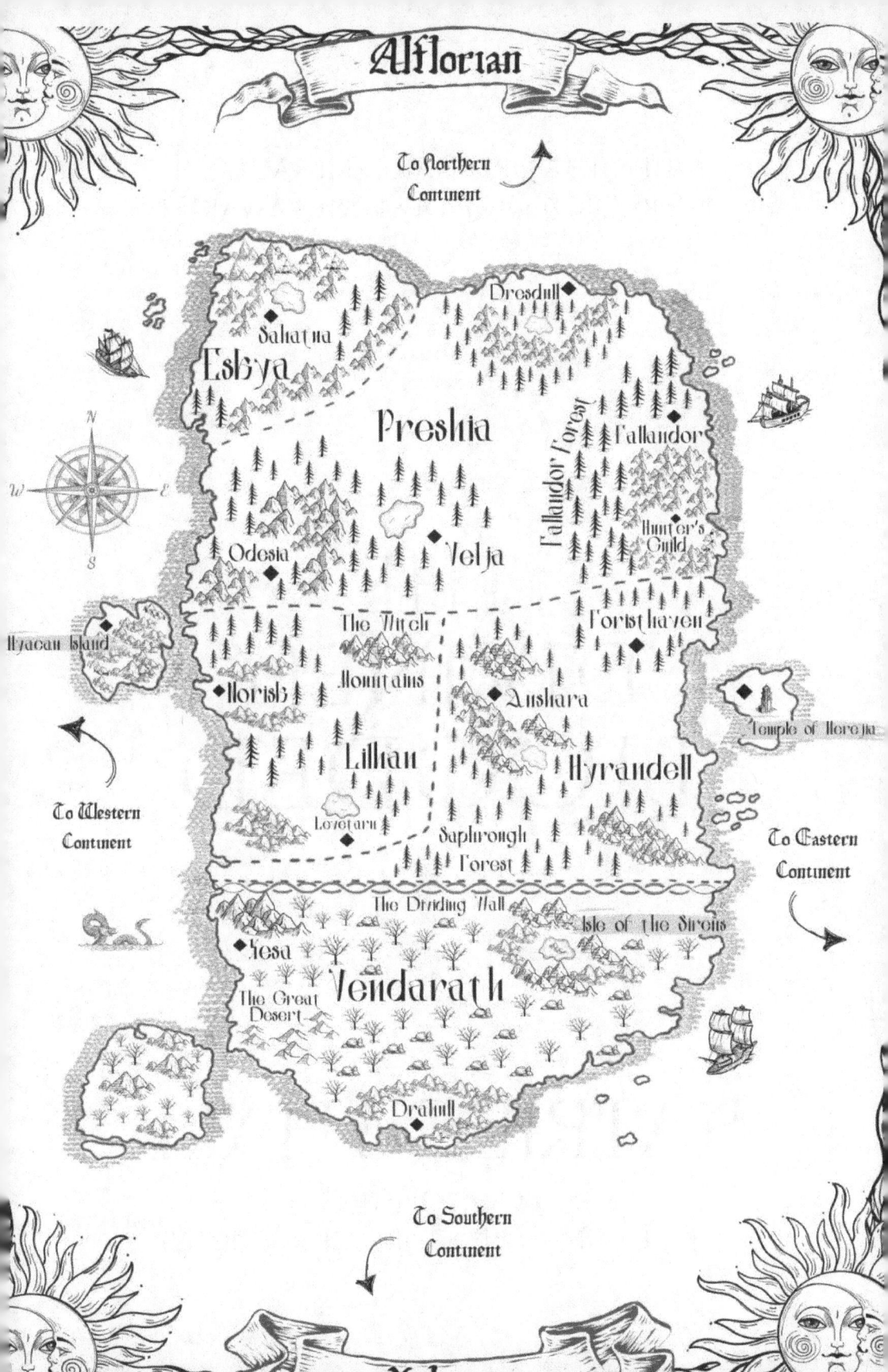

WHEN THE ORDINARY EMBRACE THE
EXTRAORDINARY, DESTINIES AWAKEN.

THE DIVINELY BLOODED

KATRIECE HALL

BOOK ONE IN
THE DIVINELY BLOODED CHRONICLES

CHAPTER 1

The blaring, infuriating shrill of the seven o'clock phone alarm sounded throughout the room, filling the spring air with the dread of a new day. Friday, however. Thank god. Dawn was just breaking through the sheer-curtained windows behind Alexis' bed as she let out an exasperated groan, reaching over lazily to turn her deafening alarm off, frowning as she did so.

She slowly lifted herself from the comfort of her bed, which she could feel beckoning for her to lie back down and call in sick. The temptation was near impossible not to act upon, but she, like most people, had rent and bills to pay.

Alexis begrudgingly slipped on her athleisure wear for her morning run and tied her hair back into a ponytail.

Upon bidding *good morning* to Aspen, her young German Shepherd, Alexis found the dog was all ready to go, her neon pink lead secure between her teeth as she waited by the front door, tail

wagging excitedly. Alexis let out a quiet laugh, patting Aspen on the head and taking the slobbery lead.
She'd barely attached it to her collar before Aspen had practically dragged her out of the house.

The neighbourhood was slowly waking as Alexis noticed parents readying their kids for school and heading to work themselves. She kept a steady pace, the music blaring through her earphones as Aspen ran ahead, quickly growing tired from her earlier eagerness.

Once they'd returned home, Alexis slipped into the shower and changed into her work attire.

She poured herself a dark-roast coffee— something she needed just to get through the day, zoning out as she sipped from her mug, the neighbourhood ambience filling her ears.

Following a quick morning read of her current romance-fantasy novel and feeding Aspen her breakfast, she bid the dog farewell, Aspen's sad eyes watching on as her owner stepped out of the house. As she walked to her car, fumbling for her keys, Alexis noticed a dark figure in the corner of her vision. Snapping her head up to get a good look, however, she noticed there was nothing there. At least, nothing out of the ordinary.

With one last, longing look at the entrance to her town house, where she knew Aspen was sitting on the other side, Alexis pulled out of her driveway.

Once the long, gruelling workday was finally over, filled with irate clients and a less-than-tolerable boss, Alexis slumped into her car and switched on the ignition, pumping the heater to a warm-enough temperature to keep out the crisp breeze. Bizarre, given that summer was just around the corner. Her phone buzzed in her pocket, and as she fished it out, a text from her father appeared across the screen. *Come over for dinner tonight? The whole family will be there,* it read.

Despite preferring the alternative scenario where she instead spent the night lying in bed, Aspen cuddled by her side, and trashy-reality entertainment playing on the television, Alexis replied with a simple, *Sure, looking forward to it.*

She supposed it wasn't the worst scenario to be thrown into, despite her social metre having nearly run out. Alexis loved her family - they were genuinely great to be around and helped to distract her from the recent heartbreak she'd experienced, which occupied her mind nearly every minute of every day.

She still hadn't changed her lock screen, which she now stared at, not consciously aware of how long, exactly, she'd been staring at it for. The photo of her ex, Mitchell, cuddling Aspen close, and smiling with that gorgeous smile she loved so much made her heart ache a little. It was still fresh, had been just over a week since he'd sat her down and told her it was over.

It's nothing you've done wrong, nothing either of us has done wrong, he'd said. *We're just too different. We have different goals in life and it's only going to cause pain and confusion in the long run.*

Initially, Alexis had been mad and confused and heartbroken. She was *still* heartbroken, but with time and space, she'd realised he was completely right.

What started out as exciting and new indeed slowly became difficult and painful. It's not that they were toxic or terrible to each other - Mitchell had been perfect, at least in her eyes.

He'd been thoughtful, loving, predictable, sure... But he was the ideal boyfriend. *Had* been the ideal boyfriend.

That, however, was the key word; *ideal.* When he'd come to her and said his dreams didn't include travelling or being adventurous, or stepping out of his comfort zone, and when it had proved to be something he wouldn't budge on, they'd both realised it wouldn't work in five, ten, fifteen years.

She had settled at the ripe age of twenty-one.

Alexis was still young and full of desire to experience the best in life. Full of hope and determination and great potential, and hurt as it may, she deserved better than to settle. That fact, she was slowly coming to terms with.

At least Mitchell had finally put his foot down and spoken up. Alexis, though she tried to deny it behind her hurt, found she was becoming more and more understanding of his decision.

She let out a humourless laugh at how sad her romantic life had become, shaking her head. Alexis had always yearned to be loved in a way that made her feel breathless all the time.

The type of love she'd read about in her romance novels. The type of love she was convinced didn't *actually* exist. At least, not in this world.

It was a bitter way to think, but how could she not? Her parents had a failed marriage, her own mother skipping out on them before Alexis could even remember her. Though, despite her lack of faith in acquiring that kind of love, she still found herself quietly hopeful.

CHAPTER 2

Having already dropped in to collect Aspen on the way to her father's place, Alexis pulled into the tree-lined driveway of her family home. It was an old house; a classic. Her father had basically renovated the entire thing, so while it was an *old* house by definition, it still looked modern enough. She loved this house, and she and her siblings had spent most afternoons exploring the wooded area surrounding it during their childhood. The first time she'd brought Aspen here, they'd spent half the day wandering around the forest land, Aspen sniffing every log and tree and rock, taking in all the birds and woodland animals. It was a beautiful place filled with some of her favourite memories.

Upon entering the house, her two siblings, Amelia, her older sister, and Sam, her younger brother, greeted Alexis. Aspen immediately ran to Amelia, struggling to contain her excitement. Aspen had always been very fond of Amelia; perhaps it was her likeness to Alexis, their similar voices.

Sam gave Alexis a tight hug, towering over her by at least a foot, despite being a couple of years younger than her. They chatted about their lives, Sam asking Alexis how she was coping with, well, everything, and Alexis shrugging and giving a bland, "It is what it is," in response.

"How's your girlfriend?" she asked, trying to give off the impression that she actually cared about his not-so-likeable other half. Amelia watched carefully from the ground as Sam ran a hand through his short brown hair. Alexis looked between her siblings quizzically, furrowing her brows in confusion.

"We broke up," he finally said, wincing. Alexis tried to hide her amusement, her rejoice.

She'd never liked his girlfriend — she was entitled, selfish, rude, and didn't like dogs, much less Aspen, which was the biggest red flag of all in Alexis' eyes.

Poor Sam. He'd always worn his heart on his sleeve; he was such a sweetheart and had always treated his flings, as Alexis liked to call them, with more respect than they'd deserved. She was biased, sure, but Alexis strongly believed that Sam had always deserved someone worthy of him, being the protective big sister she was. Unfortunately, however, love often made people blind, her brother finding himself constantly victim to the notion. But, as Sam explained why he'd broken up with his now-ex girlfriend, Alexis gained a newfound respect for him. In short, he saw her for who she really was; toxic, to put it plainly. Alexis hugged her brother, trying to hide her small, grateful smile.

The irresistible smell of barbequed meats wafted into the house, and Alexis, flanked by her siblings and Aspen, walked out to the back patio to where the source of that smell was coming from. Their dad was flipping sausages and steaks when he noticed the addition of Alexis' presence, pulling the lid of the barbeque down and striding over to her.

"Hello, worry child," he said jokingly as he embraced her in a one-armed hug. Alexis rolled her eyes, but gave a small, apologetic smile.

She'd known her family had worried about her this past week, and her dodging calls and texts and communications of any kind didn't help ease their minds. Like she'd needed space with Mitch, she'd needed with everyone.

Space, if just to clear her mind and not act out irrationally, say things she might regret. Besides, it was about time she left her house for something other than work. This was good. She needed this. Alexis had told none of her friends yet, not even her co-workers, mostly because she wasn't ready for everyone to know. Plus, she was sick of explaining why they'd broken up, if only because it was a reminder of the last three years of her life she'd just lost. Her family, to her relief, didn't pry any further.

Alexis shook her head, snapping the negative thoughts from her mind. She was in her prime - she worked a job that, granted, she didn't love, but paid well. She had her dog, her family, friends, and a generally good life. A *good* life, she had to remind herself, even if it didn't always feel that way.

As she and her family sat down to eat, her stomach grumbling, Alexis again noticed a shadow out of the corner of her eye. She found herself puzzled at how it felt as though the shadow was right there, like she *wasn't* imagining it. And yet, it was nowhere to be seen when she looked up.

As she returned her attention to her plate, loading it with various meats and salad, shaking her head and scoffing at her imagination, she flinched at Aspen's sudden outburst, the dog barking angrily with her attention fixed on the wooded area behind the house.

CHAPTER
3

Aspen grew more and more agitated with each passing second, pacing back and forth, her eyes never shifting from the woods. Everyone shared confused glances before Alexis stood from the table and hurriedly walked over to Aspen, hoping to calm her down.

"Hey girl, what's wrong?" she asked whilst trying and failing to get her dog's attention.

Aspen just continued staring toward the woods, her quiet growl growing louder with each pace. The barking had ceased, but the growling didn't ease Alexis' nerves. She looked up, trying to figure out, to *see* if there was anything in particular that was setting Aspen off. A deer, perhaps? Maybe even a bold coyote. There was, however, nothing Alexis could see or hear.

She shook her head, guiding a resistant Aspen back to the table. Five minutes passed, and Aspen had seemingly forgotten about whatever was lurking in the woods, quelling everyone's anxiety and confusion.

---···⟩⟩ ☀ ⟨⟨···---

Following dinner, Alexis was finishing clearing the table when she heard a blood-curdling, animalistic shriek. Her head snapped toward the woods behind the house, the exact area Aspen was so curious about earlier. The young canine was at her side instantly, growling with a ferocity Alexis had never heard from the dog before. Aspen's hackles rose as she took up a defensive stance, growling and baring her teeth.

Amelia burst outside, asking, "What was that?"

Alexis turned to see a terrified expression flooding her sister's face, and she slowly shook her head in disbelief. "I have no idea."

As she turned back, Aspen was already running towards the source of that noise.

"Aspen!" she and Amelia both screamed in unison, but the young dog had already cleared the back fence, running with all her energy directly into the forest. Without hesitation, Alexis began sprinting after her, not entirely sure she'd even be able to catch up. She could hear her brother and father yelling after her, but she ignored them as she quickly covered the distance between the house and the woods.

The longer Alexis chased after Aspen, the less she could see her. Whatever had her so spooked, Aspen certainly wasn't slowing down to find it.

Alexis began panting, her throat growing dry, her legs aching with each rushed, desperate step. As she approached the edge of the woods, Alexis lost sight of Aspen completely.

She began scanning the darkness as best she could, scrambling for her phone and urgently clicking the flashlight button.

Alexis called Aspen's name in as quiet a voice as she could muster, not wanting to draw the attention of whatever animal had made that sound.

A low bark came from within the forest, and Alexis made her way to it, pushing her way through the tall bushes.

Her heart raced, and she carefully felt her way through the forest, stepping over logs, only to trip over a root or log. She couldn't see anything, could only hear the eerie sounds emanating from the surrounding forest. Something soft brushed against her leg, and she immediately lowered her hand to what she knew was waiting for her: Aspen.

A whimper of relief escaped Alexis' lips as she crouched and cuddled the dog close, cursing silently at her for running away.

When Alexis rose from her spot to make her way back to the house, a blinding, bright light shone in the corner of her eye, and her head snapped toward the source. She held a hand to her eyes to shield against it. Within seconds, it had disappeared. Before she could fathom the source behind it, Aspen began barking again with the same ferociousness as before.

The sound of heavy footsteps neared; one after another. Alexis began panicking as she contemplated what it could be, reaching for Aspen to urge her to quiet down. Aspen's barking only increased as the footsteps grew louder, closing in.

Tears rolled down Alexis' face as she became desperate, reaching for Aspen, trying to force her down to the ground, to force her to quiet, but nothing worked. The heavy footsteps growing nearer, Alexis whispered, "Fuck it," before grabbing Aspen's collar and hauling the dog to her feet.

They ran without hesitation, not daring to look back. Aspen yelped as Alexis jerked her collar with all her strength, but quickly broke into a sprint next to her owner, the two of them ducking under branches and bounding over logs.

Whatever was behind them began running, its footsteps becoming heavier with each passing second. Once Alexis could see that Aspen had gained a few metres ahead of her, once she could see the house only a hundred yards away, she dared a glance over her shoulder to whatever it was they'd been running from. What she saw was not explainable - something not of this world. It looked like a large canine, with deep grey fur, a red glow emanating from inside its body. Its eyes shone a dark orange, its teeth and paws the size of a bear's. Her breath caught in her throat, and she hadn't realised that she'd slowed upon taking in the creature's unrealistic, hellish anatomy.

As she turned back around, noting that Aspen was nearly at the house, Alexis bumped into something hard. No, *someone*. Before she could fall to the ground, whoever she'd run into grabbed her shoulders, held her upright and whirled her around, positioning themself between her and the creature barrelling towards them.

The stranger towered over her, speaking in a deep, masculine voice. With the darkness of the forest, she couldn't quite make out their features.

"Run. Don't look back, just *run*."

Before she could say a word, before she could even try to recognise her saviour, they'd turned their back to her, now sprinting towards that creature. She didn't hesitate as she spun toward the house, racing with all her energy, not daring to look back. Behind her, that same shriek broke out, followed by sounds of grunting, bones breaking, and metal clashing with flesh. Then, complete silence.

The bright light that shone moments ago appeared once more and died out just as quickly.

When Alexis eventually made it back to the house, after what felt like hours, her father and brother were waiting for her at the fence line, Aspen at their sides.

"What the hell was that about?" her father exclaimed.

Alexis let out a deep breath before scanning the patio and surrounding area, ignoring her father's question.

"Wait... where's Amelia?" she asked.

Sam replied, "We thought she was with you? After you ran into the forest, she followed you."

Alexis began to panic as she turned around, scanning the edge of the woods for any sign of her sister. Not that the darkness let her see much at all.

"I'll go back and find her," Alexis stammered, her breathing ragged.

Amelia was in that forest with whatever that thing was, defenceless, probably injured. Probably even...

Alexis shook the dark thoughts from her head, refusing to let that be the case.

Sam paused in voicing a reply, his wide eyes on the forest, and Alexis followed his stare. Amelia was running from the woods, blood covering half her body, splattered over her clothes, her face, in her hair. Alexis felt a wave of relief wash over her as her sister ran towards the house, though it quickly turned to panic once more as Alexis realised she *had* likely been hurt by the amount of blood covering Amelia's body.

It was a surprise she could even run.

The adrenaline, perhaps, if she'd experienced the same hell as Alexis. Alexis began running towards her sister, who showed no sign of slowing, no sign of exhaustion or blood loss.

She was just *running*.

They met halfway, embracing each other, relief taking over once more. Alexis scanned Amelia, trying desperately to figure out where she'd been bleeding from.

"It's not mine," Amelia breathed. Alexis looked her up and down, confusion and worry taking over.

CHAPTER 4

Amelia had run into the forest after her sister and Aspen, ignoring the cries of her father and brother - no doubt they'd heard that screech, too. It would have been impossible for anyone within a three-mile radius to *not* have heard it.

"Lex," Amelia whispered as she neared the edge of the forest, completely losing sight of her sister and Aspen.

She hadn't seen where they'd entered the woods. In this darkness, it could take forever to find them, or, at least, before whatever had made that sound did.

"Lex!" Amelia whispered again, an octave higher than before. Only the silence of the forest filled the air, even the crickets quieting their tune. Amelia gulped as she realised what the silence meant — there was a predator in these woods, so deadly that even the animals of the forest had gone deathly quiet.

She heard a rustle of leaves to her left, but only the darkened shapes of trees filled her vision. Just as she was about to change her direction, a brief, blinding light shone to the north of her. Amelia raised an arm to her face, trying not to lose her vision from the source of that brightness, before it disappeared.

"What the hell," she whispered, as a low, guttural growl sounded to her right. Amelia peeled her eyes away from whatever had been shining ahead of her, and her body went limp.

Her heart raced as an enormous creature emerged from the bushes. It was easily the size of a grizzly. Grey coated its fur, a bright red emanating from within its body. Glowing orange eyes sized her up before settling on her own.

"What the hell…" Amelia repeated in a trembling voice, slowly backing away a step, not sure what to do or how to act. She nearly tripped over a stick as her eyes darted between it and whatever was now stalking her into a corner. Amelia considered what a flimsy weapon it would make, if it would even give her an advantage in this impossible situation. She ever so slowly leaned down to grab it, never once taking her eyes off that hellish creature now only twenty feet away from her, closing in quickly.

Her eyes scanned the surrounding area, hoping she could at least see that Aspen and Alexis weren't, in fact, in the immediate area, lest they avoid the inevitable danger she was about to face. So long as they were safe, she could serve as a distraction, even if she didn't favour the idea of being mauled to death.

Taking her eyes off the beast was a mistake, because in a split second, the creature was now barrelling toward her, teeth gnashing, its giant paws making the earth shudder with each heavy step. Accepting her fate, Amelia knelt, pointing the stick upwards toward her impending doom, averting her gaze and burying her face in her shoulder, her heart beating rapidly. The footsteps halted suddenly.

After a moment, Amelia dared to look in front of her to see a figure now stood in her path, their back to her. She could see blood dripping between the figure's legs, the creature standing limp. In a swift movement, the figure removed what appeared to be a knife — no, a *dagger* — from the creature's head.

Blood sprayed, coating them both from head to toe. Still kneeling, Amelia lowered the stick and could have sworn her heart stopped. Her body trembling, she raised her shaking hands in front of her face, taking in the gore and blood bathing her.

Looking up at the figure now facing her, Amelia took in her impossible beauty. It was a woman, tall and lean, with beautiful brown skin and light blue eyes, cleaning her dagger on her clothes. Her moonlight hair was braided from root to end, tied back to keep out of her face. She wore onyx leathers, and more daggers were strapped to her thighs. Her face was grave as she stared down at Amelia, a hint of concern in her expression. Instantly, her face snapped into a warrior focus as she offered Amelia a hand. Still shocked, Amelia slowly accepted the woman's hand, her eyes darting between her saviour and the creature that had nearly claimed her life.

Amelia rose to her feet, noticing just how much taller the woman stood over her, and their eyes met. She could have sworn the ocean shone in those eyes — they were the most beautiful blue she'd ever seen.

"Run, now," the woman whispered, an urgent command.

Amelia suddenly found herself doing just that, stumbling out of the woods before she could even collect her thoughts. In all her shock, she'd completely forgotten that Aspen and Alexis could still be in there. Just as a shriek broke through the air, that light returning and disappearing once more, she turned to look, but only found woodland behind her, darkness once again falling upon it. No bright light, no sign of the warrior. No sign that any of what had just happened *actually* happened, other than the thick, red blood coating half her body.

CHAPTER 5

Sam and their father looked as though they'd seen a ghost, rightfully so, the former going deathly pale and falling mute as he took in Amelia's clothes, her hair, her skin. Their dad, however, just continued to ask Amelia what had happened for her to be covered in so much blood. She and Alexis shared a look, still attempting to catch their breath as they struggled to comprehend what had just happened.

"You didn't hear?" Alexis stammered, trying to steady her breathing as she signalled to the forest behind them with a hand.

"We were attacked," Amelia coughed out. "It was... a wolf — it had to have been, because what I saw— what I *thought* I saw couldn't possibly be real."

"It was real, Mill's. Because I saw it, too. Whatever *it* was," Alexis mumbled, a hand rubbing at her chest as her unfocussed eyes fell to the ground.

Suddenly remembering those who had helped them, Amelia and Alexis snapped their heads toward the forest. "Where did they go?" they both asked in unison before meeting each other's eyes.

"Who?" Sam said, finally appearing to re-centre himself.

"There was someone who helped me. A woman," Amelia replied, sounding as though *she* didn't even believe the words coming out of her mouth. "She… killed that thing. She's the reason I look," a gesture to herself, "like this. She saved my life."

"Someone helped me, too. Unless I hallucinated," Alexis murmured, chuckling to herself in disbelief.

What the hell just happened? She tried to gather her thoughts, tried to understand what she'd just witnessed, *experienced.* None of it made sense. That thing… it didn't exist outside of scary movies, fictional books, and general folklore.

"Helped you why?" Sam and her father both asked, interrupting her thoughts.

"Why the hell would there be other people out in the forest at this time of night?" Sam scoffed, clearly unable to comprehend the situation. Alexis didn't blame him.

"I don't know, okay? I don't have an explanation for any of this," Alexis shot back defensively. "Aspen made a break for it when she heard that shriek—"

Their father swallowed as he met Alexis' eyes, his own wide with terror, before falling to Amelia's bloodied clothes once more, his nostrils flaring. Alexis could have sworn he was shaking.

Suddenly, Sam was in Alexis' face, gripping her shoulders as he said with frightened urgency, "Alexis, you aren't making any sense right now. There was no *shriek*, there was just you and Aspen freaking out and running into the forest for god-knows whatever reason, and Amelia chasing you shortly after," he shot a look in Amelia's direction, "also freaking out."

Sam's own hands, still gripping her shoulders, were shaking. Of course they were. If she were in their shoes, Alexis would react the same way — worse, even.

Their father began pacing back and forth as he rubbed at his face.

"I can't make any sense of this. You are *covered in blood*, Amelia," he exclaimed, trying to keep his voice low. "We're wasting time arguing when we should be getting you to a hospital!"

Amelia observed her body, suddenly remembering that she was, in fact, covered in blood, and hurried inside, pushing past Sam and their father. The two men called after her, their pleas cut short when they remembered the neighbours might hear the commotion and come investigating — or worse, call the police. They scoffed in disbelief as they watched Amelia disappear into the house, the sound of her footsteps ascending the stairs to the bathroom quickly replaced by the ambience of running water.

"Are you on drugs?" their father snapped at Alexis, who raised her eyebrows incredulously. "Look, I don't care what you do in your spare time, but I expect you to keep it out of this house, and especially away from family gatherings."

"I'm *not* on drugs, dad. We were attacked! Why didn't you come looking for us?" she shot back accusingly.

"Because you were only gone for a minute before you came running back as if something were chasing you!" Sam exclaimed, removing his hands from her shoulders but keeping his stance.

No, it couldn't be — they were gone for *at least* ten minutes. Had it really only been *a minute?* She turned around, studying the distance between the forest and her father's house.

"No. No, no, no. That's all wrong. It had to have been longer?"

Sam and her father shared a look of doubt, of confusion, as though Alexis had been speaking gibberish this entire time.

"Alexis," Sam said, his voice defeated. "You all ran in and then ran straight back out. There were no sounds other than your screaming for Aspen as you ran off. So please, just tell us the truth of it — what the hell happened?"

Alexis couldn't believe it - how had they not heard any of that? How did they not see…

"The light!" she exclaimed, gesturing towards the forest, glancing between them and the area behind her.

"What light?!" Sam asked, clearly losing patience.

Alexis just slowly lowered her arm as she stared at Sam, before shifting her gaze to her father, hopelessness overtaking her emotions.

"You truly didn't see or hear *anything?*" Her voice had become hollow, hopeless. It was more of a statement than a question. As she stood there, scrambling through the memories of what had just happened, she could just faintly hear her father and Sam whispering to each other, though she couldn't make out what was being said, didn't care to.

Finally accepting defeat and the fact that this argument would have no end, she pushed past her father and Sam, despite their protests. With Aspen trailing her, Alexis walked into the house without uttering another word, not even bothering to look back at her father or brother.

CHAPTER 6

The following day, Amelia and Alexis were sitting on the latter's bed trying to piece together what had happened the night before; whether it was worth calling the police, what they'd even tell them. Alexis had gotten little sleep, both her and Amelia having washed up, changing into some spare clothes, and silently agreeing to meet up at Alexis' place, saying only their goodbyes to their brother and father, who had been begging for answers, begging for Amelia to go to the hospital, but were left speechless when the sisters walked out the door without another word.

On the way, they'd stopped at an abandoned lot and burned their bloodied clothes, erasing any physical proof, any reminders, of what they'd experienced.

It appeared Amelia also got little sleep, if the bags under her eyes were any indication. That, and the stress of trying to figure out what had happened to them last night.

Alexis only managed two hours of sleep, trying to otherwise piece together everything. What was *everything?* How could anyone explain what she saw? Was she just supposed to continue living her life, pretending she wasn't suddenly traumatised?

When she wasn't sorting through her thoughts, her memory, she was having repeat nightmares of that monster barrelling towards her before she woke up in a sweat.

As if reading her mind, Amelia asked, "So what are we meant to do? Just keep on living life as normal?"

Alexis gave her sister a defeated look before shrugging her shoulders. She shifted her gaze to Aspen, who was lying on the floor watching them both. The dog was mostly back to normal, albeit a little more protective than usual. Alexis found herself hoping that whatever had happened was just a one-in-a-million impossible chance event.

"Do you want me to stay over again tonight?" Amelia asked, cutting into Alexis' thoughts.

"Up to you. I'm still spooked, but I don't think us being together *or* apart is going to stop something else from happening, if anything else *were* to happen."

Amelia looked at Alexis, attempting to read her blank expression, before giving up, agreeing, and standing from the bed. "I'm ordering take out, then."

Alexis tried to continue her life in as normal a manner as she could. Things went back to the way they were. Everything was… normal, as though last Friday night had never occurred.

Aspen was back to her usual self; still alert, but nothing out of the ordinary. Amelia had kept in constant contact via phone calls and texts, but she, too, seemed relatively normal. Though, given their sisterly likeness, she was probably just hiding her true emotions, shoving them down deep into a place she could easily ignore them. Much like Alexis.

Sam and their father had only taken a day to move onto different, boring matters, likely giving up on the entire situation once they'd realised Amelia and Alexis had nothing else to say about it, making it easier for them *all* to move past it.

This time next week, it may have all just seemed like a bad dream. Alexis had attempted to find images of that animal — creature, really — in the first few days following the incident, scouring the internet for anything that looked similar. The words *hell hound* appeared here and there, but otherwise, nothing of value or sense came from her short research. So, she gave up, feeling silly about the whole thing.

Alexis wasn't sure what could have caused such an intense hallucination, since that's what it had to have been, but she chose not to dwell on it any longer. With her life returning to normal, Alexis had also noticed the shadow she'd been seeing out of the corner of her vision slowly diminishing, becoming less frequent with each passing day.

It was Friday afternoon and Alexis had just clocked off from another gruelling week of work. Amelia had called the second Alexis stepped out of her office doors, telling her not to commit to anything because they were both going for dinner that night. Alexis had wanted to dine alone in her bed with some ice cream, Aspen, and something to binge on her TV.

Amelia, however, had other plans.

Alexis was more of an itinerary, a plan and ample notice kind of girl, whilst Amelia was quite the opposite — spontaneous and impulsive. And yet, they were the best of friends.

Sure, they had their qualms and disagreements here and there, like any other siblings would, but they shared a special bond.

Walking through the front door, Aspen wagging her tail in the kitchen and struggling to contain her excitement, Alexis headed straight for her fridge. She grabbed out a half-finished bottle of wine and poured herself a generous glass.

Amelia had offered to drive, which meant Alexis could enjoy herself a few well deserved big-girl drinks, as she liked to call them. Walking up the stairs, a wineglass in hand and Aspen on her heel, Alexis made for her closet. Being newly single, she felt like putting in the effort tonight. She had *always* put in effort to an extent, but had grown lazy towards the end of her relationship, and since she was turning over a new leaf, starting fresh, Alexis had decided it was time to celebrate rather than mourn.

After rummaging through her overflowing closet for about ten minutes, she had decided on a black, short-sleeved mini dress, sheer black stockings, heels and a white coat.

The square neckline of the dress complimented her chest, giving it a more generous appearance, which she certainly wouldn't complain about. She finished off the look with a messy bun, red lipstick and sharp eyeliner.

Her bangs sat beautifully on either side of her face, bringing out the sharpness of her jaw and cheekbones. She was certainly pretty, especially when she put in the effort. Nothing phenomenal, certainly not supermodel standard, but she had to give herself props where due. Alexis was slowly learning to love herself again, to find confidence in herself again, and, to her surprise, it was easier than she'd expected.

Being single after three years was new to her, and she needed to adjust, needed to discover who she was on her own, as a single, independent woman. She was scared, as was normal for anyone in her position, but she was also excited at all the possibilities and opportunities that now lay ahead of her.

With one last look in the mirror, Alexis grabbed her clutch and headed downstairs. She decided that she would allow herself to feel good, to *enjoy* feeling good for the first time since last Friday. Since even before then, really. It was exactly as she'd anticipated — the attack had felt like a dream, a faint memory. In all honesty, not that she'd admit it to anyone but Amelia, Alexis wasn't even sure it had ever actually happened.

She poured herself another generous glass of wine before tossing the bottle into her recycling bin, taking a seat at the kitchen table and lazily patting Aspen on the head, who chewed on a bone. Amelia was in the driveway by the time Alexis had fixed up dinner for Aspen, beeping obnoxiously to get her attention.

Alexis swore, shaking her head at how ridiculous her sister was acting. Bidding farewell to her dog, Alexis hurried out the door, looking around at her neighbour's houses, some of them now peering through their curtains at the commotion with distaste.

"Dickhead!" Alexis exclaimed in a hushed breath as she hurriedly slipped into the passenger side. Amelia chuckled, waving her sister off with a dismissive hand.

"No, seriously Mill's! I'm on great terms with my neighbours! Old Lady Dorothy next door gives me free fruit from her garden. Guess I can kiss that kind gesture goodbye, now."

Amelia turned to Alexis with a mocking-shocked expression on her face. "You were getting free granny-grown fruit and didn't think to share?"

Alexis rolled her eyes and gave Amelia's arm a shove before they drove off.

CHAPTER 7

The car park was empty by the time the girls had finished dinner, both very full and satisfied.

"Damn, how late is it?" Alexis exclaimed, looking down at her phone to see **11:30 PM** displayed across the screen. The girls had gotten to talking over dinner about basically everything that was happening in their lives currently, purposely avoiding the topic of the Friday a week ago.

As they neared Amelia's car, the parking lot lights began sporadically flashing.

Amelia and Alexis paused their walking, taken aback by the strange occurrence.
After a few moments, they hesitantly continued their walk towards the car, and Alexis noticed that same shadow out of the corner of her eye.

She turned her head to face it, finding only scattered cars.

Suddenly, a harsh ring rippled throughout the surrounding space, and Alexis quickly placed her hands over both ears, turning to see Amelia doing the same.

The ringing sent a sharp pain through Alexis' head before the sound ceased. Her eyes fell on Amelia once more, who stood still as a statue, her breathing deathly quiet as she eyed her car. Alexis followed her gaze and beheld what had her sister so shocked. There, peering at them from the other side of the vehicle, stood a tall man wearing a black suit, his raven hair combed back to reveal a handsome face. His eyes glowed red, and he stood casually, hands in his pockets. A wicked smile formed on his face, and he cocked his head to the side, sizing them up.

"Well, well, well. What beautiful women you've grown up to be," he crooned.

Alexis tilted her head in confusion, glancing between the man and Amelia, trying to figure out what kind of situation they were in whilst slowly inching closer to her sister's side. She removed her hands from her ears to find the ringing had stopped. Amelia just continued staring at those crimson eyes, and Alexis, in turn, stared at Amelia.

"Can we help you?" Alexis finally piped up, trying to hide the fear in her voice as she returned her gaze to the man.

"Yes, actually. You can," he replied coolly, extending a hand. "Come with me."

Alexis, taken aback by the command, narrowed her eyes as she finally reached Amelia's side. She grabbed her sister's arm from behind, quietly urging her to go back the way they came.
"Hey, Mill's. We forgot to grab our leftovers from the restaurant."

Amelia dropped her gaze from the man and turned to Alexis, her expression shifting into a look that said she understood what her sister was thinking.

They both rushed to make their way to the elevator, when the man in the black suit appeared in front of them, blocking their path. *How in the hell had he gotten to them so fast?* Alexis held Amelia close behind her, phone in one hand, ready to speed-dial the police.

"What the hell is your issue?" Alexis exclaimed, trying her hardest to sound brave, despite the fear coursing through her veins.

"I simply wish for both of you to come with me," the man said politely, though his growing impatience began to show. "I'll not harm you. I just wish to end this ridiculousness, and for you both to just *come with me*. I really do not want to have to resort to more drastic measures."

Alexis stared the man down, her blood thrumming in her veins.

"Please," he added, his English accent deep, the *smoothness* of it caressing Alexis' ears, as if it were a song. The redness of his irises, still glowing, beckoned for her to take his hand. *No.*

She fought the urge and backed away a step. Why wasn't she more afraid? Any normal, sane person would probably be terrified and running, *screaming* for help. Even Amelia didn't look as frightened as she should have been, but in awe of the situation.

The man reached his hand out further, and a bright light flashed from behind them, dimming just as quickly as it had appeared. He straightened himself, as if suddenly bothered by whatever had interrupted them just now.

Alexis didn't dare take her eyes off him, afraid that if she did, he'd whisk them away.

"Dimitri," a male voice sounded from behind.

Amelia turned her head, her curiosity winning out. The man's eyes faded to a deep brown, the red glow disappearing altogether. He held up his hands in sarcastic defeat.

"I'm not here to harm them, hunter," he said coolly to whoever was standing behind them.

Alexis, noticing Dimitri was distracted, finally dared a look behind her and found two more gorgeous figures. A man and a woman, clad in black leather and armed to the teeth with daggers and swords. They looked like warriors, or assassins, perhaps, right out of a fantasy show or book. The man was tall and muscled, and his short brown hair, cropped shorter around the sides, accentuated his gorgeous features. He was handsome, probably the most handsome man she'd ever laid eyes on, aside from the one who still stood in front of her. The woman was shorter, only slightly, with a lean build, her moon-white braided hair tied at the top of her head in a ponytail that snaked down her back. Her beautiful, sky-blue eyes seemed to glow under the parking lot lights.

Alexis couldn't decide who she found more beautiful — maybe they were both equally stunning as each other. She noticed Amelia staring at the woman, and her sister's throat bobbed. Not in fear, she realised, but in admiration.

Were *these* the people who'd saved them that night? There *was* an odd familiarity she could sense, looking at them both.

Suddenly remembering the man who stood in front of them, Alexis returned her attention to him. His eyes met hers, and he smirked, both hands now resting in his pockets again.

God, he was handsome.

Holding her stare, he said to the two strangers, "I have to take them with me, though. Can't leave without them, you see." He clicked his tongue. "Orders from the king and queen."

He shrugged, as if he hadn't just threatened to kidnap them. An intense fear finally crept in as Alexis processed his words. *King and queen? What was he talking about? And how much had she had to drink?* This had to be some kind of dream.

She and Amelia shared a glance, that same fear now overtaking her sister's features.

"Look," Alexis finally piped up, her voice shaking. "I'm not sure who any of you are, but we're not going *anywhere* with *anyone*." She grabbed Amelia's hand and tugged her to walk around Dimitri, who shifted to step in their path once again. Alexis stared up at him, putting on a brave face, despite her hands shaking. The sound of a sword being unsheathed came from behind them, and both sisters turned to see the tall man holding it in one hand, the woman now sporting twin daggers in both of hers.

"Come now, Dimitri," the woman crooned, a sweet venom lacing her words. "I've had a long day, and I really don't feel like making a mess of King D'Roghal's lackey."

Dimitri just huffed a laugh. "Sweet child, you really think a young, hot-headed huntress would be any match for me? I've been alive longer than your grandparents."

Huntress? Hunter? Who were these people?

Alexis glanced between them all.

"It would certainly make for an interesting fight, leech," the woman replied in that cool voice.

"Enough, I'm bored with this," her male counterpart piped up, looking as though this entire thing was, in fact, an inconvenience for him.

"Do you *really* wish to upset the king and queen, boy?"

The man in leather just shrugged. "They're not *my* king and queen."

Dimitri considered for a moment, his eyes locked with the man's, before he retreated a step, averting his gaze and staring at Amelia, then Alexis. His eyes glowed red once more.

"Very well. I don't feel like picking a fight with the Hunter's Guild, anyway."

Before Alexis could react, the parking lot lights flickered as they had not five minutes earlier, and Dimitri vanished, as if he'd never been there. She reached a hand in front of her, where he'd been standing, and waved it back and forth, trying to feel for… anything. It was empty, not a hint of Dimitri left.

"Okay, what the fuck is going on?" she asked as calmly as she could muster, turning to the two still standing behind her and Amelia.

They were sheathing their weapons, a hint of amusement flickering on both their faces, before walking toward the girls. Alexis still held a tight grip on Amelia's arm as she continued with that fake calmness, willing herself to appear brave.

She was sure the two strangers weren't fooled one bit, but it certainly didn't hurt to convince herself, at least, that she wasn't intimidated.

"For whatever reason, the King and Queen of Vendarath want you both. Given that you *appear* human, and that you're not of our realm, makes their hunt for you all the more suspicious. But we can't afford to have things like *him*," the man gestured to the area where Dimitri was seconds before, "and those Inferno Hounds strutting around your realm."

Realm? Inferno Hounds? What was this guy on?

The man crossed his arms, evidently growing impatient, and his white-haired friend stood by his side, arms also crossed, as she looked Amelia up and down, a half-smile appearing on her face. Amelia blushed, shifting her gaze to the ground, as if she'd just found something that required her attention.

"Who are you, anyway?" the woman asked before shifting her gaze to Alexis.

Alexis angled her head, clearly confused.
"Why does that matter?"

The man, still looking at her, chimed in. "Why are you being so cagey about it?" His white-haired friend snickered.

Amelia cut into their conversation with a deep sigh. "Can we please just go home? I'm so tired, and I have no idea what in the *hell* just happened, but I need to sleep it off."

All three of them looked at her, baffled at her lack of visible trauma. As Amelia reached for the keys in her pocket, the woman grabbed her wrist with unnatural swiftness.

"We need to take you to Preshia, where you will be safe and hidden," she warned gently.

Amelia slowly looked up at the woman, blushing again as she removed her hand from her pocket. The man walked to Alexis' side, gripping her arm just above the elbow. Alexis turned to face him in defiance, trying, and failing, to free her arm.

"Look, I appreciate you both saving us from," she waved a hand to the area behind them, "whoever the hell that was, but we don't *know* you, and we're not going *anywhere* with you."

Alexis tried again to free her arm from the man's grip, to no avail. He simply looked down at her, not a hint of amusement on his features, and said, "Let's go."

CHAPTER 8

Before Alexis could continue her protest, the surrounding parking lot they'd just been standing in had completely vanished, and they'd suddenly appeared in her house. She stood still for a few seconds, feeling as though she'd just risen too quickly and was now feeling dizzy.

Nausea hit her, and she tried not to bring up her dinner as she covered her mouth with a hand. The world spun as she attempted to focus, breathing in and out slowly and steadily.

Alexis noticed Amelia to her right in the same daze before realising that the man's hand was still gripping her arm.

She whipped her head around to him, instantly regretting it as the world spun again.

"What the hell," the man murmured, slowly taking in their surroundings as his obvious confusion grew. His gaze shifted to his comrade, who appeared equally baffled.

"What the hell happened?" he asked an octave higher, shifting his gaze back to Alexis. He pinned her with an accusing glare. "What did you *do*?" He let go of her arm and shook his hand, as if trying to rid himself of something stuck to it.

Alexis ignored his question, looking around again before she finally focused her eyes on Aspen, who was watching warily from the laundry, growling. Aspen locked eyes with Alexis, and her growls turned to whimpers.

Alexis swiftly walked to her dog, kneeling to calm her down.

"What just happened?" Amelia murmured to no one in particular.

The woman clicked her tongue before turning to her friend. "Rhipley, this isn't the Hunter's Guild."

The man, Rhipley, closed his eyes and let out an exasperated sigh. "I can see that, Yaz. Thank you."

He continued to glare at Alexis, who returned it with one of her own, cuddling Aspen close.

"What did you do?" Rhipley repeated.

Alexis raised a brow. "Come again?" Her voice was quiet, but she didn't hide the tinge of annoyance in it.

"What. Did. You. Do?" Rhipley asked once more, enunciating each word.

Alexis slowly rose from her spot, her blood boiling at his offensive tone.

"I don't know what you're talking about," she hissed. "You two show up not once, but twice. You don't even bother to offer an explanation, and now you're not only accusing me of god knows what, but you're also *kidnapping* us?"

Rhipley and Yaz exchanged a look Alexis couldn't quite decipher. She glanced at Amelia, who watched the exchange with wide eyes. Alexis took a deep breath before murmuring, "Thank you. For saving us. We appreciate it, but you need to leave."

She walked to the front door, pushing past Rhipley, who watched on in awe.

"You can't stay here," he argued, his eyes following her as she strode past him. "The Inferno Hounds, Dimitri — they *will* keep coming for you if you stay here unprotected."

"And, as exciting as this mysterious turn of events is panning out to be," Yaz added, "The Hunter's Guild needs us back home."

Alexis looked over a shoulder to where Amelia still kneeled, her sister returning her stare before shrugging her shoulders.

"Do you realise how ridiculous you sound? *Inferno Hounds?*" Silence. She went on. "We can't just leave. We have a father, a brother, jobs, friends, *responsibilities* here."

Alexis shook her head in disbelief before adding, "This can't be real."

"Where is this *Hunter's Guild* you speak of?" Amelia quietly asked the two strangers, though her attention was fixed on Yaz.

The woman looked down at Amelia, smirking.

"Why, only the training-grounds of the best of the best of Xalentya's hunters." She fluttered her lashes, tossing her hair over a shoulder. "And huntresses, of course."

Amelia raised an eyebrow. "Xalentya?"

Before Yaz could respond, Alexis interrupted.

"Look, it's been a long night. If you will not leave and you insist on *kidnapping us*," she slowly ground out the last two words, "I'll need to call the police."

Yaz and Rhipley shared another glance.
As Rhipley made to approach her, Alexis suddenly felt lightheaded. Her vision blurred, and as she stepped away from the door, looking to lean on some furniture for support, she collapsed to the ground.

CHAPTER 9

Alexis awoke the next morning in her bed to see Aspen cuddled up at her feet. Sitting up, she brought a hand to her forehead and winced as a mildly sharp pain shot through her.

Great, a hangover headache.

Aspen's head lifted as she eyed her owner, a glimmer of worry in those deep brown eyes. Memories from the night before began to flood back in, and Alexis huffed a laugh to herself.

"What in the hell kind of dream was *that?*" she said to Aspen, who tilted her head. The sound of a chair scraping on wood came from the corner of her bedroom, and she whipped her gaze in its direction, her heart pounding as she took in the tall man now striding for her bed.

"About time you woke up," he said gruffly.

Alexis panicked. *No, no, no!*

She hadn't dreamed — everything that had happened last night was real. This *man* she didn't know was real and was now standing only metres from her bed.

"Tell me who you are," Rhipley demanded.

Alexis tried to gather her thoughts, shaking her head in disbelief before replying in a stammer, "M-my name is Alexis, and my sister is Amelia, but I told you last night — we're nobody. At least, not of importance."

She turned her gaze back to where Aspen was lying before adding, "And I feel great. Thanks for asking."

Rhipley quickly replied, ignoring her sarcasm, "I don't believe you. You *hijacked* our Realm Walk and transported us to your *house*, I assume. And before you go denying it, I felt your magic zap me." Holding up the hand he'd gripped her with last night, he glared at her as he had before. "You're not just *some* human. You're a human with magic. Not very common in your world."

She could have sworn curiosity shone in his chocolate brown eyes, despite his serious expression. "Which makes you *very* interesting."

Alexis asked, "What do you mean, *your world?*"

A sly smile tugged on the corner of his mouth as he replied, "You didn't really think this world was the only one, did you?"

Alexis let out a breath of disbelief, before realising that Aspen had been calm since she'd awoken. No sign of her protectiveness that showed last night.

"Ah, yes," Rhipley said, following Alexis' gaze. "Fae have a way with animals. I can't believe you keep that poor dog cooped up in this tiny house." He looked around, distaste in his features.

"Actually, I leave her at my dad's house when I'm at work, so she can run around and explore."

He ignored her, continuing to take in the room, and she wasn't sure why she was even explaining herself to him, of all people.

There was a knock at the door before his white-haired friend strode in, taking up a seat at the end of the bed like she knew her way around.

"Elves also have a way with animals," Yaz exclaimed, a sarcastic tone of offence in her voice as she referenced Rhipley's earlier comment. "They like us better," she whispered loudly, scratching Aspen's ear.

Aspen wagged her tail and made to lick the woman's face, which Yaz narrowly dodged.

Fae? Elves?

Alexis closed her eyes, covering them with her hands as her head began to spin again. Rhipley sighed from his spot, still standing only a couple of feet from the bed.

Alexis brought her knees to her chest and breathed slowly, her eyes still closed.

"How is any of this real?" she asked finally.

"We'll explain in Preshia," Yaz replied, still petting Aspen.

Alexis opened her mouth to protest, but a sharp pain in her head stopped her.

"Get dressed. Don't bother packing anything," Rhipley commanded.

Yaz rose from the bed, kissing the air between her and Aspen, and she and Rhipley made to exit the bedroom before Alexis piped up. "What about my dad? My brother?" She looked at her dog. "Aspen?" Her voice broke upon saying the name and tears welled in her eyes as she choked on a sob. "I can't...I can't leave them."

Rhipley and Yaz shared a glance.

"Yazmin," Rhipley warned.

Yazmin ignored him and said cheerily, "Bring her with us." Rhipley groaned with annoyance as she blurted, "What? There're dogs in Xalentya. She'll fit right in."

Rhipley glanced at Alexis, then Aspen, then Yazmin, before letting out a defeated sigh and walking from the room. "Fine. Bring the dog."

Alexis again asked, "But what about my brother and father?" Yazmin's expression turned serious, but a knowing look lingered. "They'll be safer here."

"But those things?" Alexis shot back, panic coating her voice.

"The Inferno Hounds were chasing you and your sister, not them. If we leave — if *you* leave — they'll have no reason to come back here."

Inferno Hounds.

She still couldn't believe what she was hearing, what she was *thinking.* None of it felt real, but it was. It *all* was.

Alexis lifted her gaze to Yazmin, who was in the middle of turning towards the door when she asked, "What's it like? Where we're going?" She could barely imagine another country, let alone another world.

The corner of Yazmin's mouth lifted into a smile as she replied, "You'll see."

Yazmin descended the stairs as Rhipley stood in the kitchen, looking out the window and assessing the street for any threats.

Gods above, why him? There were other Realm Walkers in the guild, so why him?

He furrowed his brows in annoyance as Yazmin reached his side.

"We can't linger in this world any longer. Not with them," she whispered, glancing towards where the other sister was sitting at the table, sipping from her cup of coffee and staring at nothing in particular.

Rhipley followed her stare before returning his gaze to the street.

It was quiet in the early hours of the morning. He noted every human who passed by the house, not that there had been many.

Hopefully Dimitri was gone — he couldn't figure out what the vampire could want with these two human girls.

Worse, what the King and Queen of Vendarath wanted with them. But if two of the most powerful immortals of Xalentya were pursuing them, then the girls needed to be protected at all costs. One Inferno Hound was bad enough, but two?

Despite Alexis' denial of their obvious importance, who they were *had* to be vital. King D'Roghal didn't just chase *anyone*, and he especially didn't send his right-hand man after them if they were simply "not-of-importance".

Rhipley needed to get to the bottom of it, and fast.

Maybe taking the girls to Preshia, to his world, would get him the answers he needed, for the questions the Head Guild Master would surely ask. And, perhaps, would put his *own* mind at ease.

Steps sounded from the left, and he shifted his focus to where Alexis was now descending the stairs, her hair tied back in a high braid, clothed head to toe in black.

Not bad, he caught himself thinking before shaking the thought away.

She wore black boots that stopped at her mid-calf, laced up and worn in, he could see, and fitted clothes. He found himself grateful for the fact that she was at least smart enough to dress appropriately for their journey ahead, before side-eyeing Amelia, who wore what looked to be a cardigan and blue-grey pants, with shoes that were laced as well, but only came up to her ankles.

Interesting choice of clothing.

Perhaps waiting a night to leave for the girls to get things in order hadn't been such a bad idea. Especially because it would have been interesting to see the two trek through Fallandor Forest in the clothes they'd been wearing the night prior.

He still hadn't informed the girls that they couldn't Realm Walk to the doorstep of the Hunters Guild, and that after they stepped into Xalentya, they'd still have a day's trek ahead of them. Not that it mattered, since the girls didn't quite understand what Realm Walking was, anyway.

Alexis strode towards Rhipley and Yazmin, stopping a few feet away, a letter in her hand.

"For dad and Sam," she said, looking at Amelia, whose own eyes were on the letter.

"Don't worry," Yazmin replied in a particularly perky voice. "We will temporarily wipe any memories of you. Any proof that you were ever here will be erased, your homes warded and hidden from prying eyes. If and when you see your family and friends again, it will be as if no time has passed."

Alexis wasn't entirely sure she liked that idea, but what other choice did they have? She could either risk staying here and allowing those creatures, that *man*, to hunt them down for whatever reasons, or trust in these strange people she didn't know and keep her family safe. As she weighed the options, she realised that their new companions likely wouldn't allow for them to stay, anyway.

She ripped the letter apart before throwing it in the bin, realising that with fake memories, it would be of no use to her father and Sam.

As Alexis scanned Yazmin and Rhipley's features, she recalled how they'd referred to themselves as elf and fae, yet they resembled ordinary, albeit beautiful humans with their rounded ears. Perhaps elves and fae looked different in their world, as opposed to the ones in her books.

"Ready to go?" Rhipley finally asked, still facing the window.

Alexis looked down at her phone, before Yazmin announced, "You won't need those where we're going."

Alexis and Amelia looked at each other tentatively.

Rhipley cut a warning glare in her direction that Yazmin ignored, and Alexis and Amelia hesitantly placed their phones on the kitchen table.

Aspen was sitting at Alexis' side, looking up at her, a flicker of excitement in those eyes.

Alexis let out a sigh, taking in her home once more before saying, "I feel like we're going to regret this."

CHAPTER 10

In what felt like only seconds, they'd all suddenly appeared in a forest clearing. Large, sprawling pine trees and oaks surrounded them, and the sound of crickets chirping came from within the darkening woods.

Alexis' vision was blurry as she attempted to regain focus. She gazed around the area they'd landed in, trying to make out where they were, what to expect. Her head began spinning as it had last night, and the queasiness hit her almost immediately.

After she'd regained composure, breathing in and out deeply as she had the previous night, Alexis realised that the meadow appeared surprisingly normal, as opposed to what she might have otherwise expected.

The sky looked to be nearing late afternoon, painted with orange, pink and yellow hues. Alexis remained crouched as she took it all in. As she did so, she found that the air smelled, even *tasted*, clean and fresh. Alexis looked to her right, finding Amelia there in a similar position, her face more pale than usual.

Apparently, she didn't take well to the Realm Walking, either.

Aspen was lying in the grass in front of Alexis, panting.

Alexis leaned forward to comfort the dog as her other hand ran through the grass that surrounded them, and it felt unrealistically soft against her fingers.

Rhipley clearing his throat sounded from behind them, and she turned to see him standing only a few feet away, looking down at her. As she met his eyes, he held her stare for a long few seconds before turning his gaze to their surroundings, as if monitoring the woods.

"We can't stay here long. Nocturnal creatures will begin lurking in the forest, and we don't want to be their dinner," Rhipley announced nonchalantly.

Amelia said from her spot, to Alexis' surprise, "Well, wouldn't we technically be their breakfast if they're nocturnal?"

Yazmin snorted, and Rhipley just ignored them both, continuing to monitor the forest. Alexis returned her focus to the grass below her, having shifted into a cross-legged sitting position, completely mesmerised by the softness of the grassy bed.

She lifted her eyes to observe the area again, now noticing twinkling lights appear throughout the forest.

Following her gaze, Rhipley said, "Fireflies are common in Fallandor Forest."

"Fallandor Forest?" Amelia asked before Alexis could. She, too, was caressing the soft grassy bed beneath them in complete awe.

"Fallandor Forest is the wooded area that surrounds Fallandor, the nearby kingdom," Yazmin answered, her eyes on Amelia as a faint smile teased on her lips.

Amelia smiled back, and Alexis glanced between the two curiously.

"A kingdom?" Alexis asked, a tinge of excitement in her words.

Yazmin smirked and said, "Indeed, a kingdom."

She winked before turning to also monitor the forest.

Rhipley huffed a sigh. "Come on, let's go."

Alexis got to her feet and wiped off her clothes, letting out a quick whistle to get Aspen's attention. As she once more raised her eyes to the clearing they'd been sitting in for the past few minutes, she noticed the grass was now also lit up with fireflies, and various wildflowers were scattered throughout, painting the area in whites, yellows, pinks, and blues.

It was truly beautiful, like art come to life.

Rhipley walked ahead, with Yazmin taking the rear to cover their backs from any danger, Alexis supposed.

She took one last, longing look at the meadow, storing a mental picture of it, unsure of when or if she'd ever be able to see it again.

Rhipley and Yazmin had set up two separate, decently sized tents while the sisters strode off into the bushes to relieve themselves. Where they'd gotten the tents and bedding from, Alexis wasn't sure. It was as if they'd appeared out of thin air.

She studied both warriors, noting that they still only carried their various weapons. She couldn't quite recall them having anything more on them.

However, given what had occurred this past week, she chose not to dwell too much on it, along with all the other unexplainable experiences she couldn't begin to fathom.

Alexis stood in the centre of where they'd set up, glancing between both tents.

"One's for you," Rhipley said, "and the other one is for us. Choose whichever you'd prefer."

Alexis looked at him before striding towards one of the tents and opening the flaps to peer inside.

"So, are you two together or something?" Alexis called from where her head still poked inside the tent flaps.

Rhipley choked on a cough, and Yazmin scoffed.

"He wishes," she responded mockingly, glancing in Amelia's direction. "I much prefer the other sex, however."

Alexis returned her attention to their overnight accommodation — there were sleeping bags, or whatever they called them in this world, set up on either side of the tent.

They were lined with fur, and all Alexis could think about was how warm they must feel, especially with the air growing cool as the sun set. A small lamp sat in the middle, keeping the tent alight.

She ducked back out of the tent, noting an unlit campfire now set up where she'd been standing minutes ago.

"That was quick," she murmured.

Yazmin smirked, clicking her fingers as the campfire disappeared, then reappeared when she clicked her fingers again.

Alexis just stared, trying to hide her shock, though she was sure she wasn't fooling anyone.

"Us magically gifted folk have some tricks up our sleeves," Yazmin announced proudly. "Well, only if you're lucky enough, that is. Not all who are magically gifted are so… gifted."

Amelia asked, "There's magic here? So, magic *actually* exists?"

Rhipley interrupted before Yazmin could answer. "There's magic everywhere here. This world is abundant with it. Your world has magic, though it's not quite as potent as it is here."

Amelia looked at Alexis in amazement, before turning her attention back to Yazmin.

"And not everyone is magically gifted. But, unlike in your world, humans here are far more likely to have access to it, though it's still not as common as you'd think. It's very rare for the humans in your world to have it, however, let alone even knowing it exists," Yazmin added to Rhipley's comment.

"You said there're humans here, too?" Alexis asked of Yazmin's statement.

She replied, "Among other creatures."

Yazmin noticed Alexis studying her before quickly adding, "Shoot, I completely forgot." She flicked her hand, and as though some shield had come down, her appearance suddenly changed.

In place of her rounded ears now sat pointed ones, and she was somehow even more beautiful than before.

Alexis whirled around to view Rhipley, who also adorned pointed ears, and was just as radiant as Yazmin.

Although, she noticed, glancing back and forth between the two, his ears weren't quite as elongated as Yazmin's.

"Elves have longer ears. We came first," Yazmin stated, noticing Alexis' observations.

"So, elves *and* fae? You're... different?" Amelia asked from where she was now sitting at the centre of the camp.

Yazmin took up a seat on the log next to her, and Alexis and Aspen joined as Yazmin explained the difference between elves and fae.

"We're related. Loosely, that is. Fae derive from elves and humans mating, a sort of hybrid-offspring. Then, when there were enough fae to mate amongst themselves, they became their own species. Demi-fae are the offspring of humans and fae, their ears even shorter than ours. It's all very confusing." Yazmin shook her head.

Rhipley stayed where he was, taking it upon himself to stand guard for any unwanted company.

Yazmin must have noticed Alexis eyeing him as she whispered, "Don't worry. We've placed a masking shield over the campsite. No one will even know we're here."

She gestured to where Rhipley was now surveying the invisible barrier around their campsite. "But, as an extra precaution, we'll take turns throughout the night guarding you, so you needn't worry." Yazmin looked down at Amelia, who was staring at the unlit yet perfectly assembled pile of sticks in front of her, and waved a hand, the wood catching fire.

Alexis echoed her sister's gasp at the sight.

"It's okay to be impressed, or mesmerised, or shocked," Yazmin boasted, flicking her braids over a shoulder.

Alexis let out a dry chuckle, her eyes remaining on the fire.

Yazmin clicked her fingers again, and four skinned rabbits appeared above the fire, skewered to sticks and rotating on their own.

Alexis' stomach grumbled, and she realised just how hungry she was. She wanted to question how Yazmin was doing such things, but she quickly guessed that magic was always going to be the answer, confusing as it may be.

"I've never tasted rabbit..." Amelia whispered.

Yazmin just smiled slightly, as though every word out of Amelia's mouth piqued her curiosity.

"Will we be doing that… vanishing thing you guys do again anytime soon?" Alexis asked sheepishly.

"Realm Walking? Oh, no. The Hunter's Guild is warded. It's a day's walk from here."

"You couldn't just Realm Walk us to the entrance of the wards?" Alexis replied, the sounds of the creatures within the forest growing louder, her nerves growing with them.

"Where would be the fun in that?" Yazmin replied in a tone too eager for Alexis' liking.

"Well, if we're on the run," Alexis gestured to herself and Amelia, "shouldn't we be trying to get to the guild as soon as possible?"

Yazmin clicked her tongue. "Realm Walking isn't easy for mortals, and it can take a toll on you if done too often. Sure, it might be easier to Realm Walk to the entrance of the wards, but then your brains would turn to mush, theoretically. Better to rest up and recover." She took a bite of her rabbit. "Plus, there're five of us. Our abilities aren't as accurate when there's a bigger load to carry. We transported the closest we could with what we had. Even *our* magic has limits."

Alexis hadn't considered that — not that she could have possibly known. She gulped at the idea of her brain becoming fried and dropped her argument.

"Besides," Rhipley added, Alexis and Amelia whipping their heads towards him. "D'Roghal's forces wouldn't be stupid enough to cross the border into Preshia."

Alexis let herself feel a small bit of relief at that.

CHAPTER 11

Alexis struggled to fall asleep that night, the sounds of various unknown creatures emanating from the surrounding forest. Aspen had been growling on and off at every single sound, but calmed somewhat when Alexis cuddled her close.

It was more for Alexis' peace of mind than Aspen's, who didn't appear scared in the slightest, rather just protective as per usual. Alexis turned over, Aspen now lying on her side, and gazed towards Amelia's half of the tent.

"You awake?" Amelia whispered.

"Yeah," Alexis replied just as quietly.

After a few seconds, Amelia said, "I miss them - Sam and dad. I wonder if they miss us."

Alexis chewed on her lip before responding, "Given what Yazmin said about erasing our very existence from their minds with magic — however that works — I doubt they miss us."

Amelia huffed a laugh. "I don't even want to begin to think about how that works. The idea alone makes me feel uneasy."

Alexis let out a long sigh, but didn't respond. She wasn't even sure how to, if any words she spoke would offer comfort.

"Did you know? That you possess magic, like Rhipley said?" Amelia asked after a few moments.

"Of course not, Mill's," Alexis replied quickly, trying not to sound offended. "I didn't even believe in this stuff until today, honestly. I still don't think I believe his assumption about me having magic. Until we got here, I thought I'd just been in one long dream."

Amelia huffed another laugh. "Some dream."

Alexis turned onto her back and stared at the roof of the tent. "Some dream," she echoed.

The forest stirred as Yazmin monitored their campsite. She had just taken over Rhipley's watch when she'd heard the two sisters talking in their tent. They'd been whispering, though Yazmin had heard every word.

She felt bad for the girls, despite the fact that she and Rhipley had saved their lives not once, but twice, for gods knew whatever reason. If it weren't for the Head Guild Master sending them to their world, they'd likely be dead, or in King D'Roghal's clutches already. She'd pondered why the Headmaster sent she and Rhipley to the Mortal Realm, what importance the sisters held for their protection and rescue and, now, retrieval.

Neither she nor Rhipley could begin to fathom why King D'Roghal, of all people in Xalentya, would be hunting them.

Alexis had displayed a shred of magic when she'd somehow transported them to her home, but as far as she could tell, Amelia was normal.

Still, she had to admit that hijacking a Realm Walk, especially in the hands of not one, but two experienced Realm Walkers, was quite impressive, even if Rhipley didn't care to admit it.

Yazmin gazed at their shared tent, where her friend was now sleeping, and smiled at the thought of the day ahead of them, with Alexis and Rhipley no doubt at each other's throats.

She returned her attention to the tent where the girls slept, and a warm feeling filled her chest as she thought of Amelia, whose breathing had now slowed, likely having fallen asleep.

For a human, she was pretty. Yazmin had had many beautiful women warm her bed over the past century, but she'd only ever bedded a single human, who *was* a woman compared to Amelia, with her innocence and blissful unawareness. Why she was thinking of Amelia in such a way, why she was drawn to her like she'd never been drawn to anyone, Yazmin didn't know.

She shook her head, wiping the thought from her brain — she couldn't be thinking like that, s*houldn't* be thinking like that.

No matter how attracted to Amelia Yazmin was, she was still a lady, and needed to act like one. Not like some hungry animal looking for its next meal. So Yazmin stepped past the tents and circled the area, keeping an eye out for any danger as she tossed a dagger in her hand.

CHAPTER 12

Rhipley woke everyone before dawn had broken. With King D'Roghal's intentions with their new companions still unclear, they couldn't risk being out in the open for too long.

The sisters stirred within their tent as Yazmin stood beside him, buckling her daggers onto her fighting leathers — the leathers that all established hunters wore as their official uniform.

Aspen emerged from the tent and stretched, wagging her tail as she sighted Yazmin, who walked to where the dog met her halfway across their campsite, showering his comrade with kisses.

Rhipley returned his eyes to the forest, scanning for any danger, though his ears would hear anyone, or anything, approaching before his eyes did.

Fae sight was extraordinary compared to that of humans, but their hearing was nearly equal to that of elves. *Nearly.*

As much as the fae hated to admit it, elves really were their superiors, despite their close relations.

The only other creatures that could rival fae and elves were demons of the night — vampires.

With their human-like appearances, they were likely the deadliest creatures in Xalentya, especially given that whatever — *whoever* — they fed on masked their scent, making it nearly impossible to identify them.

Witches were also known to be powerful and dangerous. Gifted with magic, like that of fae and elves, but not limited to the elements. And a hunger, a taste, for anything with flesh. Preferably humans, though, they were said to feast on anything with a heartbeat, or so the rumours claimed.

Rhipley had only come across a couple of witches in his lifetime, both nasty and dangerous.

Both now dead by his hands, and Yazmin's.

Upon deciding there was no imminent danger, he turned to where Alexis and Amelia had finally stepped out of their tent.

With a swift flick of Yazmin's hand, both tents disappeared into thin air, returning to where they'd been whisked away from.

Yazmin had already taken care of the campfire, leaving no sign of their ever being there.

Rhipley looked at Alexis, who had wrangled her hair into a low bun, and Amelia, whose hair was down but in a clearly tangled mess. She poured some water from their waterskin onto her head, combing her hands through her long, red strands.

"Good," Rhipley finally said when Amelia was done, and all appeared in order. "Now that that's settled, let's go."

He gestured for Yazmin and the girls to go ahead, choosing to flank the rear this time. Yazmin walked past, shooting him a grin, and he returned it with a look of his own that said he was already growing tired of babysitting these humans.

Aspen, Alexis and Amelia followed close behind, and Alexis glanced at Rhipley, a gleam in her eye, before quickly averting her gaze. Anyone else might not have noticed, but he did, and he wasn't sure why.

They'd been trekking through Fallandor Forest for hours now, only stopping to relieve themselves when necessary. It'd been a while since Alexis hadn't had the luxury of a bathroom, only when camping in the wilderness with her family the few times that they had. She hadn't realised how much she missed it — missed having a comfortable bed to sleep in, missed having a roof over her head, missed *knowing* what was going to happen, how predictable her life was. She'd certainly never had to deal with any sort of danger, had never had to run from anyone.

Alexis hadn't let herself think too much about how her life, how her sister's life, had been turned completely upside down. It could be worse though, she supposed.

Was it fate that led them to Rhipley and Yazmin, or rather, led Rhipley and Yazmin to them? If anyone had asked her a few weeks ago, she'd have laughed them off.

But now... she'd decided that the word *impossible* had little meaning anymore. She'd always been open-minded, but, like any sane person, to things that *actually* made sense — not to the possibility of a fantasy world, or that the creatures she'd read about in fictional books could be real.

Are real, she corrected herself.

Yazmin, Aspen and Amelia were walking ahead, Amelia keeping close to the white-haired woman, asking her questions every now and again. Questions that Alexis couldn't hear, but that Yazmin was seemingly more than happy to answer.

Yazmin had so obviously been flirting with Amelia, out of curiosity or legitimate interest, Alexis wasn't sure.

Though, her sister was pretending to be completely oblivious to it, and that only seemed to entertain Yazmin more.

She looked over her shoulder to Rhipley, who had been surveying their surroundings, before noticing Alexis' gaze and furrowing his brows.

"What?" he asked, and her mouth curved into a tight line as she replied, "I — never mind."

She returned her stare to where her sister was now walking alongside Yazmin. Aspen, on their trail, made a point to look back at Alexis every so often.

She let out a sigh before asking, "Have I done something to offend you?"

Rhipley scoffed, replying, "I think you forget that you haven't been very nice to me, either."

She turned to face him, stopping in her tracks. "Because I thought you were insane until I witnessed it for myself. Not that that's an excuse…"

He stopped next to her, looking down to where her face was now angled to view his. She tried not to shy away from his lean body towering over her — his leathers were intimidating, as were the many weapons strapped to his body, the hilt of his sword peaking over a shoulder.

She dared to hold his gaze, trying not to drown in his rich brown eyes, a red tinge to them in the afternoon sunlight.

God, he was beautiful.

Her heartbeat quickened as he studied her for a moment, waiting for her to go on.

"You couldn't seriously expect me to face all this, all that's happened, and *not* be completely dumbfounded?"

He glanced around them before returning to her. "You seem to have adjusted quickly, though."

She huffed a dry laugh. "I clearly put on a good face."

Alexis noticed a hint of a smile on his mouth and held his stare for a moment longer before blinking and turning away, clearing her throat. She started into a walk again, and Rhipley quickly caught back up to her, keeping a few paces behind.

Alexis kept her eyes ahead, trying to appear calm and collected. She wondered if he could hear her rapid heartbeat, if he even noticed. His lack of acknowledgement said he didn't, or just that he didn't care.

She shook her shoulders, removing the thought from her head.

Why *did* she care? She barely knew the guy.

"Are you okay?" Rhipley asked, catching her off guard.

She ignored his question, instead countering with one of her own. "What is the Hunter's Guild? Explain it to me as someone who doesn't actually know."

Rhipley was quiet for a moment, before replying, "It's an organisation here in Xalentya, though each guild has its own rules, regulations, and traditions."

Alexis waited for Rhipley to go on, not daring to look back at him.

"It's half an academy, half an established unit. Elves, fae, and even humans enrol, or are enlisted to train with the best of the best in Xalentya. We're trained to hunt down those who would threaten peace in our realm. But only when, and if, we're enlisted to do so. We cannot hunt unauthorised."

Alexis considered for a moment, asking quietly, "So, you're sort of like pest control?"

Rhipley chuckled. "Of a sort. But we don't go blindly killing anyone, or anything. We're sent to protect against danger. If we must put someone or something down because they pose a threat, then we abide by our code. Killing without authorisation or reason is classed as treason of the highest order. We aren't exempt from the law."

Alexis finally looked at him, and noticed his eyes were already upon her, his features unreadable.

"You were sent to rescue us."

Rhipley just nodded.

"By who?"

"The Head Guild Master. He overlooks the operations of our guild here in Preshia and dispatches us when necessary. He sensed danger in your world and sent us to look into it. And that's when we found you — twice."

"How?" Alexis asked.

"Rampier— The Head Guild Master," Rhipley corrected himself, "has a very specific type of magic. He can sense danger within our world, and yours, I suppose. But he can also sense when something or someone from our world has left the confines of this realm. He sensed it with the Inferno Hounds, and then with Dimitri."

"Surely, if there are others like you, that must happen a lot?" Alexis pushed.

"The Head Guild Master doesn't like to give specifics. He sent us on a mission — two missions, really — and we obeyed. Without question."

Alexis tried to hide her curiosity, biting down on the plethora of other questions she wished to ask.

She thought about the night they first met.

"My father and brother — they said they didn't hear or see anything out of the ordinary. Why is that?"

Rhipley shifted his focus to the ground, furrowing his brows in concentration, trying to come up with an answer.

"I can only guess that it's because they don't possess magic like you do. Amelia has shown no physical signs, though it would be wise to assume she's also gifted, since she could also see the event from our Realm Walking."

Alexis just looked at Rhipley, remembering the bright light she saw both times they'd appeared, and disappeared.

"If anyone can give us answers, it's the Head Guild Master, which is why we're taking you to him — under his request."

Alexis pondered that — why them? What was so important about them? She'd never been important in her life.

"One more thing," she blurted, and found Rhipley looking at her patiently. "When we ran into the forest, it felt as though we were in there for *at least* ten minutes. But when we came back out, our brother and father said we'd only gone in for a few seconds?"

Rhipley just nodded, and replied, "Time dilation because of the Realm Walk. You experienced time normally, thanks to your magic blood, but your father and brother experienced it far differently, due to their lack of magic. It's increasingly confusing the more you dwell on it."

Alexis nodded.

Suddenly remembering her other responsibilities, she asked, "What about my job? My work colleagues. My friends?"

Rhipley just waved her off as if her question didn't faze him.

"All taken care of, don't worry. Mortal minds are far easier to manipulate than you'd think." He chuckled, then caught himself, before adding, "I mean no offense."

Alexis shot him a mocking glare, but said, "It seems that in this world, where creatures like *you* exist, humans are so… average. Less-than-impressive. I mean, even the humans in this world are more impressive than the ones on Earth."

Rhipley looked ahead, not offering a response, a retort, as if unsure what to say.

The sound of Yazmin's nearing footsteps interrupted her, drawing Alexis' focus away from Rhipley.

"We're nearly there," she informed them before looking at Alexis, excitement dancing in those sky-blue eyes.

Alexis chuckled nervously.

"You'll love it."

Rhipley responded drily, "You don't know her well enough to make a statement so bold, Yaz."

Yazmin rolled her eyes at the retort before grabbing Alexis' hand and dragging her to where Amelia and Aspen were standing on a small hill ahead. "Keep up, Rhipley. So slow."

Rhipley shook his head as he huffed a quiet laugh.

The breath was blown out of Alexis as she beheld the buildings that stood before her and the mountains that towered behind them. Built into those mountains, it seemed, was a large fort.

More like a small castle.

Tall, grey stoned walls surrounded it where she could just barely make out archers atop keeping a lookout for any guests, both wanted and unwanted.

A long flight of stairs built into the ground led to the entrance, and Alexis let out an exasperated groan.

"Really? We've been walking all day, now we have to walk up *those?*" she said, motioning a hand ahead of them.

Yazmin and Rhipley walked ahead, clearly no longer worried about any danger, considering the archers closest to them atop the wall with their bows drawn.

"Don't complain now, not when we're so close," Yazmin called from where she and Rhipley were now easily twenty feet ahead of them, walking down the forest path leading to the Hunter's Guild. Alexis and Amelia shared exhausted glances, Alexis' skin beginning to crawl with nervousness.

She reached for her sister's hand, looked down at Aspen, who was wagging her tail and smiling, and walked towards the guild.

CHAPTER 13

As they neared the gates of the Hunter's Guild, Alexis immediately noticed the green and gold banners hanging on either side of the gate, flapping gently against the wall.

They were decorated with intricate sun and moon symbols; the fabric glinting in the sunlight.

Two guards stood at the gates, clad in the same black leather both Rhipley and Yazmin wore, though adorning deep-green cloaks in addition, trimmed with gold stitching and armour built into their leathers. They each held a sword and shield in their hands as they angled their heads towards Rhipley and Yazmin, as if waiting for some kind of confirmation.

Not a second later, the two were tugging up the left sleeves of their leathers, revealing small, detailed tattoos.

Alexis stepped closer, peering down at the intricate inking, as she noted Aspen wandering around and sniffing the ground out of the corner of her eye.

There, on the inside of both their left wrists, were twin artworks of a sword flanked by a sun and crested moon. She gazed up at the banners again, then looked to Rhipley, who was still staring ahead at the guards now bowing their heads in recognition.

"What's with the sun and moon artwork?" Alexis asked no one in particular.

Rhipley, rolling down his sleeve, glanced sidelong at her. "It represents the Sun and Moon Goddess and God; Luzhula and Brundhul. Our ancestors believed that they, at the dawn of time, created this world and brought balance."

Alexis looked up at the banners once more.

"And," Yazmin chimed in, "in times of chaos, it is said that two beings, one of dark and one of light, will come together to bring about peace when it's needed most."

She smirked. "Though it's really just an over-hyped wives' tale now. There are still those who worship them, yes, but most others these days don't *really* believe in them. They just need someone to blame when things go wrong. Or, when things go right, they have someone to thank."

Amelia asked quietly, "So why do you bear their crests on your banners, then?"

Yazmin turned to her, still smirking. "We worshipped them for so long that their crests became our recognisable country symbol."

Amelia simply replied with an, "Oh."

"Also, the Preshian empire still celebrates them, so we get plenty of holidays and celebratory parties, which isn't so bad," Yazmin stated cheerily.

"It's annoying and overwhelming," Rhipley muttered from his spot.

The guards peered down at Aspen, who was now sitting quietly beside Alexis.

"The dog is with us," Yazmin announced.

The gates, two large wooden doors lined with iron, opened, and the guards stepped aside, giving another slight bow of their heads.

Whether they'd caught onto the sisters' lack of knowledge regarding this country, they didn't say.

Rhipley and Yazmin dipped their heads in return and led Alexis, Amelia and Aspen through the gates.

Alexis had seen nothing even remotely close to a castle, or fort, in real life. Only in movies or books or games. What she took in now was like fantasy come to life; a large courtyard where open hallways lined with arches led down either side, and another set of gates to the north of the walls, likely leading to an outside area.

The surrounding fort stood at two stories high, stairs on either side leading to the upper level, where there were more hallways lined identically to those below and doors that she could only guess opened to rooms.

The area they were standing in had beautifully maintained, almost glowing grass throughout, with a few paths cutting across to either side.

Then she beheld what stood in the centre; a large tree, surrounded by sitting benches, and a beautiful garden of flowers of every colour at its base.

She walked closer to it and noticed a plaque in the centre of the enormous trunk.

The words were in a language she didn't recognise, and she let out a quiet sigh.

Different world, different language.

Alexis felt someone at her back, and half-turned her head to see it was Rhipley towering over her, also looking at the plaque.

"It says *This is the Resting Place of Aurelia Wyntersier — Head Guild Master, Cherished Daughter, and Beloved Princess.*"

Alexis asked, "The previous Head Guild Master?"

Rhipley nodded, still eyeing the plaque, before shifting his gaze to the tree, its leaves swaying in the light wind.

"Did you know her?"

Rhipley squinted slightly, trying to find an answer. "Yes. She died twenty years ago."

Alexis could hear something like an ache in his voice, though he tried to hide it. His jaw was clenched, his nostrils flaring slightly as if he were remembering a painful memory, before refocussing himself and looking down at Alexis.

"She raised me, along with the current Head Guild Master, who you'll meet soon. They were the only parents I ever knew."

Alexis furrowed her brows a little, a tinge of sadness coursing through her.

"I showed up here when I was a baby. Was left at the front gates, so I'm told. This," he gestured to the general area around them, "is all I've ever known."

Alexis considered for a moment, before asking, "Were… Aurelia and the current Head Guild Master together?"

Rhipley huffed a laugh, shaking his head. "No, they were old friends, and both raised me. She was sort of like a grandmother to me, a mother figure to Rampier." The corner of his lips tilted upward in amusement. "Despite her young appearance, thanks to her fae blood."

"And she was royalty? A princess?" Alexis asked, returned her attention to the plaque.

Rhipley nodded. "Her family ruled Preshia, from Fallandor. They were widely loved and admired."

He smiled sadly, all too aware of Alexis watching him once more. "When Aurelia died, and her sister was…" He trailed off, choosing to leave that detail out. "Their parents passed due to a rapid decline in their health. Rumours say they died of sadness, of depression, at the loss of their two daughters."

Alexis' chest ached as she tried to imagine it, what that family had gone through. She wondered what Rhipley had chosen to leave out regarding the sister, but chose not to pry.

"They had likely just come to the end of their lives, and the heartbreak of losing their daughters accelerated it. We fae live for at least a thousand years, but we don't live forever. Eventually, every fae gets to a point where our bodies, our souls, naturally pass on."

Naturally — as if the fae were natural. As if living a thousand years was natural. Though, Alexis supposed, for this world, that was considered natural.

Rhipley gestured to the tree, taking a long look at it. "We like to believe that Aurelia's soul now lives on in this Red Oak, where she watches over the guild, this land, this country."

Alexis looked up at the tree, trying to figure out where the *red* in its name came from, given that the leaves were a vibrant green. Suddenly, that same shadow appeared in the corner of her vision. Alexis snapped her head, seeing, yet again, absolutely nothing out of the ordinary.

"Wait until you see it in autumn, and you'll understand why we call it the Red Oak," Yazmin said from where she approached behind them.

Alexis glanced around the courtyard, and noticed the lack of people around, the only ones of note being the guards who stood outside the now-shut front gates, and those stationed atop the walls.

Yazmin seemed to notice her observation, because she said, leaning in, "They're training, or in class, or out on patrol. Give it half an hour and this place will be crawling with students, hunters and teachers."

"Speaking of," Rhipley piped up, now turning to face them. "Unless you enjoy being gawked at and whispered about, I suggest we take you to see Rampier."

CHAPTER
14

The doors to the Head Guild Master's office were essentially a smaller version of those at the guild's entrance. The iron, however, was replaced with a darker wood, intricate symbols and artworks carved into the surface.

Two large, rounded door knockers adorned either side, and Rhipley gave a singular knock before entering. There, sitting at the end of the room behind a large desk littered with papers, was a man who looked to be in his fifties, had he been human.

His grey beard matched his equally greying hair that was cropped short and combed neatly atop his head. His ears, Alexis noticed, were pointed like Rhipley's.

Fae.

Rampier's eyes were fixed on the paper in his hand, and he didn't bother to look up from behind the glasses that sat halfway down his nose. Rhipley and Yazmin walked ahead, motioning for the sisters to stay a few feet behind.

They stopped ten feet from the desk and stood silently, arms behind their backs as they waited for the Headmaster to finish whatever he was reading.

Finally, after what felt like hours, Rampier looked up from his paperwork, shifting his hazel eyes from Rhipley to Yazmin, then to the girls standing behind them, Alexis holding Aspen by her collar to keep her from exploring.

"Welcome back, Haldier and Solarnia. And who have you brought to my guild?" he asked, as if he wasn't the one who'd requested their rescue.

Rhipley cleared his throat, replying, "The two humans King D'Roghal was after, master, that were attacked by the Inferno Hounds. We encountered Dimitri hunting them shortly after, though Dimitri let us go without so much as a scratch."

The Head Guild Master huffed a laugh, as if he didn't quite believe what Rhipley had just told him. "Dimitri doesn't just *let* his prey go. Did he try to bargain?"

Yazmin spoke this time. "No, master. Though, as you're aware, Dimitri is known to be a recluse. He is, after all, the only being under King D'Roghal's rule who has any sway, small as it may be."

Rampier's eyes settled on Alexis for a heartbeat before shifting to Amelia. He squinted before tilting his chin upward, motioning for the girls to step forward.

"What are your names?" Rampier asked curiously.

Alexis and Amelia shared a look before the former answered, "Alexis and Amelia Rainier, sir. But, we're not important. There has to have been some kind of… mistake."

The Head Guild Master just smirked. "If you were not important, King D'Roghal wouldn't be hunting you now, would he?"

Amelia asked this time, "Who is this King D'Roghal you all speak of?"

"He is the King of Vendarath, the country that sits at the southernmost point of this continent," the Head Guild Master replied, motioning with a hand to where large maps were displayed behind him.

Rampier must have sensed their curiosity as he added, "It's a safe haven for creatures of the dark. Creatures like those you encountered."

Alexis sucked in a breath, trying, and failing, to hide her shock.

The Head Guild Master stood from his spot, walking around to the front of his desk before removing his reading glasses and giving a light dip of his head. "I am Rampier Draghone, the Headmaster of this here Hunter's Guild."

Alexis and Amelia dipped their heads too, offering polite smiles. "Thank you for having us," Alexis said. "And for saving us." She glanced to where Rhipley and Yazmin still stood.

Rampier's eyes settled on Aspen, who was quickly becoming restless, wanting to explore and sniff wherever she could.

"And this is?"

Alexis' attention also shifted at Aspen, who returned her stare with irresistible puppy eyes. "My dog, Aspen. I'm sorry, I know it's inconvenient, but I couldn't leave her behind."

Rampier waved his hand in dismissal. "Do not apologise. I'm sure we can find a spot for her here. After all, there are a handful of hunters and students who house their own Daeanimus' here, so it's really no hassle." Alexis angled her head in confusion, before Rampier added, "You'll learn all about it, all about this world, in time."

Alexis let out a sigh as she chewed on her lip. *Guess we aren't going home anytime soon.*

"There is something else," Rhipley said, clearing his throat, and Alexis could have sworn he shot her an apologetic look for just a second. "Alexis can Realm Walk."

If Rampier was impressed, or surprised, it didn't show. He just looked at Alexis for a long minute before finally asking, "And what of Amelia?" He slid his gaze to her sister.

"We haven't yet seen any signs of her having magical abilities. But, given that they're related, we cannot yet rule out any suspicions of her having any in her blood," Rhipley replied, repeating what he and Yazmin had told the sisters earlier. "Plus, they both saw the

Realm Walking event both times we appeared in their world. That, in itself, is proof enough."

Rampier stroked his facial stubble as he thought. "I will extend a formal letter to the King of Preshia, requesting that our two new guests be brought to him where *he* can decide what course of action must be taken."

Rhipley and Yazmin shared a look, an unspoken conversation passing between them, before shifting their attention back to Rampier and bowing their heads.

"Until you are summoned, Yazmin and Rhipley will show you to your quarters. Please, make yourselves at home." Rampier gave a sincere smile to each of the girls before returning to the papers on his desk.

Rhipley and Yazmin escorted them out of his office doors, Rhipley remaining inside as he said quietly, "Just give me a minute. I'll catch up with you later." With that, he shut the doors.

Yazmin blew out a breath before looking at both sisters and smiling. "Well, follow me."

Yazmin escorted the girls through the corridors where what appeared to be students were now exiting their classrooms, and who were now gawking and whispering to each other.

Alexis forced herself to avoid looking into their curious eyes and kept her chin high as she followed Yazmin to their sleeping quarters. Some students smiled at Yazmin in admiration, while others shied away and averted their eyes altogether, as if in fear of her.

Yazmin ignored them all, leading the girls through the growing plethora of students.

The crowds in the hallways parted for her, as though she were some queen making her way through the streets of her kingdom.

Alexis dared to glance at various students as they passed and noted mostly fae, a handful of elves and a few humans, who observed her and Amelia the most, it seemed. Some students noticed Aspen and even leaned down to pet her.

Eventually, they were led out to the courtyard they'd first stepped into, and it was, indeed, now filled with students, teachers and hunters alike, along with their Daeanimus', all keeping themselves busy. Some were sprawled on the grass studying or reading or writing, while others were standing idly by or sat on the benches by the Red Oak, chatting away and laughing.

Yazmin led them to the southern end of the courtyard, to where the other set of large gates were. She said over a shoulder, "The hunter's quarters are separate from the students. Until you've been summoned by the king, you'll be staying there with us."

Alexis chewed her lip in anticipation.

CHAPTER 15

Rhipley stood before his Headmaster, his father figure, and waited just as he had not five minutes before. Rampier was studying the paper in his hand once again, and didn't bother to look up as he said, "You have thoughts."

Rhipley cleared his throat before asking in as calm a tone as he could, "Why do you think King D'Roghal wants them? And once King Mikkel finds out that they're wanted, and by who, don't you think he'll try to use that information for his own personal gain?"

Rampier looked up from beneath his reading glasses and thought for a moment.

"Whether the monarch finds out about those girls from us or from his own spies, it's completely out of our control. All we can do is what we're instructed to do. We may be our own private organisation, Rhipley, but we're still under their employ when and where they see fit."

Rhipley tried to keep his features calm, but Rampier could see right through him as he added, "Is there something else bothering you, son?"

Rhipley simply replied, "I know it's not my place to question, but I have to ask — why them? I understand that they have power — Alexis, at least, has significant power — but why *them*? Why send Yazmin and I to not only protect them, but retrieve them and bring them here?"

Rampier remained quiet as Rhipley continued.
"I can sense that there's something about them, master. Something about Alexis. The pure fact that she can Realm Walk is enough to question her origins, the depth of her power, but would we not have been better off leaving them in the Mortal Realm? Bringing them here attracts too much danger."

Rampier sighed and placed his papers onto the desk before cupping both hands together beneath his chin.

"You're correct, Rhipley. It is not your place to question my commands. However, I need you to trust me when I say those girls are special. Whether we'd left them in the Mortal Realm or brought them here, the circumstances surrounding them do not change. For now, that's all you need to know."
Rhipley stared at his master for a few heartbeats before regaining his composure, nodding his understanding and schooling his features into the hunter's calm he'd come to perfect over the years. "Should King Mikkel agree for the girls to be kept here under our watch, I will have you personally assigned to overlook them. Yourself *and* Yazmin," Rampier added.

Rhipley huffed a laugh at that. "Yazmin would be more than happy to oblige where Amelia is involved, I'm sure."

A hint of a smile appeared on Rampier's lips, then vanished just as quickly.

"Remember, the information you've brought to me today stays between those of us who were in this room. No one else must find out, lest it fall into the wrong hands, as you suggested."

Rhipley nodded in understanding, and as Rampier returned to his papers, he took that as dismissal, leaving without another word.

Yazmin walked the girls through the southern gates of the courtyard, and Alexis beheld an entirely different environment than that of their initial encounter.

More large, cobblestoned buildings stood before them, with training grounds throughout, most hunters sword fighting or practising hand-to-hand combat.

Yazmin announced, "These are the hunter's grounds, where students who graduate will come once they've proven they can make it as an established hunter. Unless they transfer or become independent contractors, that is."

She angled a hand to those who were fighting, some packing up for the day. "Here is where we practise our sword fighting, hand-to-hand combat, anything requiring a hunter to be in close range with their target, really."

Amelia let out a breath of astonishment, and Alexis tried not to look too impressed, given the multiple eyes now looking in their direction.

Yazmin motioned her hand towards the buildings now.

"Here are our sleeping quarters, the library, our dining hall, armoury..." She trailed off, listing each of the different buildings, but Alexis didn't hear her as she took in the two figures now approaching them.

A young man, tall and lean, more muscled than Rhipley with shoulder-length black hair that was half tied in a knot above his head, olive skin and slightly up-tilted golden eyes with tattoos covering half of his neck, and a girl who looked to be only a few years younger than Alexis, with chin-length hair that was white-blond, violet eyes and pale skin approached them.

The man clapped Yazmin on the shoulder, looking Alexis over in amusement, and the girl just gave a slight up tilt of her head in greeting, Yazmin doing the same in return.

"Fresh meat, Yaz?" the man said with a wide grin, turning his attention to Amelia, then eyeing Aspen, who now sat next to Alexis, scratching her ear with a foot.

Yazmin just grinned, replying, "Rhipley and I grew bored looking at your dull faces all the time."

The girl, who'd only glanced at them once before seemingly finding them uninteresting, replied, "Speak for yourself."

Alexis and Amelia just glanced at each other, not entirely sure what to say or how to act. Yazmin threw a thumb over her shoulder to where the girls stood.

"This is Amelia," a bow of Amelia's head, which the man found amusing, "and this is Alexis."

He seemed to size Alexis up again, a half-smile plastered on his face and curiosity dancing in his eyes. A tut from Yazmin's direction had him looking back at his comrade, who added, "Hands off, Lukai. Rhipley already called dibs."

Alexis' mouth formed a tight line as she looked at Yazmin, who laughed. "It's a joke. Calm down." She quickly added, looking down at Aspen, "Oh, and this is Aspen, my new best friend."

Lukai scoffed. "Makes sense. You elves are such suckers for animals."

Yazmin smiled at Aspen and responded with, "They make for better company," before winking at Lukai.

The blonde-haired girl was now sizing up the Rainier sisters, glancing between the two. "Care to show us your skills?"

Amelia and Alexis both let out a choked cough at that, before Yazmin quickly replied for them.

"They're new to all this. We're just hosting them for now. Rampier's orders."

The girl and Lukai shared a look that conveyed exactly what they thought of that. *Freeloaders.*

"So, kitchen staff for Cook? Or stable hands?" the girl drawled, her lips now curving upwards at the corners in a sinister smile.

Lukai spat out a laugh at his friend's comment, and Yazmin just rolled her eyes.

"Ignore Zailah and Lukai. They're just hangers on that we can't seem to get rid of."

Lukai muttered a sarcastic, "Ouch," to which Yazmin returned with a show of her middle finger.

"Where is that dreadful brother of mine, anyway?" Lukai asked, his eyes darting around the area.

Alexis blurted, "Brother?"

They looked nothing alike, aside from the same smirks they seemed to share. That, and their height.

"We were raised together. He showed up a few years after I was dropped off here by my parents. I was freshly ten when a slobbering babe was brought in by then-Headmaster Wyntersier and current-Headmaster Draghone."

Alexis took in his appearance — he looked no older than twenty-five.

Zailah spoke this time. "We fae and elves stop aging when our brains reach maturity. For most, that's usually somewhere in our twenties. Some, though, not all. After that, we age slowly. Though the lifespan of elves far outweighs that of us fae. Where we can live for only a few thousand years, elves can live ten times that."

Alexis let out a low, impressed whistle, nodding as she asked, "How old are all of you?"

Before they could answer, a familiar voice sounded from behind.

The group whirled to see Rhipley approaching, a portrait of complete nonchalance.

"Haven't scared them off yet, have you?" Rhipley asked, clapping Lukai on the shoulder and giving a nod to Zailah, who barely gave him a second glance. "Do you girls know your way around a kitchen? Stables? General duties?"

Alexis frowned and said, "We're grown women. Of course, we know how to help out with household duties."

She felt offended that he thought so little of them to even ask.

Rhipley only smirked and replied, "Good, because until we've received word from Rampier, you'll be pulling your weight with the rest of us."

Amelia spoke this time. "Will we be… training?" She glanced towards where some hunters were still practicing combat, and nervousness clouded her face.

"Not until we know *how* long you'll be staying with us," was Rhipley's only response.

Yazmin grabbed both Amelia and Alexis by their elbows, and said, "Well, hate to cut this conversation short, but I have a tour to continue."

Lukai just called after where Yazmin was now dragging the girls. "Don't let her boss you around."

Alexis gave a nervous smile in return.

CHAPTER 16

After Yazmin had finished giving the girls a tour of the Hunter's Guild, she'd shown them to their sleeping quarters — a room with two single beds on either side, adorned with fur pelts and soft-looking pillows. Two large armoires stood on either side of the room a few feet from the ends of the beds, and a large fur rug sat in the centre of the room, with a small dresser between both beds, a lamp resting atop it.

Alexis and Amelia took in their new sleeping quarters, impressed with how cosy it appeared, while Aspen didn't waste any time in jumping onto the bed that sat against the far-right wall, to which all three girls chuckled at.

Alexis wasn't sure what to expect, if she was being honest, but this was far more generous than she'd imagined. She turned to where

Yazmin was standing by the door, arms crossed and taking in the room herself.

"Does every hunter share a similar room?"

Yazmin's lips tilted upwards in a mischievous grin, and she replied, "Not every hunter. The best of the best have rooms to ourselves, but most hunters share a room like this, yes."

Amelia glanced over her shoulder at their white-haired friend, and asked, "So you're the best of the best?"

Yazmin's gaze shifted to Amelia, and she fluttered her eyelashes. "Why, of course. Why do you think Rampier sent myself and Rhipley to your world? He doesn't send just anyone to Realm Walk between lands."

Amelia smiled, impressed by Yazmin's complete lack of humility. "Well, I look forward to seeing you in action, then."

Yazmin's own smile turned from mischievous to sincere, as if the compliment genuinely surprised her. She shook her head, refocussing herself, and announced, "Supper is at sundown. I'll come to retrieve you when it's time. Until then, as Rampier said, make yourselves at home. And don't tell *anyone* who you are or where you're from."

Amelia and Alexis shared a glance with raised brows, then looked back to Yazmin before they replied in unison, "Thank you."

Alexis was lying on her bed, looking at the ceiling when Amelia piped up from where she was sitting atop her own bed.

"So, this is our lives now."

Alexis let out a sigh. "Guess so. Not sure how I feel about it just yet, or our new... *friends,*" she mumbled.

"I don't know. Yazmin seems nice, albeit a little intimidating. She certainly loves talking about herself, not that it's a bad thing."

Alexis looked over at her sister and smirked. "That's not surprising." Amelia raised an eyebrow in question as Alexis went on.

"Are you truly oblivious to her flirting with you every chance she gets?"

Her sister blushed at that and blurted out, stammering through her words, "I-I don't know what you're talking about. She's just being friendly."

Alexis rolled her eyes and sat up, the movement waking Aspen, who'd been laying at the foot of the bed snoring away, and faced Amelia fully. "Maybe if you weren't so shy, you'd notice how she looks at you. How she *smiles* at you."

Amelia blurted, "Like you can talk! Have you even noticed the way Rhipley stares at you when you're not paying attention?"

Alexis let out a short breath, words escaping her.

"Besides, you know I've never been with a girl before. I don't know how to act. Maybe... maybe she's just curious about me."

Alexis stared at her sister for a few seconds, weighing the words she'd just heard. "Well, she's amused by you, at least. Rhipley, on the other hand, couldn't care less about me — about either of us, really. He's so dismissive, and he's honestly probably just waiting for us to be taken off his hands."

Amelia laughed drily before her expression turned worrisome. "What do you think is going to happen when we're summoned by the king?"

Alexis looked at the floor, trying to think of all possible scenarios, as if she could even conjure up a thought of how just one of those scenarios might play out.

"I don't know, Mill's. I don't know what *tomorrow* will even look like." Amelia's brows furrowed as she peered out the window between their beds. "But as long as we're together, as long as we *stick* together, we'll be okay."

Her sister's eyes met hers again, and Amelia gave a half smile that Alexis didn't believe for a second. She reached down to pat Aspen, who had now rolled over, belly exposed, glancing side-long at her sister, who'd returned to gazing out of the window once more, and Alexis followed her gaze to find that the sun was setting, darkness quickly enveloping the guild. A knock sounded at their door, drawing their attention from the window as Alexis said, "Come in."

Yazmin's head peeked in from the now-ajar door, and a grin cast across her beautiful features. "Time for supper."

She strode in, closing the door behind her, and tossed a bundle of clothes on either bed.

Alexis reached down to examine the clothes that now sat before her, gripping what appeared to be brown pants, a white linen shirt and knee-high chestnut boots, as well as some under garments.

"They aren't our hunter's leathers, but it'll have to do for now. It's essentially what we wear when we're not hunting and fighting and working to the bone. I guessed your sizes — if they end up being too big or small, just let me know," Yazmin said from where she now stood in the centre of the room. Amelia hummed, examining her own clothes.

After a few quiet moments, the girls shared a wary glance before looking at Yazmin, who took the hint and blurted, "Oh, sorry! I'm so used to being unbothered by my cohorts changing in front of me that I forgot not *everyone* is quite familiar with it."

Yazmin backed away and winked in Amelia's direction, a blush clouding her freckled face as she quickly lowered her eyes to pretend to examine the clothes once more.

"I'll be right outside," she said before ducking out of the room and shutting the door behind her.

As Yazmin led them down the corridors that were lined with rooms housing other hunters, Alexis took in the clothes she was now wearing, surprisingly not so different from those she'd arrived in just hours ago. She'd left Aspen in her room, Yazmin supplying some food and water and a cloth should the dog need to relieve herself.

Amelia appeared to be in a mood as she said, "If she shits in our room, I'm not sleeping there." She shot a pointed glare in Alexis' direction.

Yazmin replied, "She relieved herself earlier, didn't she?"

Alexis nodded.

"Well, she should be fine until after supper. Then you can just take her out again."

Alexis looked at her sister this time, a smug smile forming on her lips, which Amelia just rolled her eyes at.

Other hunters were quickly filling the corridors, making their way to the dining hall where Yazmin said their dinner would take place every night, and breakfast every morning.

Though, she'd added, it was completely voluntary.

Some hunters skipped breakfast or dinner in place of practice, some ate in their rooms, and some weren't even present to eat.

"How many hunters reside here?" Alexis asked from where she walked behind Amelia and Yazmin.

"A couple hundred or so. It changes often due to some hunters changing guilds, some being summoned back to their home country, and some due to… casualties," Yazmin said over a shoulder.

Alexis gulped at that last reason.

Amelia asked before Alexis could continue her questioning, "How often does that happen?" Though she spoke quietly, every fae and elf in the corridors could easily hear her, the evidence clear as some turned to watch them.

Yazmin sucked in a deep breath before responding, "Not as often as you'd think, much less to those who are more skilled. Though, even the best of us understand that when we leave these grounds, there's a chance we may never return."

Alexis felt saddened by that; by the fact that so many of these people around her had accepted that choosing this occupation meant also accepting their possible demise.

Yazmin clapped her hands once, ripping Alexis away from her grim thoughts, and announced, "Enough of that. It's your first day here. Let's not spend it speaking of the doom and gloom that is being a hunter."

Amelia and Alexis both made sad attempts at smiles, which Yazmin saw right through with a scoff.

Finally, she led them into a wider hallway than the one they'd just been walking down, where another set of large oak doors were already open to reveal a ridiculously large dining hall.

Students and hunters alike, it appeared, shared this space.

As if Yazmin had read Alexis' thoughts, she said, "This is one of the few spaces where hunters and students mingle, really. Why have this large a room when there're barely enough hunters to occupy it at a time?"

Alexis nodded in agreement, taking in the wooden tables scattered throughout, matching wooden seats accompanying them. At the very back of the dining hall sat a table with nine chairs lining it, the central chair the largest of them. Yazmin followed her gaze and supplied, "For the Headmaster, senior hunters and academy teachers."

Indeed, Rampier and his colleagues were now walking up the stairs to the dais where the table sat to take up their seats, the Headmaster heading for the one in the centre.

The students and hunters stood with their hands clasped behind their backs as they faced the table at the back of the dining hall. They stood in complete silence, waiting.

Yazmin quietly led the sisters to a table on the right, only a few spots left where others stood. After a few moments, Rampier gave a bow of his head and sat down, everyone else following suit.

Alexis and Amelia took up their seats, Yazmin choosing a spot across from them, and as they observed those they now sat with, they quickly realised who was in their company.

Alexis, in her hurry to sit down, hadn't noticed Rhipley positioned directly beside her, along with Zailah and Lukai across from them, next to Yazmin. An unknown girl sat on the other side of Rhipley, paying the sisters no heed.

Yazmin chuckled. "Sorry we're late. I was busy being a tour guide." She flicked her braids over a shoulder dramatically, now swaying freely from the updo she'd adorned earlier, as if being their personal tour guide was tiresome work.

Lukai gave her a flick on the nose, which she responded to with a chomp of her teeth. Rhipley was seemingly deep in conversation with the girl who sat next to him, and Yazmin interrupted, "Wow, Tatiana. You could at least introduce yourself to our guests."

The girl, Tatiana, just glared at Yazmin, which she returned with a smirk. Zailah spoke this time, her voice just as bored as it had been earlier. "Don't mind her. She's too good for anyone, just likes to sit with us for charity."

Tatiana gave Zailah the finger, which Zailah returned with one of her own. Tatiana angled her head around Rhipley, taking in the sisters. She looked them both up and down before returning to her conversation.

Alexis scoffed and muttered, "Nice to meet you, too."

Just as quickly as she'd said it, she remembered that everyone at their table could hear her.

Rhipley and Tatiana halted their conversation, both slowly turning to face Alexis.

"Pardon?" Tatiana asked in a hostile tone.

Yazmin awkwardly picked at her bread roll, and Zailah and Lukai watched Alexis in amusement.

You've done it now, their expressions seemed to say.

Alexis returned her attention to Tatiana, who was still waiting for a response. "What, nothing to say now?"

Rhipley quietly said, "Tatiana, drop it."

She ignored him, jerking her chin for Alexis to respond.

Alexis held her stare, and finally said, "Where I'm from, we're polite to those we're meeting for the first time. We don't just ignore them."

Lukai let out a low whistle, and Zailah smirked. Amelia sat silently next to Alexis, suddenly finding interest in her plate and the food now atop it.

Tatiana tensed her jaw, observing Alexis' rounded ears, and replied, "Where *are* you from?"

Alexis went still and looked to Yazmin for help.

Yazmin took the hint, saying, "They're from Lilhan. We're hosting them for a while, so be nice." She pointed her fork in Tatiana's direction, narrowing her eyes.

Tatiana side eyed Yazmin, before returning her attention to Alexis, leaning in and saying with a serpentine tone, "So you're humans?" Alexis and Amelia both nodded, the latter gulping.

"Well, in that case, I couldn't give less of a shit about who you are." She gave a smug smile and flicked her long, black braid over her shoulder before standing from the table and walking away.

Rhipley let out a sigh, not daring to meet Alexis' stare before he, too, stood and followed Tatiana.

Alexis could feel her heart beating out of her chest, but not out of fear or intimidation. No, the exchange with Tatiana had made her temper rise so high that her heart was thumping out of pure anger. She breathed in deeply, trying to re-focus herself.

Trying and failing.

She turned back to where Lukai was slowly clapping, and where Zailah had returned to her food, as if nothing had happened.

"Congratulations," Lukai said sarcastically, and Alexis glared at him. "You'd have been better off keeping your mouth shut."

She furrowed her brows in confusion, and Amelia spoke as Alexis struggled to find the words. "Why?"

Lukai smirked, but his eyes stayed on Alexis as he said, "Tatiana is fae nobility. Her mothers are highly powerful and important amongst our kind, so, in turn, Tatiana believes she's the queen of this Hunter's Guild. I'm surprised you've never heard of them, though I suppose you humans *do* prefer to keep to yourselves."

Alexis held his stare for a few seconds before looking down at her empty plate. She'd lost her words, couldn't think of anything to say. So, she remained quiet as her sister, Zailah and Yazmin began speaking amongst themselves.

She stared at her plate for long seconds before she felt a thud on the seat next to her, and she turned to see Lukai now taking up Rhipley's spot.

"Can I help you?" Alexis asked, a little too coldly.

Lukai put a hand over his heart in mocking anguish, as he replied, "Is that any way to treat a friend?"

Alexis just raised an incredulous brow. "Friend?"

Lukai grinned at her, and she had to appreciate his beauty, how utterly handsome he was. His golden eyes danced with amusement as he noticed Alexis admiring him, and he responded, "You're not too bad yourself."

Alexis blushed, looking away in an attempt to hide it, though she knew he'd seen. She grabbed a bread roll from a basket sitting in the centre of the table before dipping her knife in the butter on her plate, as she asked, "Does she hate humans or something?"

Lukai let out a sigh. "Humans killed her parents. She holds a personal grudge against your kind, though deep down she knows *you're* not responsible for what happened to her parents, nor any of the other humans here, so try not to take it personally."

Alexis scoffed. "Bit hard when she practically spat in my face."

Lukai just huffed a laugh and nodded. "True, true."

They sat in silence for a few moments before Alexis asked, "Her parents? As in her birth parents?"

Lukai nodded. "Her mothers rescued her when they were visiting the Eastern Continent. She was just a girl, no older than five."

Alexis let out a short breath.

"I don't know all the gory details, but apparently her parents were commoners, and they were walking home one night when a gang of mortals attacked them, demanding their money, and when her parents had nothing to give them, they…"

He trailed off, but Alexis could guess what had happened next. "Before they could harm Tatiana, her mothers caught a whiff of the blood from the scene, from what had been done to Tatiana's parents, and they stepped in to save her. I never saw the reports, but from what I've heard of the aftermath, *I* wouldn't want to cross them."

Alexis was speechless, unsure that anything she'd have to say would even add meaning to their conversation. Lukai gave her a small smile, and she found herself once again lost in his beauty.

"She's… difficult to deal with, obviously. But she's got a good heart, and she's fiercely loyal to those she loves. So, like I said, try not to take her indifference personally."

Alexis gave him a half smile in return, and replied, "Well, I doubt we'll be best friends."

Lukai chuckled, his golden eyes sparkling, and Alexis couldn't help chuckling herself. Yazmin, despite the conversation taking place around her, looked at Alexis, a sly grin forming on her lips.

Alexis' brows bunched as she subtly shook her head, to which Yazmin returned with a slow nod of her own, her sly grin growing. Alexis rolled her eyes at that.

CHAPTER 17

Rhipley stood silently beside Tatiana as she filled her plate with different fruits. He didn't dare say anything, not until *she* was ready to. Quietly, she eyed her plate, then his, still empty, and began piling the same fruits onto it.

He didn't object; didn't need to, since she knew him well enough to guess which foods he would and wouldn't like. Finally, her gorgeous brown eyes, twin to his, met his gaze. She furrowed her brows in irritation and asked flatly, "What?"
Rhipley just shrugged his shoulders and replied simply, "Nothing, just wanted to make sure you're okay."

She didn't smile, though he knew she was trying her best to hide her gratitude at him choosing to join her when she'd so abruptly left the table.

"I'm fine," was all she said before turning to head back to their friends. They walked silently for long seconds before she asked quietly, "Did you have a hand in bringing them here?"

Rhipley just nodded, his lips becoming a thin line.

"Why?" She stopped abruptly, halting him by grabbing his arm as she stepped closer, her words now a whisper. He looked down at where she'd grabbed him, then met her wary eyes.

"They're innocent, Tatiana. I don't even think they'd know how to wield a sword if given the chance."

She didn't return his smile as she replied, "I don't care. Humans can't be trusted, even the few who reside here. Not really. They're selfish and cruel and take what they believe is theirs, not caring about who they hurt in the process."

His heart ached at the words, at the hurt in her eyes, as he leaned down to place a kiss atop her forehead. "*They're* not. Give them a chance."

She didn't back down, instead leaning away from him. "Why would you let Yazmin introduce them to our group?"

He sighed, accepting that this was an argument he wouldn't win. "You know what Yazmin's like. Leave her be, leave *them* be."

Tatiana didn't move. She just stood there, her chocolate eyes piercing his.

"We didn't have a choice, Tat. Rampier gave us a task, so we have to see it through."

She held his stare for a few seconds longer, before dropping it and gazing toward the table, where Lukai was now entertaining Alexis. Rhipley followed her gaze, and something in his chest tightened at the sight, though he wasn't sure why. He shook the feeling away, baffled at the strange, fleeting emotion.

Rhipley returned his focus to Tatiana and cupped her cheek in one hand, her beautiful brown skin soft to the touch.

"You don't have to pay them any heed. You don't even have to talk to them if you don't want to. But please, just give them a chance."

She let out a defeated sigh and said quietly, "I don't care who they are or why they're here. If they leave me be, I'll do the same."

That was good enough an answer for Rhipley as he gave her a grateful smile and Tatiana stood on her toes to plant a brief kiss to his cheek.

Alexis watched the intimate encounter between Rhipley and Tatiana, ignoring the strange, jealous pang in her chest as she shifted her gaze to Lukai, a silent question in her eyes.

"Don't even bother trying to decipher whatever is going on between those two," Zailah drawled, her fork angled towards the two.

Alexis looked to Zailah, biting her lip. She was right — Alexis shouldn't care, shouldn't pry. It wasn't her place to.

She tried to subtly look in Rhipley's direction again, who was now smiling down at Tatiana as they approached the table once more, and forced the feeling of jealousy down deep.

Amelia, bless her, shifted the conversation. "So, how did the rest of you meet?"

Zailah and Lukai shared a knowing look, the latter grinning from ear to ear, and Yazmin leaned back in anticipation, trying to quickly chew her mouthful of food.

Before she could speak, Zailah instead piped up, "I've been here the longest. I was here when Princess Aurelia had just been named Headmaster, may her soul rest in peace."

The others followed suit, murmuring those same words.

May her soul rest in peace.

"Lukai, as you know, showed up when he was ten. He's been a thorn in my side ever since, but I just can't seem to shake him."

A pointed glare in Lukai's direction, which he returned with a grin.

"You love me. Don't be afraid to admit it."

She returned his comment with a middle finger, her attention already on her food once more.

Lukai's stare, however, lingered on the petite woman.

Yazmin spoke this time, finally swallowing her mouthful of food. "I came here when I was twenty, as was requested by my family. I've been here ever since."

"And," Lukai said, clapping Rhipley's shoulder as he sat down, "We've been *inseparable* ever since."

Rhipley just huffed a laugh in response. "I've tried to shake you all off, but it's proved impossible."

Lukai and Yazmin opened their mouths in mocking, shocked expressions, placing their hands over their hearts.

"You take that back," Yazmin said, putting on a fake, trembling voice.

Lukai glanced between Alexis and Rhipley, asking, "Would you like me to go back to my seat?"

Before Alexis could speak, Rhipley quickly blurted, "No, it's fine."

Alexis scoffed quietly, returning to her food. Lukai, however, seemed completely unfazed by the exchange as he turned to Alexis and asked, "Want a *fun* tour guide after supper?"

Yazmin let out a gasp and glared at Lukai. "I *am* the fun tour guide."

Alexis laughed nervously, glancing between the two.

"Yazmin *is* fun, but it wouldn't hurt to have the perspective of someone else. Maybe you can take Amelia separately, Yaz?"

Yazmin and Amelia shared a glance, the former grinning wickedly.

Yazmin huffed an exasperated breath before saying, "Fine. If you want the boring, overbearing tour guide, be my guest."

Alexis tried not to glance sidelong at Rhipley, who had remained quiet throughout the conversation, Tatiana doing the same.

She decided then and there that it wasn't worth her worry, and turned to Lukai before announcing, "I bet we can make it fun."

Lukai's answering smile told her he had exactly that planned.

CHAPTER 18

After they'd finished supper and everyone went their separate ways, Alexis had returned to their room to fetch Aspen, who couldn't help her excitement and jumped to lick her owner upon stepping past the threshold.

Sure enough, she'd relieved herself on the cloth Yazmin had supplied earlier, but, to Alexis' relief, it wasn't the *shit* Amelia had warned her of. Amelia and Yazmin had ventured off to god knew where following dinner, and Lukai, currently waiting by the door, had accompanied Alexis to retrieve Aspen.

"Cute dog," he said, smiling down at the excited German Shepherd who eyed him warily.

"She's cautious of newcomers, so don't be surprised if she doesn't take an immediate liking to you," Alexis warned.

Lukai simply strode into the room and crouched, not making a single move to touch or pet Aspen, instead allowing her to choose to come to him. Alexis stood still, observing the interaction about to take place, nerves wracking her emotions at the uncertainty of what might happen. Aspen's hackles were standing, but she didn't growl, didn't bark. She simply sniffed the ground, slowly prowling closer and closer to him. Long seconds passed, but Aspen finally approached Lukai, sniffing his now outstretched hand before licking his fingers and wagging her tail. Lukai looked up at Alexis smugly. "She likes me."

Alexis just shook her head and chuckled, relieved that Aspen had chosen to trust rather than attack him.

Aspen's kisses had become an onslaught of affection as she stood on her hind legs, her front paws now resting on Lukai's shoulders, Lukai narrowly dodging the slobbery attack.

He looked up to where Alexis stood, her back now against her armoire as she smirked at him, his expression a silent request to be rescued.

Alexis chuckled again as she said, "Hey, you asked for it when you approached her. Deal with the consequences."

Once they'd finally been able to calm Aspen down, Alexis had gone to collect the bowls and cloth, but Lukai had stopped her, saying that the cleaners would come around and "take care of it."

She'd sighed with relief at that, not particularly wanting to deal with it after she'd just eaten.

Stepping out into the hall, she noticed hunters of all sorts were now walking up and down the corridor, some standing idly by, chatting away with each other, their Daeanimus' with them. Alexis eyed each animal, noting birds of different varieties, canines and felines, and even some rodents. She turned to Lukai, who was smiling and waving at the hunters as they passed.

"So, what exactly *is* a Daeanimus?"

Lukai looked down at her, his eyes searching hers before answering, "I'm surprised you don't know."

He raised his brows at Alexis, who only waited patiently, blank faced.

"Their souls are tethered to their companions. The stronger the bond, the stronger the connection." He glanced to where Aspen walked anxiously beside Alexis, her eyes darting between each Daeanimus.

"You *should* know, after all. You and Aspen have the bond."
Alexis stopped her walking, brows bunching together in confusion as she, too, glanced down to where Aspen now halted, the dog's beautiful brown eyes looking up at her curiously.

"She's my... Daeanimus?"
Lukai stopped a few feet ahead, turning to face her. His hand beckoned for her to continue walking, to avoid crowding in the middle of the hallway as he offered a warm smile.

"Of course you are. I scented it the second we met."
She returned her gaze to him, continuing her pace alongside his as they exited the dorms and walked out onto the grounds.

"You can sense those kinds of things?"
He just gave her a sly smile before replying, "You mustn't have much experience with our kind, huh?"

Amusement danced in his golden eyes, and Alexis forced herself to look away as she thought of an excuse, a lie.

"Not really. Where I'm from, it's only humans. We don't get a lot of... your kind around our lands."

Lukai hummed in understanding before continuing. "Fae and elves can sense how anyone is feeling, what emotions they're going through. Anyone who has heightened senses can, really."

Alexis' heartbeat quickened, and as though he was confirming her exact thoughts, he added, "And I can sense when you're nervous. I can hear your heartbeat, after all."

She couldn't fight the blush that rose to her cheeks, and she looked away from him, trying to find something, anything else, to focus on. Alexis finally said, her eyes now roaming over their surroundings, "So Yazmin and Rhipley knew? And Zailah?"

Lukai nodded. "They probably didn't think to tell you, likely so they wouldn't overwhelm you. Though, I'm surprised you don't know about humans having Daeanimus bonds if you're from Lilhan. Is it not common for the Griffin Riders of Norisk to have the bond?"

She fumbled for the words, unsure how to even respond. "Well, I suppose I'm one of the few who's lived under a rock this whole time."

Lukai huffed a laugh. "I suppose so."

They walked in silence for a long minute, before Lukai asked, "So, which town *do* you hail from?"

Alexis tried with all her might to keep her heartbeat steady, to appear calm as she responded, "You probably haven't heard of it. It's more of a village, really."

He clicked his tongue, replying with a simple, "Oh."

Night had fallen, and the sky was alight with stars.

She hadn't noticed how clear the sky was in this world on that first night, though. The constant cover of trees didn't give her much opportunity to peer up during their trek through Fallandor Forest.

The sky twinkled, shooting stars racing across the endless black expanse. She couldn't help the gasp that came out of her, as she appreciated the beauty of it.

The lack of light pollution in this world was so apparent, she found herself grateful for it, to be given the chance to actually appreciate the night sky in its entirety.

Alexis could feel Lukai staring at her, and she dared to look over at him, meeting those beautiful golden eyes. He was smiling sincerely, whether out of amusement or adoration, she didn't know.

Alexis didn't want to think about it. *Couldn't* think about it — she and Mitchell had just broken up, and even though she knew she'd likely never see him again, Alexis couldn't help the twinge of guilt that rattled through her.

The thoughts she couldn't keep at bay, telling her she was a traitor, that it was too soon to be moving on.

"What's wrong?" Lukai asked.

Alexis quickly dropped his gaze, trying to find the words. "I'm just trying to figure out why you're looking at me like that."

He didn't hesitate as he said, "I find you to be very beautiful."

She chuckled in disbelief. Not at the compliment, but at how bold he was. "You don't even know me."

He just smirked and replied, "Do I have to know you to appreciate that you're beautiful?"

She narrowed her eyes at him. "Well, attractiveness isn't all that matters if you truly want to get to know someone."

Lukai just shrugged his shoulders and returned his gaze to the sky.

"Are you always this forward?" Alexis asked when he didn't say anything, following where he watched the endless black sea of stars.

"Only with beautiful women."

She rolled her eyes, but smiled faintly to herself. Even if she shouldn't be moving on so quickly, it wouldn't hurt to entertain this little flirtation.

The faint chatter of hunters filled the quiet space as the two continued to watch the sky, and though Alexis watched the stars intently, she could still feel Lukai watching her every now and again.

Snapping her out of the zone she'd become engulfed in, Lukai asked, "Care to see the Red Oak at night?"

Alexis smiled with anticipation. "Is it just as beautiful?"

He returned her smile with one of his own, before gesturing towards the gates that led to the courtyard.

The tree was even more stunning at twilight, fireflies sitting within the branches and lighting it up like a Christmas tree. Alexis couldn't help the audible, impressed gasp that came out of her at the magnificent sight. Lukai stood next to her, grinning from ear to ear at her reaction.

She asked quietly, "Were you close with her? Princess Aurelia?"

Lukai's grin turned into a soft smile as he replied, "Rhipley and I are like brothers, thanks to her."

Alexis angled her head in confusion, and Lukai went on.

"We didn't get along for a while. Rhipley was angry, resentful, after learning that his birth parents had *abandoned* him here, as he likes to say. It wasn't easy getting close to him for some time because of that, but Aurelia refused to have us fighting and arguing. She forced us to get along. If it weren't for her influence, I don't think we'd be where we are today."

Alexis sensed someone approach from behind, and she could only guess who it was before she'd even turned around.

Rhipley and Tatiana stood there, the former gazing at the tree with sad eyes, the latter refusing to meet Alexis' stare, her arms crossed and looking none-too impressed.

Alexis didn't dare speak first, instead willing her mouth into a smile; the best smile she could possibly muster.

"So, are you done giving her a tour of the grounds, Luke?" Rhipley asked as he rested his hands in his pant pockets. The clothes he wore now differed from his leathers, rather similar to hers and Lukai's — a white linen shirt and brown pants.

Though she didn't want to admit it, least of all to Rhipley, she had to appreciate how attractive he looked. He could probably wear a potato sack and still look gorgeous.

As if sensing her shift in thoughts, the three fae looked at her.

Alexis didn't dare let her smile falter as she met their eyes, and she wondered if they could also hear her thoughts. When Tatiana rolled her eyes and Rhipley continued talking to Lukai, she guessed that they couldn't. Or that they simply just didn't care.

Alexis tried not to stare at Tatiana, but she couldn't help herself — she was truly beautiful, her brown skin glowing under the lit-up tree and various lampposts.

She wore the same white linen shirt and brown pants — the day clothes for the hunters, she recalled Yazmin saying. Her long black hair was tied back from her face in a braid that snaked down her back — the same braid she wore at dinner. Her eyes were of deepest brown, identical to Rhipley's aside from the slight down-tilt of them, and gold jewellery adorned her pointed ears, climbing their way up her lobes and cartilage.

Another singular gold ring sat at her septum, complementing the curve of her nose, the gold radiant against her skin tone.

Alexis didn't think before lightly touching her own ears, where jewellery also snaked up her lobes to her cartilage.

Tatiana finally turned to her and asked, "Can I help you?"

Alexis shifted her smile into something sweet and said, "I think we got off on the wrong foot earlier. I'm Alexis."

She reached out a hand, waiting for Tatiana to shake it in return. Tatiana simply looked at her outstretched hand and chose to ignore the gesture.

Alexis retracted her hand, biting her lip as Tatiana let out a sigh. "I'm Tatiana Elrin, daughter of Ladies Chanti and Marlene Elrin."

Alexis pretended to appear impressed, despite having not a single clue who her parents were, other than recalling the fact that they were rich and noble and… deadly.

Tatiana studied Alexis' expression for a few long seconds, and Alexis couldn't help but hope she didn't see through it.

Instead, Tatiana let out a slight hum of approval, then turned back to the conversation still taking place between Lukai and Rhipley.

"Well, I'm going to head to bed," Alexis said after some time, interrupting them.

Lukai halted and looked down at her, worry on his face. "Are you alright?"

She nodded, offering him her pathetic attempt at a half smile.

"I'm just tired. It's been a long day. I'll see you tomorrow."

She reached for his hand and gave it a brief squeeze before adding, "Thank you."

Lukai returned her smile, and as she turned to walk back through the gates to the hunter's quarters, Aspen strolling at her side, she could feel the three fae staring after her.

CHAPTER 19

The days that followed were filled with chores upon chores, the guild's faculty constantly
 expressing how grateful they were to have extra helping hands in the kitchen with the food preparation, in the dormitories and classrooms with the general cleaning and in the stables and grounds tidying up after the various animals and Daeanimus'.
It wasn't quite what the girls were used to, but they didn't dare complain, especially given the protection from D'Roghal's goons and scouts they were
receiving in return.

When they weren't cleaning or washing dishes, the girls were hanging out with their new friends at dinner or between breaks. When they could, at least, and when their friends were actually at the guild and not out on missions.

Sometimes, the hunters would be sent out for days at a time and return either cleaner than they'd left or covered in substances of different kinds.

Blood, mud, dirt.

One day, Yazmin and Rhipley had returned covered in so much blood, Amelia had nearly had a heart attack. Almost none of it was ever theirs, thankfully, but it didn't make the girls worry any less. Though, Alexis had to remind herself that Rhipley, Yazmin and the rest were trained professionals — she and Amelia's need for worry was null and void.

Oftentimes, Alexis would find herself lying awake at night, Aspen at her feet in her preferred spot, thinking about their old lives, and how different everything was now.

She'd wonder about what Sam and their father might be doing. What Mitchell and their friends might be doing. Whether she might ever see her brother and father, her friends, or her ex again.

Sometimes she could keep the thoughts at bay, especially when she was so busy with the various chores, too drained to even conjure a single thought at all.

But when she was lying in bed at night with nothing to distract her, the thoughts came flooding in. Sometimes she cried.

Quietly, so Amelia wouldn't notice, and sometimes she was so sad that she couldn't even muster a single tear, but the ache in her chest was still prominent no matter how many days passed.

Whether or not Amelia struggled with the same thoughts, she wasn't sure. Alexis had wanted to bring it up, but had known it wouldn't help their situation, especially with no way to return home. And so, despite her sorrowful thoughts, she woke up every day nonetheless and dealt with her new life as best she could.

Alexis and Amelia woke on an already-warm day before the sun had even risen to help set up the dining hall for breakfast when Rhipley appeared at their bedroom door, only knocking once before opening it.

"Excuse you! What if we were indecent?" Alexis exclaimed.

Rhipley simply smirked and replied, "Nothing I haven't seen before."

Alexis found herself speechless at the comment, and she didn't hide the disgust that coated her emotions, knowing Rhipley could sense every shred of it. Whether he'd actually cared to sense it, he didn't say, and instead leaned against their doorway with crossed arms, donning his hunter's leathers, his usual sword sheathed at his back, the onyx hilt peeking over a muscled shoulder.

Alexis tried not to pay him too much heed, choosing to not give him the satisfaction of her attention. Aspen, much to Alexis' dismay, had walked up to Rhipley and leaned against his legs, waiting for ear scruffs, which he'd happily obliged. Given that the girls had, thankfully, already gotten dressed, Alexis asked, "What do you need?"

Rhipley looked her up and down, then glanced at Amelia, who was sitting on her bed, and said, "The king has summoned you."
Alexis' heart thundered in her chest, and though she attempted to appear calm, she knew Rhipley's heightened hearing could detect it from a mile away.

"When do we go?" Amelia asked when Alexis didn't respond.
"Today. We need to have you prepared, which means appropriate attire and a quick lesson on how to speak and act in the presence of royals, which, if I'm correct in assuming, neither of you has ever done before."

When neither sister answered, he clicked his tongue and turned from his spot in the doorway, signalling for someone the sisters couldn't see.

Before they could react, three women, all appearing human, walked in carrying various dresses, cosmetics, hair accessories, and shoes. How they were carrying *all* that without struggle, Alexis wasn't sure.

"Pepper, Joan and Matilda will assist with your appearances, and when they're done, Yazmin will be down to fetch you for some quick lessons."
Without another word, he walked away and left the handmaidens to their work.

The three women had finally finished their hard work after two hours of making the girls over — Amelia's hair had been curled, two gold clips pinning her red locks back, the loose curled strands falling neatly down her back, while Alexis' hair had been fashioned into a low bun, her bangs left out to shape her face.

They'd put either sister in the most beautiful gowns, Alexis' green with ivory details, and Amelia's a gorgeous cobalt blue and gold. As she admired herself, then her sister, Alexis realised they looked almost exactly like how the maidens in her novels back home were always described. She made a quick mental note to find something to read in the library at some point, if and when she got the chance. Perhaps their meeting with the king might grant her that privilege. Or strip it away completely.

Once the three women had left, giving small bows of their heads before walking from the room, Yazmin appeared in the doorway. She gawked at both girls, quickly sizing Alexis up before turning her attention to Amelia, who blushed at Yazmin's admiration, averting her eyes.

"You look… beautiful," Yazmin muttered mostly to Amelia, though Alexis thanked her all the same.

Amelia gave her a sincere smile in return, muttering a *thank you* Alexis could barely hear.

As if remembering why she was there in the first place, Yazmin re-composed herself, standing straight and announcing, "Follow me. We're going to the library to give you a brief rundown of what to expect before our meeting with His Royal Majesty at two."

As if her wish to see the library had been granted, Alexis gave a silent thanks to the universe.

The library, which was fairly secluded from the rest of the buildings, was absolutely glorious — large wood-carved doors opened to a long, tall room adorned with desks and chairs neatly set up in vertical rows, and towering bookcases filled with various publishing's graced either side of the building. Various sets of spiral stairs that led to the upper floors were scattered throughout, and a large tree stood at the very back, surrounded by a small pond filled with lotus flowers, lily pads and golden, white and black fish.

When Yazmin had given them the tour, they'd only briefly seen the library, and it had merely been the outside given that Yazmin didn't wish to disturb those studying inside.
Alexis and Amelia gaped in astonishment at the building's interior, unable to help their admiration of the beautiful architecture surrounding them.

The library was empty, minus a librarian and some bookkeepers, with students all in their various classes, Yazmin had said.

As Yazmin gave the girls some time to explore while they waited for Rhipley, Alexis looked to the ceiling where the sun shone through the glass roof; it would take her forever to explore this place, but she didn't mind.

She'd already decided then and there that on her days off, she'd come here and read to her heart's content.

As Alexis made to explore the book shelves closest to her, Amelia and Yazmin chatting quietly a few feet away, a ray of sunlight from outside shone through from behind her, lighting up the space further. She snapped her attention to the doors, seeing Rhipley now standing there.

"Are you *finally* ready?" was all he said before making his way to one of the tables.

"Hey, beauty takes time," Yazmin quipped, earning a giggle from Amelia.

Rhipley just rolled his eyes and sat down at the table, pulling a chair out next to him for Alexis to take up. Yazmin clicked her fingers and various history books appeared, most labelled in that language Alexis didn't understand. With a wave of Yazmin's hand, the words appeared in English, or whatever they called it in this world.

"What did you do?" Alexis asked, noting one book that now read *The Royal Houses of Xalentya.*

Yazmin replied, "I simply made the First Language appear as something you can understand. Think of it as the dust being wiped away."

Amelia asked curiously, "How do you do that… thing, where you make things appear out of thin air?" She snapped her fingers for emphasis.

Yazmin considered for a second before saying, "Think of it as Realm Walking, only this particular power," she clicked her fingers, and the books disappeared, then re-appeared with another click, "is more common amongst magic wielders. Not *very* common, but still more common than Realm Walking. As for *how*, I couldn't tell you. I'm sure there's someone who *can*, but I'm not that person. Magic is a mysterious thing." Yazmin held her hand up, flexing her fingers.

Amelia's mouth quirked to the side, her eyes falling to the books. Yazmin continued, "However, we can't make just anything appear — it needs to be within a certain radius."

"So, that first night we came here — the rabbits, the tents, the firewood…?" Amelia asked quietly.

"From a house nearby. But don't worry, we returned what we borrowed, along with a handsome sack of gold — minus the rabbits," Rhipley said. The corner of his mouth tugged up into a smirk.

Alexis thought about that for a second, scoffing and shaking her head in disbelief, then remembered that she, too, could Realm Walk somehow. As if it were so easy to forget.

"Is Realm Walking a desired magic in this land?" she asked, Yazmin's words of how uncommon the power was echoing through her head.

Rhipley said, "It's sought out by many, and given that it's rare, powerful people protect or hire most Realm Walkers. Some Realm Walkers are even in hiding, choosing seclusion to protect themselves and their families. Yazmin and I, for instance, have the protection of the Hunter's Guild here in Preshia, and the royal family that resides in Fallandor. Most of Xalentya's population isn't even aware that some of us can Walk between worlds. They assume our power is limited to this realm. But, some radicals believe our kind shouldn't exist in the first place, that walking between worlds should be forbidden, that it defies the gods. The laws of nature. So, they hunt us down, either to eradicate us or use our power for their own deeds."

Yazmin chimed in, clicking her tongue as she leafed through one of the books. "You can't blame their logic, though. In the hands of the wrong person, Realm Walking *can* be dangerous. We're just lucky that so few of us can Walk between worlds. That so few are aware that it's even possible."

Alexis asked quietly, "Does the King of Preshia know I can Realm Walk?"

Rhipley and Yazmin shared a look, before Rhipley replied, "No. Not yet. Rampier is still unsure on whether to tell him. King Mikkel is an… *interesting* male. If he were to get his hands on your power, who knows what he might do? We wouldn't have the authority to hold you from him, since you're not technically a part of this guild. The only reason he hasn't used myself or Yazmin is because Rampier promised to cut ties with the royal family if he so much as tries to cross that line." Alexis gulped.

"Which, as I'd like to remind you, is why we're here now. To teach you about the royal family." He tapped a finger on the book that Alexis had been holding.

And so, Yazmin and Rhipley began schooling them. As they did, Alexis pondered what Rhipley had said.

Male — because that's what fae and elves, she supposed, were referred to. Not women or men, or guys or girls. *Males and females*.

Try as he might, Rhipley couldn't stop thinking of Alexis in that dress.

Every chance he got, he found himself watching her, admiring her. Sometimes, however, he'd find Yazmin watching *him* below her lashes, a smirk plastered on her face.

He, in turn, would give her a light kick to the shin, puzzling the sisters when she'd yelp, and when Rhipley would act equally puzzled by her outbursts.

If it weren't for their utterly human clumsiness and overall obliviousness, Amelia and Alexis could very easily pass for fae nobility upon first glance.

If they hid those rounded ears of theirs, at least.

Thankful for the fact that Alexis' human senses weren't nearly as honed as his fae ones, and therefore couldn't detect his emotions, he brushed away that small feeling of annoyance at her utter lack of delight at his presence.

Rhipley needed to remind himself, though, that she didn't really owe him anything. Sure, he'd saved her twice, but she was being looked after by his friends and the Headmaster, too.

Everyone at this guild looked after them now, really.

Perhaps she just saw him as some other male, or guy, as they were called by mortals in her world.

He shrugged off the thought and put on that face of cool demeanour. The one that Alexis, apparently, wasn't too fond of.

He tried to ignore that fact, too, as he continued tutoring Alexis, who was quickly revealing herself to be a fast learner.

CHAPTER 20

Mid-day rolled around quickly, and Alexis was struggling to keep her eyes open as she realised how mentally drained she was from all they'd just learnt.

King Mikkel had been the ruler of Preshia for nearly twenty years, and he resided in Fallandor, the largest city in this country, with his wife, Queen Ida, and his son, Prince Frederik.

They were chosen by the various council members after the previous king and queen, Princess Aurelia's parents, passed away, both their daughters unable to take up the throne and, with no living direct relatives, a noble house needed to be voted in.

King Mikkel was a generally fair ruler, in the same sense that anyone with power and greed was considered *fair*, and the opinions of him differed depending on who was asked.

All three members of the royal family were demi-fae, which was quite the controversy in a fae-dominated city, but after some time, the citizens of Preshia grew to accept their new monarchs.

Given that they were half-fae, it was more easily accepted than if they'd been human or, god forbid, anything other than elf or fae.

Yazmin had taught the girls how to properly curtsy, since bowing was for hunters, knights, soldiers and noblemen, and how to address the king, queen and prince — to speak only when addressed, and to leave any other conversation to Rhipley and Yazmin.

Alexis' nerves were like a drum beneath her skin as she, Amelia, Rhipley and Yazmin Realm Walked to the outskirts of the city. They couldn't transport into Fallandor as it, too, had a ward surrounding it, Rhipley had mentioned.

Luckily, however, the walk to the city was a mere ten-minutes, unlike the entire day hike they'd had to endure to get to the Hunter's Guild. As they followed the cobblestone pathway that would led to the main bridge into Fallandor, Rhipley muttered, too quiet for Yazmin and Amelia to hear, who were walking ahead, "You look nice."

Alexis chose not to look at him, as she scoffed. "Wow, thanks. You certainly know how to make a girl swoon."

Rhipley ignored her comment, and she huffed a laugh. "Well, I suppose your *girlfriend* wouldn't like you telling other girls how beautiful they are."

Rhipley looked at her and said, "She's not my... girlfriend, not that we even use that term here. We're just... friends."

Alexis replied, "Ah, yes. Your *friend*. With benefits, of course." Rhipley snapped back, "Why are you so bothered by it, anyway? You seem perfectly content with Lukai's attention."

Alexis clicked her tongue, finally meeting Rhipley's stare. "Are you jealous?"

Rhipley ignored her, exhaling a deep breath and rolling his eyes. She let out a dramatic sigh of her own and added, "Yes, Lukai is quite the gentleman. I'm glad to know not all male hunters are assholes."

She could have sworn he smiled slightly, amused at her comment, despite the fact she meant it as a jab.

"Tatiana and I have history. She's not nearly as awful as you make her out to be. She's just wary of humans, especially those she has never met, and who are treated as top-priority cargo for reasons unknown to her."

Alexis scoffed. "Oh, I see, so we're cargo now? Understood. I guess *now* your lack of manners makes perfect sense."

Rhipley sighed. "I didn't mean it like that."

But Alexis was already walking ahead to Amelia and Yazmin, holding the sides of her dress with both hands and pretending her ridiculous shoes didn't hurt her feet with every step.

Alexis huffed to herself, irritated at what Rhipley had said, even though deep down she knew he didn't mean it negatively. As she caught up to her sister and Yazmin, she found that both were sharing a knowing look, tight-lipped, as if trying to keep from laughing.

"What?" Alexis barked, her temper rising.

"Nothing, nothing. It's just funny seeing you and Rhipley get so riled up over each other. He's never been like that with Tatiana, or anyone, for that matter," Yazmin said over a shoulder.

Alexis rolled her eyes and let out a long sigh as she came up next to them, keeping pace. "Well, I don't really care to talk about Tatiana or Rhipley. Let them have each other. Let them bathe in their shared bitterness."

Yazmin couldn't hold in her laugh at that, and she clapped Alexis on the shoulder, Amelia hissing in amusement. For a time, there was only the sound of boots and heeled shoes clicking on the grey-stoned pathway, until Amelia and Alexis let out gasps of wonderment in unison at what stood before them.

Building tops peeked over the crest of the hill ahead, and as they gripped their dresses and hurried along the cobblestone to get a better look, a large city, alive with distant chatter and music, welcomed them.

CHAPTER 21

Fallandor was beautiful and lively, and better than Alexis could have ever imagined. From where they stood atop the hill, still gawking, she could see the castle where the royal family resided overlooking the large expanse of city.

The sparkling blues and greens of the ocean could be seen to the far right of the kingdom, where ships and boats were either docked at the harbour, approaching, or departing. A long bridge just north of them led into Fallandor itself, busy with citizens and horse-drawn carriages.

"Stay close," Rhipley ordered from where he now stood beside Alexis, keeping a respectful distance.

She mentally acknowledged his command, but chose not to speak on it, instead linking arms with Amelia and following him as he walked ahead, leading them down the hill to the bridge, Yazmin on their trail.

They were barely acknowledged as they entered the city, the only looks they received aimed solely at Rhipley and Yazmin — and those looks were purely out of both caution and admiration.

Alexis took that as good a time as any to note the various species they now walked among; mostly fae and humans, an occasional elf here and there.

There were likely other creatures mingling throughout that she wouldn't be able to identify on her own, but she didn't want to imagine what they could be.

Every citizen socialised as if there were no differences between them, though she supposed the humans of this world were used to their immortal peers.

She smiled to herself, realising it may be easier for them to blend in than they'd anticipated.

The streets were bustling with activity, cafés and restaurants alike busy with patrons. The sounds of rowdy customers came from the north, where various bars lined some of the streets — the drinking quarter, Alexis assumed.

Delectable smells filled the air, and a distant strum of music cascaded into her ears. Alexis didn't know where to look as she took in everything around her, sniffing the air, listening to the beautiful melodies, and admiring her surroundings. It was a far different world, indeed. She noted the guards posted at every street, made up of both fae and humans, each donning green and gold uniforms like that of the Hunter's Guild, with that same sun and moon emblem stitched on the right side of the chest of their uniforms.

Alexis leaned back slightly and whispered as quietly as she could to Yazmin, remembering the heightened hearing of some of those around them. "I guess we fit in better than we thought we would."

Yazmin chuckled and replied with equal quiet, Amelia now leaning back to join in on the conversation, "You'd find fitting in even easier if we were in Lilhan. Mortals are everywhere down there."

Amelia and Alexis shared a look, raising their brows.
"Is it far from here?" Amelia asked.
"Why? Wanting to leave us so soon?" Yazmin teased, and Amelia rolled her eyes. "It's to the south of here, bordered with Preshia and Hyrandell, the elf lands. Where I hail from."

Alexis noted Yazmin's sombre expression as she spoke those last few words, but it vanished just as quickly as it had appeared.

The streets grew busier as they neared the centre of the city, with various shop owners calling out their deals for the day, some even being so bold to attempt to grab at the girls.

All it took was a flash of Yazmin's teeth and her hunter's leathers for them to back off.

As Alexis looked forward to where Rhipley still walked ahead, pretending not to listen to them, she felt a pang of guilt at how she'd treated him since they'd met. Though *he* hadn't been much better.

His onyx sword glinted in the afternoon sun, and she couldn't help asking, "Does your sword have a name?"

Rhipley turned his head slightly and glanced sidelong at her before answering, "Wraith."

Alexis let out a hum before responding sarcastically, "Makes sense." She let him see her smirk — the intended friendliness in it, and the unspoken request for a truce.

Yazmin and Amelia snorted, and though he'd turned to face northward again, Alexis could have sworn she saw Rhipley smile.

Tatiana stood in the archery field, an arrow knocked and aimed for the target fifty feet ahead of her as Lukai and Zailah watched from behind. Aspen, Alexis' dog, sat next to Lukai, accepting his gentle pats.

"I don't trust them," Tatiana said, letting loose the arrow before turning to her friends, not needing to see that she'd hit the target perfectly, as she always did.

When Zailah and Lukai didn't respond, she added, "I can't put my finger on it. There's just… something not right about them."

She leaned down to give Aspen a pat — despite not particularly liking her bonded human, it didn't mean she had to hold that same feeling for her dog.

"Rhipley says the specific details of where they're from and who they are, are classified. Only he, Yazmin and Headmaster Draghone know. Perhaps we should keep our noses out of it," Lukai muttered, sending a pointed glare in Tatiana's direction, who simply rolled her eyes before grabbing another arrow and settling it against her bow. She owned only one bow — this one, which she loved more than anything else she owned. She'd been given the bow as a Donumas present for her sixteenth birthday by her mothers.

It was certainly expensive, made of pure mahogany, both ends dipped in gold from the mines deep in Aspal's mid-east.

The price of her possessions never occurred to her, though, since she'd only known riches after being adopted by Chanti and Marlene, two of the wealthiest noble-fae in both Preshia and Aspal, her home country. After so many years, she'd essentially forgotten her former life as a commoner. Had even forgotten her commoner birth parents. But she'd never forgotten how much they'd loved her, up until their last dying breaths.

As the faint memory rang through her, she knocked the arrow and let it fly with more velocity than before, anger and hatred overtaking her emotions at the unwelcome memory. The arrow pierced the target with such force she had to catch herself from grabbing another arrow and snapping it in two. Tatiana let out a few long breaths, calming her temper before once again turning back to her friends, a hand gripping her glowing necklace.

"You okay, Tat?" Zailah asked in that usual bland tone of hers, her lavender eyes cautiously dropping to the necklace.

Tatiana simply nodded, and continued firing arrow after arrow after arrow, shaking the painful memory from her thoughts.

Rhipley stood before the gates of the castle, where guards were lined up metres apart along the wall guarding the palace. Though they couldn't see through the giant gates, he knew from memory that there were hundreds more guards inside waiting to greet them. After he'd announced himself and his companions, one guard waiting by the gate had rushed inside to tell the king, no doubt. And now they waited — for how long, gods only knew.

Rhipley tried his hardest not to look at Alexis too much — tried not to note how beautiful she looked in that gods-damned dress.

Tried not to give in to his temptation to brush her hair out of her face, as she kept trying, and failing, not to do.

Given the slight breeze on this beautiful spring day, the earlier heat seemingly diminished for the moment, he could only guess that the constant flapping of Alexis' bangs was slowly getting to her.

For the past five minutes, she had been fighting a constant battle of brushing her bangs behind her ears before pulling them out again, apparently remembering the time and effort it took for Joan, Matilda, and Pepper to craft her appearance.

Rhipley's gaze shifted to where Yazmin had Amelia practically pinned to the wall, whispering something in her ear that set Amelia giggling, her face flushed with red.

Yazmin may as well have just taken Amelia against the wall right then and there. He scoffed at his friend's blatant lack of care for those who watched. Amelia, apparently, didn't seem to mind, either.

Rhipley noticed Alexis watching him out of the corner of his eye, and turned his complete attention to where she stood a few metres from him, her hands clasped in front of her, fiddling with the fabrics of her dress. She noticed his eyes watching her nervous hands and halted her fiddling, clearing her throat.

"What is it?" she asked, her eyes now fixed on the gate ahead.

Rhipley shrugged and replied coolly, "You're the one who was staring at me."

She huffed and looked at Amelia and Yazmin, still giggling and whispering to each other. Alexis gave a small smile at that, though her eyes didn't meet it.

"Is Yazmin... good? Can Amelia trust her?"

Rhipley just scoffed and said, "Well, she's never had a serious partner. She's a bit of a flirt, has had many lovers, but none past a week or so. She doesn't believe in settling down unless she finds her mate." Alexis' smile disappeared, and he added, "But I don't think she'd ever hurt Amelia. She's different around your sister — in a way I've never seen before."

Alexis' mouth pulled to the side as she pondered what he'd just said.

"When you say *mate,* what do you mean exactly? Like a soul mate?"

Rhipley tried to hide his amusement, and once again had to remind himself that she wasn't from his world.

"Don't you read about them in your books?"

She rolled her eyes but said quietly, "What are they *here?* Since this world is real and the worlds in my books aren't."

He looked to the ground and kicked some dirt before responding, "A mate is more important than just a girlfriend or boyfriend, as you say in your world. More important than a wife or husband — they're soul bound, your best friend, the one you turn to when you feel lost, a lone star in the night sky, the light in a dark room, the one you can't bear to be without. When your soul knows, it knows. It's a... powerful thing. But humans aren't known to have mates. At least, not that I've heard of."

Alexis finally looked at him again, her blue-grey eyes glistening in the sunlight.

"Are you and Tatiana mates?"

Rhipley snorted. "Gods, no. We have a bond, but certainly not a mating bond. We'd have both known by now if that were the case."

Alexis let out a sigh through her nose, out of relief or frustration, he wasn't sure, as her face had once again tightened like she was deep in thought. She finally asked, stepping slightly closer, "What happens when either of you finds your mate?"

Rhipley scanned her face, her stunning eyes, her pink, full lips and said, "I don't know. I've never considered the fact that I even have a mate out there somewhere."

Her face turned sympathetic as she looked at him, lost for words, but the interruption of that same guard had them both looking away.

"Follow me," the guard announced gruffly, turning before they had a chance to answer.

CHAPTER 22

The guard led Alexis, Amelia and their comrades into the castle and down a long hallway lined with windows, artwork and more guards. Various expensive-looking pieces of décor sat upon separate pedestals all neatly lined up, leading towards two large doors where two more guards were posted.

Their escort, a human man if his ears were any sign, hadn't said a word to them the entire walk. Alexis supposed he didn't need to say anything, really, and that his job was merely to bring them to the king and queen.

He stopped before the doors abruptly, giving a nod to the two guards, and as the doors opened to the massive throne room, he led the four inside. The throne room was like nothing Alexis had ever seen — to her credit, she *hadn't* ever been inside a throne room, let alone a castle.

Gold and green paint coated the walls, with large pillars lining either side where more floor to ceiling windows could be seen overlooking the city on one side and the palace gardens on the other.

Alexis lifted her gaze to the roof and noted beautiful artwork where a man and woman were depicted staring towards each other, one dressed in black, the other in white, a sun behind the woman and a moon behind the man.

The God and Goddess of Preshia.

Smaller figures surrounded them, creatures of all sorts — fae, elves, humans, and other creatures she couldn't quite decipher.
Though she knew she had to brush up on the history of this world, of the Moon God and Sun Goddess, she supposed the Preshians truly believed Luzhula and Brundhul brought about life if the ceiling artwork was any indication.

Despite this castle being thousands of years old, as Rhipley had mentioned in their earlier study session, it looked immaculate, as if it had been built just yesterday.

Alexis lowered her gaze to the three thrones at the end of the room where two figures sat, the third chair empty. Remembering where she was, *who* she was in the company of, Alexis subtly fixed her posture, her dress and hair, and settled her gaze completely on the King and Crown Prince of Preshia.

She willed her heartbeat to steady, her breathing to calm, though she knew any effort would be useless given the heightened senses of those around her. She dared a sidelong glance at her sister, who had squeezed Yazmin's hand as if to calm her own nerves. The exchange was swift, but Alexis' heart softened at the interaction. She made a mental note to talk to her sister about what was going on between them later.

As the guard finally brought them within ten feet of the stairs leading to the throne, Alexis noted how handsome the prince was. His dirty blonde hair was slightly curled, a few longer pieces falling around his face, and his eyes were a beautiful hazel colour, his sun-kissed skin radiant, and his face soft and kind.

Alexis caught herself staring and quickly averted her gaze to the king, a man who appeared to be in his fifties, had he been mortal, his long greying hair resting on his shoulders, matching that of his full beard.

His face, unlike his son's, did not appear kind but rather grave, giving off a no-nonsense feeling. Alexis couldn't help the uneasiness that flooded her at the sight of the monarch, his heir by his side, both looking as regal as she'd imagined.

Sure enough, both males had pointed ears that weren't as elongated as Rhipley's or the other fae, but their features alone showed their fae heritage.

She couldn't quite figure out why King Mikkel appeared so old compared to other fae, even Rampier, though she guessed that demi-fae perhaps aged differently. Another question for another time. The guard announced them in his gruff voice, cutting into Alexis' observations.

"Presenting Rhipley and Yazmin of the Preshian Hunter's Guild and their guests, Your Majesties."

Rhipley and Yazmin bowed low at the waist, while both Alexis and Amelia curtsied, as they'd been taught. In unison, the four said, "Your Majesties."

King Mikkel simply returned their gestures with a slight dip of his head, and Prince Frederik echoed his father's movement, offering a warm smile that Alexis felt inclined to return.

Rhipley had noticed the way Prince Frederik eyed both girls with something like excited curiosity in his hazel eyes, though he wasn't sure if either Alexis or Amelia had dialled it down to anything more than a nicety or general politeness.

Given the Crown Prince's reputation for being quite a male-whore, Rhipley wasn't sure he wanted to let him near the girls at all, if he could help it. He'd also immediately noticed the lack of Queen Ida's presence, and when he and Yazmin shared the same knowing look, King Mikkel had clearly noted the question in their features as he said, "Queen Ida has fallen ill these past months. I'm afraid she'll be unable to join us today."

Queen Ida was the more soft-mannered out of the two to deal with, the one with the most sway.

Guess we'll be doing this the hard way.

Several council members also stood in the throne room, posted on either side of the dais, looking rather displeased with this meeting. All a mixture of fae, demi-fae and human, and all of them every bit the grumpy, entitled pricks Rhipley had known them to be.

Tatiana's mothers were nowhere to be seen, though given their ties in Aspal, he'd assumed they were likely residing across the sea in their other gargantuan home — the home Tatiana grew up in before joining the Preshian Hunter's Guild.

The home he knew she missed and thought about daily.

When Rhipley and Yazmin didn't speak, King Mikkel asked, "Why have you come?"

Yazmin stepped forward to speak on their behalf, Luzhula praise her.

"Your Majesty, as was outlined in the letter you received from Headmaster Draghone, this matter is to be discussed privately, if you please."

Her eyes settled on the councilmen and soldiers standing by, and after a brief, hesitant moment, King Mikkel dismissed them all. Only Prince Frederik remained, sitting perfectly in his chair and clearly anxious for what was to come as his eyes darted between his father, their guests, and the departing council members.

Had he not been made aware of the letter? Perhaps not, if his cluelessness was any indication.

"Now, speak," King Mikkel said, his impatience growing by the second. Yazmin's ears flicked slightly toward the throne room doors behind them, and Prince Frederik spoke this time.

"This room is now warded against those who might listen from outside these doors. You're free to speak without concern of who may be eavesdropping."

Yazmin didn't return the prince's smile, but instead dipped her head slightly in recognition. "Your Majesties, as you would have read in the letter you received, the Mortal Realm, known as Earth, was recently attacked by Inferno Hounds. We have confirmation that the attack was orchestrated by King D'Roghal of Vendarath."

Prince Frederik's eyes grew wide as he turned to his father, who only beckoned for Yazmin to go on, ignoring his son.

"His right-hand man, Dimitri, confirmed it the night we rescued the two humans behind me. Dimitri had also been sent to hunt them."

She turned and signalled for Amelia and Alexis to step forward.

Rhipley could hear their thundering heartbeats, despite their calm features.

As he peered down to where Alexis now stood beside him, indeed, he could see that she was shivering with nerves.

He lightly brushed his arm against hers in comfort. To anyone else, it may have seemed like an accident. Given her quick breath of relief, though, he knew she understood and appreciated the gesture.

King Mikkel leaned forward in his throne and asked, "And who are you?"

Alexis didn't dare take her eyes from the king as she answered for both herself and her sister. "I'm Alexis Rainier, and this is my sister, Amelia Rainier." They gave perfect curtsies once again.

"They were being hunted by King D'Roghal's agents, Your Majesty," Yazmin repeated, her voice unwavering.

"Why?" King Mikkel asked.

"We don't yet know," Yazmin offered, and the king sat back in his chair, doubt on his face.

"But we're aiming to find out the reason as fast as we can. We're hoping, with your permission, that we can continue to house them at the Hunter's Guild and determine whether or not they're gifted with magic. If, perhaps, it can give us a lead."

Rhipley, Alexis and Amelia tried not to stiffen at the blatant lie.

King Mikkel considered for a second before saying, "Amity."

Not a moment later, a beautiful woman with flowing, curled red hair that reached her waist, wearing a white caped gown, emerged from one of the doors at the back of the room, her hands clasped together in front of her.

The way she walked looked as though she was floating.

She appeared human, though she certainly didn't smell like one. She walked to the foot of the dais, curtsied low, and met King Mikkel's gaze, his expression softening slightly.

"How can I be of service, Your Highness?" she asked in a delicate voice.

Rhipley didn't recognise this woman, didn't recall having ever seen her before in all his visits to the palace. Had never *heard* of her before — perhaps she was new in the king's employ.

"I need you to test these two human girls for magical abilities, if you will."

Rhipley and Yazmin's breathing hitched as Amity turned from her spot and looked both girls dead in the eye before smiling sweetly.

CHAPTER 23

Amity approached Alexis and Amelia with feline grace, reaching into a pocket of her gown and retrieving a small, sharp knife. Alexis wasn't afraid of pain, even had a high tolerance for it, but her sister was quite the opposite.

She tried not to let her nerves show, willing her body to remain steady despite her shaking hands, now clasped behind her back. King Mikkel smirked at the obvious fear she knew he could smell on them, and Prince Frederik looked on in curiosity, now sitting forward in his seat in anticipation, both hands gripping the arms of his chair. Alexis looked to Rhipley, whose eyes were on her, darting between her face and that of Amity's knife.

Yazmin's throat bobbed as she stared at Amelia, who was visibly shaking now.

"This will only hurt for a second," Amity purred, reaching for Alexis' hand. Alexis looked her dead in the eyes and sucked in a deep breath before bringing her hand out from behind her back and placing it in Amity's. Her skin was like velvet, so soft and beautiful to the touch. Amity breathed in sharply through her nose before asking too quietly for anyone else to hear, "What are you?"

There was no cool amusement in her eyes anymore.

No, whatever she sensed made her look almost... scared. Alexis couldn't quite decipher what emotions the woman was feeling, what she was even *talking* about.

She furrowed her brows as she slowly shook her head in confusion. "I'm... human?" Alexis said with equal quiet, forcing herself to avoid looking at her sister, Rhipley, Yazmin, or the royals.

Amity's face turned into something of slight disbelief, though rather than questioning her further, she brought the pocketknife down and pricked Alexis' finger. A sharp pain shot through her hand and just as quickly as she'd pricked her, Amity lifted the knife to her mouth, licking the blood away as her eyes clouded over in white. Alexis held onto her finger with her other hand, attempting to stop the bleeding, while she watched Amity's clouded eyes in awe and slight horror. She'd guessed that the woman wasn't human, but she'd still seen nothing like what she was seeing now.

Amity, tasting the blood, kept her eyes on Alexis', having now returned to their beautiful hazel colour. Alexis still couldn't decipher Amity's expression, how she was feeling, what she was seeing, though allowed her own face to appear completely neutral.

Amity continued to stare at Alexis for a few seconds longer, before finally walking over to Amelia.

As she'd done with Alexis, she pricked Amelia's finger and tasted her blood. Amelia had flinched at the pain, though didn't curse or make any noise of discomfort. Amity studied them all, her eyes darting between each of the four of them, as if trying to catch out Yazmin's lie.

King Mikkel spoke up, piercing the deafening silence. "Well, Amity?"

Amity stood facing them for a few long seconds as she continued to taste the blood in her mouth, before turning to walk back towards the stairs and addressing the king's question.

"I can only taste a hint of basic magic in their blood, Your Highness. Nothing of importance."

Rhipley and Yazmin didn't dare let their simultaneous confusion and relief show as Alexis and Amelia took up their spots behind them again, both girls confused at how Amity hadn't tasted the obvious Realm Walking magic in *Alexis'* blood, at least.

King Mikkel considered for a moment before announcing, "Very well. In that case, I'll allow you to return to the Hunter's Guild with these humans and protect and train them as one of your own."

Rhipley and Yazmin bowed in thanks before King Mikkel cut them off, raising his hand to stop them.

"However, given that King D'Roghal is pursuing them, I'll be sending my son to overlook your operations. Think of it as an extra form of protection. Considering we don't wish to start a war with Vendarath over two mere humans, I trust you'll keep them hidden behind your wards."

Alexis tried not to take offence at his words, but Rhipley and Yazmin replied, "Yes, Your Highness. Thank you."

Prince Frederik slouched in his chair, apparently unimpressed with his father's decision.

King Mikkel nodded in appreciation and continued. "There's just one thing I can't understand. Why would King D'Roghal, of *all* beings, want two human girls? Especially from the Mortal Realm. *Especially* ones with barely significant magic."

The disbelief in his voice set Alexis on edge as she surveyed his face, trying to read his expression, though it revealed nothing.

"Given that we have had no attacks on our wards since we arrived back in Xalentya, Your Highness, Headmaster Draghone suggested King D'Roghal may not know the girls are even here with us, rather that they're still in the Mortal Realm. If he knows they're here, he'll know they're under our protection and, therefore, the protection of Preshia. A wise king will not attack an entire country unless the prize is deemed worthy of war."

Yazmin sounded so confident that Alexis couldn't help a sidelong glance at her in equal admiration and disbelief.

King Mikkel sat in silence for long seconds, brushing his hand over his beard as he considered Yazmin's words.

Had she just messed up their chances of returning to the Hunter's Guild by suggesting war was a possibility?

Given her assumed age and experience, Alexis had to guess Yazmin was smarter than that.

Prince Frederik spoke this time, his voice coming out with such grace. "Father, would it be worth sending spies to Vendarath to, perhaps, figure out what King D'Roghal has planned?"

The king didn't bother looking at his son before he said, "Yes, that may be worthwhile looking into." He stared at Rhipley before adding, "Will your Headmaster offer some hunters to accompany our spies into their lands?"

Rhipley responded in a curt voice. "I'm sure he will be happy to oblige, Majesty."

Not that he has a choice, Alexis knew he wanted to add.

Whether King Mikkel had noticed Rhipley's unhappiness at his request, he didn't say. Amity now stood to the left of the dais, her eyes on King Mikkel, admiration sparkling on her face.

Alexis was usually quite good at reading people, and if the king and Amity's behaviour these past minutes indicated anything, it was that there was perhaps something more going on between them. Though, it was just an assumption, and one that she wouldn't dare think about any longer, given that it wasn't any of her business.

"Amity, please escort our guests to their rooms," King Mikkel commanded with a wave of his hand.

Amity bowed her head and walked towards them again, her face in a perfectly calm expression.

Rhipley cut in.

"Majesty, it's appreciated, but unnecessary. We can find other suitable accommodation in the city."

The king just waved Rhipley off in dismissal, and as they bowed one last time, Alexis and Amelia curtsying once more, Amity led them from the throne room.

Prince Frederik's eyes followed them as the guards and council members walked back through the doors, some of their faces appearing unimpressed.

"Grumpy assholes," Yazmin muttered when they'd exited the throne room.

Alexis and Amelia tried to hide their smiles, and Rhipley just agreed with a hum.

As Amity led them to their rooms in the left wing of the castle, Yazmin asked, "So, what are you? Your gift seems unusual."

Amity simply replied, not bothering to look back at them, "I'm a Magus Depre."

Yazmin and Rhipley both let out impressed whistles, and Alexis asked, "What's a Magus Depre?"

Yazmin responded, "They're extremely rare. I didn't even think they existed. They can sense the magic in another being's blood and the strength of that magic."

Amelia spoke this time. "So, are you human, after all?"

She looked at Amity's ears, noticing their roundness.

Amity was silent for a moment before responding, "I'm a witch."

Yazmin sniffed the air, earning a muffled giggle from Amelia and a roll of Rhipley's eyes.

"Strange, you certainly don't smell like a witch."

"Well, I haven't been around my own kind for many years. I suppose the stench has worn off," Amity replied, though none of them missed the jab in her remark, the slight disdain in her voice.

A witch.

There was an actual *witch* in their presence.

Alexis' heart thundered as she remembered what Rhipley had told them about a witch's primary source of sustenance being human flesh, and she gulped.

"I've been in the royal family's employ for almost twenty years, when House Koschier was voted into power. I was a handmaiden to Queen Ida. That is, before my power was revealed, and King Mikkel chose me as his personal Magus Depre."

Rhipley muttered, "That explains why I've never seen you before." Alexis looked at him in question before he continued, "Queen Ida isn't one for attention, and usually keeps to herself and her personal staff. If the matter is of importance, she'll make an appearance, but it seems now she's keeping out of even those discussions."

Amity responded quickly, her tone blunt, echoing the words the king had uttered earlier. "Queen Ida has been quite unwell these past months. It's not a matter that is discussed lightly, so the royal family hopes you can keep the queen's condition quiet and out of the public ear." She glanced back this time and shot a pointed look at all four of them. They all nodded, and she returned her gaze to the hallway ahead. Her walking slowed as they approached four sets of doors, all within a few metres of each other.

"Here are your sleeping quarters for the night. Under different circumstances, you'd be invited to dine with the king, queen and prince, but given that that's no longer an option, your dinner will be brought to you."

Alexis' stomach rumbled, and she blushed, placing a hand over her belly. "Sorry," she whispered, and Yazmin snorted.

Amity offered a flat smile and said, "If there's anything you require, please ask the servants. We hope you enjoy your stay."

She dipped her head and walked off. Floated, really.

Once Amity was out of view, the four looked at their doors, intricate patterns carved into the wood, adorned with golden doorknobs.

Alexis opened her doors first and peered inside, gasping as she took in the wondrous room. It was white and gold, the floors of finest, polished mahogany.

"My goodness, this is… insane."

Amelia pressed up behind her, peering over a shoulder and gasping all the same. Alexis could hear Rhipley and Yazmin opening their doors, too, though they didn't show any sign of astonishment — they were likely already used to this kind of thing, given that they'd visited the palace on several occasions.

Alexis walked into her room, Amelia following, as they took in the massive space. A four-poster bed sat to the far left, a large fur rug positioned beneath it. From which animal, she had no idea.

A too-big armoire sat in front of the only window in the room, albeit a grossly large window that overlooked a section of the beautiful gardens she was dying to explore, though she knew she'd never get the chance to. As she slowly walked around the space, her eyes lighting up at each new detail, Amelia fell onto the bed and sighed. "It's so comfortable."

Alexis chuckled and joined her sister, letting out a sigh of her own as she lay there, staring at the roof of the bed. They settled there quietly for long minutes before Yazmin and Rhipley returned, standing in the doorway, amusement on their beautiful faces.

"Not bad, huh?" Yazmin said smugly.

Amelia sat up and replied, "I wish we could take these beds with us."

Yazmin huffed a laugh and Rhipley smiled, his eyes falling on Alexis, who met his gaze and blushed. She quickly shifted her stare to a sizeable painting on one of the walls of the royal family — a young Prince Frederik, likely ten or so years old, King Mikkel looking many years younger and standing with his arms behind his back and his face in that same, unimpressed expression she'd witnessed moments ago, and who she could only guess was Queen Ida, holding Prince Frederik on her lap and looking as beautiful as Alexis had imagined.

The painting depicted her as young, in her thirties, if Alexis had to guess, with breast-length red-brown hair, beautiful green eyes and fair skin. All three members of the family shared the same half-pointed ears that all demi-fae supposedly adorned, Prince Frederik's a little big for his head at the time, if the painting was accurate. She smiled, then a wave of sadness crept over her as she thought of her father and Sam back home.

With each passing day, she felt as though she missed them even more. Wondered if they were okay in that big house, eating by themselves, their family now halved. Turning back to where Rhipley and Yazmin were standing, the former's eyes still on her, now wary, she plastered on a fake smile, but his sympathetic eyes told her he knew it wasn't genuine.

Prince Frederik sat at one end of the large dining table, his father at the other chewing on his steak. They both ate silently, Frederik's thoughts a jumbled mess as he pondered the information they'd been given earlier by those two famed hunters, Rhipley and Yazmin. Pondered why King D'Roghal would be after the humans, if they were to be believed. Pondered *why* his father felt the need to send *him* to the Hunter's Guild when he could have sent his general. Perhaps it was punishment for his whoring and general disregard for royal duties. Perhaps it was because his father was bored and wished to sneak around with his mistress, Amity, without his son's prying eyes and ears.

His gut twisted in disgust at his father's unfaithfulness to his sick mother, and at the fact that his mother had no idea it was even happening — *had* been happening for as long as Amity had been in their employ.

He hated his father.

He hated Amity.

He hated that his only loving parent was practically on her deathbed, barely able to hold conversation for little more than a few minutes. Frederik looked at his father, his eyes narrowing, and King Mikkel returned his stare before asking flatly, "What is it?"

Frederik chewed on his lip before responding, "Why do you really wish for me to attend the Hunter's Guild, father?"

King Mikkel placed his cutlery on his plate before wiping his mouth with a napkin, dismissing the staff. Once the dining room was empty, he responded in a gruff voice, "I want you to find out the truth about those girls and why King D'Roghal is after them. I do not believe it is mere coincidence that that *murderer* sent his beasts and his right-hand man after them if they're simply mediocre humans."

When Frederik didn't respond, his eyes searching his father's face, King Mikkel returned to his meal.

"So, you wish for me to spy?" Frederik asked at last, disbelief in his voice. His father looked up from his meal again, his expression unimpressed, as if he couldn't believe his son's daft response.

"No, son. I'd like you to do as you please, as you always have. I wish for you to whore your way through the guild and come back to me with feedback on your time there."

Frederik let out a sigh before wiping his mouth with a napkin and standing from his seat. "Very well. When do I leave?"

"Tomorrow morning. I'll send some guards to escort your carriage. Given that it is around a day's ride from here, thanks to their wards, I trust you'll appreciate the extra protection of General Burnell and his men."

"I hope you do not mean for General Burnell and his men to accompany me during the entirety of my stay at the guild?" Frederik asked, unable to hide the sharpness from his voice.

"Only if you wish it. I would hope you, a grown male, would be able to defend yourself if the need arose. You will have two guards, of course, watching over you during your stay at the guild, as is customary for any member of the royal household."

The king shook his head, as if he truly believed his son wished for a full guard when it was actually the other way around.

A feeling of disgust coursed through the Crown Prince's body at the mention of the distasteful general.

Of all his father's men, he hated General Alexander Burnell the most. He *and* his men.

Though Frederik knew better than to frequent the various brothels in Fallandor, instead preferring a selection of only the finest courtesans, he'd heard stories of Burnell leaving certain whores — a word he hated — battered and bruised.

However, given his importance and ties to the king, the owners of the brothels would simply allow General Burnell to leave without so much as a slap on the wrist. Besides, what could they do other than patch up their employees and hope their regular clients still visited after the "goods" had been damaged?

With one last, hateful look at his father, accepting the task he'd been bestowed, Frederik bowed, the gesture ignored by the king, and left the dining room without another word, his fingers flexing in frustration.

CHAPTER 24

Alexis wasn't the least bit surprised that she'd slept like a log, given how comfy her bed was. She could get used to being a guest of the royal family of Fallandor if these were the living arrangements.

As she lay there, cosy under the covers and still in her nightgown, Alexis stared at the roof — barely visible through the sheer cloth placed over the four posters of her bed — and thought.

Thought about their new, permanent lives at the Hunter's Guild — in *Xalentya*. Thought about Prince Frederik joining them and overlooking their operations.

She didn't believe for a second that King Mikkel didn't have something else planned, but given that there was little she could do about her theory, she chose to let it go.

A light knock sounded at her door.

"Come in," she called sleepily.

Rhipley entered, already in his leathers with his weapons strapped on securely, the onyx hilt of Wraith glaring over his shoulder. He gave her a bored look, and she retorted, "Hey, I've been trying to get out of bed for half an hour, but it's just so comfy."

His lips tugged upwards into a small smile, and she couldn't help sheepishly smiling back.

"So, now that we've seen the king and the prince, do I still have to wear that ridiculously heavy dress and those terribly painful shoes or can I wear what I would at the Hunter's Guild?"

Rhipley simply tossed some hunter's leathers on the bed, the boots making a heavy thud before falling to the floor.

"No more ridiculous dresses or painful shoes. Unless you *want* to wear them."

His eyes roved over her body as she sat up, reaching for the clothes, complete bewilderment on her face as she examined what now lay before her.

"As pretty as I felt, I don't think I could make them an everyday attire." She held the leathers up. "I'm to wear these?"

"You both are. We need to blend in — it'll be far easier to convince anyone who might wish to report something amiss that we're a group of hunters and nothing more."

Alexis' mouth quirked to the side as she thought about it before nodding once as she examined the clothes once more. After a few moments, her eyes slowly lifted to where Rhipley leaned against the door frame, watching her.

When he didn't move or speak, she asked, "Are you going to let me change, or would you rather stay for the show?"

Was she flirting?

Why was she flirting?

Rhipley had a... whatever Tatiana was, and she didn't want to be *that* girl. Before she could apologise for her playful banter, Rhipley chuckled and said, "As tempting as that offer is, I should probably leave you to it."

Alexis blurted, "Please don't tell Tatiana I said that. I was just joking."

Rhipley turned from where he'd stepped past the threshold and raised a brow. "What has Tatiana got to do with this?"

Alexis stammered her response, dropping her stare from Rhipley's and focusing on the clothes in her lap as she fiddled with the fabrics and details, the inbuilt hood.

"I know you're not mates or whatever," she raised her fingers in quotations as she said it. "But I'd imagine you have feelings for each other, nonetheless." Rhipley opened his mouth to speak, but Alexis cut him off. "I don't want to get between… whatever you have going on between you." She waved a hand and chuckled drily.

Rhipley crossed his arms and resumed his position against the doorway. "Since you refuse to drop the subject, Tatiana and I are old friends. The way we feel about each other is strictly platonic, and we're certainly not exclusively seeing one another. We're just comfortable. It's a comfortable dynamic."

Alexis quirked her mouth to the side as she continued staring at her clothes.

"It's… complicated," Rhipley added as he brushed a hand through his hair. Alexis just nodded.

There was an awkward silence between them before Rhipley said, his tone far less serious than before, "But you never have to feel guilty for simply being unable to resist flirting with me. I mean, I can't blame you." He grinned that usual cocky grin of his, and for once, Alexis didn't roll her eyes as she raised her gaze to his once more, admiring his smile, the way his dimples showed. Unsure how to respond after realising she'd been gawking at him, Alexis let out a stammered, "Right."

Rhipley's brows furrowed as he asked, "What, no snide remark? That's not the Lex I've come to know."

Her ears pricked up at that. "Lex?"

He simply replied, "Yeah, Lex. It's my new nickname for you."

She huffed a laugh before saying, "Only my family and friends call me that."

Rhipley replied in a sarcastically offended tone, "Are we not friends?"

Alexis gave him a smug look as she tilted her head to the side. "I don't know, are we?"

Rhipley just stared at her, as if he were contemplating something she couldn't quite understand, his eyes lit up in amusement. "I suppose I could try to be friends with you. Only if you promise to be kinder to me."

Alexis scoffed. "Goes both ways, buddy."

Rhipley returned her scoff with one of his own, and a smirk that Alexis wouldn't dare admit set her heart racing as she prayed her face wouldn't flush.

Silence filled the air between them once more as they stared at each other for long seconds, before Rhipley's eyes fell on the clothes still in Alexis' lap and he cleared his throat. "I'll leave you to it. We depart after breakfast."

With that, he left the room, closing the door behind him. Alexis raised her brows as she shook her head, feeling stupid for the giddiness that threatened to take over.

"What the hell just happened?" she whispered to herself as she undressed.

As the quartet departed the city of Fallandor, the girls' dresses travelling with Prince Frederik, his carriage and cavalry, Alexis admired the view atop a hill outside the city.

"Please tell me we'll be coming back here?" Amelia asked, a hint of sadness in her voice as she fiddled with her leathers, clearly trying to find comfort in her new attire.

Yazmin gripped her hand and smiled. "Of course we will."

The two grinned at each other, and Alexis felt a tightness in her chest at the exchange, both out of happiness and slight envy. However, no matter how envious she was of her sister's new romance, she wouldn't dare dampen it with her own issues. She side eyed Rhipley, who also watched the exchange before his eyes met hers, a brief smile tugging on his lips. Alexis chose to ignore him, instead turning her attention back to the city. "Where will we be staying tonight?" she asked curtly.

"An inn. It's right outside the ward surrounding the guild," Yazmin offered, turning from her spot. "Let's just hope they have room for us, or it's back to camping."

Amelia crooned, still holding Yazmin's hand, "I don't mind camping."

Yazmin returned her comment with another beaming smile. Rhipley shifted uncomfortably, and Alexis felt inclined to join him.

"Can we get you ladies a room before we leave?" he asked sarcastically, though Alexis was thinking the same thing.

Yazmin shot him a glare and Amelia blushed, turning away to view the city again.

Though she was happy for her sister, something about public displays of affection made Alexis feel strangely uncomfortable. Perhaps it was due to her lack of public affection in her previous relationship that conditioned her to be that way.

"How come we could Realm Walk out of the Hunter's Guild if we can't Walk back in?" Alexis asked finally, piercing the awkward quietness.

Yazmin spoke this time. "The wards are to keep threats out, not in. Same as any ward, really, though they can be worked around to do the opposite, I suppose."

Alexis just hummed her understanding — there was a lot about this world she had to learn, and now that their living here was a definite given thanks to King Mikkel's orders, she supposed she'd need to start brushing up on that information soon.

The group had been walking through Fallandor Forest for hours now, the spring sun glaring overhead, the cool wind from earlier evidently vanished.

They'd come more prepared this time, however, with not one, but four water-skins filled to the brim with fresh, tasty water. There'd been an awkward silence between Rhipley and Alexis since their brief flirtation earlier, and he wasn't sure whether it was because she had regretted flirting with him, or because she didn't wish to get on Tatiana's bad side.

Perhaps both, if he was being honest. Even though he'd assured her that truly wasn't an issue, that he and Tatiana didn't do jealousy, she still seemed hesitant.

Though, he had to remind himself that his closest friend, his brother, was back home pining after Alexis, and that to come between them would be cruel.

So, despite the temptation to continue their shameless flirting, he had to restrain himself. Behave, hard as it may be.

Rhipley looked down at Alexis at his side — unlike the rest of them, her skin was free of sweat, not a single bead to be found upon her sun kissed skin. Her blonde hair was unbound, flowing in the wind behind her, and she seemed unfocussed — as if her thoughts, too, were elsewhere.

Rhipley glanced over his shoulder to where Yazmin and Amelia were walking a few feet behind, Yazmin whispering something in Amelia's ear that set her giggling, a wicked smile on his friend's lips. He truly hoped that Yazmin had good intentions with Amelia — half to save her from Alexis' reprimand if she broke Amelia's heart, and half because he wished for his friend to finally find true happiness. Though this *was* the first time he'd ever witnessed Yazmin so smitten.

Usually, she made it obvious when she was attracted to someone, though never went out of her way to display that attraction in front of others to such lengths, and with such sincerity. He also hoped that Amelia cared about her the way Yazmin did — Yazmin's love life was closed off enough. If she were the one to have *her* heart broken, he couldn't imagine what that might look like, what it might do to her.

He returned his focus to Alexis, who was now drinking from a water-skin, and he wondered why the heat didn't seem to bother her. His eyes settled on her lips around the opening of the water-skin, the liquid dripping down her mouth, her chin. He noticed the bob of her throat as she drank.

His heartbeat quickened as thoughts about her mouth, what it might do behind closed doors, raced through his mind.

Rhipley set his eyes on the path ahead as he forced the thoughts from his mind.

Stop thinking about her like that.

Stop thinking about her.

Alexis cut into his contemplations as she politely offered him a drink. He obliged with a tight smile, taking the water-skin from her delicate hand.

"Does the heat not bother you?" he finally asked, glancing sidelong at her nonchalantly, as if the idea of her pleasuring him wasn't just overtaking his brain.

Her eyes once again on the road ahead, Alexis replied, "It's never really bothered me, honestly. I love the heat. I love summer. When the sun's out, I'm at my happiest." Her gaze shifted to the sky, to the sun, and she closed her eyes as she tilted her head back, taking in the warmth. Rhipley watched her for a few seconds — watched how her mouth tilted upwards into a gentle smile, how she breathed in and out deeply, how the golden rays on her skin made her glow.

When she opened her eyes again, he was already looking away as he drank deeply from the water-skin.

CHAPTER 25

The inn they'd stopped at just after nightfall was nice enough, Alexis supposed.

Situated on the edge of a small village in Fallandor Forest, it was essentially exactly what she'd expected it to be — cosy, large and alive with chatter and music. The village citizens, a mixture of fae and humans, kept their distance from the group, given that they all appeared as hunters, although two of them were completely untrained and, if Alexis was being honest, not a threat to anyone.

The inn was just as busy as it had sounded, patrons sharing their stories and playing card games, and a man with a fiddle played upbeat medleys in a corner of the bar.

The entire building had quieted upon their entrance, every set of eyes instantly settling on them, their faces concealed by the hoods built into their leathers. Though once they'd walked to the bar, ignoring the ogling of everyone in sight, the patrons had returned to their chatter, music, and games.

The bar staff, seemingly familiar with the Hunter's Guild given their immediate recognition of Rhipley and Yazmin upon arrival, began pouring them generous pints of ale. Alexis had decided on a cider of sorts, and Amelia a water — her sister had never been a big drinker, usually opting for sobriety over getting silly drunk.

With the drinks in hand and a hefty tip left on the counter, the group headed for a secluded spot towards a dark corner of the room, choosing to keep a low profile as Yazmin and Rhipley subtly scanned the area for any danger or unwanted visitors who might choose to approach.

Rhipley handed Alexis her cider as he continued to monitor the inn before taking up a seat beside her. The booth was small, leaving little room between them.

Yazmin took it as a chance to invite Amelia to sit on her lap, the latter obliging with a blush.

Alexis tried to ignore her thigh touching Rhipley's, his scent, their closeness.

God, he smelled good.

"You know, you two should wear our hunter's leathers more often," Yazmin purred, letting out a low whistle as she looked Amelia up and down.

Alexis smiled as she took in her own leathers. They *did* look good.

Beneath her hood, Alexis scanned the room as she lazily sipped from her cider. Like in the village outside, in Fallandor, the patrons of this inn were a mix of humans and fae.

At least, she assumed *some* of those with rounded ears were human. She wondered if any could be witches. Like Amity, with her human, albeit flawless, appearance.

Though she couldn't pick their conversations apart in the din, Alexis picked apart the expressions each patron made, who they looked at when they spoke, when they laughed.

She noticed their mannerisms, wondered how they might know each other, what their trades were based on their clothes, tools and even weapons, for some.

Her eyes roamed to the bar, where a couple of rowdy fae males were heckling a poor bartender who was doing her best to ignore their snide remarks. Alexis gritted her teeth at the sight, her heartbeat quickening.

Rhipley's eyes followed hers as he whispered in a disgusted tone, "Assholes."

Alexis felt his hand slide to his thigh, and her eyes fell to his lap, where he now held his dagger securely in one hand.

"Just in case. We don't know what they might be capable of," he whispered.

Alexis raised her eyes to his as she said, "I bet I could guess."

They returned their attention to the bar just in time to see a tall woman approach the two males, who were now making sloppy attempts at grabbing the barmaid, lazily reaching over the counter as she backed away, her irritation turning to worry.

The unknown woman smashed one heckler over the head with an empty glass bottle, the act drawing the attention of the whole room as the male fell to the floor, unconscious.

Alexis felt Rhipley stiffen beside her, and out of the corner of her vision, she noted Yazmin doing the same, a dagger no doubt in her own hand.

The entire room fell silent, and Rhipley and Yazmin shared cautious looks. Alexis' eyes shifted to her sister, who was visibly shaken, her own attention wholly on what was unfolding.

Alexis' heartbeat quickened as she returned her focus to the male on the ground, blood now leaking from his head.

No one got up to help. No one dared move, everyone too stunned to even breathe. The other male swung sloppily at the woman's head, which she avoided with ease before kicking him in the gut.

Winded, the male fell to the ground, vomiting his guts up. The woman kicked him once more in the same spot, and he groaned in pain, curling up on his side.

She stepped over him and his friend before taking up a seat at the bar with a casual grace.

Alexis didn't know whether to be frightened or in awe of the woman.

Two bar staff dragged the males away, and within seconds, the room erupted with noise once more. Alexis observed the woman — her long, dark hair, styled into dreadlocks, was tied back into a high ponytail, the sides of her head shaved.

Small, golden cuffs were wrapped around several singular locs of hair, and her beautiful brown skin was covered in swirls of tattoos. The grey long-sleeve top she wore looked slightly tattered, tucked into dark, equally tattered pants, her chestnut knee-high boots now perched on a small ledge at the bottom of the bar counter.

The woman's ears were rounded, so she certainly wasn't fae or elven, but Alexis couldn't ignore how utterly beautiful she was as she rested her chin on one hand and smiled sweetly at the barmaid, who shot back a flustered glare.

Alexis supposed they must have known each other prior to the woman's enthralling entrance.

The barmaid, her blonde hair tied back into a bun, wiped her hands on her apron and approached the woman with crossed arms. She quietly whispered something to her in a rushed manner, as if scolding the woman. The barmaid's eyes darted to another staff member mopping up the blood and vomit, her features sympathetic as she half paid attention to her friend.

Alexis continued watching the exchange between the women beneath her hood, hoping the garment would hide her obvious curiosity. She sipped from her drink casually, shifting her focus from table to table every now and again in hopes of masking her prying.

She felt Rhipley sheath his dagger, though his body still felt tense beside her.

She could sense Yazmin still consciously observing the women at the bar, too.

Daring to take her eyes away, Alexis looked over at Rhipley. "Is everything okay?" she asked quietly.

Rhipley's jaw tensed as he dropped his eyes from the woman and met Alexis' worried stare.

"She's a witch," was all he said before taking a chug of his ale.

Alexis' heart thundered — another witch? And which woman was it?

"The stranger?" Alexis asked softly. Rhipley nodded as he once again side eyed the woman — the *witch*.

She drank deeply from her cider this time, forcing herself not to look up at the bar any longer.

With perfect timing, another barmaid approaching with their food cut into their shared tension, Alexis' stomach letting out an audible grumble that set her blushing with embarrassment. She dared one last glance at the bar, where the witch was throwing her hands in the air as she argued something inaudible, the barmaid shaking her head in response as she whispered back.

Alexis returned her eyes to Rhipley, who was drinking from his spoonful of soup.

"How could you tell she was a witch?" Alexis asked softly, breaking apart some bread.

"I could smell her. Her scent is pungent," he replied.

"Could the others?" she asked, angling her head towards the room full of scattered fae.

"If they sensed her, they certainly didn't show it," was all he offered. "But our occupation also requires us to hone our skills, our senses. Most fae aren't as in tune with their senses as we are."

Alexis wondered to herself what witches might even smell like, given her lack of heightened abilities.

Remembering their earlier encounter with Amity, she asked, "Why couldn't you sense the king's Magus Depre?"

"She probably used magic to mask her scent," Yazmin replied as she chewed on a piece of meat.

"People can do that?" Amelia asked, wide eyed.

"We did it with you," Yazmin said nonchalantly, grinning at Amelia.

Alexis shot the elf a puzzled look.

"We can't have everyone knowing you're... well, you, so we masked your scents for the first few days you were here. That is, until your odours mixed enough with the scents of this world, with those around you. You reeked of the Mortal Realm, and if we hadn't masked you, everyone would have known the second you stepped within the guild." Yazmin shrugged her shoulders as she chewed.

Alexis cleared her throat. "So, your friends..."

"Are on a need-to-know basis, as is everyone else at the guild. And it will remain that way for the time being," Rhipley said in a commanding tone.

Alexis knew well enough not to argue or question him.

As they continued to chatter amongst themselves in between mouthfuls of food, Alexis noticed the witch eyeing their table — eyeing *her* and *Amelia*. She tensed, dropping her gaze to her nearly empty bowl, but she could still feel the witch watching, her stare like an invisible brand that made her skin crawl.

After some time, the sound of a chair scraping against wood came from the bar, and the witch's lips were upon the barmaids, a single finger slightly tilting the blonde woman's chin upwards.

The barmaid blushed as she appeared somewhat dazed from the sudden show of affection, before she recomposed herself and turned away, picking up a glass to shine. The witch said something as she pivoted, looking at their table once more and smirking, before walking from the inn and vanishing into the night.

CHAPTER 26

The room the inn owner had assigned them was big enough — the only issue being the lack of four individual beds. Alexis had let out a long exhale when the owner had apologised but said they'd been quite busy and this was the only room available, and given the time of night and their desire for sleep after a day of journeying, their group had given in and decided it would have to suffice.

Alexis had just returned from bathing when she'd realised one bed was taken by both Amelia *and* Yazmin, who were cuddling close and whispering to each other.

Her heart pounded as she realised what that meant — that she'd be sharing a bed with Rhipley. She hadn't shared a bed with anyone since Mitch — had *never* shared a bed with any man, or male, *but* Mitch. Had never shared her bed with a *male*, period.

Goosebumps formed on her skin as she also realised that Rhipley would likely return from his own bathing any second now to come to the same conclusion.

Yazmin's head popped up over the blanket at Alexis' lack of sound and movement.

"Sorry!" she exclaimed upon noticing Alexis' eyes on the free bed. "You'll be fine — Rhipley doesn't bite." She briefly paused before adding brashly, "Unless you ask him to, so I've heard."

Amelia snorted as Alexis let out a huff of annoyance, placing her leathers and towel on the windowsill in a neat pile before collapsing onto the bed. She splayed her arms out, feeling the soft quilt beneath her — an oddity in contrast to the firmness of the mattress.

If she'd had more to drink tonight, she might not have even cared or noticed how uncomfortable the bed was.

It's only for one night, she thought to herself.

As she slid under the quilt, the nights still quite cool despite the spring days growing warmer, she peered out the window to watch the stars twinkle, the moon illuminating the darkness of Fallandor Forest outside. The downstairs bar had quieted an hour ago, patrons either leaving to be on their way or heading upstairs to get some sleep.

They hadn't seen the witch again after she'd left, though the barmaid had been not-so-subtly looking in their direction every now and again for the remainder of the night. The blush on her cheeks hadn't disappeared for a time, either.

Whoever the witch was to her, she sure knew how to charm the woman. Alexis' eyes became heavy as she slowly dozed off to the sound of crickets outside.

Rhipley returned from his bathing to a quiet and darkened room, the lamps blown out and the girls all asleep in their beds.

He'd noticed upon walking into the room that Yazmin's white hair was pooled over Amelia's chest, Amelia's red hair entangled in Yazmin's fingers, the other resting on her cheek as they slept intertwined.

As his eyes roamed to the other bed, he noticed Alexis' small frame curled up under the quilt in a foetal position facing the window; the moonlight illuminating her sleeping face.

Inching closer to the bed and peering down at her, he watched her as she slept, simultaneously drying his hair with a towel. She looked so peaceful, so calm. He leaned down to brush a strand of hair out of her face ever so gently, trying his hardest not to disturb her slumber. Thankfully, she didn't stir.

As he tossed his dirtied clothes and towel onto the floor, not caring how they looked, his eyes rose to Alexis' own clothes and towel, piled neatly by the window. He let out a light chuckle and shook his head at her constant need for cleanliness.

Rhipley walked around and ever so slowly slid into the bed, careful not to wake her. As he got comfortable, Alexis' back facing him, her soft hair spilling onto the mattress, she turned over sleepily to face him. He stilled at that, hoping he hadn't woken her, before her tired eyes slowly blinked open and she peered up at him, the grey blue of them glinting despite the darkness now enveloping her face.

He couldn't read her emotions, couldn't quite decipher if he was in for a scolding or not. As he lay there, still as a log, she closed her eyes again and settled back into the bed, inching slightly closer to him. Rhipley allowed his body to relax as he whispered, "I'm sorry I woke you."

Alexis' eyes remained closed as she replied with equal quiet, "It's fine. I'm a light sleeper."

Silence filled the air once more as Rhipley continued to stare at her, studying her face, her steady breathing. He resisted the urge to brush her hair out of her face once more, before she rolled onto her back and opened her eyes again to stare at the ceiling, letting out a huff. "Alright, well now I'm awake."

Rhipley cringed.

"Talk to me, if only to help me fall asleep again," she requested, angling her head to meet his gaze. She smiled softly, not a hint of irritation on that warm face.

The corner of Rhipley's lips tugged up as he, too, rolled onto his back, placing his hands on his stomach. "What do you want me to talk about?" he asked, echoing her movement as he, too, angled his head to meet her stare.

"Can I interrogate you?" she teased, her smile turning into a smirk.

Rhipley huffed a laugh as he said, "Ask me anything. I'm an open book."

Alexis scoffed. "Clearly we have different ideas of what *open* means." Rhipley gave her an incredulous look as she added, "I barely know anything about you."

"I could say the same about you," he shot back, raising a brow.

"Touche."

After a beat of silence, Alexis asked, "What's your favourite colour?"

Rhipley huffed another laugh. "Starting off strong, I see." Alexis batted him gently with a hand.

"Dark green. Like the forest. It reminds me of home — makes me *feel* at home," Rhipley said softly as he thought of the guild, the forest outside.

"I like green," Alexis replied, offering a sincere smile. "It's such a gentle colour."

Rhipley smiled back as he asked, "And yours?"

Alexis chewed on her lip as she thought. "I don't really have one, honestly."

"So mysterious," Rhipley teased.

Alexis rolled her eyes as she asked, "Do you have a favourite animal?"

"Really getting down to the nitty-gritty questions, I see," Rhipley replied.

"I can just go back to sleep if you'd prefer," Alexis replied, beginning to turn over.

"I've always wanted to meet the Wolf Riders in Hyrandell. When I was young, I wanted to *be* a Wolf Rider."

He chuckled at the memory. Rhipley had the vague sense that Alexis was watching him as he looked at the ceiling. "You?"

"Well, I think it's pretty obvious," she responded, and he met her stare again.

"Aspen is a pretty neat pet," Rhipley said. Alexis nodded, her face shifting into something solemn.

"I miss her," she whispered, smiling sadly.

"We've only been gone a day," he replied, trying his hardest to hide the teasing in his voice.

Alexis rolled her eyes. "I wouldn't expect someone like you to understand."

Rhipley scoffed as he said, "Someone like me?"

Alexis nodded. "You don't seem to let anyone or anything affect your emotions."

Rhipley kept his eyes on hers, and she lifted her eyes to meet his stare without hesitation — a challenge.

After a quiet moment, he returned his eyes to the ceiling and said, "It's easier that way. Fewer chances of getting hurt, especially in this field of work."

Alexis sighed. "I've never had to think like that. I suppose I'm lucky in that regard." A few more beats of silence passed.

Finally, Alexis asked, "How can Dimitri Realm Walk? Isn't he a vampire?"

Rhipley clicked his tongue as he said, "Yes, but it's the kind of vampire he is that enables him to possess such power, which makes him all the more dangerous. Luckily for us, his particular species isn't very common, but they're out there, obviously." Alexis waited for him to continue.

"He's a Leichar — at least, that's what we call them. They're a rare species of vampire who can steal the abilities of those they feed on and kill — *only* if they kill their victim. They're not necessarily any more dangerous to humans than regular vampires. That is, unless the human is gifted with magic. Otherwise, they're just that; regular vampires, given the lack of varietal magic found in humans. However, to us fae and elves and other creatures whose blood flows with magic, they're some of the more dangerous beings in this world. Dimitri is the only one I've ever come across, and until that night we rescued you, Yazmin and I didn't know he was a Leichar. We'd heard rumours of his power, his influence amongst his kind, but we'd never learnt the extent of the threat he posed until then."

Alexis continued to stare at him for a moment before lifting her eyes back to the ceiling and letting out a long exhale.

"Well, shit," she muttered, and Rhipley huffed through his nose.

"Shit indeed. Which is another reason we need to keep you hidden and your family back in the Mortal Realm unaware of your whereabouts. Keeps King D'Roghal from sending Dimitri back if he believes they don't hold any valuable information."

Alexis let out a sigh of relief at that and smiled, though it didn't meet her eyes. "Well, as much as I miss them, I'm glad they're safe. Thank you."

Rhipley returned her smile and replied softly, "You're welcome, Lex."

She rolled her eyes before closing them again. The room was quiet for a few moments before Alexis swiftly sat up, positioning herself on her elbows as she looked to Rhipley, as if remembering vital information.

"How does he *know* us?" Her words were hurried, hushed due to Yazmin and Amelia sleeping only metres away, but there was an urgency in her words. Rhipley angled his head in confusion as she stuttered, trying to recall something. "D-Dimitri, when we first encountered him, he said that we've grown up to be beautiful women, myself and Amelia." She quickly glanced to where Amelia lay before returning her gaze to Rhipley.

"I… honestly don't know, I'm sorry," Rhipley said softly. Alexis dropped his gaze, a defeated expression on her face. "We'll find out, okay? I promise."

The corner of her mouth twitched up, but she didn't meet his eyes as she lay back down.

"Tell me a story about one of your missions," she requested, closing her eyes once more.

Rhipley's eyebrows furrowed as he asked, "Are you sure? They're not all pleasant. In fact, few of them are at all."

Alexis just nodded, her breathing beginning to slow as she tried to regain her slumber. So, Rhipley began recounting one of his less gruesome missions as he gazed upon Alexis' calm face.

The morning sun shone across the room, piercing the windows and awakening the group as the space grew brighter with each passing moment. Alexis groaned from beneath the quilt, shielding the sun from her face. Rhipley laughed quietly as she finally emerged, her hair in a tangled mess.

Yazmin and Amelia, however, didn't hide their amusement at the sight. "Wow, Alexis. I'm loving this look on you," Yazmin barked, Amelia's hand over her mouth as she tried to stifle her laughing.

Alexis patted down her hair as she glared at them. Her eyes met Rhipley's before falling to his naked — albeit beautifully muscled — torso, then the undershorts he wore. A blush enveloped her face as her eyes returned to his and she said, "Do you always sleep in… just that?" Her hand gestured to his undershorts as she tried to keep her gaze from wandering, before working her hair into a messy braid.

Rhipley's own eyes searched his body as he responded nonchalantly, "It's far more comfortable in the warmer months than wearing my usual bedroom attire. Though, given your presence, I wore *these* to be a gentleman. Usually, I opt for… less."

He couldn't help his smirk at her blushing further, her eyes trying to find literally anything else to focus on.

Amelia peered over Yazmin's shoulder to see what had her sister flushed with embarrassment, and she let out a low whistle.

"Damn, Rhipley. I didn't realise you were hiding those under your terrifying clothes."

Rhipley shot Amelia a grin.

"Don't stroke his ego, Mill's. He doesn't need it," Alexis mumbled as she glared at all three of them.

Rhipley let out a sarcastic "Ouch," at the comment, placing a hand over his heart.

"She's not as fun in the morning," Amelia replied, shrugging her shoulders.

Yazmin let out an amused hiss, biting down on her laughter as she avoided Alexis' glare.

"I'm going to wash up," Alexis said to no one in particular as she slid from the bed, collected her clothes, fresh and clean thanks to the magic of the inn, and walked from the room.

The group arrived at the quiet Hunter's Guild just after mid-morning, the students and teachers in their various classes and the hunters, or those who remained at the guild, out training. As they entered the hunter's grounds, Aspen ran up to Alexis and tackled her to the ground, swarming her with kisses as she let out excited whines. Alexis couldn't help the tears that welled in her eyes at the sight of her dog, her *Daeanimus*.

Zailah, Lukai and Tatiana followed, the latter approaching only Rhipley without uttering a single word, simply looking him over and then taking him in a warm embrace. Rhipley hugged her back deeply, his eyes briefly meeting Alexis' before he dropped her gaze just as fast as he'd held it.

Lukai approached Alexis, offering a hand, and as she reached for it, she wiped the dirt off her leathers left behind by Aspen. He let out a low whistle as he took in her new clothes, giving an approving nod. Zailah didn't say a word as she looked the girls over once, her face unreadable. Though she was tiny, easily a couple of inches shorter than Alexis, who was only of average height herself, there was something intimidating about her.

Alexis could tell that the female liked it that way — liked knowing she made people feel uneasy with her presence, liked intimidating those around her.

Zailah noted Yazmin's arm clamped lazily around Amelia's shoulders then and lifted her chin. "Finally scored, huh, Yaz?"

Amelia blushed and ducked her head in embarrassment as Yazmin grinned. "Jealous, Zailah?"

Zailah's stone-cold features revealed nothing, though when she noted Amelia subtly shaking Yazmin's arm from her shoulders and stepping away, the corner of her mouth twitched upwards in a sly smirk. Yazmin pretended not to notice, though Alexis knew the dismissal from Amelia would have stung.

"So, what's the verdict?" Lukai asked finally, the question not aimed at anyone in particular as he kept his focus on Alexis, his arms crossed over his chest.

"You tell me, Luke," Rhipley replied sarcastically, and Lukai returned his comment with a show of his middle finger, chuckling as he once again took in the sister's leathers.

"Well, minus the unmarred skin and lack of muscle, you two certainly look the part," Lukai said, poking Alexis on the shoulder for emphasis, which she batted away with a hand, narrowing her eyes.

Tatiana muttered something too quiet for Alexis or Amelia to hear, but it had Zailah replying with, "Harsh, Tati. They're part of our group now. You should welcome them with open arms."

Alexis ignored the obvious sarcasm in the female's tone.

Tatiana shot a glare at Zailah, who just smirked right back.

"Like you can talk," Tatiana muttered. Before anyone else could speak, Tatiana turned and made her way to the archery field, taking up an arrow and knocking it against her bow. Alexis admired the expensive-looking weapon, noting the ends dipped in gold, the high-quality appearance.

She watched as Tatiana breathed against the drawn arrow and let it fly after a brief moment; the arrow piercing a target with perfect precision. Alexis let out a low whistle at that, though Tatiana didn't seem phased in the slightest at her perfect aim and execution, instead taking up another arrow and firing again and again and again.

Before thinking, Alexis turned to where Yazmin still stood next to Amelia, the tension now hanging in the air between them, and asked, "Can I learn to do that?"

Yazmin's eyes followed to where Tatiana was about to fire another arrow, and she smirked. "Sure, but if you want to learn to be as good as her, she'll need to be the one to teach you."

Alexis' heart dropped into her stomach as the realisation hit her: she would *never* convince Tatiana to teach her.

Tatiana hated Alexis at the best of times — there was no way she was about to teach her about archery.

Rhipley stood before Rampier Draghone, his Daeanimus, a snow-white owl, perched on the back of his chair above his head, watching Rhipley like he was going to be the owl's next meal.

"Hello, Zula," Rhipley purred, and the owl simply ruffled her wings, refusing to drag her stare from his.

Rampier lifted his eyes from the unbound scroll in his hands and smiled warmly at the exchange, an expression so few ever saw.

"Zula just returned from our Sister Guild in Tietnam." He held the scroll up, then lifted a hand to pat his Daeanimus, who leaned into the touch, her features softening.

"And what does Princess Yuki have to say?" Rhipley stood with perfect posture as he always did when addressing his Headmaster. Rampier removed his glasses, holding them in one hand before tossing the scroll across his desk for Rhipley to read.

Rhipley picked it up without hesitation and skimmed through the words so neatly written across the paper, before lifting his eyes to meet Rampier's, then read it again. Twice. Thrice.

"How does she know this?" he asked finally, dumbfounded.

Rampier simply reached for the scroll, taking it from Rhipley's outstretched hand and gazing down at it.

"It appears one of her Shima Gai has been stationed here for weeks. A woman by the name of Freya."

Rhipley's brows furrowed as he asked again, "But *how* does *she* know *this*? *Why* does she believe this information is accurate?"

Rampier clasped his hands together under his chin, his face turning contemplative. "Her spies are highly skilled, as you well know. Freya, for instance, has been spying on King D'Roghal's agents for a time now, and it appears she picked up some interesting information."

He tapped a finger on the scroll.

"Does she know who, exactly, he's after? If this information is, in fact, true — that the Divinely Blooded have returned?" Rhipley asked as he attempted to calm his breathing, despite his anxiety clawing at him.

Rampier shrugged, unable to give him an answer. "Though, if this *Freya* uncovers any more information, I've requested that Princess Yuki inform us of it as soon as she can."

He lifted another scroll, clean and freshly bound, to where Zula now reached out a foot to grasp it. Rampier stroked her wings before letting out a sharp whistle, and the owl was gone, flying swiftly out of the open window. When the flapping of her wings faded, Rampier gave Rhipley a knowing look and said, "No one must hear of this. Not even Yazmin. This information does not leave this room until we know more."

Rhipley simply nodded, unsure how to process what he'd just learnt, and departed his Headmaster's office.

CHAPTER 27

Alexis stood before the Red Oak, peering up at the leaves, now a brown-red colour. She watched as they began to fall, one by one. They landed as thick, hot blood on the ground around her.
She stood there, unable to move, unable to react, as she watched the blood rain down, the Red Oak now burning, the flames threatening to consume her if she stepped too close.

Suddenly, that same shadow she'd been seeing out of the corner of her eye so often appeared again. Though she couldn't will her body to move, Alexis managed to turn her head in the direction of the shadow. This time, it hadn't vanished, instead taking on a corporeal form. A dark figure stood in its place, watching her from a distance. Alexis tried to speak, but words escaped her.

The blood was coating her now; the tree burned to smouldering ashes as she watched the dark figure approach.

Was it friend or foe?

She was terrified, yet felt an unexplainable, underlying sense of calm simultaneously. The figure was standing within arm's reach now, and Alexis' eyes grew wide as she saw what emerged from the shadow, the darkness slipping away from the body beneath: a woman.

No, not a woman, but a *female,* for those were fae ears peeking out from beneath her long, black hair. Alexis recognised her — her pale, beautiful face, her piercing green eyes.

Recognised her beauty from the paintings she'd seen at the Hunter's Guild, in Rampier's office: Princess Aurelia.

Her emerald eyes appeared to be both joyful and sad, a hint of longing in them that Alexis couldn't quite grasp.

Alexis remained still as she watched Aurelia approach, so close she could have touched her had she been able to move her arms.

"Is it really you, child? After all this time," Aurelia asked, her delicate hand coming up to graze Alexis' cheek, though she didn't feel the touch.

Alexis tried to speak again, but found no words.

Aurelia's eyes scanned Alexis from head to toe before settling on her ears.

"You're still human," Aurelia stated more than questioned, her voice uncertain.

Alexis inclined her head in confusion, Amity's question from their visit to Fallandor echoing through her mind.

What are you?

Finally, Alexis found her voice again as she asked, "What do you mean? How do you know me?"

Aurelia ignored the question, her eyes now fixed on Alexis' own, the greens of them piercing in the darkness.

"You must stay hidden until it is safe. You cannot tell anyone who you are," she demanded.

"How do you know me?" Alexis asked, hoping Aurelia might answer her question this time. "How am I seeing you?"

The princess simply met her stare with sad eyes and said quietly, "I *knew* you. Once, very long ago."

She took in her own body, before adding, "As for how you're seeing me — it is because I am projecting myself to you, to your dream state, from the After Realm."

Before Alexis could continue her questioning, she snapped awake, shooting upright in her bed. For a few moments, she didn't know where she was, the room bathed in darkness, the only source of light coming from the moon shining in through the window.

As she tried to catch her breath, her pants coming out hurriedly, she wiggled her toes and found something heavy at her feet: Aspen.

The dog was watching her through tired eyes, as if she, too, had been startled awake. Alexis reached down to hug Aspen close, and she glanced over to her sister's bed, where Amelia was sleeping soundly.

Alexis let out a sigh of relief as she laid back down, Aspen now cuddled by her side, Alexis' hands brushing through her coat.

She tried to remember the dream, tried to piece together what Aurelia had said to her, pondering it.

You're still human.

What could that possibly mean? Hadn't she always been human? As the words rattled through her mind, she dozed off again, sleep consuming her once more.

The following morning, Alexis sat at a table alone in the dining hall, having arrived well before breakfast would be ready. Cook and her new kitchen hands had just finished bringing the food out, and Alexis was quietly grateful that it was no longer *her* job — she liked Cook, but she wasn't a fan of the early wake up's or the late nights, though given that she would now train to be a hunter, as was confirmed by Rhipley yesterday, she supposed the lack of sleep, early mornings and late nights may become a routine for her once again.

She'd helped herself to some bread and jams as she sat at her secluded table, enjoying the peace and quiet before every hunter, student and teacher came through those doors with their chattering.

She'd struggled to stay asleep after her initial dream last night, the image of the Red Oak burning constantly plaguing her mind whenever she managed to doze off, waking her again and again.

Though Aurelia hadn't visited her after that initial dream; it was just the tree, burning away as the blood dripped down.

It was the second recurring dream she'd had, the first being her repeat nightmares of the Inferno Hound chasing her and Aspen through the woods. Alexis weighed the idea of whether or not to tell her comrades, whether they might even know what it meant.

Alexis allowed herself to feel some semblance of relief at the fact she'd now identified the source of the shadow — at least, in this world. Had it been Aurelia's spirit visiting her back home?

She didn't want to think about it — was too tired to think about it.

As she sat there, picking away at her bread, the doors opened, and footsteps and chattering encompassed the dining hall.

Various passers-by glanced in her direction — some judging, some smiling and others ignoring her altogether. Finally, her friends walked in, Tatiana with her arm through Rhipley's, Zailah reading a book, Yazmin and Amelia walking silently together, and Lukai, who was muttering something to Rhipley that had the latter laughing.

Alexis gave the best smile she could conjure as they approached, and Amelia asked cautiously, "Where were you this morning? I woke up, and you weren't in your bed."

Alexis' eyes fell on her food as she lied. "I came here. I was starving."

While it was true that she'd been here all morning, before the sun had even risen, she hadn't really been starving, but had instead needed a quiet place to sort out her thoughts, though she wouldn't voice that truth — not yet.

"I'm surprised Cook let you eat before anyone else got here," Yazmin said, impressed as she looked at the half-eaten bread roll, her stomach grumbling.

"Well, I think Cook was grateful for my help these past weeks, so she went easy on me."

Lukai took up a spot next to Alexis, playfully elbowing her as she smiled and elbowed him back. She noticed Rhipley watching them from the corner of her eye, despite Tatiana rambling to him about god knew what.

"How's my favourite hound this morning?" Lukai asked cheerfully, taking a piece from Alexis' bread roll.

"I took her to the Daeanimus Grounds before coming here. She's made a new friend, one of the hunter's wolves, I believe. She's more excited about seeing him than me these days."

Alexis shook her head, smiling at the thought of Aspen and the wolf playing together.

"How do the Daeanimus' play a role here? I mean, do hunters take them on their missions?" Amelia asked, placing a fisted hand under her chin.

"Well," Lukai said, clearing his throat. "Some hunters do, since their Daeanimus' can be quite helpful in certain situations. For instance, if a hunter had a mouse for a Daeanimus, the mouse could get in and out of small spaces. Headmaster Draghone's Daeanimus, Zula, is his messenger and occasional spy. She's an owl."

"A nasty little thing," Tatiana muttered, Rhipley and Yazmin humming their agreement.

Alexis turned to Lukai and blurted, "I didn't see his Daeanimus when we first came here?"

"She was on a mission," Rhipley said lazily as he shoved spoonfuls of soup into his mouth.

Lukai went on, the others at the table now listening in. "Though some hunters choose to only bring theirs along on safer missions, since they're too afraid to put their Daeanimus in danger. Given our special bonds with our Daeanimus', we can also give them our power if and when necessary. Some people even share their own life force, so their Daeanimus can live as long as them." He eyed her for a few seconds before adding, "Although, since you're human, I don't believe you can even give anything like that to Aspen."

Alexis stilled at the word.

Human.

Aurelia's words to her last night struck again, and she gulped as her eyes fell to her plate.

"Well, isn't that unfortunate," she mumbled.

"Why don't any of *you* have a Daeanimus?" Amelia asked, sipping from her juice. Zailah, to Alexis' surprise, went deathly still, but didn't speak.

Yazmin said cheerily, "I do. Her name is Mollurie, the finest pure-blooded Equois in all of Xalentya. She's back home."

Amelia and Alexis shot her puzzled looks.

"A horse," Tatiana mumbled.

"She's more than a horse. There are horses, and then there are the elven blessed Equois. They're descended from unicorns. So, no, they're not *just horses,*" Yazmin drawled, and Tatiana rolled her eyes.

"What about the rest of you?" Alexis asked, making a point not to look at Zailah, who had withdrawn into herself.

Lukai sighed. "Rhipley and I just haven't bonded with any, yet."

"Neither," Tatiana added, not looking up from her soup.

Alexis hummed, before her thoughts drifted back to her dream from last night, that word.

Human. Human. Human.

It clanged through her. She'd never given any thought to the word before, and now, it's all she could think about.

"Are you okay?" Lukai asked warily, putting a hand on her shoulder.

"I'm fine. I'm just tired," Alexis said curtly, before standing from her spot and leaving abruptly, rendering her friends completely speechless.

Amelia found herself in her room after breakfast, sitting on her bed and attempting to read — decipher, really — a book that she'd found in one of the drawers in the bedside table, written entirely in the First Language.

As she flicked through the pages, a light knock sounded at the door and she angled her head to see Yazmin standing there, arms crossed and a sheepish look on her face.

Amelia lowered her eyes back to the book as Yazmin stepped in, closing the door behind her.

"What's up?" Amelia asked drily, pretending to focus on whatever was written in the book.

Yazmin clicked her fingers, and it appeared in the Common Tongue, as they called it in Xalentya.

Hiding her surprise and relief at the gesture, she flipped through the pages. Yazmin's sigh sounded from the door, cutting into the quiet as she approached the bed before plunking down next to Amelia.

"I wanted to apologise for yesterday," Yazmin said sheepishly, hesitantly reaching for Amelia's hand. When Amelia didn't flinch away or protest, Yazmin gave her fingers a light squeeze.

"Whatever for?" Amelia responded, playing dumb as she kept her focus on the book.

After a few seconds, Yazmin reached over, grabbing the book from Amelia and placing it on the bed behind her, before lifting Amelia's chin to meet her eyes. Amelia held her gaze as Yazmin said, "I don't think you're some prize or some new notch in my belt, if that's what you think."

Amelia furrowed her brows at the words before Yazmin backtracked. "Well, you certainly *are* a prize, but not in the way Zailah was interpreting. I mean, if that's how I truly felt, I'd have already slept with you and thrown you away like you were just some other fling." Yazmin laughed awkwardly, then stopped when she realised Amelia wasn't amused. "Sorry to be blunt, but I'd prefer to be honest."

"If you really think I'm that easy…" Amelia grumbled, trailing off.

"No, no, I don't. That's my point," Yazmin blurted.

She struggled to explain, sighing as she grabbed for both of Amelia's hands. "I want this to work. I can't explain it, but there's something about you. Something special. You're unlike anyone I've met, both in this world and the other. I want… you. *All* of you."

Amelia searched Yazmin's pleading eyes, before her own fell to where she still held her hands.

"And what if you grow bored of me?" Amelia mumbled.

Before she could react, Yazmin's lips were on hers, the kiss filled with need and desire.

Amelia hesitated, drawing back with surprise, before bringing her lips back to Yazmin's.

Yazmin lifted her hands up to cup Amelia's face, the kiss soft, no urgency in it, no rush. They moved in perfect sync, Yazmin leading and Amelia following patiently.

Amelia leaned back onto the bed, beckoning for Yazmin to follow. She obliged, deepening the kiss, moving one hand to cup Amelia's waist. Amelia's hands tangled in Yazmin's hair, the touch full of lust.

Suddenly, Amelia broke the kiss, her face flushed.
"I've never been with a woman before, Yaz," she muttered, embarrassed. "Female, either."

Yazmin smiled softly, brushing a strand of hair out of Amelia's face and placing a kiss atop her forehead. "We can take it slow, if that's what you'd prefer."

Amelia searched her eyes, hesitant to answer, contemplating what Yazmin had offered, how much it meant to hear it. After a few quiet moments, Amelia nodded, sitting up to kiss Yazmin once more.

CHAPTER 28

Rhipley sat at a table littered with books in the quickly emptying library, the sound of shoes scuffling, books closing and quiet chatter filling his ears. He'd been waiting for Alexis for twenty minutes now, coming to the library after he'd showered following his training with Lukai earlier.

Surprisingly, Lukai had been unusually quiet during their session, giving bland answers to Rhipley's questions when they weren't clashing swords or fists, but otherwise remaining relatively silent. If Rhipley hadn't suddenly remembered his tutoring lesson with Alexis, he'd have stayed to ask his friend what was bothering him so much to render him so quiet.

Though he had a feeling it had to do with Alexis' abrupt exit from breakfast.

As he glanced around the library again, still no sign of Alexis, he realised he could have stayed back, after all.

Rhipley exhaled sharply through his nose, tapping a finger on one of the books.

Another few minutes went by, and he grunted in frustration as he flicked open one of the books, lazily reading the first page.

From the corner of his eye, he saw Alexis finally walking into the library, smiling at various students passing her by as she held the doors open for them.

Her eyes met Rhipley's, and she shot him a sorry smile, approaching him with hurried steps. She was wearing her usual attire — at least, her usual attire since she'd arrived at the guild. The clothes fit her body perfectly, accentuating certain... aspects, and though he did his best to hide his ogling, he found it difficult to remove the thoughts from his mind.

"I got held up. I'm sorry," Alexis said when she reached the table, slipping into the seat across from Rhipley's.

He closed the book, sliding it across to her. "Is everything okay?"

"Lukai wanted to check in on me after my little episode this morning." She blushed slightly, as if embarrassed.

"*Episode?*" Rhipley scoffed, resting his chin on a hand and staring at Alexis with a raised brow.

She opened the book, titled *The First Language,* without hesitation.

"I'd hardly call *that* an episode." After he'd briefly run into Rampier following breakfast, who'd advised he and Yazmin on what they'd be teaching both Rainier sisters, Rhipley had decided to begin with the First Language, the oldest of this world.

Though most folks in Xalentya now spoke in the Common Tongue, or English, as they called it in the Mortal Realm, Rhipley knew the girls would need to learn the First Language, eventually.

Then, there were the languages of other countries, like Tietnam on the Eastern Continent, or Paravka on the Western Continent.

"The First Language?" Alexis asked, flipping the cover over as she read the title, which was displayed in the Common Tongue.

"Being a hunter means having knowledge of this world. You may come across villages and folks who *only* speak the First Language, and it certainly helps if you can converse with them. Believe me, there's nothing worse than hunting down a creature and having no clue what the townsfolk are trying to tell you about it."

Alexis let out an exasperated sigh, but rather than shying away, she met Rhipley's eyes and said, "Alright, let's do this."

"Magus Depre," Rhipley said, waiting for Alexis to answer.

"To detect magic. A magic detector, essentially," Alexis replied in a dull tone, both hands cupping her temples as she stared down at the pages of the book littered with hundreds of other words she had yet to learn. Perhaps knowing that Amity was a Magus Depre, having some insight, helped her just now.

She huffed out an exhausted breath, and Rhipley angled his head to meet her drooping eyes. Alexis scowled right back at him as he smirked.

"I'm so mentally drained," she grumbled. "Can I please have a break? Even just to look around."

Rhipley's eyes scanned the empty library, even the librarian and bookkeepers having already retired for the night, the only light in the area offered by the lamp on their table. Neither had realised how long they'd been here, how long Alexis had been studying without a break. It was the least she deserved.

After a few moments of silence, Rhipley snapped the book shut, and Alexis became alert again, barking an angry, "Hey!" at him in response.

He huffed a low laugh at her reaction and said, sweeping his arm toward the many shelves behind him, "Have at it."

Her eyes lit up instantly as she stood from the table and practically ran to the nearest bookshelf. Rhipley stood too, following her in a less-hurried manner.

"I thought you were drained," he called as she disappeared into the bookshelves on the bottom level, the walkways between darkened without the lamps to light the many corridors.

Alexis didn't answer, too eager to see what books lay within.

Catching up, Rhipley retrieved a lamp off of a nearby desk and approached Alexis from behind, where she was running a finger along the spines of various books. As she tried to read them, her human eyes so poorly adjusting to the darkness, Rhipley held the lamp out to her.

She gave him a sheepish grin as she took the lamp and studied one particular book that had piqued her interest. He remained behind her, the warmth of him at her back, his breathing quiet. Trying to ignore his comfortable presence, she pulled the book she'd been eyeing off the shelf and turned it over to view the cover.

The book, bound in leather and tied shut with some string, offered no explanation for what might lie inside. Handing the lamp back to Rhipley, she unbound the book and opened it to read its contents. Upon skimming the first page, she shut it and returned it to its spot.

"What's wrong?" Rhipley asked finally, stepping closer.

"I think it's a diary," she replied softly, turning to explore some more. "I feel strange reading it."

"Why?" Rhipley asked.

Alexis scoffed as she looked over a shoulder. "How would you feel if someone read your diary?"

"I wouldn't care because I don't keep one," he replied coolly, smirking.

Alexis rolled her eyes. "Of course you don't. God forbid you write down your feelings instead of keeping them hidden."

"Is writing in a diary not keeping them hidden?" Rhipley asked, amusement in his voice.

"You know what I mean," Alexis replied. "It's better to understand how you feel rather than shutting your emotions away. It's *healthy*."

Rhipley chuckled. "I deal with my emotions in a *very* healthy way, thank you very much."

Alexis turned at that, challenge in her eyes. "And how do you do that?"

Rhipley smirked again as he leaned down and whispered, "Physical activity."

Alexis blushed, her heart beginning to beat rapidly as her traitorous eyes fell to his lips, realising what, exactly, he meant. She stumbled over her words as she finally said, "Good for you," and turned once more.

By the time they'd finished their lesson, it was nearly ten o'clock at night. They'd missed dinner, had missed seeing their friends, but Alexis didn't mind. Despite how annoying Rhipley could be, she quite enjoyed his company, when he wasn't being an ass.

They'd spent far too long exploring the library, and had it not been for Rhipley accompanying her, Alexis was sure she'd have become lost. She was certain, however, that the only reason Rhipley had let her have such a long break in between tutoring was because he was just as bored as she with all the studying.

Though she had to give him credit where it was due — he certainly made a good teacher.

After a long day, and night, of studying the First Language, which she'd also discovered was used mostly by elves, she'd managed to add a few new words to her vocabulary.

Daeanimus, she already knew, thanks to Rampier and Lukai.
Magus Depre, another one she'd learnt before the tutoring.
Donumas — a winter celebration of gift giving, similar to Christmas in her world, to celebrate the goddess of giving, Donuma.
Hyacan — to hatch or be born.

Rhipley had advised her before dropping her off to her dorm that they'd be spending one day at a time on different topics — tomorrow would be the layout of Xalentya, where the different continents and countries were situated, who ruled each country, where the populations of different species differed.

Despite the lack of physical labour, she was still *mentally* exhausted. Though, if this tutoring would help her in the long run, she supposed it would do more harm than good to not participate. That, and the fact that being a part of this Hunter's Guild required teachings both physical and mental, whether or not she liked it.

Amelia was sitting on her bed, staring at the ceiling and playing with the ends of her hair, when Alexis had walked through the door. Unsurprisingly, Aspen was sprawled on Alexis' bed, belly facing the roof and legs in every direction. Alexis huffed a laugh at the sight, and Amelia perked up from her spot, greeting her sister.

"How was your session with Rhipley?" she asked politely, her face flushed and eyes glowing.

"I'm more interested to hear about *your* session with Yazmin," Alexis replied coolly, kissing the air mockingly, which had Amelia blushing further before tossing a pillow at Alexis, who batted the pillow away just before it hit her in the face.

"It's... whatever," Amelia said quietly, refusing to meet her sister's eyes.

"How are things between you? I mean, only if you feel comfortable telling me," Alexis asked as she sat on her bed, bringing her knees to her chest. Amelia turned to face her sister, her eyes settling on the floor as she braced herself on the edge of the bed, trying to find her words.

"We kissed today," she finally said.

Alexis furrowed her brows in confusion. "As in... for the first time?"

"Well, I'd hope so," Amelia snapped back, her face enveloped in red now from her embarrassment at the confession.

"Sorry, it's just... with how close you've been over the past few days, I guess I'm just surprised that this is the first time you've kissed. Was it good?" Alexis asked, fiddling with her hands.

Amelia let out a deep breath. "Yes, it was. But I told her I have no interest in being her... fuck buddy, for lack of a better term. And I also told her I've never actually been with the same sex before..."

Alexis considered for a moment before replying, "And how did she take it?"

Amelia's eyes finally met hers. "She actually took it really well, to my surprise. Whether or not she remains interested in me after is yet to be seen, but I'm just trying to take it one day at a time." She shifted her gaze to the window, chewing her lip.

Alexis stood and walked over to her sister, kneeling before her and grabbing both hands in her own.

"Mill's, you're a beautiful, intelligent, caring and amazing woman. If Yazmin can't see that, or chooses not to, then it's her loss.

However, if you want my opinion," she paused, and Amelia looked at her, waiting for her to continue. "From what I can see when you're together, she's crazy about you. Just give it time. After all, we already have enough on our plates with tutoring and training and whatever else life is going to throw our way."

Amelia chuckled drily, and Alexis offered her a sympathetic smile.

"Plus, don't forget your birthday," Amelia added, and Alexis exhaled a long breath before shaking her head.

"I don't think it's worth celebrating this year, with all this going on." Alexis gestured to everything around them.

Amelia furrowed her brows in disappointment, opening her mouth to object before Alexis added, "Plus, no one here knows it's my birthday tomorrow, anyway. So let's just keep it between us."

Amelia sucked in a sharp breath before reluctantly nodding.

CHAPTER 29

Alexis awoke to Amelia sitting on the end of her bed, one hand lazily scratching Aspen's ear, the other donning a wrapped present.

"Happy Birthday," Amelia said excitedly.

Alexis hissed, bringing her index finger to her lips before Amelia cringed and whispered, "Happy birthday."

"We don't need every person in this guild with super hearing knowing what day it is, remember?" Alexis warned as she gave a half smile, accepting the present in Amelia's outstretched hand.

"Well, considering what kind of people this guild is crawling with, I think you'll find it increasingly difficult to keep them from finding out as the day goes on," Amelia replied, her eyes on the gift.

"Shouldn't be too difficult so long as those who know keep their mouths shut, right Mill's?" Alexis teased, one brow raised as she shot her sister a warning look.

Amelia waved her off. "I think it's silly that you don't want anyone knowing, but whatever."

Alexis rolled her eyes as she returned her attention to the gift now sitting in her lap, neatly wrapped in brown parchment paper secured in twine.

"Your wrapping skills have certainly improved," Alexis noted. Amelia simply cleared her throat awkwardly as she looked down at Aspen, avoiding Alexis' eyes.

"You did wrap this, didn't you?" Alexis pushed, angling her head to meet Amelia's averted gaze.

Before Amelia could answer, a brief knock sounded at the door, and hiding the gift under the covers, Alexis announced, "Come in."

Within half a second, Yazmin was opening the door and walking in, a wide smile on her face as her eyes danced between the sisters.

"Did you give it to her yet?" Yazmin asked Amelia, who bit her lip and shot Alexis an apologetic look.

"Mill's?!" Alexis exclaimed.

"It's not her fault — she mentioned it weeks ago in passing. I just have an excellent memory," Yazmin responded, taking up a spot on the bed next to Amelia. "You know, you two have lucky birthdays."

The sisters shared quizzical looks before turning their full attention to Yazmin. "How so?"

"You were both born on the Summer and Winter Solstice's, respectively. The days that we in Preshia celebrate Luzhula and Brundhul. You're God's chosen." Yazmin gave a mocking bow.

"I thought you said people here don't really believe in them?" Alexis challenged.

"Well, I may have been exaggerating. Many people still do, to a degree — the religious fanatics, especially."

Amelia seemed to clock Yazmin's earlier comment as she asked, "Wait, today's the Summer Solstice?"

Yazmin nodded her head. "We aren't celebrating it today, though. This year, things have changed — the councillors who organise the festivities were both found dead a few days ago, so they're rescheduling it for the end of the month."

"That's... concerning," Alexis said, raising her brows in question.

Yazmin simply shrugged. "The officials aren't classing their deaths as suspicious, so we're not asking questions."

"Is it not your jurisdiction?" Alexis pushed.

"If they were killed by creatures, yes. But, if their deaths were, as the officials stated, not cause for suspicion, then we have no choice but to move on from it. Unless we're asked to investigate personally, it's not our place to intervene." Alexis just hummed doubtfully.

"Open your present!" Yazmin ordered, rubbing shoulders with Amelia, who smiled now, too.

Alexis chuckled as she undid the twine and carefully unwrapped the parchment. She gasped quietly as she peered at what lay inside. "How did you get this?" Alexis asked, tears beginning to well in her eyes.

Yazmin smirked as Amelia replied, "Yazmin may have taken a trip home to find it."

Alexis looked at Yazmin, who shrugged, a smug look on her face. "You did this for me?"

Yazmin's smug smile turned into something warm and sincere as she reached for Alexis' free hand.

Alexis obliged, gripping it tightly. "We're friends, now. Of course I did. Happy Birthday," Yazmin said softly, squeezing.

Alexis wiped her tears away with her free hand. "How did you even remember this book existed?" she asked Amelia, whose eyes were also filling with small tears at the sight of her sister's happiness.

"I, too, have an excellent memory. It was your favourite book as a kid, after all — the reason you began reading in the first place. As your big sister, of course I remembered it. I love you."

Alexis gently pushed the book to the side and embraced her sister tightly. "Thank you," she whispered.

Aspen, displeased to be missing out on the love being shared, pushed her head between the sisters and began kissing Alexis all over her face. The three chuckled as Alexis embraced her dog, her Daeanimus. "Thank you, too, Aspen."

Following breakfast in the dining hall, left undecorated given the postponement of the Solstice festivities, Rampier giving a speech announcing the deaths of the council members, the new date of celebrations and a moment of silence, Alexis found herself sitting on her bed, rejoicing in the fact that she'd successfully hidden her birthday from her friends — from Rhipley.

It hadn't been difficult, given how sombre the atmosphere was — she'd never experienced a Solstice celebration, but considering how grey the mood had felt within the guild, she was glad to have not brought it up. The last thing anyone needed was to celebrate her birthday.

She felt guilt at even acknowledging that it was her birthday.
As she traced her fingers over the book cover, nostalgia coursing through her, she heard a light knock at the door. "Come in," she said politely, hiding the book under the covers as she had this morning.

Rhipley appeared on the other side, his hand gripping the doorknob as he stood there, his typical smirk on that too-handsome face of his. Alexis met his eyes and smiled gently.

"What was that you just rushed to hide from me?" he asked, gesturing with a slight up tilt of his chin.

Alexis gave him a bemused look as she shook her head. "I genuinely have no idea what you're talking about."

He stepped into the room, taking up a seat on Amelia's bed, his elbows resting on his knees as he clasped his hands in together. "If it's smut, you don't have to be embarrassed," he teased.

She rolled her eyes. "*It* is none of your business."

"Hey, I'm not judging," Rhipley replied coolly, his smirk growing.

Alexis found herself wanting to flirt with him, but remembered Tatiana and Lukai. Not that there was anything between her and Lukai — nothing of note, at least. He hadn't made any further moves, and she wasn't going to push it. To her surprise, Alexis was actually enjoying being single.

"Some Summer Solstice, huh?" Rhipley said, shifting his gaze to the window.

Alexis huffed a dry laugh as she took the chance to look at him — his muscled arms, his tensed jaw, his strong facial features, his chocolate brown hair, his gorgeous eyes that glowed with a tinge of red in the sunlight. When he returned his gaze to her, she looked away, pretending she hadn't been ogling him.

"It's not usually this depressing, I promise," he added with a light chuckle.

"I'm sure the festivities are grand," Alexis replied as she pondered *what* those festivities might be like.

"They certainly are," he said softly, and she caught him watching her, his face unreadable. As he cleared his throat, standing from the bed, Rhipley asked, "Ready to go?"

Alexis nodded, gesturing for Rhipley to lead the way as she subtly took the book from under the covers and stashed it in the bedside table.

If Rhipley noticed her scuffling, he said nothing.

Rhipley hadn't known it was Alexis' birthday initially. Not until Yazmin, the blabbermouth she was, had slipped up and mentioned it this morning at breakfast. After Alexis had left — rushed, really — to go to her dorm, and the only ones left at the table were himself, Lukai, Zailah, Amelia and Yazmin, Tatiana off on some mission with another hunter, Amelia had elbowed Yazmin in the ribs, though it had been too late. The table had been silent for minutes before Lukai spoke up.

"Why didn't she mention it before?" His brows had furrowed in frustration, though Rhipley knew it wasn't aimed at Alexis, but his lack of knowledge that it was her birthday today.

After glaring at Yazmin, Amelia had said, "Well, she doesn't think it's important enough, with everything going on."

Zailah had dismissed herself shortly after, and though Rhipley tried to ignore it, he'd noticed the way Lukai watched after her. When he'd returned his attention to the table, Lukai had said, "This day is depressing enough as it is. We could use a celebration right about now."

Yazmin, being the sarcastic ass she was, had raised her cup of juice and said, "Here, here," before taking a long sip, earning a middle finger from Lukai and a displeased look from Rhipley and Amelia.

"What? I'm agreeing with him," Yazmin had retorted, though her tone suggested otherwise.

Wiping his mouth with a napkin, Lukai had said, "Well, she's Goddess Blessed — she's obligated to celebrate one way or another."

"Don't push it, Lukai. If she doesn't want to celebrate, that's her choice," Rhipley had replied sternly, though he knew his brother meant well.

With that, they'd departed the table, Rhipley making his way to Alexis' room. He'd known that what she'd stashed beneath the covers was likely a gift from her sister, and if she wished to keep it to herself, he wouldn't push her to reveal it to him.

Now standing in the meadow, Rhipley having Realm Walked them once they'd exited the dorms, he held Alexis against him, trying his hardest to ignore her backside against his front. Begging his body not to betray him. How it felt having her pressed up against him like this.

He leaned down and whispered in her ear, "Open your eyes."

As she did so, a small gasp escaped her lips. She raised a hand to her mouth, and Rhipley had to focus on her heartbeat to ensure she was still breathing, her stillness unnatural — as if she, too, were fae.

Small tears welled in her eyes as she took in the meadow, realising it was the same one they'd stood in the first time they'd come to Xalentya.

"Why are we here?" she asked quietly, her eyes darting around the field before rising to meet Rhipley's. "I thought it would be a nice change of scenery," he said, shrugging his shoulders as he stepped around her, walking backwards and donning his usual smirk.

"But why here?" she asked again, her brows furrowed.

Rhipley simply beckoned Alexis to follow him.

After a few hesitant seconds, she did, her eyes never ceasing their roaming of the beautiful nature that surrounded them.

Rhipley led Alexis to a lone tree, a soft rug waiting beneath laden with food and books.

Alexis raised her eyebrows, an impressed expression on her face as she focused her attention on what lay before her. "This is quite the setup for a study session."

Rhipley, with his typical swagger, lazily took up a spot and patted the rug. "I'm known to be quite the generous tutor from time to time."

Alexis chuckled, and Rhipley found he had come to love the sound — it was like a symphony in his ears, the sound so pleasant, so… happy and genuine. When Alexis took up a spot across from him, inspecting the laid-out foods, Rhipley threw a book at her feet.

"The maps of Xalentya," he said, tossing a grape into his mouth.

Alexis looked the cover over before opening it, coughing as years' worth of dust flew into her face. Rhipley cringed as he added, "Yeah, sorry. That one hasn't been touched in a while."

"I can see that," Alexis replied, wiping at her face.

After a few quiet moments, Alexis reading the contents of the book and memorising the maps, only speaking to confirm the pronunciation of certain countries, she asked, "So why are we really here? You could have taken me to the library."

Rhipley stilled his chewing, exhaling a long breath before sitting upright.

"I thought it would be a nice surprise for you. You know, since we're friends."

Alexis angled her head, the realisation hitting her. "Which one of them told you?"

Rhipley bit down on his laugh as he replied, "Yazmin. She means well, she just needs to learn to hold her tongue."

Alexis huffed in annoyance before returning her attention to the book. A few more quiet moments passed, Alexis' attention wholly on the book as she murmured to herself, and Rhipley took the chance to appreciate her in this moment.

The way her eyes squinted as she tried to pronounce names and countries and cities, the way her golden hair sprawled over one shoulder, the strands swaying in the wind. The way her jaw tensed with frustration. Suddenly, she snapped the book shut and looked at him, catching him off guard, to his surprise.

"Who else knows?" she asked.

Rhipley ran a hand through his hair. "Everyone. Well, except for Tatiana, but that's only because she isn't here at the moment."

Alexis looked at the sky and exhaled a long breath through her nose. As the sun hit her face, Rhipley could have sworn her skin glowed — as if small diamonds danced on her skin, a shimmer cascading across her features. The sight had him admiring her once more, mesmerised.

Alexis had felt Rhipley watching her, but she wouldn't dare meet his eyes.

Instead, she tilted her head back, exposing her face, her neck, and her chest to the sunlight streaming through the overhanging leaves. She let the warmth encompass her and she closed her eyes — breathed it in, let it melt her core. She loved this weather, this heat. Loved the peaceful sounds of the forest, the woodland animals chattering away; the birds singing their sweet melodies; the tree leaves rustling. She could stay here forever — content and satisfied.

Remembering Rhipley beside her, Alexis opened her eyes to finally meet his own.

He watched her with an unreadable expression on his face — but his eyes said everything.

It was lust that crept in those chocolate irises, though she wouldn't allow herself to think about it, to accept it as such. So she just smiled and returned to the book of maps, laying on her back as she held the book above her head, thankful for its surprisingly lightweight.

Seconds later, she felt Rhipley's presence next to her. He was lying on his back, too, reading the book she held. Despite the tension that lingered in the air, he thankfully carried on as if all was normal, pointing out a country or a city or village and asking her to pronounce it. Then, he asked her who ruled over said country or city or village.

After hours of studying, Alexis had fallen asleep. She'd had the faint sense of a hand brushing hair from her face, the touch so gentle, light as a feather. Unsure whether it was actually happening or if she was just dreaming it, Alexis allowed herself to fall deeper into her slumber.

Rhipley didn't protest when Alexis had tossed the book aside and fallen asleep, exhaustion taking over. She'd done well with their lessons, despite it only being day two. To his surprise, she *was* a quick learner, as she'd said weeks ago. He felt guilt claw at him for assuming she'd be any less, for assuming she was just a clueless girl. No, Alexis was a woman — a smart one at that. A woman with determination and a hard will. He was impressed and thankful, and he allowed himself to admire her for it.
As she lay there sleeping just centimetres from him, her breathing so calm, her face so peaceful, Rhipley dared to brush a hair from her face.

Her body twitched at the touch — a natural reaction — but she didn't wake, though he stilled his hand, anyway.

He wasn't sure why he was acting this way — he'd never been like this with anyone before, not even Tatiana. He'd never allowed himself to feel anything more than friendship for anyone before. Sure, he'd felt lust and desire for his past lovers, for Tatiana, when he'd found himself in her bed, or she in his, but never anything like this.

Because feeling anything more was dangerous, and being a hunter was dangerous. He didn't want to end up like Rampier — heartbroken and alone. He couldn't allow himself to ever feel that, experience that. And so, he retracted his hand and opened a book, turning onto his back once more and trying his best to ignore the sleeping woman beside him.

Having woken an hour later, Alexis apologised for falling asleep, but Rhipley just brushed it off. Something was different about him, like his demeanour towards her had changed.

"Is everything okay?" Alexis asked warily, dusting herself off.

"Everything's fine," Rhipley assured her, giving her a smile that didn't meet his eyes. With a click of his fingers, the books and rug and food disappeared, likely returning to the guild.

"That's a helpful trick," Alexis joked, trying to pry some light humour from Rhipley, who just nodded before offering her a hand.

"Ready to go?" he asked, his eyes emotionless.

Alexis hesitantly gripped his hand, narrowing her brows in confusion at this sudden shift. But, knowing Rhipley, prying would be useless.

If he wanted to shut her out and be alone with his emotions and thoughts, she wouldn't push the matter.

Their friendship was only new, and she hadn't learnt his boundaries yet.

"Wait, we're Realm Walking back?" she asked suddenly.

"We'll Realm Walk to the gates. I have used little of my power today, so it's not a gruelling task."

Alexis nodded, stepping closer. Within seconds, they were whisked away, appearing at the steps leading to the guild. Without uttering another word, Rhipley walked up the stairs and through the gates, Alexis following behind a few steps.

Once they stood in the courtyard, she stopped, letting Rhipley walk ahead to the southern gates. When he passed through without looking back, her heart sank a little. She didn't know why — they were friends, and yet she felt like her heart was being crushed inside her chest.

He felt nothing for her, or anyone, and he didn't owe her anything more than friendship, nor she him. Interrupting her thoughts, she heard Lukai shout from across the courtyard, drawing her attention from the southern gates.

Plastering on her best attempt at a smile, she faced Lukai, who was holding two cupcakes, one adorned with a lit candle. Chuckling, she met his eyes and said, "You really shouldn't have."

"Nonsense. Your birth should be celebrated," he replied, handing her a cupcake.

"Did you make these?" she asked, noting the intricate icing in the shape of a sun atop both.

"Not quite — I may have agreed to wash dishes for Chef for a week. If I attempted to make these, you'd have been eating charcoal."

Alexis snorted. "Well, I appreciate the gesture, but you really didn't have to. I worked for Chef, remember? Washing dishes isn't a pleasant task."

Lukai shrugged a shoulder. "I've been through worse." Alexis nodded in agreement, not wanting to think of what, exactly, he'd experience during his time as a hunter — what any of them had experienced.

"Make a wish," Lukai whispered, angling his head towards the Red Oak. Alexis turned her head to look at it and imagined Aurelia standing there as she had in her dream. Imagined the princess watching them — watching her — doing something that seemed so... trivial, in the grand scheme of things.

"We really don't have to," Alexis mumbled.

Lukai met her stare. "If you don't blow it out, I will."

Alexis, allowing herself to have this one day, allowing herself to enjoy this last bit of it, obliged, and blew the candle out, earning a cheer from Lukai, who bit into his cupcake, the icing sticking to his lips.

She laughed at the sight, and the aching feeling Rhipley had left her with slowly diminished as she lost herself in this moment with Lukai. From the corner of her vision, Alexis noticed Prince Frederik watching them — watching *her*, his face unreadable.

CHAPTER
30

Rhipley and Yazmin stood in their headmaster's office, the latter competing in a staring contest with Zula, who was perched on the back of Rampier's chair. Rampier reached up to rub Zula's chin with his forefinger, smiling softly at the majestic bird, her white-grey feathers almost glowing in the morning sunlight streaming through the large window to the right of the room.

After a few quiet minutes, Rampier said gruffly, "I have a mission for you both, and it's imperative that it stays between *us.*" He cast a pointed look at Yazmin in particular, whose mouth formed a tight line at the words Rampier didn't need to add.

"Is everything okay?" Rhipley asked, attempting to sound calm, though something made his skin crawl at Rampier's grave tone.

Rampier's eyes still on Yazmin, he said, "We received a request for help from a village on the outskirts of Lilhan. There's a demon wreaking havoc."

Yazmin spoke this time, and Rhipley wasn't at all surprised at what came out of her mouth. "It'd be convenient if D'Roghal could keep his mutts on a leash."

Rampier's eyes narrowed at her comment, though he didn't disagree.

"We don't know that it's from Vendarath, Yaz," Rhipley said in a hushed tone, though Yazmin ignored the warning.

"Actually, we do," Rampier interrupted, earning a swift turn of the head from both of his finest hunters.

"How?" Rhipley asked, his anxiety threatening to surface.

Rampier's eyes locked on his, and though his master didn't utter a word, he immediately knew the answer.

Yazmin glanced between the two and asked, "Is there something I'm missing?"

Rhipley dipped his head at Rampier's unsaid words and met his friend's eyes. "Let's just go take care of this."

Yazmin's brows furrowed as she gestured for him to explain what was going on. Rhipley ignored her, returning his attention to their master. Yazmin let out a defeated grunt, but wisely didn't object further.

"Who's going to be taking care of the Rainier girls?" Rhipley asked sternly, pretending he wasn't the least bit concerned.

Rampier sat back in his seat, shuffling a few papers on his desk. "Zailah and Lukai offered." Rhipley and Yazmin shared a doubtful glance, knowing Zailah wouldn't have offered anything. "They haven't been assigned any missions that require their particular skill sets for now, so I've asked them to remain here while you're otherwise occupied. Besides, aside from you two, they're the hunters the sisters are most comfortable with." *Comfortable* was an interesting word for it.

Yazmin chuckled, something presumptuous coating the laughter as she muttered, "I'm sure Lukai is pleased with that."

Rhipley tried to ignore her comment, and though he kept his eyes on Rampier, he could feel Yazmin watching him for some sort of reaction. He didn't dare give her one, didn't dare let her know how he truly felt for Alexis, how he was *beginning* to feel something deeper than simple friendship, though he denied it even within himself. He couldn't hurt his brother like that, especially after he'd heard about Lukai's grand gesture just days before, on the afternoon of Alexis' birthday. Cupcakes, baked by Chef, of course. Though he knew Alexis would have loved it, nonetheless.

She'd loved his gesture as well, he knew, even though he kept telling himself it was simply a kind act of friendship — a gift for one's birthday, from one friend to another. Nothing more. Rampier dismissing them with a map to the village and the report he'd received, the two stepped from the office.

In the time since she'd awoken, from the moment the sun broke through the clouds, Alexis had learnt how to hold a sword, a bow, and most other weapons the guild had on offer.

Wielding them as well as a hunter was expected to, however, had not come so easily.

She hadn't realised how heavy a sword might actually be until she'd held one, and Lukai, who appeared quite amused at her lack of knowledge and experience, couldn't help the grin that cast across his face when Alexis grabbed the sword from him with such confidence, only to drop it instantaneously, followed by a few colourful words.

The bow and arrow was even worse, not nearly as heavy as the sword, though trying to aim the arrow and keep it nocked against the bow wasn't as easy as it had looked in movies.

Zailah had watched her and Amelia attempt, and fail, quietly from her spot perched on a bench with a book in her lap.

No emotions showed on her youthful face, though Alexis wasn't surprised.

The few reactions she'd seen from Zailah were half-assed in their own regard - *barely* reactions, if they could even be called that.

Amelia had gone off to continue training with Zailah, while Alexis had stayed with Lukai. She felt sorry for her people-pleasing sister, knowing how awkward she'd be feeling. As she bent over, trying to catch her breath after finally commanding enough strength to hold the sword long enough to swing it a few times, Alexis found herself missing home, missing her *normal* life. Once she was able to stand straight again, Lukai confiscated the sword, deeming her unfit to wield it just yet. He pinched at her skinny arms and said, "We need to get some muscle on those things before you accidentally hack off my favourite part trying to simply pick up the sword."

Alexis huffed a breath, accepting her fate, stretching her arms behind her head.

Exhausted from the basic but gruelling exercises Lukai had her do, Alexis panted from where she sat against a tree. Lukai chugged from a waterskin, and Alexis watched as his throat bobbed with each swallow, as stray droplets slid down his tanned neck.
Then, her eyes roamed to his muscled arms on full display in his hunter's vest, made from the same materials as their usual hunting attire, though made more breathable for the warmer months. He could have been carved by the gods themselves, if Alexis didn't know any better.
His sleek, shoulder length black hair was gleaming in the sunlight, the top half tied back in a messy bun. Alexis couldn't help but to admire him — he was unnaturally beautiful.
Fae beauty was certainly something else.

Feeling her gaze, Lukai stopped drinking, his mouth still on the opening of the skin. His eyes met hers as the corner of his mouth tugged upwards in a smirk.

"Enjoying the view?" he asked slyly.

Alexis blinked, chuckling awkwardly and averting her gaze. "When's lunch?" she asked sheepishly, dusting off her pants before standing.

Lukai offered her the waterskin, and she didn't hesitate in accepting it, gulping down mouthfuls of water herself. When she'd finally finished, wiping her lips with the back of her hand, Alexis met Lukai's eyes again.

He was watching *her* this time, and she tried to ignore how his expression made her feel. The look that had her core heating.

"I suppose we can stop for lunch," he finally said, pushing off the tree. "You've earned it."

"All I've done is stretch and work out a little," Alexis replied.

"Not true — you've also made some interesting attempts at weapon-wielding," Lukai offered sarcastically. Alexis rolled her eyes as she laughed, making her way over to one of the outdoor lunch tables, Lukai on her trail.

Lunch consisted of bread, soup, and the creamiest butter Alexis had ever tasted.

Each bite felt like heaven, her stomach's grumbling lessening with each mouthful. Whilst she ate, she listened to Lukai school her on different fighting tactics — how to take down various opponents she might come across. How to use her small, petite frame and speed to her advantage, and to keep her wits about her whether on the offence or defence. Fighting wasn't just about physical blows, but also about using your cunning to figure out the best way to come out the victor.

"Do you miss your family?" he asked in between bites of his own food, taking Alexis by surprise.

She drew in a deep breath before replying, "Yes, every day."

"And what do they think of you being here?" he asked thoughtfully, sympathy in those golden eyes. She looked at him for a second before dropping her eyes to her emptying bowl of soup, swirling her spoon around it aimlessly. "They know it's what's best for us, no matter how much it hurts."

Silence filled the air between them for a brief moment, the ambience of hunters training in the distance. Lukai's warm hand closed around hers, and she looked up to see him looking at her intently, his mouth curved into a warm smile. She returned his smile with a half-assed one of her own, her heart thundering inside her chest.

When they'd finally finished eating, more stretches and exercises followed before Lukai handed Alexis a smaller, skinnier sword. To her surprise and relief, it wasn't nearly as heavy as the previous one she'd held. Gripping it firmly in her hand, the balance far better this time around, Lukai gave her an assessing look before nodding and instructing her on how to stand and how to disarm an opponent.

After her arms had grown tired — her entire body, if she was being honest — he'd confiscated the sword once again, instructing her to finish up with a final round of exercises and stretches; ones she knew would help build some muscle on her arms and legs. "You need to be able to comfortably hold a sword before using it against an enemy."

Though Alexis was tired of push ups, lunges and crunches, she knew he was right, and she found herself thankful for it, if only because it kept her mind off of Rhipley — wondering where he was, what he was doing, and why he'd drastically changed his tune the other day. With each exercise, the thoughts of him dissipated.

It was late afternoon by the time Rhipley and Yazmin reached the village Rampier had sent them to, the pair having to take small breaks in-between Realm Walking to avoid their magic and energy depleting before their mission. The village was quaint, and the summer heat had certainly set in. Yazmin and Rhipley rolled up the sleeves of their leathers as they wiped the sweat from their brows. Upon arriving, the villagers noticed them immediately, some offering smiles, others steering clear and making their caution of the famed hunters evident.

A middle-aged human woman was the first to greet them. Though her hair was grey and her skin wrinkled with age, she showed no sign of frailness, her energy matching that of someone in their youth.

"Thank you for answering our call," the woman said, giving a dip of her head, to which Yazmin and Rhipley returned. Before Yazmin could inquire about the demon, a loud flap of wings sounded above them as something large descended from the skies. The two hunters simply shielded their eyes with their hands, the rest of the villagers, including the woman in front of them, covering their faces, their children's faces, with the fabric of their clothes, some even shielding the elderly and youth with their full bodies to protect from the gusts of wind summoned by those strong wings.

When the creature had landed in the village square they stood in, Rhipley huffed his annoyance at the realisation of who now joined them.

A human woman with long, black hair tied back into a braid, fair skin, and piercing bright blue eyes sat atop a monstrously large griffin, the eagle-lion hybrid as tall as the houses.

Yazmin, however, smirked at the realisation of who was now in their company.

"Hello, Evera," she crooned.

Evera didn't smile, didn't show any sign of amusement, her beautiful stone face as emotionless as Rhipley remembered it.

She sat perfectly still atop her famed war griffin, Reaper, Rhipley recalled his name being, and stared both hunters down for a few heartbeats before gracefully descending from her saddle, her mount lowering himself to allow her departure.

"About time you showed up," she replied gruffly, not bothering to address them by name.

Yazmin tutted. "What, no hug? No warm greetings?"

Evera shot her a pointed glare that would have sent lesser folk running, though where Evera was cold as ice, Yazmin was a hot, burning fire.

"When I see someone worth the warm greeting, I will act as such," Evera said coldly, patting Reaper on the side, the griffin shooting into the skies once more.

"What are you doing here?" Rhipley cut in, his cold tone echoing Evera's. There was no warmth on his face, no light in his eyes as he beheld his ex-lover — the lover he'd had on past missions that had brought him to this mortal country. His ex-lover — though Rhipley used the term loosely to describe their past relationship — who was fantastic in bed, but cold as steel otherwise. Though Rhipley hadn't minded. He'd never yearned for romance, and thankfully, Evera had offered nothing more than a body to warm his bed.

Despite his past relations with the brutal woman standing before him, he felt nothing more for her — platonic or otherwise. She might as well have been a stranger — in truth, he knew nothing about her, nor she him. Nothing that mattered, at least.

Evera stood her ground, arms crossed from where she'd approached, and now stood beside the village leader.

"Lady Evera is the guardian of our village. We are forever indebted to her," the village leader said warmly of the Griffin Rider, who dipped her head in thanks, an unusually soft smile on her lips meant only for the human woman and the village citizens.

"*Lady* Evera?" Yazmin retorted, making no attempt to hide her amusement.

"Yes, I've been wedded to Lord Baelin. Not that it's any of *your* concern." Evera's warm features vanished as she levelled a look at Yazmin.

Anyone could cut the tension with a knife, though where the villagers watched on with caution, Rhipley simply rolled his eyes at the interaction.

"Are you sure he's man enough for you? I mean, I doubt he's the one who wears the pants in your relationship," Yazmin snickered.

Evera scowled. "At least I've found someone who actually wishes to warm my bed for more than one night. Tell me, are you still sleeping your way through Preshia? After all, I doubt you've found anyone who is *actually* willing to put up with your bullshit."

Yazmin's features faltered for a split second, and had Rhipley not known her as well as he did, he'd have assumed she had been unaffected by the cruel comment. Instead, Yazmin continued to don her smirk as she addressed the village leader. A few silent coughs and mumbles sounded from within the crowd at the uncomfortable interaction.

"Where is the creature now?" Yazmin asked, side-eyeing Evera.

"We believe it is hiding out in the forest during the day. It has already stolen some of the children of this village. We hear their cries every night — some outlasting others." Someone within the crowd began sobbing. "A few brave souls have ventured into the forest in hopes of retrieving the children, but I'm sure you can guess how they fared," the village leader added solemnly, angling her head to observe the mourning crowd.

"Brave?" Yazmin hissed, lowering her voice so the villagers wouldn't hear. "It's suicide for an untrained mortal to go after a demon, which, by the way, is what you're dealing with."

Rhipley placed a hand on her shoulder, his eyes urging her not to add salt to the already painful wound. Evera grunted in distaste, but the village leader just nodded sadly.

"You are right — it wasn't the best option. But it *was* our only option. Until you answered our call." She smiled, the genuine kindness taking Rhipley by surprise.

"Are there no other hunters stationed nearby?" Yazmin questioned, looking at Rhipley.

Rhipley didn't speak, keeping a lock on the secret he held onto, the information he knew.

The village leader clicked her tongue. "There are, but your Head Guild Master said they weren't equipped nor trained for something like this. He said *you* were the two best suited for this job."

Yazmin's eyes darted between the village leader and Rhipley, her face growing more confused, more frustrated.

"If it's a demon who feeds on children, we need to act now. The fear of youth is far more potent than that of matured adults. It's likely growing stronger the longer it goes unchecked. How long *has* it been here?" Rhipley asked, his eyes on the village leader as he ignored his friend. He hated lying to her, hated keeping her in the dark — but it was necessary.

"It has been three nights. It creeps into the village when the lights have been dimmed and those within have turned in for slumber. In the dead of night it arrives, and soon after departs with a child in tow. We do not know how. It has not yet been seen, but rather heard. When the parents wake to find their child missing, it is already too late."

Rhipley wracked his memory, the file they'd been given, for what kind of demon they were dealing with.

How best to hunt and kill it, and get whatever children remained out relatively unharmed.

"What does it sound like?" Yazmin asked intently.

"Like a faint whisper. Only few have heard it, but didn't know what it belonged to at first. When the children began disappearing, we connected the two. Lady Evera sent word to Rampier Draghone the second we'd informed her."

"What have you been doing this whole time?" Yazmin asked Evera accusingly.

"I can't kill it if I can't track it," she snapped back. "You hunters have that special skill that we Griffin Rider's do not. Plus, I'm human. Exceptional as I am, my senses aren't heightened. Hence, you two."

"Well, it *is* our line of work. It's a smart move leaving it to the professionals," Yazmin shot back, a smirk playing at her lips.

"You're more of a last resort," Evera said, shrugging.

Rhipley groaned, gripping the bridge of his nose with his thumb and forefinger.

"We will hunt it tonight. Figure out what it is, where it hides out, what it looks like," Rhipley said sternly, cutting into the two arguing. The village leader nodded her thanks.

"You can stay at my cottage. I have plenty of room." She smiled at both hunters, her expression sincere, thankful.

Turning to face the crowd, their eyes intently watching the interaction between the four, Yazmin said with a raised voice, "We will get your children back and restore peace to your village, I promise you that." The crowd smiled, voicing their quiet thanks and blessings.

CHAPTER 31

Lukai had instructed Alexis to perform various exercises, set after set, until her body ached, following her failure in attempting to wield even the skinny sword he'd given to her following lunch.

They'd both quickly realised that she was, indeed, in no shape to wield *any* weapons, and he'd told her firmly that she *wouldn't* be wielding any until she was strong enough, until she could hold a sword without wanting to drop it after mere seconds.

Until she could carry out hand-to-hand combat for longer than a minute without running out of stamina.

To her surprise, he hadn't asked any further questions about where she came from, or her personal life, either because he was no longer curious, or because he didn't believe her for one second, but knew not to delve any deeper.

In between their sessions of weapon holding, stretches and exercises, Alexis found herself unable to shove the thoughts of Rhipley from her mind. They always crept back in, to her dismay. She hadn't heard from even Yazmin since this morning, hadn't *seen* either of them.

"Hey, have you seen Yazmin or Rhipley today?" she asked Lukai once they'd finished for the day, hoping her tone didn't imply the worry that gnawed at her.

Lukai shook his head. "They're probably out on a mission."

Alexis chewed on her lip — it's not like either owed her an explanation, but she was a little hurt that it hadn't even been mentioned in passing, not that she and Rhipley had really spoken these past few days.

She thought, however, that maybe even Amelia would have been told by Yazmin, at least.

"I wouldn't worry," Lukai said, bumping her in the shoulder with his own as they walked back towards the dorms.

"I'm not worried," Alexis said, her eyes on the buildings ahead. "I was just curious."

She felt Lukai watching her, trying to figure her out.

She wouldn't dare let him see how she truly felt, her doubt, her insecurity.

"You did well today," Lukai said, changing the subject. Alexis let herself meet his eyes, plastering a genuine smile on her face.

"You think? You can be honest with me, you know."

"When haven't I been?" he replied, a brow raised.

"I'm just saying — you don't have to go easy on me. I may be a fragile human with no prior training, but I can take constructive criticism."

"I do not doubt that," Lukai said sincerely. "But I was being truthful — you kept up, didn't complain, didn't bitch out. I'm genuinely proud of you."

Alexis felt a warmness come over her. Lukai was sweet, despite his intimidating exterior. Perhaps she should focus her attention on him, not Rhipley.

Rhipley, who, she had to remind herself, was just a friend — who only saw *her* as a friend. And she was *single*, and should enjoy herself as such.

Lukai hadn't shown that he wanted anything serious with her, anyway. Maybe it was a good chance for them both to have some fun.

"What's on the agenda for tomorrow?" Alexis asked as they made it back to the dorms, Lukai's hands full with the two swords and bow and arrows. "More muscle building? I'm familiar with cardio, so that's something we should probably start including in my exercise regime, too." Her eyes searched the training grounds for her sister, who was nowhere to be seen. Still training with Zailah, she gathered.

"Magic," Lukai answered, his smile turning into a smirk, challenge in his golden eyes.

"Magic?" Alexis asked hesitantly, returning her gaze to his. Lukai nodded.

"What if I don't really have any? Or anything of note? What if it's a waste of time? Maybe we should wait for Rhipley and Yazmin to return first…" The words came out rushed as Alexis scrambled, trying not to let slip that Rampier, Yazmin and Rhipley *all* knew she could Realm Walk.

Lukai considered her words for a second before saying, "Well, that's what we'll work out tomorrow. Though I've been told you have *some* inkling of magic in your blood, so we'll just have to coax it out."

"Is it hard to conjure? Will it hurt?" Alexis asked, trying to regain a cool demeanour, like the thought of it didn't terrify her. All she remembered from her one and only attempt at Realm Walking was the nausea that plagued her to the point of passing out.

"It can certainly drain you if you use more than you're ready for. As for whether it hurts, it depends on the strength of your magic and how much you conjure at a time. But I — *we* will teach you how to pace yourself, take it day by day. Slow and steady is the safest option when it comes to magic. It is known to be unpredictable."

Alexis was silent for a few moments, Lukai's words repeating in her mind. There was so much to learn, with the tutoring, the physical combat and now magic.

The thought of having to simultaneously learn all three just to keep herself protected hurt her brain.

Lukai, seemingly sensing her anxiety, stepped closer, his voice low as he placed a gentle hand on her shoulder and asked, "Are you okay?"

Alexis breathed in and out slowly, letting him think it was simply anxiety over learning magic and not the thought of accidentally Realm Walking in front of him. When her heartbeat had steadied some, she met his eyes and smiled. "I'm fine — I'll be fine. I've got this."

Lukai returned her smile with a tentative one of his own.

Arriving at her dorm room following dinner, having grabbed Aspen from the Daeanimus Grounds when she remembered it hadn't even crossed her mind, Alexis stopped before the door to let the dog in, who trotted to the bed and made herself at home. Closing the door, she turned to face Lukai, who smiled, waving goodbye to Aspen. Amelia was still out training with Zailah, she assumed, so she had the room all to herself until her sister was finished.

Lukai appeared to come to that same conclusion as he asked, "Want some company?"

Alexis scratched her head. "I was actually just going to read and head to sleep."

Lukai didn't take any offence to being shut down, as she'd expected — not that he'd ever given off that impression, but she'd simply expected it out of habit.

"Sounds like a good night. I'll see you tomorrow, then," he breathed, but didn't make to leave as his eyes stilled on hers.

Alexis' breathing turned ragged as his gaze fell to her lips — curiosity and a silent question.

Her heartbeat began pounding as Lukai stepped closer, placing a hand on her cheek.

"Is everything okay?" Alexis asked quietly.

"I just really want to kiss you right now," Lukai responded in equal quiet.

"Do it, then," Alexis said, her eyes meeting his again. His own eyes grew dark as his face came down to meet hers. She tilted her head back in invitation. Lukai's soft lips collided with hers, and she let him lead. There was nothing urgent in the kiss, no pressure.

Just laziness, like they had all the time in the world to enjoy this moment. He brought his other hand to her hip as the kiss deepened.

Alexis brought her hand up to his neck and found her back suddenly against the door. She didn't break the kiss, but found herself wanting more as heat built between her legs.

Remembering those in their rooms adjacent to hers, and Aspen on her bed waiting, she pulled back.

Clearing her throat, Alexis said, "Well, that was certainly a pleasant surprise."

Lukai chuckled softly, his hand still on her cheek, fingers entwined in her hair. "I've been wanting to do that all day."

Alexis didn't hide her blush as she said, "I'm glad you finally worked up the courage to do it, then."

Lukai tilted his head to the side. "If I'd known you wanted me to do it sooner, I wouldn't have delayed myself." Alexis felt giddy — like she was some high school girl crushing on a boy.

Turning the doorknob, she said, "Maybe next time, don't wait. Just do it."

"Noted," Lukai said coolly, placing his hands in his pant pockets.

"See you tomorrow," Alexis said, her teasing tone gone.

"Good night," Lukai replied, waiting for her to step inside. Once she'd disappeared into the room, she stood against the door for a few seconds, waiting to hear Lukai leave. His departing footsteps sounded soon after, and Alexis made her way to the bed, collapsing onto it as exhaustion hit her.

Rhipley and Yazmin had been waiting inside the village leader's home since dusk had fallen, the village slowly falling quiet as each family, each individual, retired to their beds. The village leader, who'd introduced herself as Hilda, had advised the two to make themselves at home. She'd revealed that her husband and daughter had fallen ill to a plague, passing within days of each other and leaving her alone in this large house, hence the empty rooms.

When Evera visited to check in and ensure the village remained untouched — monthly, Hilda had said — she herself boarded at Hilda's home, the village leader having already fashioned her daughter's room into a living space for Evera.

Reaper had his own sleeping quarters in Hilda's large barn, finding comfort amongst the poultry who, to Rhipley's surprise, weren't the least bit afraid of the griffin, instead coddling him like a chick.

Once Hilda had retired to her own sleeping quarters, bidding the three goodnight as she gave them each a wary look before departing to her bedroom, Evera had insisted they turn down the lamps and wait by the windows, watching for anything out of the ordinary.

The target had yet to show itself, whatever *it* looked like. In their years of hunting, Yazmin and Rhipley found they were still coming across new species of creatures, and demons were no exception. All they knew about this creature was that it was indeed a demon, as Rampier had advised them, and that it came from Vendarath.

That it fed on children wasn't out-of-the-ordinary, but until they encountered it themselves, knowing what kind of demon it was, remained a mystery.

With the last lights dimming as it neared midnight, the trio watched carefully from their spots within Hilda's house. Rhipley began to nod off, the weight of his earlier Realm Walking finally taking a toll on his body. As he closed his eyes, convincing himself mentally that he was simply taking a short, well-deserved break, he felt Yazmin slide up next to him.

"Hey, you see anything yet?" she asked softly, leaning past him to peer out of the ajar curtain.

Rhipley grumbled, fluttering his eyes open as he spotted Evera across the room, silently looking between them and her own window, gruff caution on her face. Yazmin leaned down to whisper as Rhipley monitored Evera.

"Are we sure there's a demon and these kids haven't just been wandering off? I mean, how many times are we called to jobs like this where there isn't a creature terrorising the village folk, but just some creep or wild animal? Is it possible Rampier's intel was incorrect?"

Rhipley huffed a laugh in response before whispering back, "I doubt it. Rampier is very rarely ever wrong."

Yazmin slid her eyes to him tentatively before letting out a sigh. "I wish you'd tell me what you know."

Rhipley's expression turned apologetic as Yazmin added, "But I understand why you're keeping it to yourself. If it's need-to-know, I'll continue treating it that way."

Turning from the window, Yazmin and Rhipley's ears pricked up at the sound of the poultry, of Reaper, in the barn chirping and grunting, as if something had disturbed them.

Evera, appearing to have heard it too, quietly made her way across the room to where the hunters now stood, peering out that same window towards the barn doors.

Nothing could be seen in the darkness that enveloped the village, so Rhipley walked to another window. Still, nothing out of the ordinary.

His eyes darted from house to house, hoping to spot something, anything, when he heard Yazmin's low, sharp whistle meant only for his ears. He was by her side in an instant, following her stare to a small house twenty yards away. As they watched the home closely, a small girl emerged, appearing from the front door and walking as though she were in a trance.

Rhipley's eyes roamed to the edge of the village, where he could just make out a small ripple of blackness in the tree line. As the girl neared, the black fog disappeared, the child following.

"What was that?" Evera asked sharply.

"Some kind of demon, but it appears to be shielding itself in mist, so identifying it won't be easy," Yazmin said blandly, unsheathing her daggers. She shot Rhipley an incredulous look that said, *Was she not listening when we said so earlier?*

"Who cares *what* kind of demon it is — we need to go after it," Evera shot back, making for the door.

Before she could rush out valiantly, Rhipley, with his heightened speed, had his hand on her wrist in an instant, halting her. Evera glared at him.

"If we run after it without a plan, the demon and those children could disappear forever. It can't know that we're onto it," Rhipley said quietly.

"If we don't act now, that child it just took could be dead before we're able to do anything," she shot back, trying for the door handle again, to no avail.

"We need to plan an attack and rescue. We're experienced in this; you aren't. Covert missions aren't the same as leading attacks on territories," Yazmin warned.

Evera's nostrils flared with rage as her eyes darted between both hunters, but after a few long heartbeats, she relented.

"What do you suggest we do, then?" Evera asked, crossing her arms over her chest.

Alexis found herself in a castle, though not the one she'd been to in Fallandor — no, this castle was made of dark stone, the area she was standing in encompassed by dim light coming from the overhead chandeliers and candles lining the parallel walls.

She watched as a woman — a *female* — white haired and pale skinned, her fae ears poking out from beneath thick strands, played with an infant who looked no older than one. The baby chuckled as it watched the female whispering to it, the words unheard from where Alexis stood.

The female was beautiful, her deep sea-blue eyes appearing to glow even in the dim lighting. Alexis walked closer, her footsteps feeling heavy as she tried to hear what the female was saying. Standing ten feet from the female and her babe, she listened.

"My dearest Alleria, one day you shall rule this world alongside Adrenna, your shadow and light coming together as one and forming Xalentya anew. The world will bow at your feet, the citizens will chant your names. Your lives will become legend, told and re-told for years to come. My precious princess. My beautiful, sun born child."

The story of Luzhula and Brundhul repeated in Alexis' mind as the female said the words.

Alexis backed away, and the female looked up at her, confusion on her face. Those eyes — she somehow recognised them. The face was so familiar, like she'd seen it before. As the female watched her, a slender arm now outstretched, the baby babbled away, and Alexis was ripped from the castle as thousands of blurred images flashed before her eyes.

She could hear a woman's screaming, a man's angry bellowing, heavy footsteps, shouts and sobs and cries of anguish.

Then, silence, and she was once again before the Red Oak.

As if out of habit, she looked to her right to see Aurelia was already waiting, as she had been in that first dream.

Aurelia watched her, that same sorrowful expression on her face, worry in her emerald eyes as she said, "Stay hidden. You are not safe. You mustn't let them find you."

Alexis tried to speak, but words escaped her. She tried to reach for Aurelia, but her body was frozen in place.

Flames suddenly engulfed her, and she was screaming, her body thrashing as her vision blurred.

"Alexis!" Amelia was shouting as she shook her awake.

Alexis' eyes flew open, and she beheld her sister, both arms gripping her shoulders and a look of horror flooding her face.

As Alexis' eyes adjusted to the darkness, she peered around the room, catching her breath as her heart beat rapidly.

"What's wrong?" she finally asked, her words coming out in a rush. Aspen was at alert, sniffing at Alexis cautiously.

Amelia held her hands up, as if in defence, her eyes wide and words escaping her.

Alexis narrowed her brows as she asked again, "What's wrong?!"

"You were… glowing," Amelia finally murmured breathlessly. "Glowing *and* screaming bloody murder."

Alexis let out a light, tentative chuckle as she angled her head. "Amelia, be serious. What are you talking about?"

Amelia gulped as she looked her sister over, not offering any further explanation.

Alexis huffed with irritation as she pulled the covers back and scanned her body — everything appeared normal. She raised her eyes to her sister again, gripping her shoulder with a gentle hand.

"Are you sure you weren't dreaming, too?"

Amelia hook her head slowly. "I swear, I'm not lying."

Alexis gave her sister a sincere look, quirking her mouth to the side. "I'm fine. Go back to sleep."

Amelia held her sister's stare for a heartbeat longer before standing and retreating back to her own bed. When the room had quieted once more and Amelia's breathing had slowed enough to suggest she was asleep, Alexis scanned her body again. Aspen had curled back up, but her eyes remained on Alexis, worry on her canine face, in her eyes.

Alexis reached down to pat the dog, who kissed her hand, as if trying to comfort her.

"I'm fine, girl," Alexis whispered before lying back down. She held her hands in front of her face, barely able to see them in the darkness, and tried to replay her dream.

Who was that woman?

Who was she referring to?

Why was Alexis seeing her?

Aurelia's warning clanged in her mind, repeating over and over.

Stay hidden. You are not safe. You mustn't let them find you.

She considered going to Rampier to inform him of her dreams, but she wasn't sure what could even be done about it. What could he even suggest? Would he tell her not to worry herself over it?

Suddenly, she found herself thinking of Rhipley, wondering what he was doing, how he might help her through her dream crisis.

As she fell asleep once more, no further dreams haunted her, the thought of Rhipley weighing on her mind.

CHAPTER 32

As the trio approached a cave, Rhipley and Yazmin following the child's scent, they came to a halt. Searching the area, they found nothing. The forest had fallen silent, the sounds of crickets and woodland critters ceasing, indicating a greater threat loomed nearby.

Rhipley and Yazmin immediately deduced the sudden lack of sound wasn't due to their presence, the former silently commanding everyone to take up their assigned positions.

With a nod, Yazmin disappeared back into the forest, and Evera, with her mortal speed, quickly and, as humanly possible, quietly made her way over to a large boulder overlooking the cave mouth.

For long minutes, they listened for any kind of commotion, any sign of the demon or the children.

The forest remained silent, and Rhipley shifted his focus to where he could just see Evera, whose own eyes were on his in silent question. Rhipley shook his head, urging her to remain where she was.

The last thing they needed was for this mission to go belly up and for whatever information the demon had to go public. They needed to settle this as soon as possible.

Rhipley sniffed again; the girl's scent was strong. She had to be here, so where was she?

Suddenly, Rhipley's ears pricked up at the sound of soft, small footsteps coming from the cave mouth. He tightened his grip on Wraith and hid further behind the tree, his eyes wholly fixed on the cave. Within seconds, the girl emerged. He heard Evera shift, and he once again had to level her with a look of warning: *not yet.*

Minutes passed, but the demon still hadn't appeared, as if it was aware of their presence and was using the girl as bait.

Rhipley sensed nothing inside the cave. The demon must have been using some kind of warding to hide itself. He quietly ducked from tree to tree, making his way around the area surrounding the cave. The girl remained still — as if in a trance. Evera echoed Rhipley's movements, her eyes constantly darting between the cave mouth and the girl.

Something wasn't right, Rhipley knew that much. He returned to his original position, waiting for Yazmin to emerge from the cave, to give the all-clear.

From the corner of his eye, he noticed Evera moving in. Immediately, Rhipley tried to signal for her, tried to get her attention, to no avail.

She was making a beeline for the child, completely casting the agreed-upon plan aside.

Still, there was no other movement. Rhipley considered for a second that perhaps the demon had departed the area or returned to the village for a second helping, despite the forest remaining deathly quiet. Taking one second to consider whether it was worth returning to the village was Rhipley's mistake, as he returned his gaze to the clearing before the cave entrance, and noticed a black shroud of mist slowly approach Evera from behind, who had finally made it to the child, attempting to wake her from her trance.

Rhipley dared to emerge from his spot behind the tree, his eyes darting between the demon and Evera. When her eyes finally met his, she tensed her jaw, and picked the girl up, hauling her over a shoulder.

"For fuck's sake, Evera," he hissed, breaking into a run.

Where the hell was Yazmin?

Before he could reach the demon, something had secured him to the spot — a trapping spell. He had fallen for the trap, had literally walked right into it.

As Evera turned around to make a break for the village, she froze, beholding what now blocked her path. Rhipley tried to reach for her, tried to break free, but the magic holding him in place was strong. He was utterly useless as he watched Evera's demise unfold before his very eyes.

Evera had decided now was as good a time as any to rescue the girl — there had been no sign of the demon for some time now, and she wasn't waiting around for the demon to show up and make a meal of the child. As she'd approached the girl, Evera noticed her eyes were clouded over, the child unresponsive to words and touch. Yazmin had yet to give the signal, and she didn't want to risk any more precious time.

Ignoring Rhipley, who she could just see in the darkness, Evera didn't voice her apology as she hauled the girl over her shoulder and turned for her exit.

Though grateful for their help, for their answer to the plea, Evera didn't trust the hunters as far as she could throw them. They were immortal, and human lives likely meant so little to them in the end, amounting to collateral damage at best. She'd never questioned Rhipley or Yazmin about their missions, about the lives saved, but she'd always read the reports on the lives lost, and that was enough for her.

She was content with her final decision to save the girl and make a run for it, as was her original duty when the plan was set, and leave the demon to the hunters. Let them hate her, let them give her endless shit for acting too soon — she didn't care.

Didn't care for Rhipley's opinion, or Yazmin's, or anyone's, for that matter. All that mattered to her right now, in this moment, was getting the little girl home safely. She was willing to bet that the trance would wear off once the demon was dead, and it was a chance she would take.

Turning to make for the village, Evera froze as she beheld the demon, its misty form blocking her way.

She reached for her dagger, but the demon was faster, an onyx hand emerging from the fog to grip her throat. The girl dropped to the ground with a thud, and Evera screamed, reaching out for her still-entranced body, despite the claws clamped around her own throat.

Her eyes shifted back to the demon, and she levelled it with a hateful stare. Losing control of her body, her limbs, the demon lifted her with ease.

Evera was paralysed, as if the grip on her throat rendered her body immobile. She couldn't hear Rhipley, couldn't even sense his movement, as if he, too, had been paralysed. Their mission had failed, and they would die here. They had failed the village, the parents, Hilda. Evera was grateful, if only because she wouldn't have to face them, to tell them she couldn't do it in the end.

Another hand reached out of the mist and aimed for her mouth, forcing it open.
She felt her jaw break; the pain slicing through her as the demon's hand plunged down her throat.

Breathing became difficult, and Evera's eyes clouded over as she felt its oily hand wrap around her heart. With a sharp snap, the world went dark.

Rhipley watched on in horror as the demon threw Evera's lifeless body to the ground, ripping her heart free and feeding on it hungrily. He could still hear the faint heartbeat of the child, a small relief coursing through him.

His eyes fell on Evera, whose body lay next to the child's, blood dripping from her mouth, her nose. He tried to move, but the spell held strong.

He was stuck, and without Yazmin, who was gods knew where, there was nothing he could do to stop the demon from making a meal of the girl next. He racked his brain for any loopholes, but came up short. His eyes rose to the demon once more, and before he could process what was happening, a dagger had impaled it. The demon let out a horrific screech in response as black blood trickled onto the ground.

Another dagger flew out of the cave, impaling it again, its shriek growing louder. Rhipley's eyes darted to the cave entrance, where Yazmin emerged, running towards them. The demon lashed out with a clawed hand, but Yazmin was too fast, diving beneath it and retrieving her daggers, before turning on the spot and slashing at it. Once, twice, thrice.

Rhipley watched as the demon struggled to keep up with his friend's fast movements, rejoice filling him. Yazmin's eyes met his, and before she could finish the demon off, it vanished.

Not hesitating, Yazmin ran to the girl, her eyes only briefly falling on Evera's corpse.

The spell broke, and Rhipley lunged forward.

"It's not dead," he warned, and Yazmin only responded with a nod.

She picked up the girl's body with ease, gently resting her on a shoulder. "I couldn't sense it in there, and only knew it had made itself visible when I heard the commotion, but it seems I was too late." Her eyes fell to Evera once more, regret lining them.

"She made her choice, and it cost her life," Rhipley mumbled, closing her lifeless eyes with a hand.

"Brave to the end," Yazmin muttered as Rhipley picked up the body, cradling it in his arms.

As the hunters approached the village, they were greeted by the citizens, alarm on their faces.

"We heard the shriek and the commotion," Hilda said wearily, her words trailing off as she beheld Evera's body in Rhipley's arms. She raised a trembling hand to her mouth as tears filled her eyes, the villagers doing the same. A cry sounded from within the crowd as a man and woman ran forward to meet them, screaming out "Willow!"

They didn't acknowledge the hunters as they reached for the child, looking her over before taking her from Yazmin's arms, who gave a dip of her head before stepping back.

"She died a warrior," Rhipley said, addressing the village in its entirety before his eyes settled on Reaper. His heart dropped as the griffin approached, his eyes solely on his rider.

Rhipley placed Evera's body on the ground before taking several steps back, bowing his head to the proud creature.

Reaper nudged Evera's lifeless body — once, twice — before letting out a heartbreaking cry and taking to the skies, Evera grasped within his claws, the flap of his wings sending a strong current through the village. The griffin flew in the direction of Norisk, the capital of Lilhan, before disappearing beyond the horizon. The sun was not long off rising, the horizon painted with a thin golden line suggesting as much.

"Does the demon still live?" Hilda asked, tear stains marking her face.

Rhipley nodded his head apologetically but said, "We will hunt it during the day. Now that we know where it hides, we can attack it when it's weakest. We will avenge Evera's death."

Hilda, to Rhipley's surprise, clasped both his hands in hers and gave a sad yet sincere smile to both he and Yazmin, the villagers bowing their heads in thanks.

CHAPTER 33

Alexis awoke the next morning, feeling groggy from her nightmare and her sleep being broken by Amelia. She gazed over to her sister's bed, where Amelia lay cuddling her pillow close, sleeping soundly. She looked out the window to where the sun was just breaking through the clouds — it must have still been early if the sun was only just rising.

Her eyes fell to her side where Aspen lay, one eye lazily open to gaze upon her owner, before the dog rolled onto her back, belly up, expecting pats.

Alexis chuckled as she obliged, trying to rack her memory for the dream last night, what it all meant. The more that was revealed to her through Aurelia and her strange dreams, the more questions she had. Was there a bigger picture she wasn't seeing?

Something the others knew that they weren't revealing?

She shook her head, feeling guilty at even considering for one second that Rhipley or Yazmin would be purposely hiding important information from them.

They were her friends, something more in Amelia's case when it came to Yazmin. They wouldn't do that.

Flashbacks to Lukai kissing her raced through her mind, and Alexis felt her face heating as she recalled how he'd held her, how his lips felt on hers. The touch was so sensual, like nothing she'd ever experienced — not even with Mitchell.

With Mitchell, their exchanges had been more platonic, like two childhood friends who had only dated to see what might come of it, if they were meant to be together.

Since her breakup, since even *before* her breakup, she'd yearned for passion, yearned to be desired and not just simply liked, or loved, as he'd loved her. Lukai, however, hadn't hidden his desire for her, and while she'd found her thoughts always drifting back to Rhipley, the guilt of it constantly nagging at her, Lukai was... good.

She didn't let herself think it could develop into something more, given that they'd only shared a kiss — a passionate kiss, granted — but it was far too early to even consider what might come of it. Alexis wouldn't let the thoughts of *what if* consume her. She'd enjoy herself, and not set up expectations.

Plus, that she still held onto her secret of who she was and where she truly came from was reason enough to keep Lukai at an arm's length, to not let whatever was blossoming between them become anything more than physical. It wasn't just her safety she had to think of, but her sister's.

Standing from the bed, she gave Aspen a long pat on the head before striding to her armoire and dressing into her daily attire. Amelia still slept soundly as Alexis stepped from the room, Aspen in tow.

Alexis watched as Aspen played with that same wolf on the Daeanimus Grounds, the two chasing each other to their heart's content. She still hadn't seen the hunter who was bonded to the wolf, having been told by a passerby weeks ago that they had been on a lengthy mission. She wondered if the wolf missed its hunter as

Aspen had missed her when she'd been gone. Alexis couldn't even imagine leaving Aspen for such a long time.

She sat with her knees to her chest, her arms holding them close with her chin resting upon them as she watched the two continue to play, before lifting her eyes to the sky, the sun having risen as it painted the blue expanse in beautiful sunrise shades. Now twenty-two, she thought about how different her life was compared to a year ago. How quickly things had changed in an instant; twenty-one-year-old Alexis never could have guessed that this might have ever happened.

She scoffed as she pondered how a human from Earth might react to this world, these people and creatures. Were there people in her world who knew of magic? Who knew that this world existed?

As Alexis became lost in thought, light footsteps sounded from behind, approaching slowly.

She couldn't help flinching out of surprise as Tatiana sat down next to her.

"Didn't mean to scare you," Tatiana mumbled, her eyes fixed on Aspen and the wolf.

"Don't take it personally; I'm easily frightened," Alexis replied, embarrassed.

"You'll have to ditch that habit if you're to make a good hunter," Tatiana said, side-eyeing Alexis.

Despite her petiteness, Alexis felt the weight of that gaze, the intimidation in it.

Tatiana's eyes returned to the playing Daeanimus', and Alexis found herself examining the female. She wore her day clothes, same as Alexis, and her long black hair was tied back in the same braid she always adorned.

Though Alexis wasn't Tatiana's biggest fan, and vice versa, she wouldn't deny the fact that the female was one of the most beautiful people she'd ever seen. Though, in this world, where fae were all inhumanly gorgeous, it was hard to find one that wasn't pleasant to look at.

"I'm told you wish for me to train you in the art of archery," Tatiana said, and Alexis gulped.

"You don't have to if you really don't want to. I'm sure I can ask someone else," Alexis said sheepishly.

Tatiana let out an amused chuckle as she met Alexis' eyes, her jewellery glinting in the morning sunlight.

"You won't find anyone else here who can teach you as well as I can. I am the best at this Guild."

Given what Alexis had seen, she wouldn't hold Tatiana's boasting against her — the female had certainly earned the right.

After a few quiet moments, Alexis returned her gaze to Aspen, who now lay down, catching her breath.

"If you're willing to, then yes. I'd like you to teach me, please."

Tatiana let out an impressed hum. "You have manners — that's a good start."

Alexis gave her a tight smile before her eyes fell on the necklace around Tatiana's neck. It was a choker-style, the large pendant that hung from it easily the size of an egg. She tried not to stare, but she found herself almost entranced. It appeared as if storm clouds whirled within the pendant, like they were trapped within.

Tatiana followed Alexis' gaze, and she gently clasped it. "From my mother," she mumbled, her stoic face faltering for only a second, as if a painful memory lay behind those eyes.

"I don't mean to pry," Alexis stammered, averting her gaze.

Tatiana didn't speak for a time, the two sitting in silence as the sound of nearby chatter and footsteps filtered out the morning quiet.

Finally, Tatiana rose from her spot, dusting off her clothes as she said, "Meet me at the archery grounds after breakfast. I'll walk you through the basic steps."

Alexis stood too, and before she could thank Tatiana, the female held up a hand to stop her.

"It will take time, you must know."

Alexis nodded — she was an amateur and had never wielded a bow, save for when she trained with Lukai, though it had merely been holding it and nothing more.

"Be thankful that I am the one teaching you, though. If it were anyone else, you'd likely take years to master it. With me, you could be an acceptable archer within weeks."

Alexis thanked Tatiana with a half-smile, watching her leave as she shook her head, wondering if she'd come to regret her decision to accept the females help.

Rhipley stood in the village square, his eyes still on the horizon where Reaper had disappeared with Evera's body, likely having made it back to Norisk by now.
The sun had risen, and Yazmin walked towards him as she strapped her cleaned daggers to her leathers.

"Time is of the essence; we must kill it now," she said grimly, her eyes focussed on the forest.

"What do you think they will do with Reaper?" Rhipley asked — mumbled, really.

Yazmin's hands fell to her sides as she returned her gaze to him. "I don't know, Rhipley, but I don't think that's important right now."

She was right — they had a much bigger task at hand than to wonder about a riderless griffin. Still, he felt sorry for Reaper.

Whether he and Evera were Daeanimus Bonded, he didn't know, didn't want to think about it, lest the guilt distract him from performing his duty.

Turning to the forest, Rhipley unsheathed Wraith, and followed Yazmin — he would avenge Evera's death, even if the blame for it would fall on him, on Yazmin and the Hunter's Guild.

Following breakfast, Alexis stood in the archery field, hunters around her already practising. Tatiana stood at her chosen spot with crossed arms, a bow and arrows sitting neatly atop a wood block, identical to those claimed by other archers, lined side by side about ten feet apart from each other. Alexis attempted a smile as she approached Tatiana, hoping that she could slowly win the female over, or at least make their interactions less awkward.

As she reached for the bow, a simple wood carved piece, not nearly as nice as Tatiana's was, Tatiana stopped Alexis, shaking her head.

"We don't start on wielding a bow just yet. First, we do breathing, stretches, and upper body exercises."

Alexis' mouth formed a tight line as she pulled her arm away. "Fair enough, show me."

Tatiana's mouth quirked up at the corner, as if surprised at Alexis' willingness to learn. She stepped next to her and held one hand on Alexis' back, the other on her abdominal section as she said, "Now, breathe in, hold for five seconds, and breathe out, then hold for another five seconds."

Alexis did so, trying not to look over to Tatiana, whose hands were surprisingly gentle upon her body, though she supposed that being a mere human, as Tatiana would say, the female would naturally want to be gentle with her frail, mortal body.

"Tense your core as you hold your breath. The strength for wielding a bow comes from here." Tatiana's hands pressed on Alexis' core, tapping gently.

"Your breathing needs to be steady at all times. If you falter your breathing, it could affect your aim and cost you a solid mark on your target."

Alexis nodded, and as she breathed, held and counted to five, she tensed her core, and Tatiana nodded, muttering "Good." This female was far different from the one she'd first met, as if she'd tossed aside her petty dislike for Alexis and was strictly business during their lessons.

This version of Tatiana, Alexis could learn to like.

After fifteen minutes of breathing exercises, Tatiana said, "Alright, time for the physical. How experienced are you with the basics?"

Alexis gave her a thumbs up and said, "I can certainly do the basics and then some, but I'm a little out of practice, so we'll need to pace the sets. The only thing I can steadily keep at without growing too tired too quickly is cardio."

Tatiana angled her head to the ground and said, "Give me ten push ups. Cardio is necessary and helpful, but we'll focus on your upper body strength to begin with."

Alexis obliged without hesitation.

As she took up her stance on the ground, she noticed Prince Frederik watching them — no, watching *her* — at the edge of the archery field.

CHAPTER 34

Rhipley and Yazmin stood before the cave, trying to ignore Evera's blood staining the dirt. Yazmin waved a hand, and the blood disappeared into the ground, as if it had never been there, though the smell still lingered.

Rhipley's thoughts became focussed on Alexis — he hadn't thought much of her these past days, had tried not to, given his promise to himself. And, considering the mission had kept him busy, it had caught him by surprise to be thinking of her now. Though, given what lurked in the cave ahead, and what secrets it likely held, he realised thoughts of her at this time were plausible.

A pang of guilt flooded through him, and his thoughts drifted to Tatiana, and whether or not she'd agreed to teach Alexis how to wield a bow yet. He was sure Rampier hadn't given her much choice, despite her noble status.

Nobility in the Hunter's Guild didn't matter — everyone at the guild were equals, and Rhipley was glad for it, though Tatiana certainly still tried to pull rank every now and again.

Lukai flashed through his mind, and a strange pang of jealousy shot through him as he wondered if his brother had made a move on Alexis yet, given he had taken over her lessons. He reminded himself that he shouldn't care, that he had no reason to care — he and Alexis were *friends*.

Yazmin's voice cut into his thoughts, tearing him away from his internal battle, to his relief.

"Alright, what's the plan?" she asked, staring into the cave, a chill emanating from within. Just like last night, the forest animals had once again fallen quiet. There were no sounds, no signs of life coming from within the cave, and Rhipley already knew what they'd likely find inside.

"We lay trapping spells on all exits, making the demon's escape impossible."

"How do we know it's in the cave this time?" Yazmin questioned, side eyeing the entrance as she impatiently tapped a dagger against her shoulder.

"It won't risk being out in the open while it's injured," Rhipley said, and Yazmin angled her head, nodding.

"I can't smell it — the stench of rot must be masking its scent," Yazmin mumbled with disgust, scrunching up her nose.

Rhipley smelled it too — he hoped it didn't belong to the missing children, though given he couldn't hear their heartbeats, couldn't hear their voices, he knew it likely did.

"How do we know it hasn't laid any traps?" Yazmin questioned, tapping the ground and the cave walls with her daggers.

"Just be extra cautious," Rhipley mumbled back, plastering on his best attempt at a smirk.

With a sigh, Yazmin lifted her dagger, clanging it against Wraith.

"Let's do this, comrade."

Rhipley dipped his head as Yazmin disappeared inside, continuing to tap against the walls and ground. He made his way around the back of the cave, searching for any other entrances while he drew trapping spells on the ground with his blood, using Wraith to draw a continuous line through the dirt to spring any traps the demon may have laid, the faerie steel able to disable the magic if need be.

Alexis had been exercising for hours now, Tatiana only offering her small gaps for resting. Despite her love for the heat, for the sun, she wished more than anything for air-con right now as her body finally began to sweat and redden.

When Tatiana had asked, however, if she wished to quit and go back to the kitchen — an unnecessarily snide remark — Alexis had given her a firm *no* in response.

No matter how difficult she found something to be, no matter how much she struggled, she wasn't a quitter. She'd push and push and push until she saw the results she desired.

So, they'd continued to alternate between breathing exercises and physical exercises, Alexis slowly becoming more efficient at both as time went on.

Tatiana had made it clear that she wouldn't allow Alexis to fire an arrow until she was strong enough, until she could hold the bow and aim without her arms shuddering or lowering under the weight of the bow, until she'd understood how each part worked, how far to pull the string back, how to hold it tightly and when to let go.

Other hunters and students had watched as Tatiana taught Alexis, much to Alexis' dismay, though they hadn't judged, hadn't snickered or pointed. They simply watched, though she knew it was more for Tatiana, the legendary bow wielder, than it was for her, the novice human.

Once Tatiana had deemed their practice for the day to be enough — for the first day, at least — Zailah had appeared, along with Lukai, a wide grin on his face. The former had simply announced that it was her turn to practise with Alexis before whisking her away. Tatiana hadn't argued, had likely grown bored of teaching Alexis for the day, as she lazily waved them off with a hand.

Zailah and Lukai led Alexis to a clearing in the forest behind the guild buildings, the gargantuan mountains looming overhead, and claimed it was the perfect spot for magic wielding. Amelia was sitting on a boulder, waiting patiently with her legs crossed, and upon seeing Alexis, she beamed.

"What kind of magic will I be doing, exactly?" Alexis asked warily, looking between all three of them.

Lukai simply smiled and nudged her shoulder playfully as Zailah announced, "Whatever magic you can. Rampier said you both have some in your veins, so it's our job to coax it out."

Alexis' breath caught, and she bit her lip, her heart racing as she said, "Shouldn't we wait for Rhipley and Yazmin to get back first?"

"Why?" Zailah asked, raising a brow as she motioned for Alexis to stand in the centre of the clearing.

"We just don't know how much magic we have, or what kind of magic we have, and I don't want to accidentally hurt myself or any of you if it goes wrong."

Lukai chuckled and wrapped an arm around her shoulder, the movement causing Zailah and Amelia to tilt their heads in curiosity, confusion.

"Don't worry, you'll be safe. We'll *all* be safe. If you only have an inkling of magic, it won't be enough to harm us. At least, not the first time you practise." His voice was sincere, supportive, and Alexis returned his smile with a small, doubtful one of her own.

She had her doubts, knowing she could Realm Walk and that it would likely be exposed in mere minutes, though she didn't voice them, didn't protest any further as she hesitantly stepped into the centre, breathing in and out slowly.

"Amelia and I have been practising, or, at least, trying to, but her magic is stubborn," Zailah said, shooting an irritated look in Amelia's direction, which her sister shied away from with a sheepish smile. "We're hoping you can convince her magic to show itself."

Alexis looked to her sister, then to Zailah as she gritted her teeth. "What makes you think my magic is any stronger than hers?" she asked, raising a brow.

"I have my theories," Zailah replied, crossing her arms.

She dipped her head slightly, her only signal for Alexis to begin. Alexis kept her brow raised, wondering what Zailah might suspect, if she knew. If the female *did* know, she certainly didn't voice it.

"I don't know what to do," Alexis said, tapping her foot.

The corner of Zailah's lips tilted up.

"Didn't they teach you about magic in your mortal classes when you were a child?" she challenged, walking forward.

Alexis averted her gaze — they didn't know, and she couldn't tell them, so she conjured up the best lie she could think of in that moment. "They didn't deem those of us without magic worthy of learning about it."

Zailah stopped, her eyes fixed on Alexis, as if she were studying her, trying to decipher if she spoke true, or if she saw right through it.

After a couple of heartbeats, the female just hummed before approaching Alexis.

She traced a line up Alexis' arm with a finger, the touch making Alexis flinch.

"You need to feel it in your veins, recognise that it's there, that it is within you. What colour is it? What does it look like, feel like? What does it smell and sound and taste like?"

Alexis closed her eyes.

This is ridiculous.

Suddenly, she thought of Rhipley — would learning magic be easier with him since he knew her true identity? She wished he was here, though she knew he wouldn't feel the same.

Snapping the thoughts from her mind, Alexis breathed slowly — in, out, in, out. Her eyes still closed, she tried to imagine her magic, but nothing came to mind. She strained, quietly begging her magic to come forth, to show itself, but nothing happened.

Alexis thought of the night she'd Realm Walked, thought of what it had felt like, how she might have summoned it. The only thing that came to mind was her nausea after. Why had she Realm Walked? What had triggered it, and why hadn't she been able to do it again since? Her mind came up blank.

She opened her eyes, knowing defeat lay in them. "I can't do it," she mumbled.

Zailah now stood in front of her. The two locked eyes, and Alexis willed herself not to back down, not to break eye contact, no matter how intimidating the female was.

"I think you need a trigger," Zailah said, before her gaze shifted to Amelia. Zailah's comment ignited a memory in Alexis, and she remembered what it was that allowed her to Realm Walk — desperation. She was, in that moment, desperate to get herself and Amelia to safety, to go home and get away from the strangers who threatened to kidnap them.

"What kind of trigger?" Alexis asked, following Zailah's gaze.

Zailah smirked as she kept her eyes on Amelia, who recoiled, looking to Lukai for support.

"Zailah," Lukai warned, standing from the boulder he'd been leaning against.

Zailah shot Lukai an incredulous look before making to walk towards Amelia, stopped only by Alexis' firm grip on her bicep.

Zailah looked at Alexis, but she wasn't furious — no, she was impressed, as if the small show of courage was entertaining to her.

"Leave her alone," Alexis warned, not removing her hand.

Zailah, with her fae strength, simply freed herself from Alexis' fragile human grip before taking another step.

Alexis knew the female was challenging her, but she also didn't know Zailah well enough to gamble with Amelia's life. She didn't know what the female planned to do with her sister, but Lukai's warning told her enough.

"Zailah!" Lukai warned again, stepping in front of Amelia, his gaze shifting between Alexis and the petite female whose eyes were solely on her sister.

At the sight of Amelia recoiling further, the genuine fear in her eyes, Alexis felt the anger begin to rise in her veins.

Began to feel her blood heat as something foreign, something powerful formed within her very being.

The last thing she saw was Zailah's widened eyes as the female turned to her, before Alexis unleashed herself.

CHAPTER 35

Rhipley trod quietly into the entrance he'd come across around the rear of the cave, having found, thankfully, that there had been no traps hidden around the perimeter.

As he drew another trapping symbol on the walls with his blood, needing to constantly reopen the wound, thanks to his fae healing, Rhipley kept his eyes roaming, his ears open and his nose sensing for the demon. There had been no sign of it in the half hour he'd been searching, but the demon had to be here somewhere.

The darkness of the cave quickly consumed him as he ventured in deeper, keeping his footsteps light and silent, Wraith drawn as his wound began to heal once more.

For a second, he considered leaving it to heal over, considering any exits from the cave had been covered with traps.

But he remembered that the demon, like most, was drawn to blood. Whether it would be drawn to *his* blood, he wasn't sure. The demon was certainly intelligent and had likely anticipated this, so the probability of it falling for baited blood was slim.

Rhipley discarded the idea, accepting that they'd need to do this the hard way. They'd been in more impossible scenarios before and had emerged victorious, so this was nothing new.

As Rhipley came to a dead end in the labyrinth, the stench of rotting flesh filled his nostrils.

Looking to his right, thankful for his heightened sight and ability to see in the dark, he approached a small cove; the stench growing stronger and stronger.

By the time Rhipley had approached the cove, the smell was stinging his nostrils. He covered his nose with a hand as he saw what lay before him — bodies piled atop bodies, belonging to both youth and adult.

His heart sank as he realised what he already knew — they wouldn't be saving anyone today, other than those in the village.

The absence of heartbeats confirmed that none of these poor souls were of this plane any longer, and Rhipley said a small prayer used by those in Preshia when laying the dead to rest — the same he'd used in the silence of this morning to honour Evera's sacrifice.

The air grew cold, and Rhipley's attention fixed on what he knew was approaching.

As he turned, gripping his sword to ready for the finishing blow, he stopped short as he found the demon, still in its clouded form, floating only metres from him, spluttering black blood onto the dirt.

"Hello, hunter," it said in a dark, deep voice.

Rhipley only hesitated for the dagger that came flying from behind the demon, plunging right into its centre. The demon let out a pained shriek as a pool of ebony blood dripped onto the ground, the dagger's pointed end poking out of its front.

Under the clouded form, Rhipley could just make out a solid black body, coiled in on itself. A last-ditch effort to conserve its energy.

Yazmin slowly approached, flipping her other dagger in her hand. There was no rush in her actions as her eyes met Rhipley's over the demon's form.

She silently beckoned for him to finish the demon off, but Rhipley remained where he was.

"Why the hesitation?" the demon asked, its broken chuckle sending a shiver down Rhipley's spine.

Yazmin hummed in agreement, crossing her arms, her brows furrowing in frustration.

When Rhipley still made no move to kill it, Yazmin stepped forward and twisted the dagger, but Rhipley stopped her with a hand. "What is your deal? Let's kill it while we have it," Yazmin protested.

"I want to know what it knows, and who it has told," Rhipley said, his eyes remaining on the demon, who let out a spluttered laugh.

"Knows what?" Yazmin asked, stepping around to face the demon from the side.

"Everyone on this continent will know soon enough, hunter," the demon spat, its maniacal chuckle filling the air.

Yazmin groaned in response.

"And what do *you* know?" Rhipley asked.

The demon was quiet for a moment. Yazmin reached for the dagger again, twisting it once more. The squelching was followed by pained cries from the demon, but neither hunter budged — this, they were used to. Had done worse to other creatures.

"I will tell you, if only so your dog will leash its temper," the demon spat, and a sinister smile curved Yazmin's lips.

She had been called worse, and instead of wounding her, the names just encouraged her infliction of pain.

Rhipley nodded to Yazmin, who backed off, but kept a hand on her other dagger strapped to her thigh.

"They are looking for the prophesied. The *Divinius Aguris*, and they will not stop until they have found them," the demon said, spitting more black blood onto the ground.

Rhipley's eyes followed where the blood now painted a small section of dirt as he asked, "King D'Roghal and Queen Valeria?"

The demon grunted in response.

"Why?" Yazmin asked. Though Rhipley had already been made aware of the reason, thanks to Princess Yuki's letter, Yazmin was still in the dark. She wouldn't be for much longer, though.

"Because they are important for the cause. For *our* cause," the demon said, its voice smooth and serpentine.

"The cause?" Yazmin asked.

The demon chuckled once more. "You will find out soon enough."

"Where are the Divinely Blooded now?" Yazmin continued, her jaw tensing.

"You should know, huntress, since you house them at that fortress you call a guild," the demon replied. When Yazmin, in her shock and surprise, didn't answer, the demon let out an amused hum.

"You didn't know," it said, and though Rhipley couldn't see its face, he knew it was smirking.

Yazmin, clocking the word, immediately looked at Rhipley, who breathed out slowly.

"You knew?" she spat, her face in a rage, hurt in her eyes.

"I only found out days ago," he replied, trying to convey the apology in his voice.

"You knew, and you didn't tell me?" she shot back.

The demon remained silent, watching them like their argument was entertainment.

"I was under strict orders not to," Rhipley said. He wouldn't let his temper rise to meet Yazmin's, wouldn't angrily defend himself. His friend was hurt, rightfully so, and he wouldn't attack her for it.

"How did you know they were in Preshia?" Rhipley asked the demon, pointing Wraith towards it.

"Your friend's hesitation gave it away. I had only guessed what my king and queen already suspected. When the agents I was travelling with were ambushed by one of the famed Shima Gai, I was the lone survivor. I barely made it out with my life," the demon answered.

"Why are you so eager to tell us this?" Rhipley asked, forcing his eyes away from Yazmin's enraged expression.

"You're going to kill me, anyway. I have nothing left to hide," the demon replied.

The Shima Gai — which one was it? Freya?

Rhipley didn't want to know, had hoped they wouldn't run into her. Was thankful that they hadn't yet.

"Who else knows?" Yazmin demanded.

"It's hard to say. I'm not the king's sole messenger, just one of many. I came here to replenish myself following the attack. Apparently, doing so drew your attention."

"Sloppy," Rhipley replied, but then stopped himself short. Had they fallen into a trap? Had the demon intentionally drawn them here?

Before the demon could continue its taunting, Rhipley drove Wraith through it, the demon's shriek bellowing through the caves, its echo filling the space.

With a single swipe, the demon fell to the ground, its physical form a black, bloodied mess on the dirt.

Yazmin and Rhipley stood silently for a moment, Yazmin retrieving her dagger from the demon's body and wiping the blood on her clothes as Rhipley did the same with Wraith.

"What the fuck, Rhipley?" Yazmin exclaimed as she faced him.

"We need to get back to the guild," he said, his eyes roaming to the alcove where the rotting bodies lay.

Yazmin huffed, but agreed with a sharp nod, hauling multiple bodies over her shoulder.

"The villagers won't be pleased," she muttered, steadying herself beneath the weight.

As Rhipley hauled the rest over his own shoulders, he huffed. "There was nothing we could do."

"They won't care. They never do," Yazmin said, and Rhipley just hummed in agreement. Being a hunter was certainly a thankless job.

As they exited the cave, the smell of death filling their noses, Yazmin said, "Did you always know it was them?"

Rhipley didn't hesitate as he said, "No. I only pieced it together when I read Princess Yuki's letter."

Yazmin looked at him, question in her eyes.

"Rampier received a letter from her stating that the Divinely Blooded were back, and that they were in Xalentya. Speaking for her, only she and her Shima Gai know for now.

Rampier has requested she keep it that way until we know what to do about it."

"So, Rampier dispatched us to ensure the information doesn't get out on this continent?"

Rhipley nodded.

Yazmin's eyes grew wide with realisation. "Do Alexis and Amelia know?"

Rhipley shook his head, standing finally. "They can't find out, Yaz. Not yet."

Yazmin shot him a doubtful look. "Rhipley, they'll feel betrayed when they find out that we knew and didn't tell them."

Rhipley held her stare for a while longer before exhaling deeply.

He knew she was right; of course she was, but the information was too important, too dangerous, and he didn't know what the sisters might do with it. He highly doubted that they knew and were keeping it a secret all this time — they hadn't known that magic, this world, existed before coming here. How had they been so oblivious to their true nature all this time, all these years? Were there other forces involved to ensure their lack of knowledge, to keep them, their world and this world, safe from those who would exploit their powers?

Rhipley decided that once they were back at the guild, he'd get the answers he needed from Rampier. Whatever answers he could.

He hated himself for keeping the information from Alexis, but she would understand that there was far more at stake here.

When they returned to the village with the bodies, the parents and families of those deceased rushed forward, crying and screaming as they clutched the bodies of their loved ones close.

Some wore angered expressions, some wore ones of anguish, and some were just empty. They didn't speak, didn't shout words of hatred, but didn't thank the hunters, either.

Hilda was the only one to walk forth, tears in her eyes but her face set in understanding and gratefulness, as she quietly thanked them both for their efforts, embracing them both in deep hugs, which neither backed away from.

When Yazmin and Rhipley prepared to Realm Walk, pain in their hearts, they doubted anyone would care or notice that they'd left without saying their goodbyes.

CHAPTER 36

Alexis opened her eyes to find the world cast in shadows. She felt someone holding her close before she registered who it was. As she angled her body to get a better look, she saw her sister's red hair draped over her, shielding half her vision. Amelia was shuddering, gripping Alexis as though she'd disappear into thin air.

"Mill's," Alexis whispered, trying to pull herself from her sister's grip. Amelia slowly raised her head and looked Alexis dead in the eyes. Alexis flinched, jumping back as she noted what looked like her sister, but didn't. Amelia's usually hazel eyes were darkest ebony. Alexis felt her heart thunder at the sight. The black shrouding Amelia's eyes slowly diminished, replaced by the greens and browns Alexis was used to. Her sister raised a hand to her face, shaking as she touched the skin around her eyes.

"Your eyes were…" Alexis stammered, unable to finish the sentence.

The black fog surrounding them slowly lowered, and the world was once again as it had been moments ago. Amelia sat back, resting on her calves, legs folded beneath her body as her face went vacant. Alexis searched for Lukai, for Zailah, and found the former holding the screaming female in his arms. Zailah was aggressively rubbing at her eyes, sobbing and shrieking. The sounds sent chills down Alexis' spine as she watched on in horror.

Lukai was looking down at Zailah, panic on his face, before he raised his eyes to meet Alexis' own. She could have sworn he flinched away as they locked eyes. Alexis slowly rose to her feet, the movement alone making her lightheaded. She pulled Amelia with her, her sister still distant, her body a near deadweight under Alexis' grip.

"What happened?" Alexis asked no one in particular. Zailah continued to shriek, and Lukai rose, holding her petite frame in his muscled arms. His face held no warmth, but genuine fear.

"You... what did you do? What are you?" Lukai asked warily, a growl in his voice.

Alexis looked at him with narrowed brows, shaking her head as if to say, *I don't know what you mean.* At that moment, she felt a slight buzz ringing through her veins, and she dropped Lukai's gaze to study her hands. Her body was emanating a light glow, the light diminishing with each passing second. Her breathing trembled as she realised what had been done. What *she* had done. She took a step towards Lukai, who backed away, fear and panic and anger in those golden eyes.

Tears began to well in her eyes as she took in Zailah, the skin around her eyes reddened under her hands.

Zailah continued sobbing, and Lukai looked between the two sisters before turning and making a run for the guild. Alexis reached out a hand, but with his fae speed, he was gone within seconds. She turned back to Amelia, who stood still and was white as a ghost, and she could have sworn shadows swirled around her sister, as if they were snakes protecting their master.

"Amelia?" Alexis said carefully, and in an instant, Amelia's head snapped to attention, the shadows gone.

"What happened?" Amelia asked, her eyes wide as she took in the ground below them. Scorch marks stained the earth, and splotches of white and black entwined together like a messy piece of art. Alexis' body filled with heat, and despite the worry and sadness that bit at her every nerve, she'd never felt so alive, so… awake. Amelia, studying her hands, appeared to feel the same as they locked eyes.

Alexis stood before the Red Oak once again, as she had so many times before. It had burned to ashes, as it always had in her dreams, and before the woman had even appeared, Alexis looked to her right, waiting for Aurelia.

Stepping out of a shadow, Aurelia approached Alexis. Those same shadows that she'd seen swimming around her sister also surrounded Aurelia, kissing at her skin, carefully observing for any threats.

"You… you're the shadow I've been seeing all this time," Alexis stated more than asked. Aurelia simply nodded, taking up a spot next to Alexis, watching the tree wither away with sad eyes.

"What am I?" Alexis asked. Aurelia hesitated in answering as she turned to face her.

Her face looked so familiar, as though Alexis had seen it before, but she couldn't quite pin it. Not as she'd seen her in the portraits around the guild, in Rampier's office, but as though she were familiar, like someone from Alexis' past.

"You're the prophesied, the chosen one. You possess the gifts of Luzhula, Harbinger of Light, and your sister, the gifts of Brundhul, Harbinger of Shadow. You are very powerful, child."

Alexis clenched her jaw in frustration. "I don't want to be chosen or prophesied. I didn't sign up for this. I don't want it. Choose someone else." Though her words were harsh, she gave Aurelia pleading eyes.

"It does not work that way, my dear. This life chose you, *Luzhula* chose you. You must fulfil the prophesy, whether you wish to or not." Aurelia placed a pale hand on Alexis' shoulder, though she didn't feel the touch.

"Who are you? Why am I seeing you?" Alexis asked coldly, shifting her eyes to the tree.

"I've been looking over you all your life. I've been protecting you, guiding you, though you may not have known it. I did not wish this life for you, but you cannot cheat destiny."

Alexis exhaled a shuddering breath.

"What am I?" she asked again, her voice desperate but exhausted as she turned to face Aurelia fully.

Aurelia reached her hand up to graze Alexis' cheek, and as she opened her mouth to speak, Alexis was pulled from her dream.

Rhipley and Yazmin returned to the guild at sunset, aiming straight for Rampier's office to report their findings when they'd heard screaming coming from the infirmary. Usually, that wasn't uncommon, given their occupations, though the screams were familiar. Unsure whether to head for the infirmary or continue to Rampier's office, knowing they'd need to report to Rampier sooner rather than later, Rhipley looked down at Yazmin quizzically. She returned his stare with wide eyes, and he knew he didn't need to ask what she was thinking; *who was screaming*? Who'd been hurt?

They silently agreed to head for the infirmary, just to be safe, when Prince Frederik emerged from one of the hallways lining the academy section of the guild with a book in his hands, his brows furrowed.

"What is the cause of all that screaming?" he asked, and Rhipley would have assumed he'd meant it in a mocking tone had his face not shown genuine sympathy. He and Yazmin bowed low, and the prince didn't so much as speak as they rose, still waiting for an answer.

"We're going to find out, Your Majesty. You're free to join us, if you'd like," Yazmin offered, trying not to sound too rude or rushed as her eyes darted between the prince and the infirmary. Rhipley gave the prince a tight-lipped smile as he, too, tried not to show his impatience at the prince stopping them in their tracks. He appeared to consider for a moment before dipping his head and saying, "Alright, I might as well."

He offered them both a genuine smile as he held out his arm for them to lead the way. Out of the corner of his eye, Rhipley noted two guards stationed ten feet behind the prince, hiding in the shadows of the corridors, watching him, and them, carefully.

Although neither he nor Yazmin were a threat to the prince, he tried not to chuckle at the fact that they wouldn't be able to bring any of the hunters down, anyway. At least, not with ease.

"So, where are your two guests?" Frederik asked nonchalantly, flipping through the book's pages.

Yazmin and Rhipley shared a look before Rhipley responded, "I'm sure they're around here somewhere, likely training."

Prince Frederik gave an amused hum in response. "And they're adjusting well to Xalentya? I can't imagine it would be easy, having to give your old lives up and start anew."

Yazmin clenched her jaw in frustration at the prince's interrogation. After the last few day's they'd just had, answering countless questions was the last thing either of them wished to do.

"I imagine so, yes. At least, we have had no reason to believe they're struggling," Rhipley replied, trying to hide his own irritation.

Prince Frederik briefly looked up from his book to give Rhipley a tight smile. His eyes fell to Yazmin's, likely expecting a smile from her, too, but she only looked ahead.

"Does your father not trust us?" she asked, and Rhipley could have sworn his heart stopped beating at the blatant question. However, much to his surprise, Prince Frederik chuckled as he glanced back at his personal guards.

"It's just a safety precaution. You know, with King D'Roghal's next move unknown."

Rhipley nodded, humming his own response. As they made it to the infirmary entrance, Rhipley holding the door open for Yazmin, Frederik, and his two guards, the screaming grew louder, and he finally recognised who it had been coming from as he, too, stepped inside.

On one of the beds lay Zailah, bandages covering her eyes.

Lukai sat by her side, holding her hand in his as he tapped his feet anxiously. At the sound of their entrance, he whirled around to look at who had joined them, and his eyes grew wide as he stood, gently letting go of Zailah's hand and placing it onto the bed.

"What the hell happened?" Yazmin asked, her voice hushed. The infirmary was otherwise empty of other hunters, the only company being various healers walking around, cleaning and attending to Zailah, who quietly wept, her screams ceasing as she was given an anaesthetic tea.

The healers remained quiet as they noted who had joined them, and in unison, bowed deeply, whispering, "Your Majesty," before resuming their duties.

As Lukai approached, Rhipley noticed his eyes were red from crying, filled with anger and confusion and sadness, the golds of his irises bright.

"Alexis did something, I don't know what or how, but she..." He trailed off as he glanced back to where Zailah lay.

Rhipley's heartbeat quickened at the information, as he and Yazmin swapped anxious looks.

"Alexis Rainier, the mortal from Earth, did this?" Prince Frederik asked, stepping forward and angling his head to get a better look at Zailah. Lukai narrowed his brows at the information Prince Frederik had just let slip, and Rhipley gritted his teeth.

Lukai's confused eyes shifted to Rhipley as he realised the truth, but he didn't speak on it as he said, "It seems she's finally discovered her magic. She *and* Amelia." Lukai's nostrils flared as he seemed to recount the memory of whatever had happened.

He stared at Rhipley, waiting for him to offer some kind of explanation, but Rhipley subtly shook his head. *Later.*
Lukai, thankfully, understood his unspoken request and offered no further information, even as Prince Frederik asked, "What manner of power?"

Cutting in, Yazmin said, "Perhaps we should leave Zailah be and report to Rampier. I'm sure what we're seeing was just a terribly unfortunate accident that occurred upon discovering their magic." How she downplayed such a serious situation, and in the presence of royalty, Rhipley didn't know, but he was beyond grateful for it. Yazmin always had a way with words, when she tried.

When the prince didn't move from his spot, still peering at Zailah, Yazmin stepped in front of him, offering a polite smile and saying, "Please leave us to do our jobs, Your Majesty. Rampier will offer you all the information you require when necessary."

Prince Frederik dropped his gaze to Yazmin, doubt in his eyes, but he obliged and said, "Very well. I look forward to your findings. Give her," one last look in Zailah's direction, "my condolences."

The three hunters bowed their heads as the prince departed from the infirmary, looking over his shoulder once more before the doors shut behind him.

CHAPTER 37

Lukai led Rhipley and Yazmin over to Zailah's bed, the healers throughout continuing to quietly go about their duties, keeping to themselves. Zailah must have heard them approach as she whimpered, "What aren't you telling us about those girls, Rhipley?"

Lukai looked at his brother, that same question in his eyes, as he sat in the chair by the bed once more and picked up Zailah's hand. Lukai and Zailah had always shared a unique connection, though it had never blossomed into anything more than friendship, Zailah believing Lukai was too juvenile to win her heart.

Now, however, it seemed he was her lifeline, with the way her petite hand gripped his.

"I'm sorry this happened to you, Zailah. But, without Rampier's permission, I can't give out any information regarding the Rainier girls," Rhipley offered, his voice apologetic.

At Lukai's incredulous face, Rhipley added, "Any *more* information. The prince was foolish to speak so freely of what he knew."

Lukai scoffed in response, before turning fully to Zailah, his free hand gently running over her hair.

"What happened?" Yazmin whispered, all too aware of the fae healers amongst them.

Rhipley trusted that Rampier would have ordered the healers to keep any information they'd learnt to themselves, nonetheless.

"We took the girls to a clearing on the edge of the guild to train their magic. Amelia had shown no sign of hers emerging, so Zailah thought we could speed up the process with the help of Alexis." Lukai spoke softly as he recounted the moment. Rhipley and Yazmin looked on silently, patiently waiting.

"It was nothing at first. We were almost convinced that neither sister possessed any magic, that the information you had been given and relayed to us by Rampier was bad intel. That is, until…" He sighed, almost hesitant to go on.

"Until what?" Rhipley pushed.

Zailah nodded, knowing that Lukai watched her, and as if he'd been waiting for that confirmation, he said, "Zailah prodded. She… used some unsavoury tactics to push Alexis to reveal her powers. Triggered her emotions."

"How?" Rhipley asked, a hint of a growl now in his voice, though he tried to remain patient, understanding. He and Yazmin shared a look of concern, at what was about to be revealed.

"I… I threatened Amelia. It's all I could think of. A last resort," Zailah whispered through choked sobs. Her voice cracked as she said the words, and Rhipley felt his temper flare at the information. "I had no intention of actually hurting the girl, but it didn't matter."

Rhipley felt Yazmin tense beside him, sensing her own temper rising.

"Zailah was standing too close when Alexis unleashed herself. It was like a cork being unscrewed, holding in all her magic, and Zailah triggered it. The second I saw Alexis' eyes glow, I made a break for her. I could *feel* the energy, the raw power that would emerge, so I made to save Zailah from being annihilated. Amelia must have followed me, because in the split second that I'd gotten Zailah to safety, Amelia was standing before Alexis. Then, a giant ball of shadow enveloped them both. I yelled for them, all while cradling Zailah, but nothing could penetrate that dome of power. When I finally pulled my attention away from the girls to assess the damage, it was too late."

Rhipley and Yazmin looked to Zailah at that, once more noting the bandages covering her eyes.

"She blinded Zailah, Rhipley. Unless we can find a truly remarkable healer, she won't recover."

Yazmin's breathing hitched, and her eyes turned worried as she looked around the room, her anger dissipating.

"Are none of our healers up to the task?" she asked quietly.

"Not for this. This kind of magic hasn't been seen in years, not since the days of Headmaster Wyntersier. It would take an old healer, one who was around when it was last used, to fix this." Lukai closed his eyes in frustration, taking a few deep breaths.

"You know she didn't mean to do this, Luke," Rhipley offered sincerely, his features turning soft, sympathetic. His friend, his brother, didn't meet his stare. He knew Lukai was angry — understandably so — but it wasn't fair for him to blame Alexis for this. When Lukai didn't speak, Rhipley exhaled a breath. With one last look at Zailah, he and Yazmin turned to make for the doors before Rhipley felt a light tug on his arm.

"You may not be able to reveal any more information to me about them, Rhipley, but perhaps withholding it is doing more damage than good," Lukai said sternly, his voice quiet.

"Until Rampier says so, their identities remain secret," Rhipley warned.

Lukai went to speak, but Yazmin said, "That's an order, Lukai. If you mention what you heard today to anyone, it will be an act of treason."

Lukai set his angry eyes on Yazmin, his nostrils flaring.

"I wouldn't dare reveal what I heard today without permission. I just think more can be done to prevent what happened to Zailah from happening again. Their powers are dangerous," Lukai whispered.

Rhipley didn't protest — Lukai was right, and had Rhipley not been put in his current position, he'd have agreed wholeheartedly.

Before Rhipley could speak, Lukai was already walking back to the bed, his arguing ended.

Alexis sat up swiftly, her eyes flying open, as she realised she was back in her dorm room. And, sitting before her, watching her with his own solemn eyes, was Rhipley. He was *here*. She didn't hesitate in throwing her arms around his neck, holding him close as she attempted to catch her breath. She noted Yazmin sitting on the end of Amelia's bed, one hand resting on her sister's hip atop the quilt, her eyes wary as she watched the exchange.

"Are you okay?" Rhipley asked, pushing Alexis back to examine her. She tried not to flinch at his lack of response, his choice not to hug her back. She held a hand to her forehead and winced as it thumped, her brain burning as the headache threatened to consume her.

"I… had a nightmare. It's nothing," she said, dropping his stare. "How are you back so soon?"

Yazmin and Rhipley exchanged confused glances before Rhipley said, "You've been unconscious for two days, Lex."

Her eyes went wide as she looked up.

"Two days?" she exclaimed, baffled. Yazmin simply nodded before gazing down at Amelia, sleeping soundly.

"Lukai told us what happened," Rhipley said quietly.

Alexis remembered then what had occurred two days ago.

"Is Zailah okay?" she asked urgently, trying not to let the guilt of what she'd done consume her.

"You blinded her, to put it plainly," Rhipley replied, looking away, as if racked with his own guilt.

Alexis' nostrils flared at the information, and tears began running down her face as she covered her eyes with her hands.

"I'm so sorry. I didn't mean for that to happen. I didn't know," she stuttered between breaths and sobs. To her surprise, Rhipley pulled her in. Against his warm, muscled body, Alexis cried. She couldn't stop the tears and sobs that escaped from her as they held each other for long moments. The sound of Yazmin clearing her throat interrupted them, and as they pulled apart, his facial expression held a question he didn't need to voice: *Will you be okay?* She nodded, giving him a pathetic smile and wiping her eyes.

"What's wrong with Amelia?" Alexis finally asked, rising from her bed and walking to her sister's sleeping body. She looked calm, though her breathing was heavy, her slumber clearly deep.

"From what Lukai said, you both used a lot of power. Given that it was the first time for her, Amelia's body and mind likely need more time to recover." Yazmin didn't raise her eyes as she spoke softly.

"I'll stay here," she added. "I'll watch over her. You go to Rampier. He's been waiting for you to wake." Alexis bit her lip, uncertainty and anxiety coursing through her, but Rhipley placed a gentle hand on her back.

"It'll be okay," he assured her as he guided her out of the room. Aspen, who'd been watching them all anxiously, jumped onto Amelia's bed and cuddled close.

Rhipley and Yazmin had sprinted for the girls' room upon learning what had happened. Rampier had used a locking spell to seal the door to their room, only allowing one of the healers, in addition to himself, Rhipley and Yazmin, in every few hours to check on the girls, to ensure they were still breathing.

Rhipley had practically sagged with relief upon entering the room. When he'd sighted Alexis asleep in her bed, her hair, her very body untouched, as though she'd been completely still in her unconsciousness, he'd let out a thankful sigh.

Aspen had been lying next to her bonded companion, her head on Alexis' chest, watching her warily upon Rhipley and Yazmin entering the room, and, as if smelling their scents, having grown accustomed to their presence, she'd simply side-eyed them, giving a small wag of her tail, and returned her gaze to Alexis.

A day later, Alexis had sprung awake, nothing but fear on her face as she'd adjusted to the light, her room, and upon seeing Rhipley, she'd embraced him, to his surprise.

He'd wanted so badly to return her embrace, to sweep her into his arms and not let go, but he'd also needed to make sure she was okay.

Now, as they made their way to Rampier's office, having made a quick pit stop to get some food for Alexis' grumbling stomach, she fiddled with her clothes, that nervous tick making itself present.

She didn't dare make eye contact with anyone they'd passed, as if afraid of how they now saw her, like she was some monster. The other hunters and students, however, paid her no heed, for they didn't know what had occurred, who'd put Zailah in the infirmary. For all they knew, all Rampier was allowing them to know, Zailah had been sent on a mission nearby, and returned the unlucky one. The more who knew of Alexis and Amelia's powers, the more danger it put them in. Rhipley had told Alexis as much, but it didn't stop her anxiety from surfacing.

Anytime Rhipley prodded Alexis for her thoughts, she simply shook her head and remained silent. Whatever was on her mind, she was choosing to deal with it on her own. He knew he should respect her choice, respect her personal space, but he wanted to be there for her, help her through this. However, until she said the word, he'd remain as he was. A shoulder to cry on, a listening ear.

Opening the doors to Rampier's office, he sensed Alexis' heartbeat quicken, her anxiety grow. Rhipley offered her a sympathetic smile, though her own in return didn't quite reach her eyes as they strode in, Rhipley closing the doors behind them.

Thankfully, Rampier's office was warded against prying ears, like that of the throne room in Fallandor's castle. Rhipley dipped his head in greeting Rampier, Alexis following suit, though she tried not to meet Rampier's stare, still ashamed by what she'd done.

"Come forth, child," Rampier commanded softly, not a hint of anger or disappointment in his voice.

Alexis looked at Rhipley, and he simply nodded, gesturing with a hand to go ahead. She obliged, her steps unhurried, and she finally lifted her head to meet the Headmaster's stare.

Rampier clasped his hands together on the desk as he asked, "Do you know what you are? What your powers represent?"

Alexis' eyes darted around, as if searching for an answer, but she simply shrugged her shoulders, shaking her head.

"You are Luzhula Blessed, Alexis, and your sister is Brundhul Blessed. You are the bearers of their powers, and it is a great responsibility that I'm sure neither of you can even begin to comprehend. It also explains why King D'Roghal is pursuing you, which puts this guild, this country, this entire world in danger."

Rhipley stepped forward, ready to protest, but Alexis spoke.

"I don't want these powers, Headmaster. I never asked for them. I'm just a human girl from Earth, not someone special or destined for greatness. I've never fought anyone in my life, and I didn't even know magic existed until a month ago. Please, I don't want to be a part of this prophecy." Her lips trembled as she stumbled over the last few words, tears already building in her eyes.

Rampier's own eyes turned solemn as he watched her, exhaling deeply. "You are the prophesied, Alexis. I know you're not sure what that means entirely, but you can't leave, not now. Your fate has already been decided. Unfortunately, no one can stray you from that path. Xalentya is counting on you, if and when the time comes. No matter where you go, no matter where you are, you will be pursued. You and Amelia have great power flowing through your veins. Power that we will need to train you to utilise."

Alexis didn't respond, as her eyes remained on the ground. As Rhipley's eyes remained on her.

Aurelia's words from Alexis' dream clanged through her head as Rampier spoke. The more information she learnt, the more questions she had. She hadn't dared to mention that she'd been seeing Aurelia in her dreams, unsure of what it even meant.

"I'm really sorry," she finally muttered through her tears, guilt ripping her from the inside out. She felt Rhipley step to her side, his hand gliding to the small of her back; a gentle touch, though it meant so much more to her, perhaps more than he'd intended.

After minutes of silence, Rampier seemingly lost for words, Rhipley spoke up. "I can't, for the life of me, figure out how two humans from a different world are the ones from the prophesy. How does that even happen?"

Rampier's eyes met Rhipley's, realisation in them. "Unless they're not from another world, but rather this one," Rampier said quietly, his gaze sliding to Alexis.

Alexis couldn't read his expression as she angled her head to the side in question, completely dumbfounded at his suggestion.

"N-no. My father has recounted our births to us an obscene amount of times. He has photos of us as babies. I think I would know if we came from… this world." She muttered the last words, doubt filling her as she dropped Rampier's stare. "We're not from Xalentya," she finally said, her voice quiet. She could feel Rhipley watching her, studying her.

Thankfully, rather than prodding further, Rampier just hummed as Rhipley changed the subject. "Are we equipped for an attack, should D'Roghal choose to?"

"Half our hunters are away on missions. We would need to send word for them to return to the guild immediately, and even then, we couldn't guarantee they'd receive word in time. Some of our hunters aren't even on this continent currently. For those who aren't Realm Walkers, it could take weeks for them to return. And, by then, depending on the forces D'Roghal might choose to dispatch, there may not be a guild to return to." Though Rampier sounded calm, Alexis could sense the panic laced in his words as his eyes dropped to his desk.

Her heart raced at the information, the realisation. This world she'd come to love might be ripped away from her in a matter of days, and these people, whose protection she was under, might not even be able to stop it. It was all her fault — this was all happening because she and Amelia simply existed.

Though the hunters were skilled fighters, just one equalling fifty soldiers, so she'd been told, they could still be mortally wounded, able to die at the hand of a sword pierced in the right spot — the human hunters more so than the fae and elf hunters — but all could be killed, nonetheless. The thought of Rhipley being wounded in such a way sent chills up her spine. Her breathing hitched, and she gulped, trying to push the thoughts down as she closed her eyes. Alexis breathed in and out, commanding her mind, her body, to calm as she collected herself.

"Is there anything I can do?" Alexis asked, finally meeting Rampier's eyes once more, though she knew what the answer may be. The two males looked at her before looking at each other, a silent conversation passing between them.

CHAPTER 38

Alexis sat by a river that afternoon, studying her hands. The sun blazed overhead, summer well and truly in full bloom. The sounds of the water lapping at the bank, over the scattered rocks, filled her ears as she flexed her fingers.

"Come on," she mumbled, urging her power to show itself again. She thought she'd be afraid to use her magic again, afraid to hurt anyone again, though she supposed that's why she was here, alone, far away from the guild. Far away from her friends. Guilt had racked her ever since she'd learnt of how she'd scarred Zailah. She hadn't asked about the female's condition, hadn't asked whether she might recover. She wasn't even sure whether the fae *could* heal from something like that, and she didn't want to think about it.

Though she hoped, god, she hoped Zailah could, somehow.

That her eyes had reddened after the fact, with no sign of healing, didn't bode well. A knot formed in Alexis' stomach as the intrusion of thoughts hit her. She closed her eyes and breathed — in, out, in, out. Slowly, steadily.

Rampier had informed her that the fate of this world rested on her shoulders, so she needed to focus on adjusting to her powers. Her shoulders, and Amelia's. They both now needed to learn how to control their powers, should the very likely need to use them arise.

Footsteps sounded behind her, soft and unhurried, and she looked over a shoulder.

Lukai stopped a few feet away, peering down at her with sorry eyes. She quickly averted her gaze, feeling foolish for her lack of bravery to face him. For what *she* had done.

'I'm so sorry, Lukai... please know that I didn't mean to hurt her. I didn't mean to hurt anyone..." As she sniffled, angry at herself for crying, Lukai stepped closer, before sitting beside her. His shoulder brushed hers, and she couldn't help the surprise at his choice to sit so close, let alone to come and see her after what had occurred.

She finally found the courage to meet his eyes as she asked, "You're not mad at me?"

His own eyes met hers, looked into her very soul, though she didn't dare flinch away.

"I was mad, at first. But, then I was reminded that it wasn't your fault. It was your first time tapping into your magic. We shouldn't have underestimated you."

Alexis couldn't help looking away at that — at the lie, though Lukai didn't know. Didn't know that she'd previously Realm Walked, that it wasn't her first time using her magic, even though she hadn't known it was *her* magic she was using. She hated that she couldn't tell him the truth, that she couldn't be honest with him, despite it being out of her hands.

"Zailah pushed too far. She shouldn't have, and I should have taken better lengths to stop her. It's a messy situation."
Alexis huffed a dry laugh at the comment, nodding in agreement.

"Will Zailah recover?" she asked, picking at some grass.

"Rampier has requested our Sister Guild dispatch one of their healers. Luckily for us, Tietnam has the best healers in the world — and this particular healer can Realm Walk, so we expect she will be here within a week or so." He smiled softly, likely grateful that there was hope for his friend, after all. "Though there's no guarantee the healer can fix what's been done... Your magic hasn't been seen in years, Alexis. We just have to pray that Goddess Luzhula has mercy on Zailah."

Goddess Luzhula — she who *blessed* Alexis with such gifts. *Gifts,* as if they could even be called that. The word turned sour in her mind.

"I know you aren't from here," Lukai said after a few quiet heartbeats, and Alexis didn't speak, didn't know what to say in response. "You don't have to hide it from me anymore."

"What do you mean?" she asked, playing dumb, pretending she had no clue what he was referring to.

Lukai angled his head to meet her eyes, and she begrudgingly raised her own to meet his.

"You're not from this world. Prince Frederik said so himself," Lukai whispered, aware that anyone could walk in on their conversation, despite there being no one bar them out here.

Alexis swore to herself, angry that the prince had been so stupid to let such a secret slip.

Had it been on purpose, to make his investigation into their true powers easier, should more people know of their true origins?

"It wasn't my choice to keep the truth from you," Alexis said, chewing on her lip as she once again returned her gaze to the grass.

"I know, and I don't hold it against you. I don't even hold it against Rhipley or Yazmin. I understand why Rampier chose to keep it a secret, chose to only trust Rhipley and Yazmin. After all, they're the ones who brought you here, correct?"

Alexis didn't confirm nor deny the question, unsure whether to let Lukai in on any further information.

Instead, she changed the subject. "I wish none of this had happened. I wish I could take it back. I wish-"

Her words were cut short as Lukai met her lips with his own, her face softly gripped between his calloused hands. Her eyes were wide with surprise for a few moments before she slowly closed them, accepting the kiss, placing her hand atop his.

The kiss was soft, sweet, unhurried, like they had all the time in the world. This time, however, he didn't try to push further, didn't urge for something more. The kiss was simply that — a kiss. Something to show support, understanding. To make Alexis feel good. For her to understand that he wasn't mad at her, wasn't upset with her. A soft moan escaped her lips as his tongue caressed her own, the warmth of him enveloping her. They separated, Alexis looking into his eyes, the golden hues of them iridescent in the sunlight. He didn't remove his hands from her face, and she didn't move from his grasp as they both stared into each other's eyes, smiling.

Rhipley had been searching the guild for Alexis, hoping to check up on her. When he'd heard from a hunter that they'd witnessed her aiming for the river, he hadn't hesitated in making his way there, too.

Sniffing for her scent, listening for her heartbeat, her words, her footsteps, he'd sighted her blonde hair swaying in the wind as she sat on the riverbank, staring at her hands, attempting to summon her magic.

As he'd gone to approach her, he'd halted, sensing the addition of someone else. When Lukai had emerged, quiet and solemn, Rhipley remained behind the tree line, watching on.

He knew it was wrong to eavesdrop on a conversation that didn't involve him, wasn't even *about* him, but he couldn't help his curiosity.

He'd felt sad for Alexis when she'd cried at the realisation of just how bad Zailah's condition was, despite the fact there may still be hope. Then, he'd sagged with relief at her refusal to reveal any important information to Lukai about her origins. Then he'd felt sadness again — his own sadness. Then white, hot rage and jealousy, as his friend, his *brother,* had kissed Alexis.

He kissed her with such passion and desire that Rhipley knew it hadn't been the first time. He knew his friend had wanted Alexis from the moment he'd met her, but this was... more than he had expected. And when Alexis didn't balk from the kiss, but rather leaned into it, welcomed it, Rhipley felt his heart crack.

He had finally accepted his feelings for Alexis, had realised how he felt when he'd been relieved to find her unharmed, when she hadn't hesitated in embracing him. Though he'd spent the past month trying to bury his growing feelings deep, had kept his distance to avoid the temptation of kissing her himself, of taking her for all she was as Lukai was now doing, he couldn't ignore the thoughts of her, day and night, that gnawed at him.

He could have sworn she'd felt the same way, had fallen for him first, but Lukai had beaten him to it. Not that there was a race to begin with. Lukai, who had initially expressed his desire only to bed her, had been smart enough to act on his feelings, seemingly winning Alexis over once and for all. Her knight in shining armour, though she certainly didn't need one.

Rhipley had missed his opportunity, and it was all his fault. He averted his eyes, not being able to stomach the sight of Alexis with someone else, of someone else making her happy, of someone else *kissing* her, as he made his way back to the guild.

Tatiana sat on Rhipley's bed, reeling over the information she'd come back to, that Lukai had mumbled while he'd hurried with Zailah to the infirmary. He'd simply said something about Alexis and Amelia having powers of the sun and moon, and Tatiana had connected the dots after, informing Rampier at once.

Alexis and Amelia, the humans, were more than just that. They were the prophesied, the chosen ones, those blessed by the God and Goddess she had worshipped all her life.

The universe certainly had a wicked sense of humour, she had to admit. As she gazed at the floor, making out all the swirls and cracks in the polished wood, the door opened, and Rhipley strode in. She immediately sensed the utter sadness coursing through his body, the anger and betrayal.

The second he'd locked eyes with her, she was on her feet, striding for him, taking his body in her arms.

"What's wrong?" she asked, pulling back to look into his eyes, to assess his face. He shrugged his shoulders.

"Nothing, don't worry about it."

Tatiana raised a brow in silent question, but he shook his head in dismissal, making to walk around her. She stepped into his path, before looking him up and down, her eyes travelling over his body, taking in those gorgeous muscles, that gods'-made face.

Without uttering a word, she removed her leathers, not daring to break eye contact. He watched her, though not with desire.

However, instead of arguing against it, he just stood there, watching as she removed piece by piece, until she was completely naked. When he didn't speak, didn't move to touch her, she gently grabbed his hand and led him to the bed. Pushing him down, she climbed atop him. She knew he didn't love her like that, knew they weren't mates. Gods, she'd known for years, and she had completely accepted it, agreeing that they shouldn't be exclusive, not minding who else he bedded, who else he desired.

Because, no matter what, they always found their way back to each other. It wasn't healthy, but it was enough. A distraction amid a world of chaos.

So, she kissed him, and he kissed her back, removing his own clothes in unhurried movements. He was upset, and she knew he needed a distraction. So, she would be that for him, as she lowered herself down his body, her eyes on his in sultry seduction.

CHAPTER 39

Alexis chewed on her lip as she made her way back to the dorms, feeling as giddy as she had that first time Lukai had kissed her. After he'd left, hesitantly, her request to be alone clearly not sitting well with him, she'd practised her magic.

She'd managed to summon small balls of light at each of her fingertips, bright as those that she'd witnessed when Rhipley and Yazmin had Realm Walked in and out of her world, though she didn't balk from it, didn't shield her eyes. She watched the small balls dance on her fingertips, watched them come to life.

Then, they'd disappeared.
She'd repeated the process for hours, sitting by that riverbank until the sun had gone down.

Now, on her way to her room, choosing to make a pit stop along the way to collect Aspen, she smiled to herself. With the help of her friends, her gut told her she'd somehow be okay.

Despite everything going on in this world, she knew she'd be okay. Distracted, she halted as her body collided with another.

She grunted, one hand caressing her head where a throbbing pain was beginning to form.

Prince Frederik turned around, a smile on his face as he massaged his shoulder. His guards were at his side in an instant, hands on their swords as they watched her with predatory eyes.

"Stand down, it's fine," the prince said in a calm voice, holding his hand up in a dismissive signal. The guards swapped glances before stepping back, removing their hands from their swords, though refusing to take their eyes from Alexis.

"Remind me to remain more aware of my surroundings should you ever be in the same vicinity again," Alexis said sarcastically, before realising who she was addressing and bowing low. "Your Majesty. I am so sorry."

Prince Frederik chuckled at the formalities. "That's really not necessary. It's fine."

Alexis rose, tight-lipped as she slightly dipped her head, unsure how to act despite the prince's dismissal of her bowing.

"Can I escort you somewhere?" he asked when Alexis didn't speak.

"Oh, no. I'm just going to check in on a friend before heading to get some food," she stuttered, unsure why she was so nervous. The prince seemed kind, harmless, just as he had on that first day they'd met. His eyes fell to where Aspen sat patiently beside Alexis, and as he leaned down to pet her, the dog backed away.

Alexis narrowed her brows at Aspen's strange reaction to the prince, though she didn't speak on it as she met his eyes once more.

"Ah," Frederik said, before turning to the side, holding out his arm for her to continue on. "Make sure you watch where you're going in future." He winked at her, and she tried to hide her blush at how handsome he was.

"Will do, Your Majesty." With one last glance at his guards, and another dip of her head, she walked around him, Aspen walking much more closely than before as she side-eyed the prince. Despite fighting the urge to subtly look back at him, she could feel his eyes watching her as she passed, and something uneasy came over her.

Rhipley heard a light knock at his door, and, glancing down at Tatiana, asleep on his chest, made to gently move out from under her, trying not to wake the female. She'd offered him just the distraction he'd needed, as he recalled the way his body relaxed and was quickly overcome with pleasure as she'd taken him into her mouth, the motion erasing any jealousy and thoughts of Alexis and Lukai from his mind.

He knew it was wrong, knew he was using her.
Though truthfully, they were using each other. Besides, he couldn't have Alexis, and didn't want anyone else in the way he'd so badly wanted her, so why shouldn't he indulge in something he could still enjoy physically? Especially if it was being offered to him on a silver platter by someone who was more than willing to give it with no strings attached.

He'd forced himself not to think of Alexis while Tatiana rode him, while he was buried deep inside her, when his head was between her legs. Had forced himself not to imagine Tatiana's moans of pleasure as Alexis'. Had forced himself not to imagine the sounds he could coax from Alexis, how her body would tremble beneath his touch, the gentle caress of his fingers, his tongue.

Because he'd never find out, and neither would she. She wanted Lukai, and Lukai wanted her, and that was that.

He'd force himself to keep his thoughts and desires hidden, no matter how much it wracked at him, no matter how it made him feel. He couldn't — *wouldn't* — hurt his brother. Wouldn't steal Alexis' chance at happiness, even if it was only physically.

The knock sounded again, and as he pulled on some pants, gazing over a shoulder at the still-sleeping female in his bed, he made his way to the door. A similar scent hit him as he turned the knob, and before he could prepare himself for what awaited him on the other side, he found Alexis standing there, smiling.

That is, until she noticed his bare chest, the fact he was holding the door only ajar enough for her to see him and only him. Whether she suspected anything, she didn't let on as her eyes searched his bare chest, his abs, his muscled arms.

She gulped, and Rhipley tried not to smirk at the reaction, tried to push down the pride he felt at how the image of him half-naked made her feel. A sense of arousal hit him instantly, and he cleared his throat.

"Hey, what's up?" he asked, that usual cool, impassive tone coming out. She lifted her eyes to his, and as she went to open her mouth to speak, Tatiana's voice sounded from behind.

"Is that Yazmin? Tell her to mind her own business and stop being a pervert."

Hurt shone in Alexis' eyes as she realised what she'd interrupted, despite the fact they'd finished their... activity a while ago.

She shook her head, pretending she wasn't bothered, and replied in an equally cool voice, "Well, I'm glad you finally got lucky. I was sick of dealing with your brooding attitude." She said it as a joke, though he knew she didn't mean it as one, not deep down. Though he felt guilty for her obvious hurt, he couldn't help the pang of joy at her jealousy over him.

Though, remembering Lukai, and how he'd kissed her yesterday, how she had kissed him, he discarded his feelings.

"Lex…" he said, trailing off and making to step into the hallway, but she just said in a voice louder than before, "Thanks for doing us all a favour, Tatiana."

Tatiana didn't speak, was likely too puzzled to speak, and as Rhipley made to close the door, to speak to Alexis without her prying ears, Alexis was already walking away, Aspen looking back at him.

Alexis' heart had hurt, her chest caving in when she'd realised who Rhipley had in his room, what he had been doing before she'd stupidly come looking for him. She'd simply wished to ask how his mission went, how he was feeling after everything that had happened. A friend checking on a friend.

But, at the sight of his half-clothed body, his obvious attempt at hiding Tatiana, likely naked on his bed, she'd wanted to cry. She didn't know why, felt like an idiot for the sadness now coursing through her veins. Lukai wanted her. Lukai *liked* her, and he had shown it this afternoon. Sure, he may have been a little scared of her power, but that was a normal reaction to have, she supposed. He may still only want her physically, but she didn't mind, because she felt the same way. He was good, and kind, and sweet, and god-damn, was he gorgeous. Perhaps she just needed a good tumble in her own bed to get her mind off of everything. The thought had a heat between her legs building.

It had been a good while since she'd broken up with Mitchell, and she wasn't going to see him again, so it was time to move on, and not feel guilty about doing so. She hadn't indulged in sex in far too long, and the need for it was quickly growing.

As she willed her emotions to calm, she plastered on a fake smile as she headed for the dining hall. With each step, she erased Rhipley from her mind. With each step, she set her sights on Lukai. With each step, she set her mind on one thing and one thing alone — making herself happy and satisfied. She and Rhipley were friends, and she had to learn to accept that fact.

CHAPTER 40

Alexis found Lukai in the dining hall, midway through a sandwich, when she'd sat next to him. He gave her an awkward smile as he chewed, mouth full.

"Is everything okay?" he asked once he'd finally swallowed his food, eyeing her tentatively.

"Are you busy for the rest of the night?" Alexis asked, ignoring his question.

He studied her face, seemingly catching on to what she wanted as he met her eyes, the corners of his lips tugging up into a feline smile. "I can be," he breathed, leaning in.

She didn't dare break eye contact as they stared at each other, as if they were the only ones in the room. Alexis cocked her head to the side, sizing him up. "Good. Meet me at the library after dinner."

Before he could respond, she rose, taking a piece of bread from his plate and flashing him a feline smile of her own. She walked away, putting a slight swish into her hips as she felt Lukai gaze after her.

Amelia stood in one of the fighting rings at the guild, Yazmin watching on with determination.

"You've got this. Just remain calm and will your magic to come forth," Yazmin said.

Amelia glanced her way, and Yazmin returned her stare with a supportive nod, one arm gripping the other, as she rested her fingers beneath her chin, shifting from foot to foot as she waited.

Amelia's mouth went into a tight line as she returned her eyes to her hands, palms facing the sky, her body relaxed, or as relaxed as it could be.

As she closed her eyes, Amelia cleared her mind and breathed in through her nose, then exhaled through her mouth. She thought only of her magic, only of positive emotions. A ripple coursed through her body, and she began to shy away from it, but Yazmin's voice stopped her.

"Don't fear it. Accept it, welcome it. It's a part of you."

Amelia calmed her breathing once more, and the ripple continued coursing through her veins, cooling her blood. She opened her eyes, and a ball of shadow had appeared in her palm. It was so black, Amelia wasn't sure it was even there, or whether she may have just been imagining it. It didn't help that she was practising in the dead of night.

The ball looked like a small — *very* small — black hole in her palms, the edges rippling. As her eyes adjusted, she saw only the ball of darkness, as if it had enveloped all other colours, as if it had absorbed the world. She smiled in complete awe at the strange magic. Yazmin stepped closer, her own awe evident on that beautiful face.

"Alright, so *that's* nothing like I've ever seen before," she mumbled, her focus wholly on the ball.

Had Amelia's own eyes not adjusted to the blackness of the ball in her palms, she may have likened it to black light, too difficult to look at for too long at a time. Yazmin averted her gaze, clearly struggling to look at it directly.

"That's some magic, alright," Yazmin announced, placing a hand atop Amelia's shoulder. Amelia smiled before closing her hand, the black shadow ball vanishing.

"It doesn't feel real. I don't think I could ever grow used to possessing magic," Amelia said, meeting Yazmin's eyes. Yazmin's mouth quirked to the side as she studied Amelia.

"How do you feel about everything? About being *The Chosen One*." Yazmin said the last three words dramatically, earning a giggle from Amelia.

"It hasn't really kicked in yet, I don't think. But, I suppose I'm also trying not to think about it…"

Yazmin gave her a sympathetic look as she nodded. "Do you understand what it means, though?" she asked softly, stepping to face Amelia fully.

Amelia looked up at her, her hazel eyes darker than usual, as if using her magic had affected them somehow.

"I know it makes us dangerous. I know it puts you, Rhipley, and everyone else here in danger, including ourselves. I know that it's why King D'Roghal is after us."

She exhaled a long breath, turning to head back to the dorms as she recounted all that Alexis had told her. Yazmin stopped her as she grabbed her wrist.

Amelia looked over a shoulder, furrowing her brows.

"I won't ever let anything happen to you. I promise that." Yazmin spoke quietly, softly, yet there was a firmness to her voice that Amelia hadn't heard before. She smiled, her heart warming at the comment, as Yazmin pulled her in for a kiss. Amelia chuckled, and she could feel Yazmin's smile against her lips as the moon shone down upon them, seeming to illuminate brighter.

Alexis leaned against the doors to the library, having convinced the librarian to keep them unlocked so she could catch up on some late-night studying, the lie somehow rolling off her tongue so easily.

Though the librarian had given her a doubtful look, she'd obliged, reminding Alexis firmly to ensure she locked up when she was done, and to return the key to Rampier's office.

As she gazed up at the moon, particularly bright on this night, she suddenly felt someone's breath on her neck. She smiled, biting her lip as she turned her head to the side, Lukai looking down at her with a smirk on his face.

"So, what have you summoned me here for?" he crooned, curiosity in his eyes.

She smiled broadly before turning to the unlocked doors, pushing one open and striding inside, Lukai on her trail.

As he closed the door, darkness enveloped them. Though Alexis knew he could see easily with his fae sight, she couldn't see a thing.

As Lukai made to find a lit candle, more for her sake than his, she stopped him. "What's the point in having the magic I've been gifted with if I can't use it in times of need?"

Lukai stopped, crossing his arms as if to say *go ahead, then.* She closed her eyes, breathed in deeply, and called her magic forward. She heard a gasp from Lukai, and as she opened her eyes once more, the entire library was lit up. Every candle and chandelier alight with flames, brighter than she'd ever seen them in her time spent here. She chuckled to herself, taking in what she'd done.

Her quick practice sessions appeared to be coming in handy, though she couldn't yet do more than just that — conjuring small balls of light, and now, fire, apparently.

Would she need to someday conjure more than just this? More than what she'd wielded on that dreadful day she'd discovered her magic? The thought of it irked her, made her want to hide her magic deep inside.

"Impressive," Lukai mumbled, gently shouldering her.

She looked up at him and smiled. "I learn something new every day."

He walked ahead, hands in his pockets as he took in the library, completely emptied, as she'd expected it to be.

"You still haven't answered my question," he said smugly, raising an eyebrow at her as he turned around. Her cheeks heated as she understood the silent question in his eyes. She clasped her hands behind her back as she walked towards the bookshelves, her strides slow.

Huffing, she said, "I want to study, obviously." Though she couldn't see him behind her, Alexis could tell Lukai was rolling his eyes at her fake coyness.

Continuing her stride into the stacks, pretending to study each book, pretending to look for something to read, she felt Lukai approach from behind. Stopping in her tracks, a particular book catching her eye, she felt him lean in as he whispered in her ear, his warm breath tickling her neck, "*You* want to study? Or," he placed a hand on her waist, planting a soft kiss to her throat that had a soft gasp escaping her lips. She tried not to moan at the touch, tried not to give in and tackle him right then and there. "Would you rather I study you instead?"

Her breathing hitched at the request, her cheeks heating and blood boiling and heart pounding. It had been so long since someone had touched her — even she and Mitch hadn't so much as made love before they'd broken up, their sex life essentially non-existent by that point. She had craved it so badly these past weeks. Craved to be touched and kissed and worshipped. Craved to have that ache within her diminished, satisfied.

As Lukai continued kissing her neck, every plant sending vibrations through her veins, Alexis couldn't help the whimpers that escaped her lips, tilting her neck into it. Lukai huffed a laugh against her skin as he bit down gently, and a bolt of electricity coursed through her body.

She couldn't take it anymore, this teasing. Alexis turned around and pulled his body against hers as she kissed him. He welcomed her, returning each kiss with one of his own, laced with such hunger she wasn't sure she could ever get enough of it, of him. His tongue slid over hers, their lips perfectly interlaced as he lifted her up in one swift movement, her legs wrapping around his waist.

She ran her fingers through his silken hair, made to pull his shirt up, to see and feel all of him, before he stopped her, his hand gently grabbing her wrists.

She pulled back, meeting his lustful stare with a confused one of her own. As she made to free her wrists, with no luck, he smirked, the hunger evident in his eyes, his smile. He walked down the corridor of book shelves before finding a particularly shorter bookshelf and propped Alexis' body atop it.

"Convenient," she muttered, taking in her new seat. She gazed up at Lukai once more, a glimmer in her eye, a predator staring down at her prey. Given how Lukai scanned her body, however, she could have sworn it was the other way around.

He leaned in to kiss her again, though this time it was slow, patient. Alexis didn't bother guessing what his intentions were as his hands slid to her pants, unbuckling her belt in swift, smooth movements. She smiled in between kisses at what she knew was awaiting her. As if he'd done it so many times before, within seconds, Lukai had removed her belt and unzipped her pants, propping her up slightly to remove them, and her underwear. The coolness of the library, of the top of the bookshelf she sat upon, bit into her skin.

Lukai began kissing down her neck, unbuttoning her shirt. Alexis savoured the attention she was receiving, leaning into every touch, soaking it up like the warm summer sun.

As he unbuttoned her shirt, her bra underneath now on full display, Lukai took a moment to admire her before he continued his trail of kisses. He worked his way over her chest, then down her stomach.

Alexis' heart thundered as she watched Lukai descend lower, the ache between her legs growing with each passing second.

He propped each leg on his shoulders, his warm touch, his closeness, making the ache between her legs unbearable.

"Beautiful," he murmured. His eyes met hers, utter sin laced in those golden irises as he leaned in and feasted on her.

Alexis' eyes rolled into the back of her head as she welcomed his tongue, welcomed his fingers, both working in tandem movements, her whole body ready to come undone in mere seconds if he kept going like this. She didn't stifle her moan as she savoured this moment, as his tongue gently caressed up and down her centre, his fingers working in a gentle rhythm. She let the moans escape her, not caring who heard.

The pleasure coursed through her body, sending shivers down her spine as her hand gripped his hair, the wood beneath her creaking. When she finally came undone, Lukai, to her surprise, didn't cease his movements. Instead, he continued, Alexis bucking and writhing beneath him. She could lose herself in this feeling, content to remain here forever.

CHAPTER 41

Studying in the library the following morning post-breakfast, Alexis chewed on her quill as she recounted the previous night, how she'd practically been glowing with delight this morning. Upon meeting Yazmin and Amelia at the library doors, students already flocking in ahead of them, the huntress had pinched her nose between her forefinger and thumb, dramatically acting as if something smelled grotesque upon her arrival.

"Been busy, Alexis?" she'd said in a funny voice, her fingers still clamped around her nostrils.

Alexis had blushed before giving Yazmin a light shove, the two chuckling.

"What do you mean?" Amelia had asked, clueless.

Yazmin and Alexis shared a look, before Yazmin offered, "Your sister reeks of utter lust. It's all I can smell. That, and Lukai's stench."

Amelia shot Alexis a look that said, *you didn't tell me?!*

Alexis had rolled her eyes, holding her books close to her chest as she'd stepped around the two, walking through the library doors.

To her surprise, none of the library patrons had paid her particular mood, or scent, any heed, their heads all stuck in books, some chattering away quietly amongst themselves.

"Don't expect any of these students to react to your particular odour. They're young, of course they're horny, as well. Probably more so than you."

Amelia stifled a laugh as she and Yazmin shared amused glances.

"Their poor teachers," Alexis muttered.

"The poor librarian," Yazmin added.

Sure enough, the librarian was observing the students, her eyes settling on a few here and there as her face turned into something of disgust, before she continued whatever she'd been doing.

Now, having re-read the passage in her study book over and over, due to her wild thoughts and lack of concentration, Alexis felt something light hit her in the head.

"Ouch!" she exclaimed as quietly as she could.

"Girl, come on. If you're going to be emitting that stench our entire lesson, you may as well spill the beans on how this came to happen," Yazmin said in a hushed tone, her eyes narrowed in curiosity. Amelia, despite her amazing study ethic, had drawn her attention away from her own book to also corner her sister, her eyes equally as narrowed as Yazmin's.

Scanning the room, careful of listening ears, Alexis leaned in, the girls following suit until they were all as close as the table would allow.

"Please don't repeat this to anyone," Alexis whispered, the statement aimed at Yazmin in particular as her thoughts settled on Rhipley. She knew she shouldn't care. Knew Rhipley wouldn't particularly care, either.

Yazmin furrowed her brows, as if taking offence at the comment, though nodded all the same.

Breathing in deeply, Alexis continued. "It sort of just happened. We both wanted it, so we did… it. Last night."

Amelia covered her mouth, trying to cease her verbal astonishment from escaping. Yazmin's jaw had practically hit the floor.

"Damn, so Lukai took your immortal v-card," Yazmin muttered, excitement dancing in those sky-blue eyes.

"Not quite," Alexis mumbled, chewing her lip.

Yazmin and Amelia shared a puzzled look.

"We did... stuff, but not everything," Alexis said, trying not to blush as the memory flooded back in.

Amelia's face was in a state of awe, while Yazmin chuckled to herself, nodding as she returned her eyes to the book in front of her.

"Not bad," she said, flipping the pages. "Was he at least good at it?"

Alexis cleared her throat, remaining silent.

"That's not a no," Yazmin teased.

"He's surprisingly very generous. That's all I'm going to say," Alexis mumbled, a light smile gracing her lips.

"Well, well, well, who would have thought Lukai was such a gentleman," Yazmin said.

"And you didn't go all the way because...?" Amelia pushed.

Alexis felt strange talking about her sex life with her sister, but given that they were already on the topic...

"I was exhausted by the end of it," Alexis said, avoiding her sister's gaze.

Yazmin let out a low, impressed whistle. "Wow, generous indeed."

"So if you didn't do it in our room, where did you do it?" Amelia asked, before saying, "Actually, don't tell me. I don't want to know."

Alexis chuckled as she said, "Believe me, you really don't."

Her eyes betrayed her as she raised her stare to the book stacks behind Amelia and Yazmin, the two catching on before the latter exclaimed, "Here?!"

Alexis hissed, reminding Yazmin to keep her voice down.

"Not *here*," Alexis said, gesturing to the table. "But, yes, here in the library."

"Horny freaks," Yazmin muttered, amused. "Didn't realise you had a book kink; I thought you just enjoyed reading them."

Alexis flipped Yazmin the finger. "That's all I'm telling you. Now leave the subject be."

Yazmin held up her hands in defeat, before Amelia said, "Do you think Rhipley will care?"

Yazmin and Alexis both shot her looks of confusion, Alexis' more a look of warning.

"Why would Rhipley care?" Yazmin asked, and Alexis was grateful for it, if only so she didn't have to admit to anyone but herself that she had held feelings for Rhipley. Feelings she needed to force herself to let go of.

"I just thought he might like you," Amelia said to Alexis.

Yazmin scoffed. "Rhipley has never liked anyone in that way. He refuses to let himself. Smart, really, given our occupation. It's the easiest way to avoid heartbreak."

She shrugged her shoulders nonchalantly.

Amelia immediately turned her attention to Yazmin, shock and betrayal on her face.

Yazmin, realising what she'd just said, quickly backtracked as she placed an arm around Amelia's shoulders. "Not all of us are like that, obviously. Life is too short to toss love aside, even for us immortals."

Amelia's mouth quirked to the side, but she nodded, planting a light kiss to Yazmin's lips.

"Nice save," Alexis mumbled, and this time, Yazmin was the one to flip Alexis off.

Tatiana still hadn't known how to process the information regarding the two human girls, what power they possessed, how important it made them. How that power had been passed down to two mortals, she couldn't grasp. She'd known there was something off about them, but she couldn't have possibly guessed it would be this.

She'd certainly needed that tumble in the sheets with Rhipley the other night, and though she'd done it for his sake, it had equally been to get her mind off of everything, too. Rhipley had awoken before dawn to train, she'd assumed, leaving her to the walk of shame hours later.

Usually, she didn't mind. In fact, most times it was Rhipley quietly exiting her chambers. It was their thing, their agreement, and she hadn't minded at all — before. Now, sensing a shift in Rhipley's emotions, sensing how he felt about Alexis, noticing how he looked at her, how he seemed to light up slightly around her — it caused an ache in her chest, and she hated it. She and Rhipley were friends, albeit friends who liked to explore each other's bodies from time to time, but they were friends, no feelings involved.

Perhaps what irked her was the fact that even she couldn't stir any feelings in Rhipley. At least, not romantically. But suddenly, this Luzhula Blessed mortal could? Whether Alexis was aware of Rhipley's true feelings, Tatiana didn't know.

Didn't care to know.

Making her way to the dining hall, having already finished her prayers to Luzhula and Brundhul, Tatiana strode in, aiming right for her usual table. Alexis, Amelia and Yazmin were already sitting there, chatting away about business she didn't care to listen to.

She slowed, wondering whether or not it was worth joining them without Rhipley or Lukai being there, too. At least if either male were there, they could offer some kind of distraction, so, gods forbid, she didn't have to interact with the girls more than necessary.

Yazmin was all about Amelia these days, the fool. Completely love-struck.

Had finding out about Amelia's power strengthened Yazmin's feelings? Given how gods-worshipping the elves were known to be, Tatiana deemed it very likely.

As she stood there, weighing her options, Alexis' gaze slid to her. She offered a warm, sincere smile, tapping the seat next to her.

An invitation.

Tatiana didn't dare smile back, didn't dare let her surprise and gratitude at the gesture show, as she continued walking towards the table, deciding that sitting with them wasn't the worst option on her plate.

Amelia and Yazmin halted their chatter as they watched Tatiana take up her spot beside Alexis. Yazmin clicked her fingers, and a plate of food appeared before her. She'd done it in the past, many times, though given Tatiana's foul behaviour towards the girls these past weeks, Yazmin hadn't bothered with niceties of late.

Tatiana dipped her head in thanks, offering a tight smile, which Yazmin just huffed a laugh at.

"So, to what do we owe the pleasure of your presence?" Yazmin asked sarcastically. Tatiana rolled her eyes, picking up a bread roll from her plate and biting into it.

"Care for another lesson today?" Tatiana asked Alexis, ignoring Yazmin completely.

"I actually have some studying to do, but I could meet you this afternoon?" Alexis offered.

Before Tatiana could respond, Lukai came up behind them, planting a kiss on Alexis' cheek. Alexis blushed, trying to wave off the gesture. Yazmin and Amelia, now turned to each other, side eyeing them and snickering. Tatiana, apparently, was the only one taken aback by the gesture.

"Good morning," Lukai said cheerfully.

It hit her then, the scent he was giving off. That both he *and* Alexis were giving off. Something had occurred between them. Did Rhipley know?

As if in answer, she turned to see Rhipley standing by the doors, watching their table. His face wielded nothing, but she could feel, could *scent* his jealousy, his surprise.

Lukai and Alexis had engaged in conversation, something Tatiana didn't care to listen to, but she kept her eyes on Rhipley, her face sympathetic. He simply smirked back, putting on that fake bravado.

He made his way to the table, offering a wink at Tatiana.

Fine, if he was okay with *pretending* to be okay, she was, too. If that's what he wanted.

As he took up a seat beside Yazmin, a plate of food instantly appeared in front of him, too.

"Summer Solstice party is in two days," Rhipley said flatly. Yazmin tilted her head in silent question. "Rampier," he added, and Yazmin nodded, the name answer enough.

"I suppose I'll have to raid my armoire for something spectacular," Tatiana mumbled, tossing some peas around with a fork.

Alexis looked at her. "Do we have to dress up?"

Yazmin scoffed, but quickly cleared her throat at Amelia's light punch to her arm. "It's a real soiree. Of course, we dress up. The fancier the clothes, the better. People like Miss Tatiana Elrin over here have endless dresses to choose from, being a fancy rich female and all." Tatiana offered Yazmin her middle finger in return.

Rhipley glanced at Tatiana, who glanced right back, furrowing her brows in question. Rhipley, without needing to voice his plea, simply tilted his head slightly at Alexis, the mortal not even noticing the gesture. Despite Alexis practically gushing over Lukai in front of him, Rhipley still made the effort to look out for her. Tatiana scoffed. If only Alexis knew how lucky she was to have someone like Rhipley secretly pining after her.

Tatiana turned to Alexis as she said, "You can borrow one of my dresses, if you wish."

Alexis smiled, mouthing a silent *thank you*.

"You too, I suppose," Tatiana said without looking at Amelia, who she could feel watching her.

"Can't wait," Yazmin said smugly, wriggling her brows at Amelia, who giggled.

Tatiana didn't miss the swift glances swapped between Rhipley and Alexis, Lukai completely oblivious to it as he spoke about gods knew what.

Alexis made a good show of pretending she was listening, but she couldn't stop herself from looking at Rhipley every now and again.

Rhipley, unsurprisingly, pretended not to notice her watching him, only looking up when Alexis had averted her gaze. Tatiana realised, though she didn't mind one bit, that Rhipley would likely be visiting her room far more often now that Lukai and Alexis' affection for each other was now a public spectacle.

As if sensing her revelation, Rhipley held Tatiana's gaze, angling his head towards the doors to the dining hall, desire in his eyes.

Tatiana glanced between the group, ensuring they were all too distracted to notice, before standing from her spot and making her way to the doors, glancing back over her shoulder only once, accepting Rhipley's invitation.

As she glanced back, she caught Alexis watching her and Rhipley, before returning to her conversation with Lukai.

CHAPTER 42

Zailah was sleeping when Alexis entered the infirmary to check on her. Guilt had been lashing at her since the incident, more so today, given how long she'd taken to visit the female. As she'd approached the infirmary doors, Alexis had seen Lukai sitting by Zailah's bed, gazing at the female longingly, one hand stroking her hair as the other gently caressed her hand.

Alexis had briefly greeted him on his way out, choosing to wait so she didn't interrupt whatever moment they were sharing, and she'd realised then that Lukai could never feel anything for her more than lust, for his heart already belonged to Zailah, whether she knew it or not.

The healers had dipped their heads in greeting, only a couple of other hunters, and some students, occupying the space — none in nearly as bad a condition as Zailah. All were conscious, all with injuries far easier to heal.

Alexis had expected the healers to look at her with disdain, no doubt knowing what had truly occurred for the petite female to occupy one of their beds permanently. But they'd simply looked at her with sympathy, as if understanding that she hadn't meant for this to happen. What they knew, they didn't speak of. Had likely been instructed not to. For that, she was grateful.

Alexis sat there beside Zailah's bed, watching her chest rise and fall in a steady rhythm. A bandage covered her eyes, though the redness that tinged her skin that day was nowhere to be seen. Courtesy of the guild's healers, no doubt.

As Alexis sat there in silence, the only sounds filling the space the muttering of the other infirmary occupants, and the healer's footsteps, she wondered how much longer the reputable healer from Tietnam would be from arriving, how soon this terrible mistake could be reversed.

Though Rampier had said Zailah's healing wasn't promised, that the healer could all but try her hardest to fix the damage, Alexis still held hope, because that's all she'd allow herself to do. If she didn't hold on to that small slither of hope, she didn't think she could ever forgive herself. In truth, she wouldn't forgive herself until Zailah had, if she ever would.

Zoned out, a small movement brought Alexis' attention back, as she noticed Zailah shifting beneath her quilt.

Alexis sat still, not daring to utter a word as the female came to. Her brows furrowed, and despite being blinded, Zailah guessed exactly who was sitting by her bed — likely from Alexis' scent.

"Hello, Luzhula Blessed. You've come to see me at last," Zailah said simply, though her tone wasn't harsh, much to Alexis' surprise. Alexis cleared her throat. "Yes, I'm sorry it's taken me so long. I just truly didn't know how to…" she trailed off, unsure how to finish her sentence.

"Confront me? Assess your damage?" Zailah asked.

Alexis, stupidly forgetting for a split second that Zailah couldn't see, nodded. "Y-yes," she mumbled, correcting herself, silently cursing at her idiocy.

Zailah smirked, reaching out a hand. Alexis hesitated, staring at the porcelain fingers, before placing her own hand in Zailah's, the female's skin smooth to the touch.

"I'm so sorry, Zailah. I truly didn't mean for this to happen," Alexis said softly, fighting the tears threatening to emerge. She'd apologised to so many people these past days, though she didn't mind, didn't care how often she needed to apologise before all was forgiven.

Zailah, to Alexis' surprise, squeezed her hand. "You needn't apologise, girl. At least now I can brag about being attacked by one of the Divinely Blooded." Her lips curved upwards in a half-sinister smile.

The words clanged in Alexis' head. It would take some time to adjust to now being referred to as that.

The Divinely Blooded. The Prophesied. Luzhula Blessed. Harbinger of Light. The Chosen One.

Alexis huffed a laugh.

"I should be the one apologising. I pushed you too far. Granted, it confirmed you have magic — some of the most powerful magic known in Xalentya, in fact. But, my demise is of my own doing," Zailah continued, smile now vanished, her words now firm. "I told Rampier as much."

"Thank you," Alexis whispered, and Zailah nodded.

"How are you doing, despite this?" Alexis asked, signalling to the bandages.

Zailah, as if guessing her movements, chuckled, throwing her hands in the air. "Well, it hurt like a motherfucker. I'll tell you that much. But, it's actually been nice just resting, not having to hunt or work. The healers aren't much for conversation, so dwelling in this silence is my own personal paradise."

"You're not just being nice to me because I'm *The Chosen One*, are you?" Alexis asked, half sarcastically, half genuinely curious.

"Gods, no. It's certainly an ethereal feeling, being in your presence. I mean, I can literally feel your power radiating off your skin as we speak," Zailah replied. Alexis looked down at her arms, at her body, scanning for that invisible magic. "But," the female continued, "don't get used to it. Once I'm back up and running, I plan to return the favour in the training ring."

She pointed a finger at Alexis, who smiled and muttered,

"Fantastic."

Tatiana watched as Alexis finished her sit-ups, the latter breathing out of her nose in steady movements, pretending she wasn't sore or tired.

Tatiana leaned against one of the armoury walls, her arms crossed, braid swaying in the wind.

Alexis stood from where she'd been laying, dusting off her pants and shirt, before guzzling from her waterskin. Tatiana had been pleasantly surprised by the mortal's willingness to learn, to push through. And though she still hadn't grown to like her, Tatiana had decided that Alexis and Amelia still deserved her respect, nonetheless, realising that the alternative would make her a hypocrite, given her worshipping and beliefs in Luzhula and Brundhul. Though she'd never admit it, she wished so badly to see Alexis' magic herself, to marvel at the beauty of it.

She hadn't seen it at all, had apparently been the only one from their group who hadn't seen it, and she couldn't help the jealousy that coursed through her veins at that thought, despite Alexis' power landing Zailah in the infirmary.

Stepping up to Alexis, Tatiana didn't hesitate before grabbing her arms and feeling for the muscle now growing. Alexis gave her a tentative look, though didn't balk from the touch.

"Good, *now* you can learn to wield a bow," Tatiana said firmly. Alexis gave her a look of anticipation, finishing her drink and tossing the waterskin aside. Tatiana offered her a bow — one that was used by the children, granted, but everyone had to start somewhere.

Alexis looked over the bow, taking note of its size compared to her own body, compared to Tatiana's bow, and frowned.

"Really, a kid's bow?" she asked.

Tatiana simply shrugged her shoulders and signalled for her to take up a spot by the woodblock. Positioning herself as Tatiana had shown her before, Alexis eyed her target, lifted the bow with ease, and pulled back the arrow. Tatiana stepped up to better position the bow, Alexis' arms, then stepped back once more, giving a nod of approval.

Alexis side eyed her for a second before returning her focus to the target, breathing in deeply before letting the arrow loose. It landed in the grass just ten feet from where they both stood. Tatiana smiled but stopped a laugh from escaping her lips as she reminded herself that Alexis had never actually shot an arrow before. The fact that the arrow landed in the ground with such precision fared better than a lot of other first-time archers.

"Again," Tatiana ordered, and Alexis obliged, taking up another arrow. Again, she fired.

Again, it didn't hit the target, but with each fire, with each shot, she got closer and closer, her technique slowly growing, improving.

Tatiana could sense the frustration in Alexis, though even without her fae senses, she would have been able to see that the girl was frustrated by the way she tensed, by the way her brows furrowed, and her jaw clenched with each failed shot.

All afternoon, right up until the sun had set, they practised. And, though Tatiana had yet to grow to like the girl, she found herself filled with pride, filled with hope at the mortal's perseverance.

CHAPTER
43

Amelia had been more than happy to assist Yazmin with decorating the guild for the Summer Solstice party tomorrow, students and hunters alike chattering away with delight and excitement as they did so. Side eyeing Yazmin, who was looking the Red Oak up and down, assessing how to properly decorate it, Amelia asked, "So, this party tomorrow... does Alexis have to do anything? Or does she get anything?"

Yazmin shifted her attention to Amelia, quirking her mouth to the side. "Unless Rampier declares it, I don't believe so. The general public are still unaware of her true nature, and until Rampier decides to make that news known, we're to continue keeping quiet about it," Yazmin said softly, though there was a slight firmness to her voice.

"What about the Winter Solstice?" Amelia asked, hanging a streamer along a lamp post.

"That's another six months away, though it's just as beautiful. We can still celebrate you, in secret. Though, by then, I suppose the news will probably be out," Yazmin muttered, assessing the tree once more.

Amelia considered for a second, raising her eyes to the sky, the moon cresting overhead.

"So, Brundhul and Luzhula — they're the God and Goddess of Light and Shadow. Are they also the God and Goddess of night and day?"

Yazmin simply nodded, letting out a hum as some streamers appeared in her hands.

"So, the moon…" Amelia mumbled.

"The moon is Brundhul, I suppose," Yazmin finished for her. "Everything the darkness brings is Brundhul. The night, the stars in the sky. Even the flow of water."

Amelia smiled — smiled at her God, at the God who had blessed her with such gifts. Though she knew Alexis was still growing accustomed to her magic, Amelia had welcomed it fully. She had always dreamed of being important, powerful, someone who mattered. Now she was.

Though, her naivety, she supposed, stopped her from wondering about the consequences of having such power. Perhaps that was why Alexis was still experiencing growing pains — because she was all too aware of what being Luzhula Blessed meant.

Amelia looked down at Yazmin once more, who'd clicked her fingers. A variety of lights appeared in the tree, illuminating it like the fireflies had. She clicked her fingers again, and the various white and yellow streamers that she'd held now hung from the branches, cascading down at different levels. Another click, and small white flowers appeared throughout the branches.

Appearing satisfied with her work, Yazmin clicked her tongue and placed her hands on her hips, nodding to herself.

"It's beautiful," Amelia said, climbing down from the ladder placed against the lamp post she'd decorated. Yazmin clicked her fingers once more, and the ladder disappeared.

"I like to think my decorative skills are quite brilliant, indeed," Yazmin replied, grinning. "Though it would be far easier, far more beautiful, if your sister were able to assist us. We wouldn't need faerie lights, wouldn't need half of these with her power. A display of her light would be enough."

Amelia placed a kiss on Yazmin's cheek, linking their elbows as she rested her head on her shoulder. Yazmin huffed a content laugh, echoing the movement, her head a warm weight on Amelia's.

"Not bad," Rhipley said from behind.

Amelia turned to see he had his arms folded, a half-smile on his lips as he surveyed the tree.

"Have you seen Alexis?" he asked.

"She was training with Tatiana," Yazmin mumbled, not bothering to turn to look at him as she continued to admire her work.

Rhipley clicked his tongue, making to walk towards the hunter's grounds.

"Is everything okay?" Amelia asked.

She couldn't help her concern, her pity for Rhipley, who she knew, deep down, felt something for her sister, though he hadn't admitted it.

"Everything's fine," Rhipley said over a shoulder, though Amelia didn't believe his words as he departed.

Alexis lay on her bed, her arms aching as she rubbed them, and she could have sworn her muscles were literally throbbing. The constant tug and pull of the bow string certainly took a toll on her body, though she kept reminding herself that it would be worth it when she could finally hit the target.

Today had been a bust, though Tatiana said that was to be expected. It was her first day firing an arrow — no one expected her to be able to hit the target. Not yet, anyway. But, with practice, she'd get there.

A light knock sounded at the door that had Alexis sitting up.

"Come in," she said, wondering who had come to visit her.

At the thought of it being Lukai, a heat began to form between her legs, the thoughts of what they'd done the other night racing through her mind.

Rhipley, however, strode in.

He'd been smiling, but upon sensing her feelings, apparently, he tensed, the smile faltering. Whether or not he knew she was thinking about Lukai, she didn't know, didn't want to think about it.

"Yes?" she asked bluntly, straightening her posture.

Rhipley watched her with an expression she couldn't quite read as he quietly closed the door behind him. He didn't make to move as he stood there, watching her. His throat bobbed, and she couldn't help gulping herself as they watched each other.

"Can I help you?" she asked when he didn't speak, but he just continued to look at her, desire in his mahogany eyes.

A tingle coursed through her body, and that space between her legs began to heat further. He approached the bed in only a few steps, his long legs covering the space easily. Alexis backed up on the bed, unsure what his intentions were as he leaned over her, his breath warm and smelling of cinnamon.

Before she could react, his mouth was on hers, the complete desire and lust and hunger in it so blatantly obvious. Alexis couldn't help kissing him back as his strong hands pushed her down onto the bed, his gorgeous body now atop hers. She fiddled with his shirt and pants before another knock interrupted them.

Suddenly, she was alone once more.

Alexis looked around, realising she'd been imagining the entire thing. She cursed at herself, shaking the dirty thoughts from her mind as she said, "Come in."

Much like in her daydream, Rhipley strode in, though his smile didn't falter.

"Am I interrupting something?" he asked, his typical smirk on full display.

"What can I do for you?" Alexis asked, ignoring his question as she dropped his gaze.

"I just wanted to warn you about tomorrow," Rhipley replied, leaning against the doorway. Hunters walked past as they mingled and chatted, the sound diminishing as Rhipley shut the door behind him.

"Why?" Alexis asked, still refusing to meet his stare. Had he known, somehow, what she'd been imagining just now?

"It's the day of the Summer Solstice celebrations, and since no one knows of your power, and since we're still in the early days since the actual Solstice, meaning your powers are heightened, I just came to warn you to be careful, more alert. We don't want to repeat what happened to Zailah," he teased, though there was a grave undertone to it.

Alexis frowned at him, clicking her tongue, not willing to play along, even if Zailah and Lukai were past the occurrence.

"I'll be fine, thanks." She stood, aiming for her armoire. "Is there anything else I can help you with?"

Alexis side eyed him, and his face turned serious, the smirk, the teasing, gone. He made to block her path, but she quickly stepped around him. To neither's surprise, he grabbed her arm anyway — his fae speed outmatching hers easily.

Leaning in, he said in a low voice, "I'm sorry. I was just trying to make light of the situation."

Alexis shook out of his grip, rifling through her clothes, though they all looked the same. "It was a low blow, even if it was just a sad attempt at some humour," she shot back. She wasn't mad, wasn't angry. She just wasn't in the mood.

And, in truth, she was trying to mask how her daydream had made her feel, how the idea that Rhipley was about to fuck her made her feel, even if it was all in her head.

"Are you happy? With Lukai?" he asked, catching her off guard.

She looked up at him, trying to hide her surprise at his question. "I'm content," she replied, smirking in the same way he always did.

"But does he make you happy?" he questioned, no hesitation in his response.

He didn't know that they were simply enjoying each other physically and nothing more, that there was no love between them, no feelings more than platonic.

"That's none of your business," Alexis said simply.

Rhipley cocked his head to the side, his eyes falling to her lips. "Why do you care, anyway?" she quipped, not hiding the sharpness in her voice as she tried to ignore the way he was now looking at her.

"He's my friend, as are you. Am I not allowed to care?"

Alexis scoffed, pulling her night clothes from the armoire and shutting the doors with a thud.

"If I didn't know any better, I'd say you sound jealous."

Rhipley just shrugged, and his refusal to neither confirm nor deny the statement had Alexis rolling her eyes.

"If you're just going to stand there like some arrogant bastard, I'll be cutting this conversation short and asking you to leave," Alexis barked, turning to make for her bed, if only so she wouldn't have to face him anymore.

He grabbed her arm once again, but she didn't try to pull from his grip this time, rather stopping in her tracks.

He leaned down to whisper in her ear, his voice sending a shiver down her spine as his breath caressed her skin, heating her core.

"See you at the Solstice Celebrations," he said, his voice sultry.

She could practically feel him smiling as her face heated, her heart pounding inside her chest. She didn't respond, didn't turn to face him as he walked from her room.

"And try to keep your arousing thoughts to a minimum. The scent you give off is very distracting."

Alexis pointed a middle finger at the door, grunting in frustration.

CHAPTER 44

Amelia found herself standing in that same clearing where she and Alexis had first displayed their magic. The darkness of night enveloped the area, the only source of light from the moon above. *Her* moon. *Her* god.

She looked at the sky, smiling.

"Hi, Brundhul," she whispered, and she could have sworn the moon glimmered in response.

A mysterious woman suddenly appeared in the shadows, her long, dark hair swaying with each step, her emerald-green eyes nearly glowing despite the near complete absence of light.

Amelia stumbled back a step, wondering who this mysterious woman could be, how she'd entered the guild without sounding any alarms, dressed like a ghost. Amelia then realised fully that she was also, somehow, in this clearing, despite having no memory of coming here tonight.

The woman stopped, holding her pale hands up.

"Calm, child. I am not here to harm you," she breathed.

Though Amelia had never seen her before, did not know who this woman was, she felt familiar, somehow. And, as if her instincts trusted this woman, Amelia's panic ceased, her nerves calming, her heartbeat slowing to a steady beat once again.

"Who are you?" Amelia asked warily as the woman neared.

She was beautiful — a unique kind of beautiful. Her skin was moonlight pale, yet she didn't appear sickly — no, she was *glowing* under the moonlight, as if the moon favoured her just as it did Amelia.

Echoing Amelia's words from moments ago, the woman looked to the sky and smiled, whispering a quiet hello to Brundhul as she appeared to soak in the moon's energy, its light.

"I am you," she offered, her soft smile unfaltering as she returned her gaze to Amelia.

"Me?" Amelia said, dumbfounded.

"Technically, we are one and the same. I was you before you. I was blessed with Brundhul's powers before you were. And now, it is your gift and burden to carry." Her eyes turned sad, and Amelia cocked her head to the side.

"I am so sorry that this has happened to you, child. Please know that I hadn't intended for this — at least, not this soon."

"What do you mean?" Amelia asked.

The woman stepped closer, and Amelia suddenly realised who the woman was, remembering the paintings around the guild.

"Princess Aurelia!" Amelia announced, bowing her head.

"There's no need for that, my dear," Aurelia said, a soft laugh escaping her lips as she lifted Amelia's head with her hand.

"How am I seeing you? Aren't you…"

"Dead? Yes, but in this world, death is not the end." Aurelia motioned to the sky, to Brundhul. "Brundhul's essence flows through us. It flowed through those chosen before me. It will flow into those chosen after you," she continued.

Aurelia held out her hands, palms facing the sky, and in a heartbeat, two balls of darkness appeared. Amelia watched the balls closely, noticing starlight in the darkness, as if Aurelia herself had summoned the night sky. She gasped, meeting Aurelia's smile.

"Can you teach me to do that?" Amelia asked, echoing Aurelia's motion, her palms now facing the sky, too.

Aurelia continued to smile, though something like sorrow filled her eyes simultaneously.

"I can — I have been. Whenever you dream, I am here, teaching you. Though, for reasons I cannot comprehend, you never seem to remember our encounters. Every time we've met in your dream state, it is as if we're meeting all over again."

Amelia cocked her head to the side in confusion. "So, I won't remember you after tonight?" she asked sadly.

Aurelia shook her head, her ebony locks swaying with the movement. She took Amelia's hands in her own, showing her how to call forth the power of Brundhul.

Summer Solstice celebrations began the second the sun arose, Alexis waking from her slumber to loud chattering and footsteps, the sound of a distant melody filling her ears.

Despite being Luzhula Blessed, she still found waking early to be a task and a half. Amelia, however, was already awake, pulling her boots on.

"Morning," Amelia chirped, not taking her eyes from the laces she was currently tying, a grin spreading across her face.

Alexis waved a lazy hand, rubbing her eyes with the other. Aspen was standing near the door, waiting impatiently to be let out, her excitement obvious with her frantic tail-wagging and foot-tapping. Alexis huffed a laugh at the image, pulling her quilt back to rise out of bed.

"What's on the agenda today?" Alexis asked, opening her armoire to find her daily clothes.

As she dressed, Amelia said, leaning back onto her elbows, "It's a holiday, so we don't have to do any work today. That is, not if we don't want to. They have celebrations here at the guild and in the city, so Yaz and I are visiting Fallandor today."

"The wards?" Alexis asked, pulling her shirt over her head.

"They're lowered today. With the celebrations, people from all over come to visit. There are extra precautions in place, triple the guards, but Yazmin says it's completely safe," Amelia said merrily, looking at her feet as she tapped them on the ground.

"But *we're* here now. I don't think they've ever been equipped to deal with outside threats while they house the *Chosen Ones*," Alexis drawled, whispering the last two words.

"Hence the third wave of guards. Usually, Rampier only *doubles* the protection," Amelia replied, not missing a beat.

Alexis just nodded, buttoning the front of her shirt.

"Care to join us in Fallandor?" Amelia asked, assisting Alexis with her braid. Alexis hummed to herself, considering the offer.

"Perhaps. Is it just you two?"

"Well, we'll extend the invitation at breakfast. I do feel bad that Zailah is still in the infirmary," Amelia said, a hint of sadness in her voice.

Turning to face her sister, Alexis said firmly, "Don't you dare let yourself feel guilty for what happened to her, Mill's. It's my fault she's blinded. You have no reason to shoulder that guilt."

Amelia looked at Alexis with soft eyes, a sad smile forming on her lips. She grabbed one of Alexis' hands and squeezed. "It's not *my* guilt I'm feeling," she whispered.

Alexis knew she didn't mean it as a jab, but she couldn't help the annoyance that flooded through her at the realisation that her sister was feeling *her* guilt, *her* sadness at the situation. Rather than arguing, though, Alexis just squeezed her sister's hand back.

"I'll consider joining you. I'd still like to get some practice in, if I can," Alexis replied, opening the door.

Amelia rolled her eyes. "Of course. Why am I not surprised?"

Alexis playfully punched her sister in the arm as they both chuckled.

Rhipley was pulling on his pants when Tatiana spoke from her spot on the bed, the sheets covering her still-naked body.

"Yaz and Amelia are headed into the city today. Think it's worth joining them?" she mumbled. Rhipley didn't turn from his spot as he buttoned his pants, searching for his shirt.

"I hadn't considered it," he replied, furrowing his brows. Finally turning to face Tatiana, he saw her dangling his shirt from her forefinger, flashing a wicked grin. He scoffed, grabbing the shirt from her and shaking his head. As she stood, the sheet falling from her body to reveal those gorgeous curves, Rhipley pulled his shirt over his head, her footsteps fading as she approached her armoire to retrieve her own clothes.

"You never told me what summoned you to my bed last night," Tatiana teased from behind.

Rhipley huffed a laugh. "I don't know what you're talking about." Tatiana rolled her eyes as she glanced sidelong at him.

"You're telling me that was just regular sex? Not destress sex or angry sex?" She tutted sarcastically as she pulled on her blue and gold tunic. The colours were absolutely radiant against her brown skin — any vibrant colour always was.

As Rhipley sat on the bed to pull on his boots, he said, "Can't I just desire a good time?"

Tatiana turned to face him fully, a doubtful expression on her face. "It wouldn't have to do with a certain golden-haired, Luzhula Blessed mortal, now, would it?" she asked slyly.

"You mean the mortal who is likely warming my best friend's bed? And his heart," he replied sharply, cringing at the obvious irritation in his words, his voice.

Tatiana appeared to catch onto that irritation as she chuckled drily.

"Take it from me. If you actually observed them for more than two seconds, you'd notice a thing or two about their supposed attraction to each other," Tatiana mumbled, tying her long, black hair into a braid.

"What do you mean?" Rhipley asked, pretending to be unfazed as he kept his eyes on his boots.

"When you're not wallowing in self-pity or escaping to my room for a distraction, take a second to pay attention," Tatiana teased, leaning down to kiss him on the cheek.

"Have you been replaced by a nicer doppelgänger? You hate Alexis," Rhipley quipped back, fiddling with his laces.

"I've come to learn that she isn't so bad. For a human, that is." Tatiana was standing before him with her arms crossed, clearly waiting for him to finish pretending to tie his already-tied laces.

"Interesting," Rhipley replied smugly. Tatiana cocked her head to the side as Rhipley rose from the bed. She held his stare as he continued. "I always knew you'd get along if you just gave her a chance."

Tatiana let out another dry chuckle as she made her way to the bedroom door, looking over her shoulder at the unmade bed. "Don't get ahead of yourself. She's Luzhula Blessed, of course she deserves my respect. I have no intention of being her new best friend, though."

Rhipley, following Tatiana's gaze, clicked a finger, and the once-messy bed made itself, appearing completely untouched. Tatiana gave an approving nod as he followed her out into the hall.

"You females are confusing," Rhipley muttered, poking Tatiana in the ribs with his elbow.

She elbowed him back as she snapped, "Don't be a sexist asshole."

The dining hall was an array of Summer Solstice decorations, various Luzhula dedicated décor spread throughout. It looked as though not a single inch of the guild had been left untouched.

Many of the hunters and students were wearing yellow and white coloured clothing, the elves and fae in particular with painted suns around an eye, on their cheek or in the middle of their forehead. Others adorned sun and star-shaped jewels, glinting in the sunlight streaming through the windows.

Even the teachers wore lighter coloured attire, Rampier wearing a particularly handsome white and yellow tunic decorated with various swirls and sun emblems. Upon noticing the presence of

Alexis, he gave a subtle nod of his head, as if acknowledging the importance of her presence, her power, in silence. She nodded back, smiling.

"This is crazy," she mumbled as she bit into her apple. She'd noticed that even the food in this world tasted so much better than back home, the flavours erupting on her tongue and filling her stomach faster, too. What she'd give to celebrate today with Sam and her dad and friends, if only they knew this celebration existed.

"It's pretty standard," Yazmin replied, shrugging as if she were used it. Though she still didn't know Yazmin's age, Alexis supposed that she probably *had* grown used to it, as she and Amelia had with Christmas or Easter.

Amelia looked at Yazmin lovingly, realising the same thing.

"What's tonight going to be like?" her sister asked, taking in the dining hall as she held Yazmin's hand.

Yazmin, rubbing her thumb over the back of Amelia's hand, replied coolly, "It's a huge party. Today is just as important as tonight. In some cities and villages, the celebrations last a week."

Amelia and Alexis shared a look of awe.
"Unfortunately, however, given our occupations, we aren't granted that privilege," Yazmin went on, huffing a sigh.

Amelia giggled, planting a light kiss on Yazmin's cheek. Alexis' heart warmed at how loved-up her sister was — something she'd never really witnessed before. Had she not previously been so self-involved, she might have noticed all the hints pointing towards her sister's sexuality. Amelia had never had a serious boyfriend, had never liked to show public displays of affection to any man she happened to be dating.
Now, with Yazmin, she was truly in her element, truly comfortable and at ease.

Sensing the presence of someone else, Alexis didn't get a chance to turn her head before Lukai planted a kiss to her cheek himself. She tried to fight the blush that rose to her cheeks — though she'd realised it wasn't from Lukai's affection, but rather the publicity of that affection. She wouldn't have minded quite so much if she didn't already know who he likely wished to show those affections to instead. But she wasn't jealous, wasn't upset. Rather just confused as to why Lukai was parading around with her when his heart so clearly belonged to another.

"Hi, you," she chuckled, struggling to meet his eyes as the memory of him in the infirmary replayed in her head.

Lukai wrapped a muscled arm around Alexis' shoulder, and he leaned in to whisper in her ear. "Today's about you, you know." Alexis cleared her throat, subtly looking around the dining hall to ensure no one had overheard.

Yazmin, tight-lipped, locked eyes with Lukai as she raised a finger to her lips, signalling for him to keep quiet.

Lukai nodded, rolling his eyes.

Alexis ignored the feeling of Lukai's attention now fixed on her again as she picked at her food, Yazmin and Amelia sliding into conversation across the table.

"So, who's excited to get drunk?" Lukai bellowed, smacking his hands on the table excitedly. Alexis found herself quietly glad that he was no longer embracing her, his attention no longer fixed on her. Seeing Lukai with Zailah yesterday shifted something within her, made her desire to continue sleeping with him cease to exist. Yazmin, in her typical fashion, grinned, raising her glass of water and replying, "Here, here!"

Lukai returned her grin, glancing between Amelia and Alexis for their confirmation.

"I don't really drink," Amelia responded quietly, heat rising in her cheeks.

Alexis gave her a nod of understanding, but Lukai simply said, "Come on, it's Summer Solstice!"

"If she doesn't want to drink, she doesn't have to," Alexis snapped. Yazmin, taken aback by Alexis' tone, hesitated before she softly echoed Alexis' words.

"You don't have to if you don't want to." She squeezed Amelia's hand as she looked into her eyes, but Amelia just smiled and mumbled, "I suppose one drink couldn't hurt."

"That's the spirit," Lukai said, seemingly ignoring Alexis' earlier retort. Ignoring, or simply having just not noticed it.

The three looked at Alexis now, their brows raised in silent question.

"I was thinking of getting some practice in, actually," she stuttered, her mouth forming a tight line as she took in their disappointed faces.

Amelia, because she wanted Alexis to celebrate, and Yazmin and Lukai, because they wanted another drinking buddy.

Alexis shrugged as she sheepishly said, "I just want to learn hand-to-hand combat. I think it would be useful, and I'll need to learn, eventually."

"You can learn tomorrow," Lukai said, his eyes begging her to change her plans.

Alexis didn't budge, though, as she said, "I'll meet you guys there later. After I find someone willing to teach me."

"Rhipley can teach you," Tatiana said as she slid onto the chair beside Alexis, smirking.

Alexis gave her a baffled look, which Tatiana pointedly ignored.

"I doubt he'd want to," Alexis mumbled, poking at her food with a fork. Rhipley appeared at the end of the table, hands in his pockets as he said, "Sure, it's not like I wanted to go drinking, anyway." Tatiana shot him a fake-innocent smile, and he gritted his teeth.

"You really don't have to teach me," Alexis replied.

Her eyes met his when he didn't respond, and she chewed on her lip before refocusing on her food.

"I'll meet you on the grounds in twenty minutes," Rhipley said, plucking a piece of fruit from Yazmin's plate.

Yazmin barked a retort that Rhipley chose to ignore, earning a chuckle from Lukai and Amelia. Alexis simply nodded, mumbling her thanks.

CHAPTER 45

After bidding farewell to their friends, Rhipley waited on the grounds for Alexis, quietly cursing Tatiana for forcing him into such an awkward position. After how smug and jealous he'd acted yesterday, he was certain Alexis wouldn't want a bar of him.

Why had he acted like that? Why *was* he acting like that?

He'd never been jealous before, had never acted out of jealousy, especially not over a female. And being jealous over his brother's girl, or whatever she was to him? Foolish.

He needed to snap out of it, get himself together. Stop acting like an ass, for his sake, and for Alexis' and Lukai's.

His thoughts once again drifted right back to Alexis.

Alexis, who was Luzhula Blessed — not that that mattered to Rhipley. No, he'd been attracted to her well before he'd found out that titbit of information. Though he'd tried to fight it, tried to deny it, he'd had an attraction to her since that first time he'd seen her, since their first encounter.

These feelings, however, were something new that he did not know how to navigate.

When he'd approached Alexis' dorm yesterday, he'd sensed the arousal before he'd even knocked.

Anyone else might have assumed it was coming from the many hunters gathered in the hallway or in their own rooms.

But *he* knew Alexis' scent, and when he'd knocked, she hadn't answered, apparently so caught up in whatever had her so aroused. Upon the second knock, he'd been just about ready to either walk away, the mature decision, or give in to his temptation to enter, purely out of curiosity. Luckily for both of them, she'd been sitting on her bed, likely daydreaming. If he'd found her in any other position, he wasn't sure he'd have been able to help himself from joining her, enjoying her himself.

However, once he'd realised the aroused thoughts were likely about his brother, he couldn't help the jealousy that rose inside him like a flame.

Pretending he didn't care or notice, pretending the thought didn't occur to him, he'd played it off, acting as that smug asshole Alexis had come to know, though he'd failed at even that.

She'd known it, too, and he wasn't quite sure how it had made her feel, whether her rapid heartbeat was out of anger or nervousness.

Now he waited for Alexis to join him.

Rhipley hadn't bothered to tell her she wouldn't learn all there was to learn in the couple of hours they'd been granted, before Yazmin would likely Realm Walk back here and drag them to Fallandor.

But Rhipley knew Alexis was smart enough to already be aware of that.

She *was* smart, and full of drive and courage. He felt stupid for underestimating her when they'd first met, but, to be fair, she *was* a meek, ordinary human. She and Amelia had both come a long way in their short time at the guild, and he couldn't help the pride that constantly burned inside him at their progress.

As he flipped one of his daggers in a hand, tossing it in the air and catching it with perfect precision, he sensed another approaching from behind. Gently sniffing the air, he didn't bother taking up a defensive position as Alexis finally approached.

He glanced over a shoulder and gave a half-smile, which Alexis returned with one of her own, mumbling, "Hey."

Sheathing his dagger, he motioned for Alexis to stand in front of him. She obliged, and as she stood before him, shifting on her feet, her eyes not meeting his, he huffed a laugh under his breath.

"What?" she asked, levelling him with an incredulous look.

Rhipley shrugged as he replied, "I'm just surprised that you'd rather stay here and practise than go drinking."

Alexis dropped his stare once more as she fumbled with her fingers, mumbling, "I still intend on joining them. But a little practice never hurt. Plus, I still have a long way to go."

Rhipley nodded in agreement, appreciating her self-awareness.

"Now, legs apart," he instructed her.

She did so, and he came around to face her side-on, correcting her stance slightly.

"Arms up," he said, giving an example with his own arms. She followed suit, and he once again corrected her stance, fiddling with her closed fists.

"This," he showed her with his own closed fist, his thumb firmly placed beneath his other fingers, "is how you want to land a punch. If your thumb is inside your palm, you'll do more damage to yourself than your opponent."

Alexis nodded, looking down at her fixed fists.

Taking up a position directly beside her, Rhipley showed her how to punch. Simple and easy. As he punched the air several times, switching arms every so often, he looked down at Alexis, signalling for her to follow his lead.

She did so, though he could tell she was certainly trying too hard, too focused on her movements being perfect. That was easy for him to think, however, given that his own movements were perfect. Though, unlike Alexis, he'd had a hundred years of practice and experience up his sleeve.

So, he trained her. Showed her how to move, how to dodge, how to land a blow. How to use her petite figure against her opponent, and how to conduct a sneak attack from behind.

Though she had a long way to go, he couldn't help but admire her willingness to learn, her desire to see this through, to make mistakes and pick herself up again.

He knew he should keep his feelings to himself, and he would, but his feelings for Alexis only resurfaced and gnawed at him the more time they spent together.

Whenever he got the chance, he found himself watching her, admiring her, pretending it was completely out of observation as her teacher whenever she'd catch him, but when she'd look away, he let slip that stone façade, let his features soften as he admired her — admired the strong woman she was becoming.

Shit.

He was in deep, deep shit.

Alexis' lesson with Rhipley had gone as well as she'd expected, and though he'd been kind about her mistakes, she'd felt like a newborn fawn — clumsy and falling over herself. Alexis couldn't help her surprise at how kind Rhipley had been, though. He hadn't once smirked or scoffed — he was completely professional, a teacher with his student.

Every touch, though, had sent shivers down her spine. Goosebumps had formed on her skin, and something heated between her legs whenever she caught him watching her with a gleam in his eye, though he'd been quick to hide it.

She could so easily melt under his gaze, under his touch, and she hated her body for betraying her, at her heart for stupidly wanting him, defying all logic.

If Rhipley had wanted her in any way, he'd have shown it. Sure, there was that strange moment of jealousy from yesterday, but Alexis had narrowed that down to Rhipley being protective of his friend, not her.

Before ending their lesson, Rhipley announced, "Alright, now show me what you've learnt. Let's spar."

Alexis couldn't help her expression of shock, as she was taken aback by the command. "You want me to practise... on you?"

Rhipley glanced around the area, that same damned smirk appearing on his face. Alexis rolled her eyes, hiding how that smirk truly made her feel.

"I don't see anyone else here?" Rhipley replied, coaxing her to approach. He stood still, though his body was relaxed, and Alexis couldn't help but feel mocked at his utter lack of defensiveness, as if he knew she wouldn't be able to take him down.

He was right, of course, but he could at least pretend to *want* to defend himself. She held up her arms, taking up the stance Rhipley had shown her, and lunged. Her punches were sloppy, but she was fast. Nowhere near fast enough to take on a fae, let alone a fae hunter, but she could certainly try.

Rhipley dodged her blows effortlessly, ducking and stepping with ease. It felt like a dance — one where she had two left feet and couldn't follow the rhythm, and where he had been dancing for years. Each move executed beautifully.

Before long, she was puffing, air escaping her as they moved around and around, her punching, him dodging. Eventually, having noticed her growing tired, Rhipley finally took on the offensive. He didn't throw a single punch, but as he stepped around her, Alexis too tired to keep track of his movements, he grabbed her from behind and tossed her to the ground.

She landed on her back in an instant, though the impact wasn't nearly as hard as she'd expected it to be.

Rhipley, seemingly showing mercy, had softened the landing by placing his arm beneath her. As she opened her eyes, she found him above her, looking into her own. He panted slightly as his eyes roamed over her face, settling on her lips.

She watched him, panting herself as her heart thundered in her chest. Whether it was due to the exercise they'd just undertaken, or that Rhipley's face was only inches from hers, she wasn't sure. Probably a combination of both.

When his eyes lifted back to her own, the corner of his mouth tugged upward.

"I quite like this position," he murmured smugly.

Alexis let out a dry laugh as she replied, "I'm sure you do."

She huffed, trying to catch her breath as she added, "You didn't show me how to do *that*. Unfair."

Rhipley laughed again. "Sorry about that."

The warmth of him encompassed her, and though she was sweating, though the sun was blazing overhead, it didn't bother her.

As Alexis tried to figure out how to escape his grip, she focused on where he had her pinned.

One of his legs was atop hers, the other settled between her thighs, only inches from...

She refocussed.

One of his hands pinned down her wrist, the other behind her back, but gripping her at the waist.

His hold loosened slightly, as if he, too, noticed her noticing where he had her pinned, and she took that as her chance to escape.

He didn't have time to react before she was turning him over and pinning him to the ground.

How she'd managed to flip Rhipley over onto his back, how she'd been able to catch him by surprise, she had no idea, but Alexis revelled in this moment, this small win.

"You're right — this is a nice position," she said breathlessly, not hiding her grin. Rhipley was looking up at her, dumbfounded, but a smile graced his own face as he realised what she'd done.

"I'm starting to like this view much, much better," he purred back, his smile turning cocky. He didn't even attempt to move, to push her off, as he lay there, staring up at her.

Alexis, puffing, found herself lost in his eyes, her smile fading as she became entranced.

Rhipley lifted a hand as Alexis' grip loosened, and he gently brushed a strand of hair from her face, tucking it behind her ear as he searched her eyes, his own turning soft.

Alexis shook herself from her trance, realising what was occurring, and stood from her spot in a hurried motion.

She offered a hand to Rhipley, and for a second, he sat there, staring at her, before shaking himself from his own stupor, accepting her hand and rising to his feet.

Alexis averted her gaze, patting herself off as she stuttered, "Well, we should probably get going before Yazmin does, indeed, come and drag us to Fallandor." She chuckled awkwardly, and though she could feel Rhipley's eyes still on her, she ignored it.

Forced herself to ignore it, to ignore *him*.

"You're going to wear that?" Rhipley asked, and Alexis finally looked to him again as she noticed him gesturing to her, her clothes.

She looked down at her now-dirty shirt, grass stains painting the white linen material.

"I suppose I should probably change," she said sheepishly, examining herself.

Rhipley clicked his fingers, and a fresh set of clothes appeared in his hands.

"Yazmin's. I'm sure she won't mind," he replied, handing them to her.

Alexis hesitantly reached for the clothes, but Rhipley pulled them just out of her reach. She furrowed her brows at him. "Give me the clothes," Alexis ordered, angling her head in confusion.

"Come and get them," he teased, before vanishing into thin air, reappearing across the field.

One hundred metres away.

"Asshole!" she yelled, and she could have sworn a faint chuckle sounded across the way.

Rhipley held the clothes up, challenging her.

"I don't know how to do that!" she yelled again, though she supposed, given his hearing, yelling probably wasn't necessary.

"Just try," he yelled back.

She huffed, her patience growing thin, but steadied herself, breathing in and out deeply as she closed her eyes and tried to focus. She remembered how she'd done it that first night, how badly she'd wanted to get away, though she hadn't been trying.

Within seconds, the world around her disappeared, and she felt as if she was falling.

Opening her eyes once more, anxiety clawing at her, Alexis stood before Rhipley before falling to the ground and throwing up.

Rhipley's hand was instantly on her back, swirling in soothing motions.

She threw up again, tears falling from her eyes as she groaned before wiping her mouth on the back of her hand.

A waterskin appeared on the ground next to her, and she didn't hesitate before drinking from it, swirling the water around and spitting it onto the ground several times.

"You're okay," Rhipley said, his voice softer than she'd ever heard it before as his hand remained on her back.

"You owe me a drink," Alexis grumbled.

He chuckled, helping her to her feet. "You did great, if it's any consolation."

Alexis shot him a doubtful glare as she said drily, "Yeah, all I did was throw up my breakfast."

As she steadied herself, she added, "Why didn't that happen the first time? Or any other time we've Realm Walked?"

"Because that was all you," Rhipley replied, his mouth curving up to one side as if he was impressed and not at all disgusted by the stench of vomit that hung in the air.

"The first time wasn't?"

"Not entirely — you hijacked the Walk, sure, but it was mostly using mine and Yazmin's power. This time, you used your own power, and *only* your power. It's sure to take a toll, especially since you're human, Luzhula Blessed or no."

Alexis sighed, turning to head for the dorms, clothes now in hand.

"Where are you going?" Rhipley asked.

"To... change?" Alexis replied, holding up the clothes as she stopped in her tracks.

"You know, it'd be faster if you just changed here."

She hesitated before turning to face him, her heartbeat quickening once more.

"So you can have a free peep show? Yeah, I don't think so."

Rhipley rolled his eyes, but there was something sensual laced in his features.
"Change by the tree. It's not like there's anyone here. Everyone's either in the city, at their places of worship, or deep within the guild, celebrating in their own ways."

Alexis levelled a glare at him. "You're here," she said sharply.

Rhipley chuckled. "I won't peek, I promise."

Alexis gave him a look that said she didn't believe him for a second, and he held up his hands innocently. "I swear I won't. I am a gentleman, after all."

Alexis chewed on her lip, considering.

Rhipley simply angled his head towards the tree, turning as he did so. She glanced between Rhipley and the tree, before deciding to take on his suggestion, refusing to take her eyes off him.

"I swear to Luzhula herself, if you so much as try to look, I *will* blind you. On purpose," Alexis called as she took in their surroundings once more, ensuring there was no one else around, and removed her clothes.

"I would expect nothing less," Rhipley called back, and she could hear the amusement in his voice.

Within minutes, she was out of her dirty, sweaty day clothes, and now found herself in a long-sleeved corset top, giving her average sized breasts a rather generous appearance, and chestnut pants with ebony-coloured boots to match.

As she struggled to tighten the laces on the back of the corset, Alexis let out a frustrated huff.

Instantly, Rhipley was at her back.

"Let me," he whispered, and she felt the breath escape her as she pulled her hair over a shoulder.

As he pulled on the laces, a small grunt escaping Alexis every time he did so, she tried not to focus on his warm, muscled body against hers, his breath on her neck. When he was finished, he remained there. Alexis turned to face him, her lips forming a tight line as she asked, "How do I look?"

Rhipley's gaze slid over her, from head to toe, ever so slowly, and she felt her blood heat.

Finally, as his eyes met hers again, he cleared his throat. "You look good."

Alexis rolled her eyes. "You're truly spectacular at giving compliments."

She noticed his own clothes — gone were the dirt and sweat crusted clothes he'd worn before, now replaced with clean ones. The same day-clothes, just more presentable.

As they began walking to the gates, Rhipley said, "Care for a drink before we go? Some liquid courage to face our likely very drunk friends?"

Alexis furrowed her brows at him in confusion.

"Rampier has a stash of some particularly old wines in his office."

"Is Rampier not here?" Alexis asked, surprised.

"Rampier likes to spend today in his own way — in solitude. It's not an easy day for him," Rhipley said softly.

Alexis knew she shouldn't pry, knew it wasn't her business, but she couldn't help wondering what could have happened on this day for Rampier to wish to remain alone while others celebrated.

As if reading her thoughts, Rhipley said, "Rampier lost his mate and child on this day many years ago. She, like him, was a hunter at this guild. Before Aurelia passed, before the mantle of Head Guild Master was bestowed upon Rampier, his mate fell pregnant with their child, and when he was born, they'd planned to quit the guild and live in peace far away from here. Somewhere in a small village within Preshia."

Alexis watched Rhipley as he spoke, waiting for him to continue. He seemed to consider for a second before adding, "But that's not my story to tell. If and when Rampier is ready to tell you, he will."

"Poor Rampier," Alexis murmured, and Rhipley nodded in agreement, letting out a sigh.

"Anyway, enough of sad stories — let's go drink," Rhipley said, holding out a hand.

"Let's," Alexis echoed, offering a grin as she placed her hand in his.

CHAPTER 46

Fallandor was alive with music, chatter, dance and Solstice festivities. Rhipley had Realm Walked them to the same spot they'd stopped at the first time the girls had visited Fallandor, only this time, the city was in full Summer Solstice festival mode.

Alexis had beamed at the sight, and it took everything inside Rhipley to not embrace her right then and there.

Their earlier training session had taken him by complete surprise; the subtle touches, the curious looks, the way she looked so beautiful and perfect beneath him, and even more so atop him.

His body had been begging for something more, begging him to rip her clothes off and say to hell with Lukai and Tatiana, as selfish as that was.

But, his brain, his moral compass, had reminded him what a stupid idea that would be, and he'd backed off, all too aware that Alexis, too, had felt it, her scent a beautiful honey cinnamon that filled his nostrils and sent his instincts into a frenzy.

His loyalty to his brother mattered more than anything, and he wouldn't throw that away. He and Lukai had never voiced it, but there was always some unspoken promise to never let a female get between them.

As he side-eyed Alexis, who was taking in all that Fallandor had to offer, he tried not to let his gaze lower to where the top of her breasts peeked over the hem of that corset.

That damned corset.

Lukai would appreciate it, Rhipley knew, and the thought sent tremors through his body, boiling his blood.

Calm, he reminded himself as he breathed in and out slowly, steadily.

"Shall we?" he asked, extending a hand toward the walkway that would lead to the main bridge into the city.

Alexis nodded, striding down the cobblestone path. She was practically shaking with excitement, and had she not been ahead of him, unable to see his face, he wouldn't have allowed himself to grin like an idiot at the woman in front of him, giddy and happy and content with this world. *His* world.

She had come to love his world, he could tell, and he realised he loved that.

Loved…

Shit, shit, shit. *Cut it out.*

Rhipley shook the thought that took him by complete surprise from his head as he followed Alexis into Fallandor.

Alexis hadn't meant to ignore Rhipley attempting to keep up with her as she practically ran into the city, but she couldn't help it. Whatever festivities she'd experienced back home, they didn't compare to this.

The city was aglow, *alive,* unlike how she'd experienced it that first day they'd come here.

As if the sun above had literally shone down and bathed the world in gold.

The people of Fallandor were, similar to those at the guild, dressed in their finest Summer Solstice attire. Yellows and whites and golds and silvers blurred her vision as she glanced around, as she tried and tried to drink down everything she was seeing.

This was all for *her,* and none of these people knew it.

Alexis didn't mind though, since she simply wished to observe and enjoy all that surrounded her without being the main attraction.

As she made to walk into a crowd gathered around something she couldn't see, a hand grabbed her wrist from behind.

She whirled around to see Rhipley pulling her back. Not to stop her from seeing what the crowd was watching, but to keep her close for safety.

Alexis offered an apologetic smile, and Rhipley just huffed a laugh, keeping a light hold on her wrist as he motioned for her to continue forward.

Finding a gap between the crowded people, Alexis ducked and dodged and squeezed her way to the front, to find what the circle beheld.

Acrobats performing in Summer Solstice themed costumes with mask-covered faces created fire illusions, the crowd letting out sounds of surprise and awe at each trick.

Though, she supposed they weren't really trick, since she guessed that those performing truly did possess magic.

Fire magic, it seemed.

Various shapes and animals and creatures were crafted from the fire, a story she couldn't quite decipher while the acrobats sprung and flipped in the background.

To finish, two of the performers joined their power and sent this world's equivalent of fireworks into the sky, the crowd cheering in triumph as the performers bowed and accepted loose change.

Making her way back into the street, Rhipley's hold on her wrist still present as he gently pushed past the plethora of revellers, they made their way down the drinking quarter, where shop owners were, once again, yelling out their menus for the day, queues and queues of citizens lining up at the stalls, looking over the Solstice styled merchandise while others roamed the streets with various glasses of alcohol in their hands, chatting and laughing away.

String music erupted around them, as if it were coming from every direction — an upbeat melody.

"They could be in any one of these taverns," Rhipley mumbled, his eyes searching for any sign of their friends.

Unfortunately, many of the guild's hunters were at each of the taverns, so using *them* as a clue was out of the question.

As Alexis followed Rhipley's lead, letting him search, she gazed up at the castle towering over the city.

"I wonder where the prince is today," she said.

"He's probably at the castle, or at a brothel," Rhipley replied blandly.

"I haven't seen him much at the guild since he arrived. Just small encounters and sightings here and there," Alexis commented, but Rhipley simply shrugged his shoulders.

"He's probably too scared to mix with us common folk too often."

Alexis chuckled, earning a side long grin from Rhipley.

Apparently having finally chosen a tavern to explore, Rhipley grabbed for her wrist again, gently pulling her towards a particularly packed bar, patrons both outside and in.

Alexis fought the urge to cover her ear with a hand at the rowdy noises coming from within, loud cheering and chatter, glasses clinking together, music bellowing throughout.

She earned a few long glances from some of the patrons, both male and female, though the second they'd eyed Rhipley, their gazes were quickly averted.

Whether it was because they'd noted his terrifying demeanour, his grip on her wrist, or if they simply knew him as the famed hunter he was, she wasn't sure.

After pushing their way through the packed tavern, Alexis apologising softly to each person who glared at them, Rhipley came to a stop, releasing her wrist and allowing her to walk around to see a large table occupied by their friends and her sister.

Amelia was holding a half-emptied glass of ale, Yazmin sporting two of her own, one on the table, the other in her free hand, her other hand wrapped tightly around Amelia's waist.

Tatiana was sitting elegantly as she watched on, a goblet of wine in her manicured hand, and Lukai appeared to be the most drunk of them all, laughing and grinning and spilling beer all over the place. Alexis chuckled awkwardly at the sight and edged past Rhipley to walk to Lukai's side. He didn't notice her at first, still talking to a hunter Alexis didn't recognise, chugging from his beer between conversations.

When Alexis gently placed her hand on his back, Lukai swung around, his eyes glassy and his face flushed red — further proof of that drunken haze.

"There's my girl!" he bellowed, and Alexis couldn't help from flinching at the roar in his voice, how loud it was in her ears.

She cringed, but Lukai didn't notice. He simply wrapped an arm around her shoulders and pulled her into him, his shirt sweaty.

"Maybe you should slow down," Alexis whispered, plastering on her best attempt at a smile. As she reached for his glass, he chuckled, angling his head and moving his beer from her grasp.

"What makes you say that?"

"You're very drunk," Alexis replied, reaching for his glass again. This time, he blushed, clearly embarrassed by his behaviour. He obliged in allowing Alexis to take his beer and gave her an apologetic smile.

"Well, would you look at that? You're a changed male," Tatiana said from across the table, watching the exchange above her goblet.

Lukai brushed off the comment, acting as though he wasn't offended by the teasing remark, but Alexis suddenly felt a rush of guilt.

"On second thought, you don't have to listen to me," she stuttered, stepping away and releasing her grasp on the beer.

Lukai's grip on her shoulder didn't loosen as he pulled her in once more, planting a sloppy kiss on her brow.

"Nonsense, you're right. I can't still be like this by tonight," he said, far too loudly.

"How was training?" Tatiana asked blandly, her eyes now on her goblet as she swirled the wine around.

Alexis forced herself not to glance in Rhipley's direction as he said, "Good. She's well on her way to being able to kick someone's ass." Alexis gave her friends, her sister, all now watching a tight-lipped smile.

Tatiana glanced between Alexis and Rhipley, and when Alexis met her stare, she couldn't read the female's expression, what she was thinking. She raised her brows in question, and Tatiana simply smirked in return.

"Well, as long as you don't lose control again. I, for one, am excited to see your progress," Lukai chirped, grinning at Rhipley, as if waiting for a witty response from his brother.

Rhipley didn't smile, didn't laugh.

He only cleared his throat uncomfortably, taking a long chug from his beer as he glanced sidelong at Alexis.

The table went silent, and Lukai, having noticed the lack of laughter at his poor joke, looked down at Alexis. "Oh, I'm sorry, I didn't mean to-"

"Forget about it," Alexis replied sharply, moving out of his grip to take up a spot next to Amelia.

"Alexis," Lukai called after her, disbelief in his voice, but she ignored him and didn't meet his stare, didn't even meet Rhipley's stare as she sat on the stool next to her sister.

"You're drinking," Alexis said more than asked, and Amelia lifted her glass to clink one of Yazmin's.

"It's my first, and only drink. Don't worry," Amelia replied, smiling. She didn't appear drunk, thankfully, and Alexis hesitantly nodded as she took a sip from her sister's glass, making a disgusted face at the bitter taste before placing it back onto the table.

Yazmin and Amelia chuckled at her reaction as the former fell back into conversation with another hunter sitting at the table.

Alexis placed her hands on the table, fiddling with a napkin and drowning out the sounds of conversation around her as she dared a glance at Rhipley. She tried not to seem taken aback when she noticed he was watching her back.

Rhipley had never wanted to throttle his brother more than he did right now. Well, apart from when they were youths, since Rhipley was too angry to get along with anyone at that time.

It had taken all his willpower to not tell Lukai to fuck off with that comment, whether he'd meant it as a joke or not.

Not only had he nearly blown Alexis' cover, but he'd hurt her, the evidence so clearly written all over her flushed face.

Now, Alexis sat only a few seats away from him, drowning out the surrounding noises, losing herself in the apparently very interesting napkin she now held.

Her nostrils flared, and her eyes turned glassy as he glanced at her. Had there not been a million people in this establishment, Rhipley might have been able to sense her emotions.

Though, he was thankful he couldn't, because if he could, nothing would be able to stop him from taking her hand and whisking her away from this bar in an instant, if only to steer the sadness from her eyes, her face.

He glanced at Lukai, who was watching Alexis, despite being in conversation with another hunter. Tommen, if he remembered correctly. Apparently, Tommen didn't care about or notice Lukai's lack of interest in whatever he was saying.

He was probably just as drunk as Lukai.

Rhipley's eyes found Tatiana, who was watching him back, a silent question in her eyes. He lightly shook his head, wordlessly telling her to keep her mouth shut.

Tatiana just smirked, taking a swig of her wine.

Tonight was going to be interesting.

CHAPTER 47

Upon returning to the guild, Alexis was still unsure of how Yazmin had managed to Realm Walk, considering how tipsy she'd been. Everyone had gone their separate ways, some muttering about needing to get ready for the Summer Solstice Hunter's Ball.

Alexis had never attended a ball before, unless she were to count her prom. Though, she was sure her senior prom wouldn't even compare to what she was sure the Hunter's Guild had in store for tonight.

Yazmin led Alexis and Amelia to her dorm — the first time Alexis had seen it, she realised. Yazmin began rummaging through her seemingly endless armoire.

Amelia was sitting on Yazmin's large bed chatting away while she and Alexis lazily watched Yazmin, anxiously waiting to see what she'd pull out.

The bed, located against the back wall where a large window sat behind it, looking out onto the Daeanimus grounds, was probably bigger than Amelia and Alexis' dorm beds combined.

A bookshelf sat to the left of it, where neatly stacked books took up the shelves, and a small table sat to the right of the bed, a lamp atop it — and some daggers, unsurprisingly.

Alexis huffed a quiet laugh at the sight, taking up a spot on the ridiculously soft bed next to Amelia.

"So I suppose the guild *does* discriminate," Alexis mumbled, running a hand over the grey quilt.

"What do you mean?" Yazmin asked without turning, comparing the two dresses she held in either hand.

"Our room certainly doesn't look like this," Alexis replied, taking in the spacious room, the bed, once again, the general space and feel and aesthetic of it all.

"Well, it's like I said on your first day here; we're the best of the best. Which means we… get the best." Yazmin practically stuttered as she voiced her reply, still not looking at the girls.

Amelia and Alexis shared a look before Amelia rose from the bed, approaching Yazmin from behind.

"Can I try that one on?" she asked, her eyes alight with excitement. Yazmin turned, holding a sparkling onyx dress in her hand, and as she looked Amelia up and down, a sly grin cast across her face.

"So much for Tatiana offering us dresses," Alexis mumbled as she scanned the dress, her legs crossed.

Amelia took the gown from Yazmin, undressing without hesitation. And, as Alexis watched Amelia undress, completely zone out, her thoughts elsewhere, she noticed Yazmin watching her sister with a predatory hunger.

Alexis blushed at the expression, and though she was truly happy for her sister, she couldn't help the awkwardness at someone being aroused over her *sister*. At her being in the same room as them.

"Well, my dresses are better," Yazmin mumbled, her eyes growing wider as she took in the sight of Amelia.

Alexis rose from the bed and made her way to the massive window, looking out to the Daeanimus grounds, where she spotted

Aspen and the wolf playing. She smiled as she watched, finding herself thankful that she wasn't fae or elf, and couldn't sense Yazmin's obvious sexual excitement.

Alexis heard a light gasp from behind, and as she turned, she beheld something unlike anything she'd ever seen before.

Her sister now wore the floor-length onyx gown bathed in shimmering starlight, the material fitting perfectly to her body. It was as if the gown had been made for Amelia, complimenting her pale freckled skin beautifully and hugging her curves, which were much more generous than what Alexis had been given.

She couldn't help her own gasp as she slowly walked towards her sister, unsure where to even look. The gown was of deepest black, sparkling like a star filled sky, the afternoon sun casting in through the window setting the shimmers alight.

"Mill's... It's perfect," Alexis murmured, finally lifting her gaze to her sister's face.

Amelia had been admiring the dress herself, speechless as she, too, came to that same realisation.

She held out a hand and willed her magic to come forth, and as she did, a small ball of black appeared in her hand. She held it against her dress and realised they were the same — as if the dress had, indeed, been made for *her*.

"Alright, where's my dress?" Alexis asked, her eyes moving to the armoire expectantly.

Yazmin's mouth slowly turned feline as she angled her head for Alexis to follow, walking towards the endless closet of fine dresses.

Rhipley stood before the floor-length mirror in his room, assessing his clothes. He'd chosen to dress in an ebony suit, the black undershirt unbuttoned towards the top to reveal a hint of his muscled chest beneath.

He hadn't bothered to style his hair, preferring the slightly ruffled look to it being combed back.

A light knock sounded at the door, and Tatiana entered a moment later, Lukai by her side, looking recovered, thankfully.

His brother wore his hair half-down, a bun atop his black hair, and he wore a similar attire to Rhipley, though in a deep-red colour. Tatiana looked stunning as ever with her long black hair fashioned into an updo atop her head, the bun styled to look messy, though he knew it'd have taken hours to fashion, no doubt.

Her royal blue and yellow skirt was accompanied by a matching top, a long piece of fabric draped over her shoulder.
The golden jewels sitting atop her fingers and wrists, running up her ears, finished with a large golden hoop through her nose, shimmered in the afternoon sun, setting her beautiful brown skin alight. That special pendant hung around her neck, the storming clouds within dancing together.

"Don't you look handsome," Tatiana said as she walked to the mirror and began fussing over her makeup, her hair.

Rhipley gave her a slight dip of his head in thanks as his eyes, once again, travelled to Lukai.

Apparently, Lukai was still feeling sorry for himself, as he made his way to Rhipley's bed without uttering a word, and sat down with a thud.

"Still sore from your earlier fuck up, Luke?" Rhipley asked, smirking.

Lukai returned the comment with a show of his middle finger.

"Do you think she's still pissed?" he asked finally, tapping his feet on the floor.

Tatiana and Rhipley shared a look before Tatiana turned and said, "You deserve it if she is."

Lukai looked up, the image of a sad pup on his handsome face. Or a defeated male who knew he'd fucked up.

"I was just trying to help. If she loses control, it could mean a total shit show for the rest of us," Lukai said of his earlier comment.

Tatiana clicked her tongue as she replied, "She will be fine. I understand your intentions come from a good place, Luke, but we will all be there.

Rampier will be there, along with the other teachers and

established hunters. *If* she were to lose control," a glare from Rhipley, "it would be handled. Plus, her magic isn't something to be afraid of."

"Tell that to Zailah who, might I remind you, is still blind," Lukai shot back.

"She's not some monster," Rhipley said sharply, watching Lukai from his reflection in the mirror.

"Her magic is dangerous, though," Lukai replied just as sharply.

"Aren't you courting Alexis?" Tatiana questioned as she raised an eyebrow.

Lukai shifted his gaze to Tatiana as he said, "Yes, but it doesn't mean I understand her magic. Perhaps if she kept a damper on it…"

"So you want her to hide who she is?" Rhipley snapped.

Lukai looked at his brother in shock, unable to find the words. "Enough," Tatiana said, stepping between the males, Rhipley looking as though he was ready to pommel Lukai if he uttered another ill word.

"You males and your fucking dominance issues."

The two looked at Tatiana, complete offence on their faces, and she simply shrugged and walked towards the door.

"Let's go get drunk," was all she said as she stepped into the hallway.

Rhipley huffed a breath, trying to remind himself that tonight was a night of peace and celebration, and if he beat the shit out of Luke, he wouldn't be able to attend or see Alexis.

Plus, Alexis would probably kill him for hurting Lukai.

Lukai, who was *courting* Alexis.

Lukai, who was his *friend*, his *brother.*

Lukai, who he *loved.*

Rhipley and Lukai shared a look, the latter hesitant as he slowly rose from the bed.

They didn't speak for long seconds before Rhipley clapped Lukai on the shoulder and grinned.

"Sorry for being an ass," he said, and Lukai grinned back as they walked from the room.

CHAPTER 48

The courtyard had come to life, with students, teachers, hunters and what looked to be some Xalentyan officials all mingling throughout. Alexis and Amelia gasped as they entered the space, somehow seemingly larger, as if the area had been altered with magic to suit the night's festivities, the large host.

Strings of lights cascaded above, stretching between the rooftops, and beautiful music filled the air.

A large staircase had appeared from the left, and Alexis shared a puzzled look with her sister, having not seen it there previously.

The magic of this world was something else, and she wasn't sure she'd ever be able to grow used to it, despite possessing magic of her own. She reminded herself to keep that magic contained and hidden, though she could feel it begging to surface, to enjoy this night made for it.

Certain hunters and students weren't in attendance, Alexis noticed, Yazmin nowhere to be seen since she'd directed them to the courtyard and had advised that she'd join them in a moment.

That had been ten minutes ago.

Perhaps she was assisting with another matter, but it didn't help with the girls' anxiety as they stood in one of the arched hallways looking out at the festivities.

Despite having been at the guild for a month now, they still hadn't really mingled with anyone other than their main friend group. They didn't know anyone else, hadn't gotten the chance to know anyone else.

Though, it wasn't like they hadn't had time to — they could have easily attempted to get to know passers-by, but no one had really approached them, either.

Alexis spotted Cook from across the way, and waved a delicate hand, smiling. Cook dipped her head, still wearing her usual attire, apparently catering even for this party. That woman never took a day off, it seemed.

"Does she ever take time off?" Amelia whispered as she, too, waved at Cook, seemingly reading Alexis' thoughts.

"Maybe she enjoys it. I mean, she's still attending," Alexis whispered back, fiddling with the fabrics of her gown.

Yazmin had placed her in a dress almost identical to Amelia's; though, this one was a rich gold colour, and the neckline, unlike Amelia's low-cut v-line, was a halter, the back of the dress cut low, revealing her entire back as it reconnected in a ruche stitching just above her backside.

She'd fallen in love with the dress instantly, insisting Yazmin tell her where she'd gotten it from, given its likeness to Amelia's.

Yazmin had simply shrugged before mumbling something Alexis couldn't interpret.

When Alexis had pushed for more information, Yazmin had shushed her, fashioning her and Amelia's hair into respective updos.

"Is there anything you *can't* do with that magic?" Amelia had asked as she'd looked herself over in the mirror.

"Many things. But, constantly using my magic for miniscule or materialistic tasks is a waste of my energy. You'd be surprised at how quickly it can be depleted."

Alexis had barely registered Yazmin's words before she'd joined Amelia in admiring herself in the mirror. She'd looked pretty before, but tonight, she was beautiful.

They both were.

Rhipley stood by the Red Oak, sipping from his wineglass as Lukai stood beside him, anxiously tapping his foot on the ground.

"You need to calm your shit," Rhipley muttered, side eyeing his brother.

Lukai huffed, searching the area for Alexis, no doubt.

Rhipley continued to sip from his glass as he, too, searched the area, the growing crowds, for any sign of Alexis or Amelia.

After a few minutes of lazily looking around, he spotted them standing in one of the hallways, completely opposite of where he and Lukai were.

Rhipley slowly lowered his glass, taken aback by Alexis' sheer beauty, her elegance. She wore her hair in a similar style to when they'd met that second time, after he'd rescued her from Dimitri, and the gown she wore…

Gods, Rhipley needed to control his thoughts, his emotions.

Half of him couldn't help admiring her; her beauty, her grace, how she literally radiated light in that gown that was practically made for her. The other half, however, wondered how easy it would be to whisk her away and rip that dress straight from her body.

Amelia, to her credit, looked just as radiant, her red hair in a low bun, the onyx dress hugging her body in all the right places, her body curvier than that of her sister's.

If no one had guessed who they were, *what* they were, they surely would upon seeing them tonight. They *were* Light and Dark, Sun and Moon. As Brundhul began cresting above, Luzhula retiring for the night, setting the sky in beautiful hues of orange and pink and yellow, there was no denying that Alexis and Amelia Rainier were, indeed, Luzhula and Brundhul Blessed.

As if in answer, Alexis' dress appeared to dim somewhat — not in a way that made it look drab, but to almost allow her sister to shine, Amelia becoming one with the night, as her dress appeared to shimmer beneath the rising moon.

Before Rhipley could notify Lukai of his lover's whereabouts, before he himself could approach her, the chatter and music halted. Rampier appeared at the top of the steps they'd had the earth-gifted fae build into the guild every Solstice. He wore a fine black suit, a sun broach clipped on the right-hand side, Zula atop his shoulder.

Holding up a glass, he announced, "Thank you to all of you who were able to attend this year's Summer Solstice celebrations. Obviously, given the recent unfortunate circumstances, celebrations for the country as a whole had to be pushed back, but we prevail, nonetheless. As we give thanks to our Goddess of Light, Luzhula, we find ourselves appreciating each new day she brings us. To Luzhula Light Bringer."

Rampier raised his glass in salute, followed by the rest of the crowd. "To Luzhula Light Bringer."

It was subtle, but Rhipley noticed Rampier's eyes slide to where Alexis now stood, out from under the hallway, holding her own glass in the air as she stared up at the Headmaster.

Her smile was radiant, and as she chuckled at something Amelia said, Rhipley found a smile casting across his own face. Rampier began announcing each royal and noble, some accompanied by their own royal dates, some alone, some accompanied by commoners.

"Princess Yazmin Solarnia of Anshara," Rampier said, and Yazmin appeared atop the steps, hand in hand with Tatiana, who Rampier announced shortly after.

Out of the corner of his eye, he noticed Amelia stumble back, gawking at her lover now descending the stairs.

Did she not know?

Had Yazmin not mentioned her royal background?

He supposed no one had, given that they were all used to it by now, and given that royal status was null and void at the guild, aside from nights like tonight. Rhipley chuckled, realising what deep shit Yazmin had gotten herself into.

"She's a princess?!" Amelia exclaimed, watching Yazmin's every step, confusion flickering in those hazel eyes.

Alexis gently grabbed her sister's hand.

"Why didn't she tell me?"

"Perhaps she didn't want you to think any differently of her?" Alexis offered, her eyes darting between her sister and Yazmin, who was now approaching them, her grin slowly fading as she spotted Amelia's less-than-happy expression.

The elf gulped, then cleared her throat as she plastered that same grin on her face again, though unlike those in the crowd watching on, Alexis knew it was out of nervousness for what awaited her.

"I can explain," Yazmin said as she walked up to them, grabbing for both of Amelia's hands, Alexis letting go of the one she held and quickly stepping aside.

"Please do," Amelia muttered back furiously, trying not to cause a scene.

The fae and elves side eyed them, able to hear the commotion, while the humans continued as they were.

"There are many princes and princesses in our country. Noble and royal households are far more common in Hyrandell, amongst elves, compared to fae and humans." Yazmin was practically blurting the words out.

"Wow, you really *do* think highly of yourselves, huh?" Alexis mumbled back, taking a sip of her wine as she shot Yazmin a sly grin. Yazmin returned it with a nervous chuckle.

"Being a princess in our culture isn't seen as important unless you're in line for the throne. We're treated as normal, otherwise," Yazmin continued, gripping Amelia's hands, a sorry expression on her face. "I'm sorry, I should have told you."

"Why didn't you?" Amelia asked, the rage slowly diminishing as she let Yazmin's words sink in.

"I was worried you'd see me differently. Whenever a lover of mine finds out about my royal status, they fawn over me, my potential wealth, and they have no desire to get to know *me*."

Amelia's eyes turned to sadness as she retracted her hands from Yazmin's grip. "I thought we'd already discussed that I'm not like your previous lovers," she mumbled.

"I know, I know! Gods, I'm sorry, I don't know what I'm saying. It's just a defence mechanism, I suppose. Please know that I'm sorry, Mill's," Yazmin said, practically begging.

Amelia's face turned soft at the use of her nickname, and she exhaled deeply as she glanced over at Alexis.

Alexis, still sipping her wine, shrugged and glanced around the courtyard.

At that moment, she spotted Rhipley standing by the Red Oak. He was watching... *her.*

She tried not to choke on her mouthful of wine as she looked back at her sister, now hugging Yazmin closely as they whispered sweet nothing's to each other.

As the announcements finally found their end, an upbeat orchestral symphony began playing from the musicians stationed toward one corner of the courtyard, and various guests cleared the way for a dancefloor, those choosing to dance approaching the space with their respective partners.

Lukai finally found Alexis as she once again looked in Rhipley's direction.

Lukai, who now stood beside Rhipley, smiled sympathetically as he spotted her.

Alexis offered a tight-lipped smile in return, turning to her sister and Yazmin as she bid them farewell and made her way to the two lurkers ogling her.

As she approached, Lukai stepped towards her before taking her into his arms and hugging her close. The embrace was so tight, she needed to remind him she was still only human.

"I can't breathe," Alexis choked out, one hand gently tapping his back. Lukai backed off, apologising as his eyes met hers.

She gave him a half smile, which he returned with a regretful one of his own.

"I'm so sorry, Lex," he blurted.

Alexis went to respond, to tell him it was fine, and she was over it, but the nickname on his tongue stopped her in her tracks.

"What did you just say?" she asked quietly.

"It's what everyone calls you, right? Rhipley does, anyway."

Alexis looked at Rhipley, who was standing a few steps behind Lukai, quietly sipping from his wineglass.

Rhipley, in his typical fashion, just brushed it off with a shrug as he continued to sip at his wine, the glass now near empty.

Repeating the words she'd said to Rhipley all those weeks ago, Alexis said, "Usually only my family calls me that."

Lukai chuckled as he took Alexis' hand, leading her to the dance floor. "Well, surely your friends and your *lover* have that privilege, too?"

Alexis laughed awkwardly, following Lukai's lead.

"I can't dance…" she whispered, anxiety coursing through her as she watched the others waltzing effortlessly.

"Just follow my lead, you'll be fine," Lukai reassured her, planting a gentle kiss upon her cheek.

Alexis couldn't help glancing back at Rhipley, who'd now been joined by Tatiana, looking as flawless and elegant as she always did.

Tatiana clinked her glass against Rhipley's, another one in her other hand. Rhipley looked at the glass, then at Tatiana, in question.

"For you," she crooned, handing it to him.

He finished his current one before swapping it with the one she'd handed him, smiling.

"Always looking out for me," Rhipley said coolly, and Tatiana just huffed a laugh before her eyes roamed to where Lukai had dragged Alexis away.

"Lost your chance again, huh?" Tatiana said in an almost amused tone.

Rhipley rolled his eyes, but he couldn't help the ache in his chest at his brother dancing with the one he wanted. Not that either of them knew, which is how it should stay.

For all Alexis knew, their brief flirtation earlier that day had been just that — a flirtation, light-hearted and meaningless.

Moments of silence passed as the two watched on, the waltz becoming faster and faster, and Tatiana tutted as she noticed Alexis stressing.

"Poor girl, did no one think to give her dancing lessons?"

"Perhaps *you* should have," Rhipley replied sarcastically, and it was Tatiana's turn to roll her eyes. She cleared her throat after a few more quiet seconds, her voice dropping a few octaves.

"We can't sleep together anymore."

Rhipley looked down at her, angling his head in confusion.
"For the first time since I've known you, for the first time in your life, you actually care for someone more than just platonically."

"I cared for you in that way at one point," Rhipley countered, earning a smile from Tatiana.

"Only because you wanted to get in my pants," Tatiana replied, raising her brows.

"Hey, you wanted to get in mine, too."

Tatiana, with a raised brow and a smile, raised her glass as if in agreement.

"I don't want to be the one who stops you from finding true happiness, Rhip. And now you have the chance for it." She angled her glass toward Alexis, whose eyes were frantically darting between her feet, Lukai, and those dancing around them.

"Tat, she has *Lukai*. My happiness doesn't matter if it means coming between his, and hers."

"Look at them and tell me you honestly think she's happy. That either of them are," Tatiana challenged as she side eyed the dance floor before returning her gaze to his.

Rhipley sighed, watching on.

Tatiana was certainly observant, because as much as Lukai couldn't take his eyes from Alexis, the same couldn't be said for his dance partner. Not only that, he could feel her anxiety.

Not happiness.

Not love.

Anxiety, nervousness and... longing.

"Besides, if we're being honest with ourselves, everyone knows who Lukai *truly* desires, but can't have, because she doesn't feel the same way," Tatiana continued, sipping from her glass nonchalantly, as if she didn't just utter some tragic gossip.

"Speaking of, have you seen her?" Rhipley asked, trying to hide the smirk from his face at what Tatiana had said, all too aware of the truth in her words.

"When we returned earlier, yes. She's weirdly content, and I thought she'd feel left out, being unable to attend tonight, but I suppose she *has* attended hundreds of these before."

"Surprise, surprise. Zailah is content with being left alone, who would have thought?" Rhipley said, not even attempting to hide the sarcasm from his voice.

Tatiana raised her glass in agreement as they both chuckled.

Rhipley turned to Tatiana, her brown eyes meeting his.

"You're truly not upset with me? Or jealous?"

Tatiana scoffed as her free hand reached for his own. "Rhipley, you're my oldest friend. My closest friend. I only want what's best for you. Besides, I still have hope that my mate is out there somewhere. I, for one, am excited to find out who it is."

"You know, you should really let others see this side of you," Rhipley replied, the corner of his lip tugging up in a smile.

Tatiana let out a dramatic gasp. "How dare you? I quite enjoy people thinking I'm a bitch. Keeps them on their toes."

She winked at him, and Rhipley couldn't help the genuine laugh that escaped him.

He side eyed the dance floor and noticed Alexis watching them, that feeling of longing growing stronger. Longing and jealousy. Something inside Rhipley felt pride and surprise at that.

Pride and surprise at her actually *feeling* something.

For *him*.

Noticing it too, Tatiana mumbled, "Told you so."

Alexis waltzed away with Lukai, trying to focus her attention on her footwork and the music and, most importantly, her dancing partner, but she couldn't help glancing Rhipley's way every-so-often, who was chatting with Tatiana while the two watched her dance.

Or, at least, attempting to dance.

She had to give Lukai credit, though, because he certainly knew what he was doing, and with each step, she found she was adjusting to the rhythm and movement slowly.

She moved with the music, the symphony in her ears coursing through her veins as the sky descended into night.

She'd guessed that the wine must have been stronger here, because her head had begun to feel heavy, her eyes becoming blurry, tipsiness slowly taking over.

Lukai spun her, and before she could understand what was happening, she was now dancing with none other than Prince Frederik.

"Your Highness," Alexis stuttered, unsure whether to continue dancing or curtsy as she begged her head to stop spinning.

"Hello, Miss Rainier," the prince replied, his voice a smooth caress. She held his gaze and begged her tipsiness not to show. Not in a moment like this.

"I feel as though I've barely seen you around," Alexis replied, trying to keep her composure as she followed his footsteps. Prince Frederik, though it came as no surprise given his royal status, was an even better dancer than Lukai had been.

"Nonsense. We've seen each other on a handful of occasions."

Alexis gave him a tight-lipped smile as she nodded, dipping her head to watch her feet.

"I didn't wish to intimidate you, so despite what my father asked of me, I've been mostly keeping to myself. My presence here is overbearing as it is, let alone if I were to be looming over everyone night and day." He offered a sincere smile, and Alexis found herself surprised at how… humble he seemed to be.

"I don't recall Rampier announcing you?" she asked, gesturing toward the stairs the other royals and nobles had descended earlier.

"I'd rather keep a low profile. Besides, I've been announced at enough of these parties. I'd rather not steal the spotlight, especially not from someone as interesting as you." He raised a brow, a silent question.

"Whatever do you mean?" Alexis asked innocently.

Leaning in, Frederik whispered in her ear, setting her skin in a frenzy of goosebumps. "Well, it is *your* party after all, is it not?"

He lingered there for a moment before pulling back, waiting for her answer.

"It's Goddess Luzhula's party, I think you mean," she replied, her voice a cool-calm.

Prince Frederik didn't speak, instead offering a nod of his head as if to say *Touché*.

"I find it hard to believe you're able to keep a low profile if you're dancing like this," Alexis continued, changing the subject, hoping he'd take the bait.

How did he know about her? And if he did, had he already informed his father?

She needed to speak with Rhipley immediately, find a way to tackle this sudden predicament.

"Well, I still love to mingle with the ladies, and there are so many fine one's here," he purred, looking around before settling on her once more. "And you do look rather divine tonight."

Alexis forced a blush to her face, though the words didn't strike the same as whenever Rhipley complimented her. If anything, it felt like Frederik was the cat, and she was the mouse. A dangerous game.

"When do you return to the palace?" Alexis asked nonchalantly, dropping his gaze to look for Rhipley.

"Well, my father, as you know, wishes for me to overlook your training, but I can see you're in excellent hands, so I don't believe my presence here is required any longer."

Alexis let out a hum, finally spotting Rhipley dancing with Tatiana across the floor.

"Besides, I don't much like acting as his personal spy. Whenever my father wishes to learn information, it's never for a good cause. I, for one, don't wish to see you used by him. Your power, your sister's power, is too great, too magnificent to fall into the hands of someone like King Mikkel."

Once again, the prince was eyeing her curiously.

"You're here to spy on us?" Alexis asked, dropping her voice to a low murmur.

Fine, she would drop the act. If he already knew, there was no point in playing coy any longer.

The prince simply shrugged before saying, "I know what you are. I know what Amelia is. But you do not need to worry. I have absolutely no interest in informing my father of your particular gifts. When I return, I will tell him you're exactly as Amity said — standard humans with little magic."

"Why?" Alexis asked, trying to calm her breathing, her thundering heartbeat.

"My father is not a good, honourable male, which I'm sure you've come to learn. If he gets his hands on you or your sister, given your power, he will do cruel things. Our continent will break into war, and I quite like how my life is, so I don't wish to see that happen anytime soon."

Alexis found herself speechless, unsure how to process the plethora of information Frederik was practically offering her on a silver platter.

"Why are you telling me this?" she asked bluntly, holding his stare.

"Because, Alexis Lightbringer, I want us to be allies. You don't know it yet, but you are extremely important, and extremely powerful. I would love nothing more than to have you on my team when it is my time to take up the throne."

Another sincere smile, and then he said, "It was a pleasure dancing with you, Miss Rainier," before spinning her in place, and as she returned to face him, she found Rhipley, instead.

"What did he want?" Rhipley asked, his face in a stone-cold expression as Alexis tried to steady her dizziness once again.

These males needed to stop spinning her before she threw up all over the dancefloor.

"He knows. About me, about Amelia," Alexis said quietly, her breathing a rapid, unsteady rhythm.

Rhipley pulled her closer, his free hand gliding to her back and tracing circles on her spine in a calming motion.

Alexis stood at his shoulder, and as he leaned down, he whispered, "You're okay. I won't let anyone harm you."

Alexis didn't speak as she tried to slow her breathing, watching Tatiana now dancing with Lukai, chatting away as they moved.

"He says he wants to be our ally," Alexis muttered, closing her eyes and inhaling through her nostrils, then exhaling out through her mouth.

"He says his father will do cruel things to the continent if he has our power at his disposal. That he will use us as weapons."

Another inhale and exhale.

She pulled back to face Rhipley, looking into his chocolate eyes. His face was solemn now, the coldness completely replaced.

"Rhipley, someone like that shouldn't be on a throne, let alone in that kind of position of power."

Rhipley nodded and said, "I know. Hopefully, once he passes his crown onto Frederik, his son will be a better king. The king this country needs." His words were soft, but his eyes held doubt, like he didn't believe the words he was saying.

"Do you trust him?" Alexis asked, holding his gaze.

"Gods, no. I don't trust anyone outside of this guild."

"So, what do we do? He knows, Rhipley. What if he tells his father? Or sells the information to someone who would kill for it? For us?"

"Yazmin and I will inform Rampier, and he can decide what our next course of action will be." Rhipley slowly grazed his fingers up her spine, and the movement made her blood heat. The gentleness, the softness. So unlike that warrior she'd met a month ago. So unlike the cool façade he paraded around in.

"I'm sorry for how I've treated you in the past. I clearly underestimated you, and I shouldn't have. You're special, Lex."

Her heart tightened at his use of her nickname, and then the wine began to *really* kick in.

"Is it only now that I'm Luzhula Blessed that you feel the need to apologise?" She angled her head, waiting for his reply. Though she said it with sarcasm, she was still half-serious.

"No, of course not. I realised it before your powers came to light, literally. I'm just… not good at letting people in."

"I've noticed," Alexis said, smirking.

He half-smiled back, and they didn't speak for a few moments as they continued to dance and stare into each other's eyes.

"I suppose I forgive-" Her words were cut off as she heard a sharp ringing in her head, and she brought her hands to cup her temples, a sharp pain coursing through her brain.

Your loved ones are in danger, Alexis! Heed my warning. You must-

"Aurelia?" Alexis said, and she hadn't realised she'd voiced the name aloud until she noticed Rhipley looking at her, confusion on his face. He was speaking, but she couldn't hear him as another's voice filled her mind.

Hello, child. I have finally found you after all these years.

The voice was cold, like a snake given human tongue.

"Aurelia?" Alexis said again, unsure of who that second voice belonged to, wondered if it were behind the force constantly interrupting her dreams these past weeks.

As she gripped her head, groaning against the pain, she felt Rhipley's hands on her own, and as she looked up, she found him staring down at her, genuine fear in his eyes.

Tatiana was by her side in a heartbeat.

"We need to get her away from prying eyes."

Trying to stand straight once more, Rhipley taking her against him, Alexis glanced around the party and noticed there were, in fact, people staring, murmuring. She felt Tatiana's hand resting atop her shoulder, and as Alexis slid her gaze to the female, she found Tatiana staring back with what could only be described as sympathy and worry.

A look she hadn't once seen the female give anyone other than Rhipley.

They hurriedly exited the dance floor, the music continuing as some resumed their dancing, some continued to chat amongst themselves, and some continued to watch her, their eyes wide. The fae, the elves — those with heightened hearing would have heard what she'd said. There was no mistaking it.

Alexis looked ahead as Rhipley mumbled, "I suppose it's going to be far more difficult to keep your identity a secret, now."

Tatiana hummed her agreement as she left Alexis' side, walking to one of the refreshment tables, and grabbed a glass of water, handing it to Alexis.

"Thank you," Alexis said softly, gulping down the liquid as she gave Tatiana a sincere smile. Tatiana's lips twitched upwards ever-so-slightly in
acknowledgement, understanding.

"Where's Amelia?" Alexis asked, searching the premises. She hadn't seen or heard Amelia or Yazmin since she'd left their sides to speak with Lukai and Rhipley. In fact, where was Lukai? As if reading her thoughts, Tatiana said, "Lukai left a few minutes before you went down. He didn't say where he was going, just that he had to check on something."

"Zailah?" Rhipley asked, and Tatiana shrugged.

"Probably."

Alexis weighed their words, realising what it meant. Realising that it confirmed what she'd known all along.

"I saw Yazmin drag Amelia off towards the dorms. One can only guess what for," Tatiana continued, rolling her eyes.

"Yazmin can't keep her hands off of your sister, it seems," Rhipley offered, trying to lighten the situation.

Alexis simply huffed a dry laugh, trying to figure out what had happened just now.

"The prince watches," Tatiana warned, and Alexis didn't dare look for confirmation.

Rhipley side eyed the dance floor and returned his gaze to Tatiana just as quickly before nodding.

"Take care of her while I take care of this," he ordered Tatiana, subtly gripping Alexis' arm as if to say *It'll be okay,* before striding towards where, Alexis could only guess, the prince stood.

CHAPTER 49

Rhipley approached Prince Frederik's side, where he was now standing on the edge of the dancefloor, sipping on his wine and watching on as the partygoers danced in time to the music.

He lowered the glass and dipped his head as he eyed Rhipley, Rhipley bowing deeply in return.

"Your Majesty," he said smoothly, taking up a spot beside the prince.

"Hunter," the prince said in return, side eyeing Rhipley as he, too, sipped from his glass he'd just retrieved from a servant making the rounds with a tray of wines and other beverages.

"Are you enjoying the festivities? I'm sure they don't compare to what you're used to at the palace, but we certainly try our best," Rhipley stated coolly, one hand in his pocket.

Prince Frederik huffed a chuckle. "It's quite splendid, indeed. I find that I prefer the less extravagant manner in which the guild throws its parties in comparison to those held at our castle. I don't believe I've ever mingled with so many elves or humans. Usually, my father prefers to only invite the most elite of humans, fae and demi-fae. This is quite refreshing."

Rhipley hummed before saying, "Yes, well, we at the Hunter's Guild like to think that we don't discriminate."

Frederik huffed another laugh, not missing the jab, and they stood in silence for some time, sipping at their glasses.

Rhipley dared to slide his gaze to where Tatiana and Alexis still stood by the refreshment table, chatting away about gods knew what, a hint of a smile tugging at Tatiana's lips every so often as Alexis appeared to be recovered, the wine starting to take effect.

Rhipley dared his own half-smile at that, at the realisation that he was correct in his assumption that Tatiana and Alexis could be friends if they tried.

Prince Frederik, apparently having followed Rhipley's gaze, said, "She's rather magnificent, isn't she?"

"Lady Tatiana Elrin, Your Highness?" Rhipley played it cool, pretending to be clueless.

The prince side eyed Rhipley this time, a sly smile grazing his lips. "I think we both know who I'm referring to."
He took a long drink from his glass, continuing to watch Rhipley for any kind of reaction.
Rhipley dared to step close to the prince, monitoring his personal guard standing close by, their hands subtly inching closer to their swords as they watched the interaction.

Whispering in Frederik's ear, Rhipley asked, "And what do *you* know of Alexis Rainier?"

The prince's smile remained as he whispered back, "I know she's Luzhula Blessed. I know she wields the gift of light, that the sun itself shines within her. That Luzhula's very magic runs through her blood. And, I know the same applies to her sister. That she is Brundhul Blessed."

Rhipley pulled back to study the prince's face, to see if he could uncover any hint of betrayal lingering beneath the surface. Rhipley had to give credit to Frederik, admitting to himself that he'd have made a fine hunter, for his face revealed nothing.

"Should we expect your father's forces to grace our doorstep in the coming days, then?" Rhipley held his stare, promising a world of hurt should Frederik threaten this guild, his home.

The prince smiled, though there was nothing sly in it this time, but something of understanding.

"My father will not find out. Not if I can help it."

Rhipley kept quiet, furrowing his brows as he waited for the Prince to continue, his patience wearing thin.

When the prince simply shrugged, returning his gaze to Alexis, Rhipley said gruffly, "What's in it for you?"

"It's as I told Alexis — I wish only for us to be allies. The throne will be mine soon enough, and anyone with half a brain knows there is no good use in making enemies of the Hunter's Guild."

He looked over his shoulder at his guards, their hands still resting atop their swords.

"I assume just one of you could take down at least twenty of my best guards?"

Rhipley didn't confirm nor deny the claim, but it seemed that his silence was answer enough for the prince.

"I know you have no reason to trust me, but believe me when I say that a war amongst ourselves is the last thing I want. I hope that when the time comes for me to take up the throne and succeed my father, I can count on your guild's backing."

The prince's face was serious now, nothing mocking or cunning in his expression. Rhipley continued to stare at him, then eyed his guards once more, before turning back to face the dancefloor. He dipped his head, his only acknowledgement of what Frederik had said.

As Rhipley watched Alexis — admired, really — Frederik spoke again.

"I hope you know I do not say this to judge you, or to insult you, but that woman is a goddess amongst us."

Rhipley exhaled slowly, preparing himself for what the prince was about to say.

"Someone of her stature will not settle for a hunter. No matter how much you pine after her, no matter how often you dare to glance her way, no matter how you feel for her, even *you* must understand that." Frederik turned to face Rhipley, clapping him on the shoulder before bidding him farewell, disappearing into the crowd.

The words cut deep, despite whether Frederik had meant for them to or whether it was a simple observation. Rhipley couldn't help the deep pain in his chest, though his face didn't falter as he watched Alexis, now laughing away at something Tatiana had said, and he came to the same realisation as the prince.

Someone like him could never deserve her. She *was* a goddess in her own regard, and he was an orphaned hunter. Granted, he had the rare gift to Realm Walk, but that paled in comparison to her power. Alexis sighted him across the floor and smiled, and the beauty in that smile tore something in his chest open.

He smiled back, pretending he hadn't just realised that Frederik was completely and utterly correct.

Alexis would always, *always,* be out of his league, and he would never deserve her.

Alexis had convinced herself that Tatiana was finally warming up to her, though it may have just been the effects of the alcohol.

The female was actually smiling genuinely at the nonsense Alexis had been blathering on about, even if they were only half-smiles at best.

"I really love your sari," Alexis said, offering her most sincere smile to Tatiana, who angled her head in confusion.

"What you're wearing — it's similar to what we call a sari in…" Alexis didn't finish her sentence, all too aware of who might be listening.

Tatiana quirked her lips to the side as she considered.

"Sari… I like it," she said coolly, offering Alexis a half-smile as she sipped from her wine.

Suddenly, Amelia and Yazmin approached, her sister holding one hand against her head, the other interlaced with Yazmin's arm.

"Are you okay?" they both asked in unison, and Alexis placed her glass down to embrace her sister, to look her over.

"You heard it too?" Amelia asked once Alexis had searched her over.

"Yes, but I only recognised Aurelia's voice."

Amelia furrowed her brows. "You recognised Aurelia's voice? How?"

"Because... I've been seeing her. In my dreams, since we arrived. I've always seen her out of the corner of my eye — a shadow, as if someone were standing there, but I could never see her clearly until we came to this world."

Alexis glanced around the group, the women staring at her with stunned looks on their faces.

"You never thought to mention this?" Amelia asked, a sharpness in her voice that Alexis had so rarely heard before.

"I didn't know how to, if it meant anything... *what* it meant." She cast apologetic eyes on her sister, who simply crossed her arms.

"So, which one was Aurelia, then?" Amelia asked, watching Alexis, who now crinkled the fabrics of her dress in her hands nervously.

"The voice who warned us. I don't know who the other voice belonged to, though."

"What did Aurelia say?" Yazmin cut in, holding Amelia close.

"She said our loved ones are in danger, but I don't understand what she..." Alexis trailed off before realising what it meant — *who* it meant.

"Sam and dad!" Amelia and Alexis gasped in unison.

Tatiana hushed them, subtly referencing the surrounding crowd, fae and elves now watching as they had before, their hearing able to pick up even the quietest of noises. Humans, it appeared, also looked on, though anyone with even the poorest of hearing would have been able to hear the outburst.

"We must take this information to Rampier, if it is to be believed," Yazmin said in a low voice, locking eyes with Tatiana, who simply nodded, signalling for Rhipley to re-join them.

In a few heartbeats, Rhipley was at Alexis' side, his hand lightly brushing against her back, before he quickly removed it, as if scared to touch her.

Alexis angled her head in silent question, but Rhipley wouldn't meet her stare.

Sighting their Headmaster, Rhipley and Yazmin made their way to him, Yazmin quietly instructing Tatiana to take the girls to their dorm.

Before Alexis could protest, Tatiana was hauling the sisters out of the party, her arms linked through theirs — putting on a façade that they were simply three friends retiring for the night, hiding the urgency behind the movement, the situation.

Amelia sat on her bed as she watched Alexis pace back and forth, her eyes often glancing toward the window, as if she could see all the way to Earth.

Her sister's nervous tick had gotten worse since they'd realised who might be in danger, as she crinkled and folded the fabrics of her dress in her hands over and over. Alexis was biting her lip as her eyes darted between the floor and the window, as she'd been doing since they'd returned to the dorm.

Tatiana had instructed them to sit tight until news came of what had happened, if anything had happened. She wasn't sure what the plan was, what Rampier might decide, and clearly Alexis wasn't sure, either, and it was very evidently eating away at her.

"Why do you think I don't see her? Why I've never seen her?" Amelia asked as her eyes followed Alexis' pacing.

Her sister side eyed her as she asked, "What do you mean?"

"Aurelia, why don't I see her like you do?"

Alexis either didn't care for the conversation, or found the question to be bothersome, because she replied curtly, "I don't know."

Amelia sat still, quiet, for minutes as Alexis continued to pace. They'd retrieved Aspen on their way back to their room, and the dog was just as agitated as Alexis, whining softly and watching her companion with worried eyes. Daeanimus indeed — the two were definitely emotionally connected.

"Why didn't you tell me?" Amelia finally asked.

Alexis looked at her fully this time, stopping in her tracks.

"Because I didn't know what the dreams meant. I didn't know if it was a blessing or a curse that I was being visited by the dead princess and former Headmaster. And… I didn't want you to feel like you were being left out, like you weren't special or something."
Alexis quirked her mouth to the side as she waited for Amelia to speak. Amelia just watched her sister, blank faced, unsure what to say or how to react.
She didn't want to think about anything negatively right now, didn't want to even dwell on the fact that her family might be in danger, if Aurelia was to be believed. She knew she should worry, but she and Alexis were different.

Where Alexis panicked, Amelia usually became non-verbal, non-responsive, tried not to think about it, let it consume her whole.

So, rather than asking about Sam and their dad, Amelia chose to instead focus on this topic, much to Alexis' dismay.
"It certainly hurts, wondering why my predecessor doesn't visit my dreams, but I'm sure there's some kind of explanation. What hurt the most, though, was that you kept it from me. I'd prefer your honesty always, no matter how much you might think it will affect me." Amelia allowed her features to form into something of understanding, something soft, to let her sister know she was no longer pissed. When Alexis had informed her earlier of Aurelia's true origins, that she was the previous Brundhul Blessed, Amelia was shocked, surprised, unsure what to do with the information, if it even made any difference to her.

Alexis approached the bed before sitting down. Relief coursed through Amelia as she realised her attempt at distracting herself had also worked on Alexis, for the time being.

"Would you like me to ask her? If I see her again?" Alexis offered, her hand sliding to cup Amelia's.

Amelia smiled at her sister, placing her other hand atop Alexis'.

"Sure, why not? I, for one, would like to know why she has chosen not to see me."

Alexis chuckled.

"Can you summon her at will?" Amelia asked, tilting her head as she pictured it, the image of Alexis calling forth Aurelia as if she were summoning a demon or ghost at a seance making her chuckle.

"No, certainly not. If anything, she summons me. I haven't seen her for some time, though. Tonight was the first she's spoken to me in days."

Amelia hummed in curiosity, wondering why that was as she leaned over, resting her head atop Alexis' shoulder. Aspen hopped off the bed and approached them, nuzzling against their legs.

"So, what did you two sneak off for, anyway?" Alexis asked, and Amelia could hear the mischief in her voice as she bit her lip, trying not to think about what she and Yazmin had been doing only moments ago.

"We... may have... slept together," Amelia murmured, images of what they'd done, of Yazmin atop her, then between her legs, looking up at Amelia as she writhed with pleasure flashing through her mind.

"Wait, what?" Alexis gasped, pulling back to face Amelia fully. Amelia couldn't help the blush that rose to her face.

"Yeah, we did."

Alexis was speechless, words completely escaping her as she gaped at Amelia.

"How was it?" she finally managed to ask.

"It was... good. *Really* good." Amelia smiled, trying to shove the thoughts from her mind. How she'd completely given herself to Yazmin. How Yazmin had worshipped her.

"And you were ready? I know you said you wanted to take things slow with her... but that's a big move." Alexis tilted her head in question.

"I know, but tonight just seemed right. I don't know if it was the dress, how it made me feel, how it made *her* feel, or if I just realised I was ready to give myself to her completely. Something just changed, and she was respectful and didn't push me."

When Amelia had finished explaining, Alexis chuckled in disbelief before embracing her.

"I'm glad you're happy," Alexis murmured.

Amelia nodded before retracting from the hug, shaking her head, surprised at herself — at how *she'd* been the one to suggest she and Yazmin go all the way, that *she'd* been the one to initiate it.

Then, when they'd found themselves tangled together, naked beneath the sheets, staring at each other as Yazmin ran her fingers through Amelia's undone hair — which, to Amelia's amusement, had been re-done with a wave of Yazmin's hand only minutes later — the voices, the headache, had interrupted their moment together, Yazmin practically jumping out of bed to look for the nearest healer.

Suddenly, interrupting her thoughts, a knock sounded at their window.

Alexis and Amelia jumped from the bed in unison at the thud that had sounded against the window just seconds ago.

"What was that?" Alexis whispered to Amelia, her sister shrugging her shaking shoulders as she folded her arms, her hazel eyes full of terror.

Alexis signalled towards the window, questioning if she should approach, Amelia clearly too afraid.

Amelia shook her head, her eyes growing wider. Another thud filled the room, and Alexis jumped once more, Aspen now growling low at whatever — or whoever — was outside, making that noise.

"Stay here," Alexis whispered, inching closer toward the window. Amelia reached for her, but Alexis stepped away from her grasp, crouching low as she approached the window.

Slowly raising her head to peer outside, she noticed nothing at first — nothing but the illumination of the festivities from the courtyard, and... a dark figure standing amongst the trees.

Her blood chilled as she ducked down, hiding from the person's view. Another thud reverberated against the window, and she flinched, the sound so much louder now that she was mere inches away from the glass, genuinely surprised that whatever was knocking against it hadn't yet shattered the window.

Suddenly, she heard a faint voice calling her name — a male voice. As the figure called her name again, she realised who the voice belonged to as she raised herself up, looking out the window ever so slightly, to see that the figure, now stepping into the light being cast across the grassy space, was Lukai.

Alexis exhaled a breath of relief, grateful that it was friend rather than foe, her thundering heartbeat slowing with each passing second.

Standing to her full height, Alexis pulled the window up, opening it to lean out. She glanced over a shoulder at Amelia, now cuddling Aspen close, and mouthed the word *Lukai*.

Amelia quite literally sagged with relief, though didn't loosen her grip on Aspen.

The Daeanimus bond Alexis shared with Aspen showed, as the dog also appeared to relax. Facing Lukai once more, Alexis said, her voice as quiet as she could muster, whilst also projecting it enough that Lukai could hear her, "What do you want?"

The words came out sharper than she'd intended, but Lukai hadn't missed the tone, stepping back a bit in surprise.

"I came to check on you. Can we talk?"

Even from this distance, Alexis could see the sincerity on his face.

She contemplated for a moment, quirking her mouth to the side. After a few long seconds, she nodded slightly before retreating back through the window, closing it and turning to her sister.

"I need to go speak with him," she whispered, making her way to the bedroom door.

"Lex, we're supposed to stay here." Amelia's face was grave as she gripped Alexis' wrist, pleading in her eyes, on her face.

"It won't take long, I promise." Alexis offered a soft smile, but the worry didn't vanish from her sister's face. Amelia hesitantly let go of her wrist, warning Alexis to return as soon as possible.

Opening the door slowly, Alexis peered into the hall, checking for safe measure that no one — especially no one unexpected — was lurking nearby. Once she'd deemed the area safe, she stepped into the hallway, her movements quiet and careful.

The festivities outside masked her footsteps, the sounds they might have made, but Alexis still listened for anyone who might approach, her eyes roaming up and down the hallway.

The faint sounds of moaning and a bed creaking crept into her ears, and she tried to hide the smile at what she knew other hunters had snuck from the party to do.

Finally making it out of the dorms and into the gardens, she made eye contact with Lukai, who was leaning against a tree, deep in thought.

"Hi," Alexis said as she approached him, no longer on high alert.

"Hey," he returned, his eyes sad, apologetic.

"Where did you disappear off to?" Alexis asked, choosing to avoid any small talk. She already knew, but wanted to see what he might say, what excuses he might make. Not that he owed her anything, really, but if she could finally get him to admit that he was only messing around with her to avoid his hurt at Zailah's rejection, she could finally move on from him.

"I went to check on Zailah. Is that okay with you?" There was no hint of defensiveness in his tone, only calm.

"Of course, it's okay. I just wish you'd said something." Alexis let out a sigh, leaning against the other side of the tree.

"I'm sorry… I honestly thought you'd be too busy to notice. You were enjoying yourself, and it was only supposed to be for a moment…" He trailed off, exhaling deeply.

"How is she?" Alexis asked, not wanting to start any drama over it.

"She's as best as she can be. Surprisingly still chipper, though it's typical Zailah. She wouldn't let something like this, being left out of this annual party, get her down."

"Chipper? Are we talking about the same female?" Alexis asked sarcastically, and Lukai chuckled.

"She has a side to her she won't let anyone see."

"Anyone except you." Alexis let the statement hang in the air. Let Lukai realise what she already knew.

"Lex…" She heard him turn to face her, felt his body shift towards her as she angled her head to look up at him.

"Luke, it's fine, really. I think we both know that this," she angled her index finger between them, "was purely physical. You're a great guy, and I appreciate having you as my friend. I appreciate the fun we shared, but it shouldn't be at the expense of your feelings for her."

"You're not mad?" he asked softly.

God, even in almost-complete darkness, his golden eyes still shone so brightly.

"I'm seriously fine. I think we'd be better off as strictly friends, anyway." She offered a warm, sincere smile, pushing off the tree to face him.

"I think I'd appreciate that," Lukai said, smiling back.

Alexis offered Lukai her hand for him to shake. Lukai looked down at the offering before pulling her into a hug. She huffed a laugh against his broad chest, wrapping her own arms around him.

"Are you okay, though? I heard you went down, that something happened?" He pulled back, examining her face, her body.

"It's a long story. Rhipley, Yazmin and Headmaster Draghone are investigating it now. Until they have answers, Amelia and I have been told to hang tight."

She shrugged her shoulders, linking arms with Lukai as they walked back towards the dorms.

CHAPTER 50

"I need you both to go to the Mortal Realm," Rampier said gravely as he rounded the corner of his desk, taking up his seat. Yazmin and Rhipley shared a glance before Rhipley spoke up.

"Headmaster, are you sure? I understand that the Rainier sisters were warned by… Aurelia," he tiptoed over the name, swallowing as he noticed Rampier ever so slightly flinch, "But, how can we know for sure that she was referring to their family?"

Rampier gave Rhipley a doubtful look over the rim of his glasses. "Who else would she have been referring to?"

The room went silent, and Rhipley could feel Yazmin watching him, waiting for an answer.

"I understand, Headmaster. When would you like us to leave?"

"As soon as you possibly can. I have sensed no danger as of yet, but that could change in a matter of moments if Aurelia's premonition is accurate."

Rampier rested his chin on his closed fists, his eyes going vacant as he appeared to ponder.

"Gods bless Aurelia, and, of course, rest her soul, but I truly do wish she'd given either of the girls a timeline," Yazmin remarked, exhaling. Rhipley threw her an incredulous look, to which she simply shrugged at.

"There must be a reason she warned Alexis and Amelia. Had they mentioned seeing her before tonight?" Rampier asked, his eyes still vacant.

"No, tonight was the first we'd heard of it. Given that Aurelia was the previous Dark Bringer, it would make sense that she could be guiding the girls." Rhipley contemplated it, shifting on his feet.

"But she hasn't been visiting Amelia? At least, that we know of. Wouldn't it make more sense for her to visit her successor, rather than V-"

"Do not speak that name, Yazmin," Rampier cut in, cutting stern eyes to Yazmin, who ceased her talking, standing to attention once more.

Rampier waved a dismissive hand, raising the other to stroke Zula's chin, the owl perched atop Rampier's chair in her usual spot, watching the two hunters like a guard dog.

Rhipley and Yazmin shared another glance before taking each other's hands and Realm Walking to the Mortal Realm.

Alexis, to her surprise, had slept like a log, though Aurelia hadn't visited her, the female seemingly disappearing once more after her warning the previous night.

"Why don't I have a Daeanimus? I love animals," Amelia sulked as she watched Aspen and the wolf play, Aspen chasing the wolf around and around.

"I'm sure you'll find one. It's probably by happenstance that Aspen was mine — I doubt it's a common occurrence," Alexis replied, smiling as she watched Aspen wag her tail, the happiness coursing down the bond they shared.

"She has to be your Daeanimus for a reason, though, right? Like, what is a Daeanimus?" Amelia asked, tilting her head.

"Well, Lukai said they're a companion, sort of like how fae and elves have mates — it's a bond. Perhaps coming here, to Xalentya, has opened that bond up for us. With each passing day, I feel more of what Aspen feels, and vice versa, I'd assume. It's not all the time, but it's certainly becoming more evident, more common. Like, when Aspen is grumpy, I'm grumpy. Or, when I'm sad or stressed, so is she. I've been meaning to read up on it..." Alexis trailed off, quirking her mouth to the side.

Amelia let out a "Hmmm," as they continued to watch the two canines play.

"Do you think she has access to your power? Or can she help strengthen it?" Amelia asked, glancing at Alexis, anticipation on her face.

"I... never really thought of that. I know hunters here use their Daeanimus' on missions sometimes, but I know little about sharing power. They can share life spans, which is pretty cool. But..." Alexis looked down at her hands, then looked up at Aspen, who'd halted her playing to watch Alexis, as if sensing her thoughts.

Alexis inhaled a deep breath before closing her eyes and calling forth her power.

She needed only a drop for what she wanted to try.

She felt the power course through her veins, light up her blood, and when she opened her eyes, little balls of light danced at her fingertips.

She raised her gaze to Aspen, whose eyes were now glowing golden.

"Holy shit," Alexis murmured, looking over at her sister, whose face was in complete shock.

"Lex, your eyes..." Amelia touched her own face, her fingers lightly grazing just below her eyes, as if the movement would convey what her lack of words couldn't.

Though she saw the world as normal, though nothing looked different, Alexis knew what Amelia beheld.

Just as quickly as it had happened, Aspen's eyes returned to their normal chocolate brown, Alexis', presumably doing the same. The wolf watched Aspen closely, carefully, sniffing her at a distance.

Amelia and Alexis watched each other before smiling and laughing. "That's so cool!" Alexis exclaimed.

Once Aspen and the wolf had resumed playing, the use of the magic seemingly tiring Aspen somewhat, Alexis brought her legs up to her chest.

"I don't think I could ever take Aspen on a mission," Alexis finally said, her voice quiet. "I couldn't forgive myself if she were to get hurt, or worse. I don't know how anyone could do it."

She felt Amelia watching her from the corner of her eye, her sister silent. After a few moments, she felt Amelia's hand on her shoulder — a comforting touch.

"Maybe she will become more durable, like you. There's a reason hunters take their Daeanimus' with them. Maybe she's not as breakable as you'd think." The words were soft, meant not as pressure, but as encouragement, consideration.

"Maybe," Alexis murmured.

"*Maybe* you could include her in your training lessons. The physical attack and defence ones, I mean," Amelia said cheerily.

"Well, I don't think she'd be very good at reading, or dancing, or curtseying," Alexis replied sarcastically, and Amelia snorted.

"What do you mean? I bet Aspen would make our curtsies look terrible!"

Alexis began laughing at that.

She contemplated the suggestion, realising that if she were to become a hunter someday, it might not hurt. Perhaps taking Aspen on missions — the less dangerous missions — wouldn't be a bad idea.

Besides, she needed a distraction. She'd spent last night, before she'd confronted Lukai, stressing about Aurelia's warning, not that there was much *she* could do about it. Tatiana had informed them that Yazmin and Rhipley had gone to their world, just to be safe, though even *they* doubted Sam and her dad were in danger, especially since Rampier had sensed no danger.

But, Aurelia had said it for a reason, and if she wasn't talking about Alexis' family... She didn't want to think about her friends, the students and hunters and teachers, this new home she'd come to love, being in danger. All because of her, because of this power she was given, for gods knew whatever reason.

So, she'd find Lukai and ask that he train her and Aspen, in whatever way he could. If it could help, even in the slightest, she wanted to do it.

Yazmin and Rhipley arrived on Earth, right in that same forest they'd appeared in on that night over a month ago. Immediately, they smelled the blood, sensed the carnage.

"Shit," Rhipley swore, making a run for the Rainier house.

He couldn't see anything out of the ordinary, but as he and Yazmin approached the back of the house, the smell grew stronger.

A coppery tang filled their noses, like the blood was fresh. As they circled the house, each taking one side, Rhipley neared the front of the house, and saw the cause behind the smell.

Blood soaked the driveway, the deck, the front door. The bottom half of a man's body lay in the middle of it all, the top end nowhere to be seen, as if whoever — whatever — had done this, had taken their time, enjoyed it, the flesh so messily torn.

"What the fuck happened here?" Yazmin asked, her eyes dancing around the area, as if trying to comprehend the events that had taken place. Mere moments before they'd arrived, apparently.

Rhipley shook his head, walking to where the bottom half of the body lay, so much gore he didn't know where to look.

"Who is this?" he asked no one in particular.

Suddenly, the front door opened, and a young man emerged, completely dazed. His eyes were glazed over, as if he were sleep walking, completely unaware of what lay before him. Yazmin was at his back in an instant, her fae speed covering the distance in seconds. She looked him over, retrieving her dagger.

"Who are you?" she asked, that usual nonchalant demeanour completely replaced by cold ice.

The man appeared to awaken, his eyes quickly focusing on Yazmin's hand clasped on his arm, then on the dagger she now held to his throat. He swallowed, his wide eyes now searching the bloody area, Rhipley with Wraith drawn, the half-eaten body splayed on the driveway. He opened his mouth to scream, but Yazmin's dagger pressed even harder against his throat, stopping him as it drew blood. He began to urinate — a typical human response.

Rhipley neared the deck, slowly ascending the steps, his eyes wholly on the stranger.

"Who are you?" he asked, echoing Yazmin's words from just moments ago. Tears began to well in the man's eyes, and Rhipley forced himself to ignore the potent smell of urine. Forced his eyes away from the evidence.

"I-I'm M-M-Mitchell," the man stuttered, his words barely audible.

"Mitchell?" Rhipley mumbled, thinking to himself, wondering where he'd heard the name before. Suddenly, his eyes darted to Yazmin's, who still held the dagger to his throat, her eyes watching Mitchell, making the human completely aware that all it would take to make him fall was one easy swipe.

"Yaz, lower the dagger," Rhipley ordered, though he didn't sheath his sword as he listened for any other company they might still have.

Yazmin hesitantly lowered her dagger, refusing to take her eyes off Mitchell. Though she stood a few inches shorter than him, he seemed wise enough to realise she could take him down in an instant.

"What happened here?" Rhipley asked, motioning towards the viscera with his sword.

Yazmin stepped around Mitchell, unsheathing a second dagger as her eyes scanned the area, her ears twitching as she, too, listened for any danger.

"I-I don't know," Mitchell stammered.

Yazmin and Rhipley shared a wary glance.

"Okay, this time, try telling the truth," Rhipley demanded, piercing Mitchell with his stare.

Mitchell wouldn't yield, his heartbeat racing, though it was likely because of what he was looking at, his eyes focused on the carnage.

"Who is that?" he asked quietly, pointing a finger at the corpse.

"That's what we'd like to know," Yazmin said, gritting her teeth.

"I don't know! Please, you have to believe me. One second I was knocking on the door, the next, I'm walking out of the house to find you two threatening me, and blood everywhere."

His voice trembled.

"Rhipley, he's been compelled," Yazmin said quietly, far too quietly for Mitchell to hear, and Rhipley studied the man, remembered how his eyes had been glazed over, how he'd been in a trance before coming to.

"Fuck," Rhipley said under his breath. "Search the area. They might still be lingering."

Yazmin didn't hesitate as she Realm Walked around the property, the sudden disappearance, then reappearance, emitting a shocked noise from Mitchell as he watched on in disbelief.

"Who are you? Why are you here?" he asked.

Ignoring his question once more, Rhipley approached Mitchell, and maybe, just maybe, he put on a threatening demeanour to frighten Alexis' past lover, just for his own amusement.

And, perhaps, because something primal in him twisted at the idea of Alexis reuniting with Mitchell. Something instinctual made him want to leave the man behind.

He reminded himself that jealousy was not an attractive trait, and that Alexis had gotten over Mitchell in the past month. He also reminded himself that Alexis wasn't *his* to be jealous over, Prince Frederik's words replaying in his mind.

"We need to go," Rhipley said gruffly, gripping Mitchell's bicep.

He tried to shake from Rhipley's grasp, but only found an adamant grip, like trying to pull a limb from between boulders.

"Yazmin?" Rhipley called, and in seconds, the female was beside him once more, shaking her head, confirming they were alone.

"Do we just leave this here?" she asked, eyeing the body once more.

"We need to get back to the guild. If this was D'Roghal and his goons, we need to warn Rampier."

"Alright," Yazmin mumbled, using her earth magic to sink the body into the dirt, taking the blood and carnage with it.

CHAPTER
51

Alexis had been training practically all day with Aspen, Tatiana and Lukai overlooking and adding their own comments while a specialty Daeanimus trainer and hunter — Kimora, she'd introduced herself as — had spearheaded the session. Alexis took a quick liking to Kimora — the female didn't question her, didn't look down her nose at her, but rather critiqued and acknowledged where Alexis went wrong, and praised what she got right.

Being an elf, she supposed understanding Daeanimus bonds made sense given, from what Alexis had been told and had learnt over the past month, the close relationships elves shared with all living things. Aspen had never been hard to train — given her breed, Alexis had always trained her from when she was a pup. Though she only knew the basic commands, really. Walking on and off a lead, recall, sit, stay, lay down, focus.

Still, Alexis had to give herself props — Aspen was an excellent student, as much as Alexis was an excellent teacher, in her own regard. Nothing compared to Kimora, though.

The two of them had picked up Kimora's instructions quickly, working at it again and again and again, until Kimora had demanded they take a break, Alexis willing to push through until they got every exercise right. Some hunters, students, and even teachers had stopped to watch, some simply looking over as they went about their usual tasks, some stopping completely, deeming the training more entertaining than whatever they'd originally been doing. Alexis hadn't minded — if anything, the pressure of those watching just drove her need for success even deeper.

Made her hungry for a win.

By the end of the lesson, she and Aspen were admittedly exhausted, both mentally and physically, but they'd learnt how to work together, at least. Aspen could now guard and heel, among other things.

Alexis had also learnt — theoretically — how to transfer her energy, her magic, to Aspen, but had been reminded by Kimora that the use of magic, especially for a new wielder, *especially* for someone who hadn't yet learnt how to pace themselves, could be draining for both of them.

So, much to Alexis' dismay, they'd take it slow. Though, that dismay had vanished when she'd reminded herself that it wasn't just her life on the line, but Aspen's as well.

As they made their way back to the dorms, readying themselves to shower off and prepare for dinner, Yazmin and Rhipley had burst through the gates, someone hanging between them.

Alexis froze as she beheld who they carried with them — Mitchell.

Rhipley and Yazmin hadn't stopped since they'd arrived back in Xalentya. Though, Mitchell, to no one's surprise, had vomited, then passed out, thanks to the Realm Walk. He'd been in and out all day, never conscious for long enough at a time to comprehend where he was, or that he was in a completely different world entirely.

Rhipley hadn't minded one bit — the last thing he wanted to do was explain himself, or stroll down memory lane, bonding over their shared affection for Alexis. Not that Rhipley was quite ready to admit that to anyone just yet — Tatiana had been the exception, though he supposed she wasn't necessarily an exception, since she'd guessed it.

The guards at the entrance to the guild had let them in immediately, their wary eyes solely on who Rhipley and Yazmin now carried between them, their weapons drawn for safety. Thankfully, Mitchell was light. Though, given their fae and elf strength, most people were light.

Rhipley wanted to run to Alexis, to comfort her, to turn her gaze away when he'd beheld her face. Only complete shock and grief coated those beautiful features, and as she'd made a run for them, her eyes were only on Mitchell. Rhipley buried the feeling of jealousy deep down — he needed to be there for her, for Alexis. Being an asshole, an alpha, letting his primal male instincts take over was not what any of them needed or wanted.

So, he continued to hold on to Mitchell, who was currently completely unconscious.

"What happened?" Alexis asked frantically, looking Mitchell over, her eyes tearing up.

"We'll explain all that later. Right now, we need to get him to a dorm. He's been in and out of it all day. Who knew Realm Walking would take such a toll on a human." Rhipley tried to lighten the mood, tried to sound humorous, but it didn't land. Alexis just continued looking over Mitchell, her gentle hands stroking his face as she voiced a quiet thanks to the gods.

Rhipley had found an empty dorm, laying Mitchell upon the empty yet perfectly made bed. He stunk, and though Rhipley tried to ignore it, tried to mask that it bothered him, filled his nostrils, Yazmin and the others didn't so much as try to hide their feelings about the stench of body odour and sweat and urine.

"He needs a bath," Tatiana mumbled, holding her nose between her index finger and thumb.

Alexis ignored the remark as she sat by the edge of the bed, refusing to let Mitchell out of her sight.

She gently stroked his arm, her eyes looking his body over once more.

Rhipley didn't dare approach as he said softly, "We should let him rest. Leave him be."

Alexis simply shook her head without so much as looking at Rhipley. He breathed in deeply before nodding, leaving her to it.

As he exited the room, shutting the door behind him, he faced Tatiana and Lukai, their heads angled in silent question.

"Who is that?" they finally asked, Tatiana's arms crossed.

Shit.

"Um…" Rhipley trailed off as he scratched his head, trying to find an excuse. Rampier still hadn't given instructions to inform anyone of the Rainier's true origins, though his friends had certainly guessed by now, but he supposed that with Mitchell here, it would be hard to work their way around the secrets with everyone else.

"He's her ex-lover," Rhipley finally said.

He didn't miss Lukai's tensing at the words, though Rhipley only looked at Tatiana, who stared him down.

"From where?" she asked.

"I can't say," Rhipley replied. He didn't enjoy lying to his friends, but he wouldn't betray his Headmaster, either.

Tatiana clicked her tongue, scoffing.

"They're not from Xalentya, are they?" The question — more of an accusation, really — caught Rhipley off guard. He knew better than to expect Tatiana to drop it. She was far too intelligent, far too observant. She would have made the realisation the second she saw Mitchell, the clothes he wore that weren't of this world.

Lukai glanced between Rhipley and Tatiana, his face unreadable.

"Are you asking because you wish to know, or because you already know?" Rhipley challenged, and Tatiana smirked — the only confirmation he needed.

"Do you both know?" Rhipley asked sharply, shifting his gaze to Lukai. Lukai only averted his gaze, ashamed, but not sorry.

"Fantastic," Rhipley mumbled. Tatiana opened her mouth to, no doubt, spit out some bitchy retort, but Rhipley was already striding down the hall, trying not to think of Alexis alone in that room with Mitchell.

Alexis ran her hands through Mitchell's soft hair, down his face, down his arm. He seemed okay, had shown no signs of trauma.

She had seen no cuts or marks on his skin.

Though he did stink. The second he awoke, she'd need to get him to the bathing chambers.

She could only imagine how putrid he smelled to her friends, whose senses of smell were so much stronger than her own.

She watched him with careful eyes, unable to believe that he was here.

Why was he here? What had Rhipley and Yazmin discovered? She hadn't thought to ask, had instead given her attention wholly to Mitchell. She made a mental note to inquire later.

A knock sounded at the door, but she didn't speak. A few moments later, after a second knock, the door opened. She didn't look to see who entered, but as the light footsteps approached, she saw her sister's red hair before she saw her face.

"How is he?" Amelia asked quietly, taking up a spare chair she'd retrieved from the corner of the room.

"Alive," Alexis replied. She allowed a small smile to grace her lips, though she knew her eyes were full of worry.

"Do you think Sam and Dad are okay?" Amelia asked, and Alexis could feel her sister watching her.

"I don't know — I hope so, but I haven't had the chance to ask." She wouldn't let herself worry about the status of her brother and father — not yet. Not until there was need for worry.

Amelia gave Mitchell a once over before saying, "He doesn't appear to be hurt, so that's good."

Alexis nodded, gripping his hand in hers.

Amelia must have gripped her nose, because in a nasally voice, she retorted, "God, he stinks, though."

Alexis let herself chuckle, let herself be happy while she waited for Mitchell to wake. If only for a fleeting moment.

"Once he wakes, I'll take him to the baths. Surely Rhipley can find some spare clothes for him."

Amelia tossed something her way, and she took her eyes off Mitchell to see what it was. "Yazmin's already got that covered." Indeed, a pile of the hunter's guild daily clothes now sat on her lap.

"She's a real one," Alexis said cheerily, placing the clothes next to Mitchell. Shifting her gaze back to her ex, she noticed his eyelids begin to flutter.

Instantly, her attention was wholly on him as she waited for him to wake. He didn't move, as if he was slowly, very slowly, rising to consciousness.

"Do you think Rhipley and Lukai will be jealous? Of him?" Amelia asked, angling her head in Mitchell's direction.

"Lukai, no. He's in love with Zailah," Alexis chuckled at the thought.

"Why would Rhipley be jealous?" she furrowed her brows as she kept her eyes on Mitchell.

When Amelia didn't answer, she dared a glance at her.

Amelia was biting her lip, as if scared to offer an explanation. "Uh… never mind," she said hesitantly.

Alexis rolled her eyes. "I know you think he's got a thing for me, but he doesn't. If he did, he'd have said something by now." She shrugged her shoulders, watching Mitchell once more.

Amelia scoffed as she said, "You're so intelligent, yet so daft at the same time."

"Ouch," Alexis mumbled.

"It's true! You're ignoring all the signs," Amelia retorted.

"Whatever," Alexis muttered.

Mitchell's eyes finally opened as he blinked slowly, adjusting to the light. Immediately, Alexis had both hands on either of his arms. "Mitchell," she said in a voice more panicked than she'd meant for it to be.

Mitchell sat up, his eyes searching the room before they landed on Alexis.

"Lex?" he said in a soft, gravelly voice.

Alexis couldn't help the tears that fell from her eyes as she smiled and embraced him.

"You're okay," she said over and over again, crying over his shoulder. His hands gripped her back as he held her close, exhaling and inhaling deeply.

"Where are we?" he asked as he pulled back, noticing Amelia sitting to the side.

"Hi," she said, gently gripping his hand and squeezing it as she smiled warmly.

"We'll explain all that soon. But first, we need to know what happened," Alexis said. She watched him, waiting.

Mitchell just glanced between the two as he tried to find his words.

"I-I can't remember," he mumbled finally, one hand drifting to his forehead, as if a headache burdened him.

"You don't remember *anything*?" Alexis pushed. She didn't want to nag, but she needed to know. For her own peace of mind, and for Amelia's.

Mitchell simply shook his head. "I remember driving over to your dad's house to check in, since I hadn't seen him or Sam since the breakup." A wince, and Alexis just shook her head.

"And then I remember standing on the front deck, a woman's knife at my throat, and a man with his sword out, looking at me like I was a threat. And..." His eyes went vacant as he tried to recall everything.

"And what?" Amelia said this time.

"I can't remember. It's all very foggy after that," Mitchell said, giving them both sorry eyes.

Alexis and Amelia looked at each other. "You didn't see dad or Sam?" Alexis asked.

"No — at least, they weren't there before we left," Mitchell replied. Alexis blew out a deep breath.

"Why did they bring you here, then?" Alexis asked herself more than him.

"I actually don't know…" Mitchell said. "All I do know is that I have a killer headache." He hissed as he touched his forehead again, as if he'd been dealt a physical blow.

"Let's get you to the baths," Alexis offered, helping him up from the bed. Smelling his armpits, Mitchell scrunched his nose and nodded. Amelia chuckled as she followed from behind.

Rhipley sparred with Lukai an hour later, needing to expel all he was feeling, all he'd dealt with in the last twenty-four hours, through physical combat. Lukai, thankfully, was more than happy to help. As they circled each other, Rhipley went in with a punch.
Lukai blocked, and they began circling once more. They continued their little dance, neither wielding to exhaustion.

Rhipley noticed a golden head of hair approaching from the corner of his eye, and he made the mistake of looking, just for a split second. As he did so, Lukai took his shot, landing a blow to the face that had Rhipley nearly tripping over his feet.

"Don't get distracted," Lukai taunted, grinning. Rhipley spat before punching again. Lukai, again, dodged to the side, landing another blow to his ribs. Rhipley grunted.

"Come on, stop lacking. Get on your A-game," Lukai taunted again.
Rhipley could feel her standing there, watching them. He wouldn't dare let her see him go down.

So, he made Lukai think he was about to make a move, before side stepping as Lukai took the bait, and catching him in a headlock, pulling him to the ground. Within seconds, Lukai was tapping Rhipley's hand, calling for his surrender.

"That's what I thought," Lukai mumbled as he tried to catch his breath, chuckling. Rhipley simply scoffed, helping his brother to his feet. Lukai beamed as he beheld Alexis watching them.

"Enjoy the show?" he asked.

"Always," Alexis replied, smiling smugly at him.

Rhipley tried to hide his own smile as he unwrapped his hands, walking towards her.

"To what do we owe this pleasure?" he asked, not looking up from his hands.

"I need to talk to you," she said without hesitation.

Rhipley knew this was coming, knew he'd need to offer an explanation. Especially since Yazmin had worked a glamour on Mitchell's mind, making him conveniently forget that someone had been killed at the Rainier home.

Rhipley finally raised his gaze to meet hers, but only determination laced those blue-grey eyes.

"How's Mitchell?" he asked, not that he particularly cared.

"Ah, yes. The lover from your past. You sure do have a type, huh?" Lukai teased, and Alexis batted his arm away.

"What can I say? I'm a sucker for boys with pretty eyes." The smoothness in her voice was like a melody in Rhipley's ears. He cleared his throat, tugging his shirt over his head and extending an arm, motioning for Alexis to lead the way.

Alexis had practically been drooling as she watched Rhipley and Lukai spar. Her traitorous thoughts had her wondering what it would be like to be sandwiched between them, their naked bodies all tangled together. She snapped the thoughts from her head, cursing herself for being so sex obsessed lately, despite having had no sex. Well, unless she counted her encounter with Lukai.

Since then, it's all she wanted, all she desired, despite her surprising impulse control.

She couldn't help herself as her eyes roved over Rhipley's torso — the muscles in his arms, his abs, the sweat that dripped off him. She had to calm herself, needed to stop thinking of him like that — especially since her ex was literally now at this same place with her. If anyone had asked her if she'd seen herself in this position a month ago, she would have laughed them off. But, now?

She walked ahead of Rhipley, leading them to a quiet area behind a few trees, away from the training grounds and the dormitories and the academy. Somewhere they could talk between themselves.

As Alexis turned to look over a shoulder, she noticed Lukai in the distance, making his way to the infirmary. She smiled, which surprised her — though she supposed she was truly happy for him. She'd known she and Lukai were nothing more than friends and never would be. Hopefully, for Lukai's sake, Zailah would finally return his feelings someday.

Rhipley stood casually, his hands resting in the pockets of his pants, as he watched Alexis, his chocolate eyes solely on her. She forced her eyes to meet his, forced her eyes not to drift to his lips, or anywhere lower.

"So, what did you want to talk about?" Rhipley asked, cutting Alexis away from her dirty thoughts. She shook her head, stumbling over her words.

"I, uh... I wanted to ask about your mission to our home — the Mortal Realm." She shifted on her feet, wringing her fingers as she waited for him to answer.

"Yeah, um... we didn't find anything. Well, other than Mitchell." He offered a flat smile.

"Nothing? So, my dad and brother weren't there?"

"We didn't see them, no." He leaned back against a tree — a casual stance, for an otherwise serious conversation. As if he were trying to dilute the gravity of it.

"Why did you bring Mitchell back?" She didn't hide the urgency in her voice.

"He was there alone, and, given the warning you received, we figured he'd be safer here than out there in the world, where D'Roghal's goons, or anyone who wanted to hurt him, could."

"Where do you think Sam and dad are?" Alexis asked, considering.

"We don't know. But, it's not worth stressing over. Just because they weren't there doesn't mean they've been harmed. Perhaps they just weren't at home." Alexis watched him with worry in her eyes, though she eventually let out a sigh and nodded.

Rhipley practically sagged with relief as Alexis seemed to move on from her interrogation. He didn't want to hurt her, didn't want to make her think the worst when even he didn't have the answers she sought.

Yes, he'd lied about there being a literal dead body at her house.

No, he hadn't mentioned the fact that although there was no sign of her brother or father, aside from the unidentifiable body at the scene, the house looked completely untouched.

He felt guilty — so guilty — for lying to her, for keeping the truth from her, but she was finally happy. She had finally grown to love his world, his friends, this life. He'd had every intention of telling her, eventually, but he wanted to let her enjoy her life for the first time in weeks. Who would he be to ruin that, to strip that away from her? Besides, he would get to the bottom of it, and when he did, he'd reveal the truth to her.

Sure, she might hate him, but he could live with that.

Could he live with that? He didn't want to think about it.

Alexis began approaching him, her eyes on the ground, and as he stood there, leaning against the tree in a cool-calm position, pretending his heart wasn't pounding in his chest as she looked up at him with doe eyes, she said, "I ended things with Lukai."

Rhipley didn't hide the surprise from his face, but he replied casually, "Oh yeah? And why is that?"

More relief shot through him.

Not yours, never yours.

The words clanged in his mind, and the relief vanished.

"He's got feelings for Zailah. Besides, we were better off as friends." She shrugged, her glance casting off towards the training grounds he and Lukai had been sparring in just minutes ago.

"I'm sorry to hear," Rhipley said, and he meant it, if only because he was sorry that she'd had to go through it again, having gone through it with Mitchell only two months ago.

Alexis scoffed as she returned her stare to him. "Don't be. I still care for him, just not in that way."

They stood in silence for long seconds before she said, "Are you afraid of my power?"

The question caught him off guard. "Of course not. Why should I be?"

"Well, you *did* tell me to keep my magic in check, remember?" She raised an eyebrow at him.

"Yes, only because others might have been afraid, or intrigued enough, to delve deeper into your roots, which would have spelled trouble for us. Remember?" He poked her on the nose playfully.
She seemed to recall Rampier's orders about keeping their identities a secret and clicked her tongue, nodding.

Not that keeping their *real* backstories was becoming any easier with each passing day.

"Besides, I could never be afraid of your power. You're– your power is amazing."

He coughed awkwardly, hoping she hadn't noticed his slip up.

She had noticed, though, as she offered him a grateful smile that threatened to undo him entirely. It took all his willpower to not take her face in his hands and kiss her deeply.

She stepped closer, and he searched his pocket, pulling out a gift wrapped in paper and twine.

"This is for you," he said, his words rushed as he tried to distract himself. He tried not to think of the effect she had on him — how she could undo his cool demeanour by just simply existing in his presence.

She lowered her eyes to his outstretched hand, the present that lay in it, and grabbed it gently.
"What's this?" she asked, unwrapping it to find a glass sunflower sitting there.
He'd noticed it in one of the shops when they'd visited the city on Summer Solstice and, recalling Amelia's mention of sunflowers being her sister's favourite, hadn't hesitated in buying it for her — despite the hefty price tag.

Alexis gasped as she took it in, turning it over, the sunlight reflecting off the glass and casting beautiful colours onto her hand. "This is… how did you know?" she asked, looking up at him once more as she clutched the gift close to her chest.

Silver tears lined her eyes.

Rhipley smiled. "Amelia. It's your Solstice gift. I hope you like it."

She lunged at him, throwing her arms around his neck. He couldn't help hugging her back — she felt so light against him, so fragile, despite the fact he knew she wasn't. Not one bit.

Chuckling softly, he said, "You're welcome."

She pulled back, looking his face over. Her eyes fell to his lips, as his did hers, and she leaned in. His heartbeat quickened as the realisation of her intentions became clear.

Before her lips could touch his, he pulled back. He hated himself for the look that appeared on her face — complete and utter disappointment and sadness.

He'd rejected her, but not for the reason she was likely now thinking.

"We can't...I can't..." he mumbled, forcing his eyes away from her.

"I-I'm so sorry," she muttered, but before he could stop her, she ran off towards the dorms.

Rhipley remained there, his outstretched hand frozen in the air, letting her go.

CHAPTER 52

Alexis tried to calm her breathing, though it was impossible.

She was flushed with red as she practically ran from Rhipley, completely embarrassed.

She'd tried to kiss him, tried to act on her feelings for him, which she'd been trying to hide deep down inside, refusing to completely acknowledge them, and he'd rejected her.

She felt like an idiot. She *was* an idiot.

As she went to open the doors to the dorms, someone emerged from inside. She flinched back, startled by it, before realising it was Mitch who walked out.

"Oh, hi," she said, trying to hide the tremble in her voice, trying to fight back the tears that threatened to emerge.

Mitch's smile quickly faded into something of concern as he reached a hand out to gently grab hers.

"Are you okay?" he asked softly.

Alexis breathed out, slow and steady, and put on her best fake smile as she replied, "Of course, never better." Mitch sagged with relief as he offered her a smile of his own.

"So, want to give me a tour?" he asked, looking around, taking all of it in. "I don't know how to explain it, but everything here just feels more… alive. More vibrant."

Alexis nodded. "I know what you mean."

And so, leaving behind Rhipley and his rejection, shoving the sorrow deep down, Alexis gave Mitchell a tour of the guild.

Rhipley had wanted to confront Alexis and explain himself when he saw her at dinner, sitting and laughing with Mitchell.

Gods damned Mitchell.

If he weren't so important to Alexis, he'd have happily left him in the Mortal Realm, danger or no. Now he was making Alexis smile and laugh and the sight was beautiful, and Rhipley hated it. Hated him for it. Hated that he wasn't the one to make Alexis glow like that. He'd ruined his chances when he rejected her, even though it wasn't for the reasons he was sure Alexis kept telling herself. He wished he could tell her why he did it, wished he could explain himself, but how could he?

The prince told me I would never live up to your illustriousness, and I believed him and now I'm insecure about ever being with you. Forgive me?

So, putting his pride first, Rhipley had retreated to his room to eat, leaving Alexis behind. Whether she'd even noticed him in the dining hall, he didn't know.

Alexis stood in the clearing where she'd first tapped into her magic, but something felt off — like she wasn't really there, like she was dreaming. She looked to her left and, to her surprise, found Amelia standing there, realising the same thing.

"What's going on?" her sister asked, and Alexis shook her head, barely able to comprehend it herself. Out of instinct, Alexis looked for Aurelia, assuming she was behind this sudden dream. The princess was nowhere to be found. Instead, stepping from the shadows, his eyes aglow with crimson, Dimitri now approached. Alexis stepped to protect Amelia, summoning her magic, the balls of white appearing in either hand as she stared the vampire down. Dimitri, to her surprise, simply raised both palms to her in surrender.

"I am not here to harm you, child," he said coolly, his voice just as silky as it had been the first night they'd met.

Alexis didn't back down, instead asking, "Why *are* you here?"

Dimitri's eyes returned to their almost onyx colour, and he placed his hands in his pockets — the image of a perfectly respectable gentleman, not a monster of the night.

"You both need to come with me," he said, a slight urgency now in his voice. Alexis, monitoring Dimitri, glanced back at Amelia only slightly. Amelia simply watched her, cowering.

"We're not going anywhere with you."

Dimitri sighed. "Unfortunately, unlike the last time we met, I cannot take no for an answer." He held out a hand, nothing sinister showing on his face, but sympathy, as if he were hurt to be doing such a thing. "It is for your own good, Alleria-" He stopped short, as if he hadn't meant to utter the words.

"What did you just say?" Alexis asked, recalling the name from a nightmare she'd had. Of a woman, beautiful and fair-haired, saying the name to a small babe.

"I misspoke. Please come with me. I urge you." He continued to hold out his hand.

"If we're dreaming, how can we come with you?" Alexis' gaze dropped to that hand, then rose to his face as she felt Amelia cling to her arm.

"You'll understand when you wake."

"Why should we follow you? You tried taking us to your king last time. The same king who sent those creatures to hunt us down." Alexis wouldn't budge — not until she had some answers.

Maybe even then.

"They were never going to harm you."

"Sure didn't seem that way," Alexis replied, her tone sharp.

"Inferno Hounds are simply made to retrieve. They only kill if they're ordered to. In that case, they were ordered to retrieve you, nothing more."

"How did they Realm Walk?" Alexis could feel Dimitri growing tired of her questions.

"As I said, they're retrievers. They're the only known creatures, aside from Realm Walker's, who can do so."

"You can Realm Walk?" Alexis said, not hiding her accusatory tone. Dimitri chuckled. "Yes, I can. Because I took that power from another."

Alexis recalled what Yazmin had called him — a Leichar. A rare breed of vampire who could steal the abilities of those they killed. She then recalled what Rhipley had told her that night at the inn.

Rhipley. Yazmin. She needed to wake and find them, alert them.

"You… killed a Realm Walker?" Amelia mumbled.

Apparently, she'd come to the same conclusion.

"We're wasting time," Dimitri said, his tone slightly more urgent than before.

"Again, why should we?"

"Because they have your brother," Dimitri said, and Alexis felt the air leave her lungs.

"Sam?" She wasn't even sure she'd said the name out loud as she looked behind her to where Amelia still stood, white faced and barely breathing.

"Why?" Alexis asked as her heart thundered in her chest.

"They needed to get your attention. Starting a war with Preshia and the Hunter's Guild would be unwise, and the only other way for my king to have you in his possession was for you to come willingly."

"Holding our brother hostage isn't exactly giving us much choice," Alexis snapped.

Dimitri didn't speak, though shame showed on his face.

Alexis looked at Amelia, who now stood next to her.

"We *don't* have a choice," Amelia whispered, and Alexis knew she was right. She hated it, hated that they'd been forced into this position, but she'd die before letting any harm come to her brother.

"Fine, we'll go with you. Just please leave this guild untouched."

Dimitri placed a hand over his heart and bowed. "I give you my word."

Hesitantly, swapping one last glance, the sisters walked towards him and placed their hands in his. Suddenly, they were ripped from their dreams, and were now standing outside the guild gates.

Still in their nightgowns, feet bare and hair unbound, they scanned the area, searching the walls for guards. None could be seen.

Their eyes lowered to the gates.

The two guards stationed outside were unconscious. Footsteps neared, and they swiftly turned to see who approached.

Dimitri, appearing exactly as he had in their dream, stood ten feet away.

"What did you do to them? And how did you get past the wards?"

"I had help on the inside," he said, with no hint of smugness. Someone had betrayed them from within the guild?

"Where are all the guards?" Alexis asked, looking back towards the walls.

"Oh, they're up there. They, too, are unconscious." Dimitri dipped his head toward the guards at the gate for reference. Alexis glared at him. "Hey, I could have killed them. Instead, I left them unharmed." He held up his hands in defence, like he had in their dream.

"We're not equipped to travel," Amelia argued, finding her courage again.

"Do not worry," Dimitri said as he waved a hand, their noses filling with a metallic smell, before they, too, fell unconscious.

Rhipley jolted awake, sensing something was amiss. He didn't know what, didn't know who, but something in his blood screamed at him to run to the Rainier girls' dorm. The guild still slept, the world outside silent, still bathed in darkness.

As he neared their room, he immediately noticed it was left unguarded.

"What the fuck?" he muttered, rage filling him. He could have sworn he'd organised someone to be on duty tonight. Where were they?

He didn't hesitate to open the door, finding their beds empty, aside from Aspen lying on Alexis' bed, now alert and awake.

"What happened?" he asked the dog, though he knew she couldn't respond.

She'd been left untouched, unharmed, apparently unaware of her Daeanimus bonded human missing.

"Something's not right." His eyes searched the room, looking over every inch for anything left out of place.

As he quietly approached the window, peering outside, he noticed nothing out of order.

Their scents lingered, though they weren't fresh. As if they'd been gone for some time.

Yazmin appeared behind him, already in her leathers.

"What's happened?" she asked, peering past him to Amelia's bed. Her eyes widened as she came to the same conclusion.

"Someone's taken them. I just don't know who, or how," Rhipley said gruffly, walking towards her. "We need to alert Rampier and make chase. They could be miles from here by now."

Yazmin kept her breathing steady, though Rhipley could sense her heart beating quickly, her nervousness growing as she, like him, imagined the worst.

Rampier hadn't sensed the wards being down, hadn't ordered for them to be lowered, hadn't even sensed anything amiss within the guild. Like his power had been dampened, like someone had dampened it without his knowledge.

Rhipley didn't know of anyone with that kind of magic.

Great, one more thing to worry about.

After sending them on their way, advising them not to alert anyone else of the situation, Rhipley and Yazmin had departed the guild immediately.

Finding the guards waking from unconsciousness, they couldn't offer any help, any insight. They'd been awake one second, and the next, they were being awoken by a stern-faced Rampier, unaware of what had occurred.

The Headmaster had taken it upon himself to investigate the cause behind it all, and that was that.

Now, running with all their energy, picking up the girls' scents heading south, Rhipley knew where they'd been taken, and the thought made his stomach drop: Vendarath.

CHAPTER 53

Alexis remembered falling in and out of consciousness, remembered being carried, remembered travelling beneath what looked like an enormous wall, before being consumed by sleep once more.

She awoke to the sound of distant chatter, and she had the vague sense that she was being flanked by someone, or a couple of someone's. As she opened her eyes, finding a dark marble floor beneath her, her eyes adjusting to her new surroundings, Alexis realised she needed to be smart about this.

She was in a new territory — a new country — surrounded by dangerous beings, if Rampier and the rumours were to be believed. The room was dim, and she didn't dare look up as her eyes travelled to her right, then her left, and she saw a pool of red, curly hair five feet away. Amelia lay there, seemingly also rising to consciousness.

Alexis steadied her breathing, though her heart thundered away in her chest. She allowed herself a small look behind her, as much as she could, at least, and found that she was, indeed, flanked by what looked like guards. Two sets of boots stood diagonally behind her, one on the left, one on the right, and another brief look in her sister's direction told Alexis that Amelia had the same amount of guards watching her.

The chatter died down, and before Alexis could figure out how to tackle the situation, she was being hauled to her feet by powerful arms under her shoulders. She'd been changed, it seemed, for a pure white floor-length gown had replaced her nightwear.

It took a few more seconds for her human eyes to adjust to the darkness; only half the torches in this room were alight, it seemed. The throne room, it appeared, was almost completely opposite to that in Fallandor — painted in blacks, greys and reds, and a long crimson runner led to the dais. Alexis looked over to Amelia once more, finding that she was now awake, her eyes searching the room, taking it all in. Her night-black gown was a twin to Alexis' — symbolic of who they were, *what* they were.

Someone clapped from up ahead, and they were hauled forward. Alexis knew who waited upon the throne — the King of Vendarath, and his queen. Alexis searched for Sam, for their father, but could barely make out anything in this darkness.

She noted Dimitri, standing by the dais, his eyes on her, and she could have sworn she saw actual regret in them.

As if he were, indeed, apologetic.

Alexis just glared, repulsed. Finally, she lifted her eyes to the king, and was surprised by what she found. A handsome man, who appeared no older than forty, sat lazily on his ebony throne.

And, sitting beside him, looking both girls over, sat his queen, and she was truly the most beautiful woman Alexis had ever seen. Her moon-white hair fell to her hips in a sleek-straight style, an onyx tiara atop her delicate head, and those eyes — like sapphires.
She was pale, similarly to Amelia, though no freckles or blemishes marred her skin. It was as though she'd been crafted out of stone and given life. There was a strange familiarity to this woman — female,

she supposed. Not like when she'd seen her in her dream — for this *was* the female who she'd seen all those weeks ago.

It was as if Alexis truly knew her, had seen her before. One glance at Amelia told her that her sister must have been coming to the same realisation, her eyes darting between the king and queen.

D'Roghal waved a dismissive hand to the guards, who stepped back, letting go of the girls completely.

Alexis instantly hurried to Amelia, embracing her.

"Are you okay?" she whispered, despite knowing that likely everyone in this room could hear her. Amelia just nodded, her attention only half on Alexis as her eyes drifted to the sound of a door opening. Alexis followed her gaze and nearly sobbed, for between the arms of two beautiful women, both blonde haired, was their brother. He hadn't appeared to have been hurt — yet, and Alexis found herself quietly thankful to the gods.

Sam was unconscious, and before Alexis could speak, the blonde-haired women threw him to the ground like a sack of potatoes. Alexis growled, stepping towards them before being pulled back by her sister. The women just returned the sound with their own feral grins.

Amelia choked on a sob as she clung to Alexis, her eyes on their brother, and the way he was thrown to the ground visibly shook her.

Alexis wished she had heightened hearing, if only so she could confirm Sam was alive, for the way his body fell suggested otherwise. So limp, so frail, in the hands of immortals.

Alexis returned her focus to the thrones and levelled a glare at the king, who was smugly watching her, curiosity in his eyes.

"It has been far too long, my children," D'Roghal finally said, his voice smooth. This male was nothing like she'd expected — in all honesty, Alexis wasn't quite sure what she was expecting, but it certainly wasn't a handsome, silver-haired male.

A hand propped under his chin, the other tracing idle circles on his wife's knee, the king waited for the girls to speak, showing no sign of impatience.

"Let our brother go. You have us, so you have no need for him." Alexis found herself surprised at her lack of anxiety, how steady her voice sounded, but she tried not to dwell on it. If she needed to put on a brave façade to get her brother to safety, she'd do it with everything she had.

"Oh, quite the contrary, my dear. He owes us a debt," D'Roghal purred, not even bothering to look at Sam. Alexis furrowed her brows, visibly confused.

"His mother took something very important from us, but seeing as she is no longer of this realm, he must be the one to pay her debt," D'Roghal went on, his face turning serious.

"*His* mother?" Amelia muttered. "You mean *our* mother?"

The queen snapped, her voice tender but firm. "He is not my offspring."

Alexis froze, and she could sense Amelia had done the same.

Her offspring?

"Who are you?" Alexis demanded, though a part of her already knew. "And who is *his* mother?" A million thoughts were running through her head.

"My darling girl, if you haven't already guessed it, *we* are your parents. Your *true* parents, not that filth that raised you." Valeria's voice was sweet yet cruel, as if she were lavishing this moment.

"As for who his mother is, why it's none other than my dearest elder sister, may she rest in the Under Realm," the queen spat.

Alexis still couldn't grasp who she was referring to before D'Roghal added, "Yes, Princess Aurelia certainly kept herself busy when she fled this world." He chuckled at the words, a sinister smile forming on his lips as he side-eyed Sam.

Alexis couldn't breathe, couldn't think. There was no way *these* monsters could truly be her parents?

"Aurelia is... Sam's mother? You're *our*..." Alexis mumbled, unable to finish her sentence as her eyes drifted to Sam once more, then to Amelia. "How?"

"It seems Aurelia subdued your true identities, hid your true forms, making it easier to conceal you from us in the Mortal Realm. It certainly worked for twenty years. But this," D'Roghal said, disgust in his voice as he gestured to their ears, their human bodies, "is not who you truly are. Your *brother* isn't even human, though he is still half-breed trash." D'Roghal and Valeria snickered.

Alexis didn't hear anything except the ringing in her ears. "We can't be. We'd have known by now if we weren't truly human? Others would have known, sensed it?" She couldn't believe it — didn't believe it. They were lying, had to have been lying. She was human, she was mortal.

They *all* were.

"You're lying," Amelia managed to say, her voice trembling, as if reading Alexis' thoughts.

"Why would we lie when we've jumped through so many hoops to bring you back to us? To your home," the queen said, motioning to the throne room, the world that waited outside. "Aurelia's magic was powerful — of course it was. She was Brundhul Blessed, after all. But it faded, only lasted so long, before we were able to detect you once more. That is when we sent our hounds to retrieve you. Though, it appears her magic on your physical identities was made to stay." She sneered — not at Alexis and Amelia, but at their mortal bodies, at the fact that they'd been stripped of their immortality.

Before Alexis could respond, Sam began groaning, his limp body regaining consciousness as he rose on shaking arms. Alexis sagged with relief at the sight of her brother slowly rising from the ground. The two blonde women now watched him, as if waiting for orders.

"Restrain him," D'Roghal ordered, and the women hauled him upright with no hint of gentleness.

"Where am I?" he mumbled, his words slurred. He had a bruise on his left cheek — one that Alexis hadn't noticed before — and rage filled her blood.

"Don't you dare hurt him," she growled again, but the women ignored her, their eyes wholly on the king.

"How thoughtful of you to finally join us," D'Roghal said, amusement in his voice.

Sam's eyes squinted as he, too, adjusted to the dimness of the space, and as they searched the area, they finally landed on Alexis, then on Amelia. His eyes widened as he took them in their dresses, how they no doubt looked all dolled up, as if being presented to a pageant crowd.

"Lex, Mill's!" he yelled, his words suddenly cut off by a swift punch to the face. Alexis lunged for him before being pulled back by the guards.

"Let go of me!" she yelled, but they didn't listen. Immovable statues.

The king clapped, and the room went silent.

"Enough with the theatrics."

Sam was groaning in pain, blood now dripping from his lip, and Alexis felt the rage building inside her. If she could just access her magic and find a way to blind them all, surely it would buy them enough time to rescue Sam and make a run for it.

Even though they weren't sure where they could go, how far away they were from Fallandor, from the guild, their friends. But, if she could Realm Walk... it was hopeless.

She'd only Realm Walked twice, and both times were a mess. Alexis glanced at Amelia, who was still watching Sam, tears falling from her eyes.

"The road to our absolute succession can now commence," D'Roghal announced, and cheers sounded from throughout the room, from the guards holding onto her and Amelia, from the women guarding Sam, from people she hadn't even noticed.

"Now that our heirs have returned to us, we can find ourselves whole once more." The queen watched the girls, a smile on her lips and... longing in her eyes. As if she truly *had* had her children ripped from her and now returned.

"After twenty years, we've only been further exiled to this small territory we call home. We are not welcomed as we once were. We are not admired and loved as we once were. The fae of the north tell stories of our supposed evil doings, our power. They fear us, as they should, but they would also see us rid from this world if they had the chance."

Boos erupted, along with the heavy thumps of weapons — staffs, swords. "But with the Divinely Blooded once again with us, in our grasp, we can start anew." More cheers and claps. D'Roghal grinned, as if pleased with himself, but Alexis only felt hatred.

This was not her father, or her mother. These people were evil. They would use her power for their own fiendish deeds. Treat her as a slave, as a weapon, to wipe out this beautiful world she'd come to love.

"Alleria, Adrenna, display your mighty power for us now," D'Roghal ordered, beckoning for Alexis and Amelia to come forward.

They shared glances, confused.

"Ah, yes. I sometimes forget that you were given such mediocre mortal names when you were stolen from us. What were they again?" he asked, looking at Dimitri.

"Alexis and Amelia, Your Highness," the vampire responded, dipping his head in a bow.

"Terrible names," the queen muttered, shaking her head in disapproval.

The girls remained still, refusing to move an inch, before they were pushed forward once more, something hard nudging them in their backs, like the hilt of a sword or an axe. Alexis turned her head to scowl at the guards, but they didn't react, standing to attention once more.

"Show us your power, please," D'Roghal repeated, beckoning for them to take the floor with a sweep of his hand. Alexis' nostrils flared as she realised she didn't have any choice, and after a few long seconds, she willed her power to come forth, light appearing at her fingertips. Amelia did the same, complete darkness forming at her own fingers, and as they brought on their magic, their skin glowed, Amelia's giving off an almost black-light effect compared to Alexis' complete glow of the morning sun. The room applauded, and the girls muted their power, stepping back.

It had felt as easy as breathing. Each day they'd practised had made the use of their magic far more simple, more accessible, like it was second nature. And now, these people were going to exploit that magic, use it for their own evil deeds.

The king and queen were clapping, Valeria bellowing, "My

daughters are quite magnificent, are they not?" The words sounded like poison on her tongue, and Alexis refused to acknowledge it.

Suddenly, the thought of her father — her *real* father — came to mind.

"Where is he? Where is our father?" Alexis asked, looking at Sam, a defeated expression on his face.

In an instant, that expression turned hateful as he spat, "They killed him!"

The king and queen didn't show any reaction, any signs of confirmation, but Alexis' heart dropped, nonetheless.

"No, no, no," Amelia sobbed, falling to her knees. Alexis felt inclined to join her, but was frozen to the spot, unable to make a single sound as her head roared.

Dead. Their father was dead.

"They made me watch as their hounds ripped him to shreds," Sam growled between his own sobs, as if the memory was still fresh in his mind.

The two women holding him looked at each other, one shrugging as the other purred, "And he was delicious."

Sam tried to rip free of their grips, thrashing wildly, to no avail. The one with the short pixie-cut licked her lips in confirmation.

"I will kill you," Alexis said, staring the two women down. The women, to their credit, looked taken aback. Frightened, almost.

"He was not your father, child," the queen said, standing from her throne and descending the dais, holding her long red gown in either hand. She appeared to float, like a ghost, as she approached Alexis, taking her face in either hand. She stood at the same height as Alexis, but there was something intimidating about her — she appeared as dangerous as she was beautiful, like a monster lay beneath that perfect, alabaster skin. Alexis flinched at the touch, but the queen just kissed either cheek, saying softly, "You haven't the faintest idea how much I have missed you these years, my child." Alexis didn't speak, didn't move as she glared at her supposed mother.

Her *mother,* who had ordered her father, real or not, to be slaughtered.

Her mother, who wished to use her power to enact God knew what on this world.

The queen walked to Amelia, echoing the same movements, and Amelia just cried, her sobs a quiet whimper. Amelia, unlike Alexis, didn't glare, her eyes completely vacant.

"Why do you need our power?" Alexis demanded as the queen looked at her once more.

"I was stripped of my power when I chose D'Roghal as my husband, my mate. Luzhula saw to it that I would no longer be the Light Bringer if I chose to live in the shadows. And, when my sister was executed, there were no more Divinely Blooded in this world any longer. You two were brought into this world to bring about peace." The queen smiled genuinely, lovingly, and it made Alexis sick.

"You call it peace? You wish to eradicate this world and those who stand against you. How can you call that peace?" Alexis spat, not daring to hide the disgust on her face, in the tone of her voice.

"My dear child, you may be my own blood, but you certainly have a lot to learn. Do not be so naïve. You cannot yet even begin to grasp our plans. Do you merely believe the words of those you lived with? Those who would use your power to their own advantage if they had their way?" D'Roghal asked, his eyes roaming to the back of the room.

The sound of heavy doors opening came from behind, and though she tried, Alexis was unable to see who now entered, her guards blocking her view. Chains clinked, the scuff of footsteps neared, and she beheld her friends, handcuffed and battered — Yazmin and Rhipley.

CHAPTER 54

Rhipley and Yazmin had been intercepted on their way to rescue Alexis and Amelia, just outside the border between Preshia and Hyrandell. By King D'Roghal's third and fourth in his legion of vampires, according to the women who'd attacked them.
Now, they were being dragged into King D'Roghal's throne room; the onlookers snickering and
whispering.

Rhipley noticed Alexis first, her worried face, those pieces of shit guards holding her back like some wild animal. She didn't bother thrashing or breaking free of her restraints as she watched them throw Rhipley to the ground. He looked at her, and she returned his stare with one of... hate.

Her eyes burned, evidence of the tears she'd shed. But she didn't scream, didn't yell. She simply watched him, and Rhipley hated, more than anything, that she was levelling that look at *him*.

He rummaged through his memories, trying to figure out what had occurred for her silent wrath. Then, he looked up to see who he could only assume was their brother, Sam, hanging between the two vampires who'd attacked he and Yazmin.

Sam, their *brother,* who was likely attacked by whatever had torn up that body at their house.

If Sam is here, then that body was-

Rhipley shot pleading, sorry eyes at Alexis, unable to explain himself, to explain how sorry he was for lying to her. He didn't care that D'Roghal's court watched as he continued to stare at Alexis, silently conveying how apologetic he was. She practically tore her gaze away from him, refusing to look upon his face further. He hated himself — he'd hurt her, and he hated himself for it.

Amelia watched the exchange of glances between the two and realised the same thing, looking to Yazmin, betrayal on her face, before turning away in sadness.

Rhipley clenched his teeth and levelled a gaze at the vampire sisters, who stared right back, no regret in their expressions, no sorrow in their eyes. They just *sneered.*

He would kill them. He didn't know how, but he would kill them. If only to bring some closure to the Rainier's.

D'Roghal spoke up, his voice powerful as he tore Rhipley's attention away. "Enough of this façade."

Before Rhipley could react, before *anyone* could react, a ripple of invisible power washed through the room, and the girls and Sam were screaming, writhing in pain, their bodies held upright by their captors. Rhipley thrashed in the grip of the guards, but his power was spent, his energy low.

All he could do was watch on in horror as Alexis, Amelia and Sam were transformed before his eyes. Human ears grew pointed. Their hair, their skin, became softer, sleek like that of the fae. They weren't being *transformed;* they were being *returned* to their original forms. For as Rhipley had guessed and now knew to be true, Valeria and D'Roghal were Alexis and Amelia's true parents. The parents of Sam, however, he still wasn't sure, hadn't grasped. One of them had to be fae, though, for though he now *looked* fae, his features resembled those of a half-breed. A demi-fae.

The three breathed in deeply, their transformations now complete. Amelia threw up, Sam panted heavily, but Alexis just breathed in and out slowly. Rhipley watched on, his eyes solely on her.

On Alexis.

Yazmin's words cut in, drawing his attention away.

"The world is already at peace. You're chasing a foolish goal," she barked, the fresh cut on her lip dripping blood. Their injuries were healing *too* slowly, as if D'Roghal had put a damper on their healing abilities, their power.

"Is it? At peace? For you elves and fae, perhaps, but what of your other immortal brethren?" Queen Valeria motioned to the entire throne room, referencing the demons, succubi, warlocks and other creatures standing present. "We have been confined to a single country. Big as it may be, we're shunned if we so much as step outside our walls. The world may be at peace for your kind, huntress, but what of us? Or, are we not entitled to that same happiness? The citizens of Vendarath have just as much right to this world as anyone else. We are gods' made, just as the rest of you." Cheers and applause erupted around them.

"You left your kind," Rhipley spat, and Queen Valeria looked down her nose at him, her eyes darting to each ear, before returning to his eyes.

"I stopped aligning myself with the fae when they refused to change their ways, refused to accept those they deemed lesser than us." She didn't drop his gaze, didn't balk from him as he returned her own.

"So, you'd align yourself with those who would pillage and rip apart homes when left unchecked?" Yazmin didn't falter as she spoke, wouldn't back down, despite the positions they were in.

Valeria scoffed. "You don't even know the half of it, child."

Yazmin bristled, spitting blood onto the marble floors.

Rhipley noticed D'Roghal watching Yazmin, and Yazmin muttered, "Hello, *D'Roghal*."

Rhipley angled his head slightly, confused at the way Yazmin seemed suddenly familiar with the King of Vendarath.

"Hello, Princess."

Rhipley had lost his words, lost his will to speak, as he stared at his centuries-old friend, baffled by what was unfolding before him.

Yazmin wouldn't meet Rhipley's stare, not as she herself stared down one of the most dangerous people in the world.

Amelia must have been watching, too, as she exclaimed, "Yazmin?"

Yazmin instantly looked to Amelia, her face turning apologetic, and Amelia whispered, "No more secrets."

Yazmin simply mouthed, *I'm sorry.*

"Oh, yes. Please, do tell them our history." D'Roghal was resting his chin on his hand, watching Yazmin with expectation, his posture relaxed.

"He was next in line for the throne," Yazmin said. "He was to be the next King of Hyrandell: King of the Elves." Yazmin looked to the ground, spitting again.

"Before he tried to draw on dangerous magic through human sacrifice, turning to the dark side and bewitching the Princess of Fallandor. You're just a bedtime story for naughty elvlings, now. We don't speak of it to anyone on the outside. You are our kind's greatest shame." Yazmin didn't hold back as she glared at D'Roghal, the King of Vendarath looking none-too-impressed.

"You will speak of me again, very soon. You will speak of the king who bore the light and dark of the world, the Light and Shadow Bringers, the Divinely Blooded. I was meant to rule — our kind was just too stubborn to see it." D'Roghal glanced at Alexis and Amelia, and Rhipley had finally put two-and-two together. Alexis and Amelia were the heirs of both Fallandor *and* Vendarath. He had no doubt that D'Roghal planned to put them on either throne.

Alexis was now fae. Amelia was now fae. And Sam... Sam must have been half of that, for his ears, his entire being, looked like Prince Frederik, like the King of Fallandor and many of his subjects.

These were their *true* forms. The room was so much brighter, the sounds far louder. Alexis' skin was softer, her body strange, foreign, as if it wasn't hers. She could literally hear her magic thrumming inside her veins. Could literally feel and sense the life around her — the smugness of the king and queen and their own subjects, the sorrow and regret and anger of Yazmin and Rhipley, and the pain of Amelia and Sam.

"Now, you're probably wondering why we've brought you here, hunters," D'Roghal announced, addressing Rhipley and Yazmin, ripping Alexis away from her trance.

"We require you to fetch some… particular items. They're vital to our plans, you see."

Yazmin and Rhipley seemed to wait with bated breath. Alexis glanced between them and the king.

"We're not in the market for doing your dirty work," Yazmin seethed, thrashing against the guards that held her.

"On the contrary, you don't have a choice," the queen, her *mother*, replied.

Rhipley exhaled, clearly defeated, realising she was right: they didn't have a choice. Not if they wished to leave alive. Alexis didn't at all put it past these people to threaten her friends with execution should they choose not to agree. The fact that they'd kidnapped her brother, killed her father and were now holding them hostage told her as much.

"You must retrieve Relics for us. There are four in total; two in this world, two in another." D'Roghal held no amusement in his voice, on his face. As if he were ordering around his guards.

"Get them yourself," Yazmin bit back.

"Wouldn't you prefer to be our allies in whatever war is likely to break out, Yazmin?"

The threat in the queen's statement was obvious: *Work for us and be spared from death, or die, along with our enemies.*

"Please, just let them go. You have *us*. We're all you need. We will do what you ask, just don't harm them." Amelia was practically begging between sobs.

"My dearest child, you must understand. We aren't doing this to hurt you. We're doing this to help you," Valeria said softly, offering a warm smile.

"We won't," Alexis snapped under her breath, drawing everyone's attention to her. "I will not help you tear this world apart."

She could have sworn her eyes began glowing as the blood in her veins shone brightly. Valeria looked on in admiration, while D'Roghal simply clicked his fingers.

Alexis dimmed her power immediately upon seeing who'd been revealed, kneeling in a corner of the room. There was Mitchell, bending over a chopping-block, previously hidden by onlookers. An executioner stood by, holding a too-big axe. Mitchell's screams were muffled by the bandage around his mouth, his limbs immovable by the ropes that bound them together.

"No!" Alexis breathed, tears now running down her face. Had they truly gone after everyone she loved?

She calculated the distance between her and Mitchell, and realised there was no way in hell she could get him, herself, her sister and brother, *and* the hunters out in time.

Her stomach sank, her throat going dry.

"Perhaps this will give you incentive. Collect my Relics, and this will not happen to Sam next," D'Roghal drawled before snapping his fingers once more, and the axe came down on Mitchell's neck.

The world stopped, and Alexis' head went silent as she screamed. She fell to her knees as she watched Mitchell's head tumble to the ground, watched as his blood poured out onto the marble floor.

She could hear the onlookers' sounds of both shock and amusement. Then, Amelia was also screaming, Sam was swearing, and Rhipley and Yazmin were watching the king and queen in horror. Alexis just kept looking at Mitchell, his lifeless eyes.

A piece of her died with him as she just stared and stared at his limp, lifeless body.

"I hate to do this, I really do," D'Roghal said, his voice much calmer now: a manipulation. "But he was just a human, anyway. What's one human life compared to millions of immortal ones?"

"You monster," Alexis seethed, returning her gaze to D'Roghal, guilt gnawing at her for ripping her eyes away from Mitchell. D'Roghal simply returned her gaze, disappointment on his face, before nodding to his guards, and before Alexis or Amelia could react, handcuffs were being placed around their wrists. The power Alexis had been building out of anger had completely died out, and she felt nothing. Like something had been torn from her.

He'd supressed their magic: they were completely and utterly useless, as if becoming human all over again.

D'Roghal clicked a finger, and the long-haired blonde vampire holding Sam held a knife to his throat.

"Now, do we have a deal?" he asked.

Alexis looked at Sam, then Amelia. She wouldn't dare look at her friends — didn't want to, didn't care for their opinion at this time. Amelia simply nodded, defeat in her eyes, on her face, as she returned her gaze to Sam.

"We will do it," Alexis finally announced, and she heard Rhipley let out a sigh of defeat. She wouldn't let herself care, though. Not now. Her *parents* had taken too many people from her already.

If working with them meant keeping the rest of her loved ones safe, she'd do it.

"Wonderful," Valeria said merrily, offering a smile of approval.

Looking in Sam's direction, the king ordered, "Take him away."

The two women hauled him upright before turning to drag him out of the room. Sam's screaming and thrashing was all Alexis saw before the doors closed.

Alexis began thrashing again, and Amelia was protesting as she watched helplessly.

"No, you said you'd let him go!" Alexis demanded, turning pleading eyes on D'Roghal.

D'Roghal simply lifted a finger, as if correcting bad behaviour. He tutted, "I said we wouldn't kill him. I didn't promise we'd let him go. Not yet, anyway."

Alexis and Amelia returned their eyes to the doors Sam had disappeared through, tears running down their faces, white noise filling their heads.

"Harm will not come to him until you've fulfilled your mission," D'Roghal said. "You have my word."

"Your word means nothing," Alexis mumbled, eyes still on the doors.

"You will soon come to change your mind, dear one," D'Roghal returned.

They'd lost. The fates of her friends, her family, were in the hands of the enemy. She didn't want this life, didn't ask for it. But Alexis slid her gaze back to her parents. She stared D'Roghal and Valeria down, who were now ordering the guards to escort them out of the city, and she made a promise to herself: she would kill them, all of them. For what they'd done to her father, her brother, Mitchell, herself and her sister, her friends. And for Aurelia.

She would have her revenge.

CHAPTER 55

Three days later, Rhipley found himself standing in the tree line at the Hunter's Guild, silently watching Alexis as she looked into the water, the river flowing steadily in the afternoon. He'd been debating whether or not he should approach her, explain himself, but after what she'd just gone through, he hadn't had the guts to even try.

She hadn't spoken a word to him on their journey back. Hadn't even looked in his direction. To be fair, she hadn't been any kinder to Yazmin, either. Yazmin, however, had tried not to take it to heart, had practically pretended it never happened.

We have more important things to focus on than petty grudges, she'd said.

Though Rhipley agreed with her partly — they did, indeed, have more important things to focus on — how Alexis felt wasn't simply a petty grudge. They had lied, and sure, it had been his idea, but Yazmin had gone along with it. It was their responsibility to bear, and theirs alone.

He watched her silently, trying to keep his movements to a minimum — she looked so peaceful, or as peaceful as she could be after what she'd gone through. She held a small ball of light in her hands and bobbed it between her fingers, making it dance and hop from one finger to the next to the next, and back again.

She continued it for long minutes, before he heard her say, "I can hear your heartbeat."

He froze, unsure what to do. Had she known it was him, or had she simply known someone watched her?

"I can smell your scent. I know it's you, Rhipley."

His name on her lips was the sweetest sound he'd ever heard, and he treasured it, even if a part of him knew she said it with disdain.

After weighing his options of confronting her or fleeing back to the guild, he decided on the former, stepping out of the tree line.

Alexis had her ears covered by the long strands of her golden hair. He'd wondered if she hated them, hated this version of her. Hated her true form.

He didn't dare ask.

She wore a long, white gown made of linen, the skirts spooled around her. She looked like an angel, a true goddess, innocence becoming her.

Rhipley stopped a few feet away, not wanting to push his welcome, not knowing if he would even *be* welcomed within close proximity to her. He waited for her to speak, unsure of what words he could even utter that would offer comfort. For a while, the only ambience was that of the lapping water in the river, the birds chirping and singing, the trees swaying, and the distant clashing of swords and weapons.

Rhipley was glad he couldn't see Alexis' face, if only so he wouldn't feel more guilty than he already did. But he didn't feel any powerful emotions coming from her. Sure, he could sense sadness and anger, but it was as if she'd shoved them deep down, like she refused to feel them.

Like she had become a shell of a person — empty.

Upon closer inspection, angling his head so he could better watch the ball she danced between her fingers, he noticed she held the sunflower he'd given her in her left palm, the rays from the sun casting beautiful rainbow reflections onto her skin, her dress.

"Do you remember what you and Yazmin told us that first day we came to the guild? That only a select few in this world still believe in the gods, in Luzhula and Brundhul?"

Rhipley played that day through his head, had remembered Yazmin saying something along those lines as he responded with a simple, "Yes."

"If that is the case, why do so many believe in myself and Amelia? Why does bringing peace to this world ride on our shoulders, if only so many actually believe in those who bestowed these powers upon us?"

Rhipley sighed. "Yazmin was exaggerating. There are more than just a few who believe in you. It's just that some, as you'll find in your world, have given up on the gods. But we cannot rely on the gods to make all the evil and wrong in this world simply vanish. We need to evolve, need to learn how to vanquish those who would bring harm to our world on our own. Need to figure out conflict on our own." He wasn't entirely sure if she'd understand all that he'd just said, but Alexis just gave a small nod in return.

They were quiet once more for a time, but Rhipley wouldn't push. He was content simply being in her presence, being *allowed* in her presence.

"Do you know what happened to your parents?" Alexis asked, surprising Rhipley.

He hesitated, before saying, "No, I don't. But, I wish I did. I wish someone had told me, if only they knew."

Alexis scoffed before standing, and Rhipley remained still, unsure what to expect. "And yet, you didn't think I deserved to know?" She turned to face him. She looked so beautiful, though anger glowed in her eyes. Alexis looked down at the sunflower in her palm.

"You gave this to me as a token of our friendship. But all I see when I look at it now is a lie, and broken trust."

Rhipley's heart cracked, and he muttered, "I'm so sorry, Alexis. If you're going to believe anything I say, please choose to believe that."

"I don't want to hear anything you have to say," she spat back, tossing the sunflower to him. He caught it, but kept his eyes on her, pleading.

"Alexis, please," Rhipley said softly.

Alexis' eyes began to glow with white light, and her magic sang at her fingers. "Leave me alone. I don't want to see you. I don't want to talk to you."

Rhipley's eyes dipped to her hands, before rising back to her face. He wasn't scared of her, could *never* be scared of her.

She knew that, and yet she'd still try, if only so he'd back off from her.

So, rather than fighting, rather than forcing himself, his apology, he let out a sigh and turned to walk back to the guild.

Alexis didn't hate Rhipley, could never hate Rhipley, but she'd hated that he'd kept the truth from her. She knew, deep down, that he meant every word of his apology, but she didn't care to hear it.

She didn't want to feel, because feeling only hurt. She'd felt her father's death, had felt Mitchell's death, had felt Sam being taken away, had felt the betrayal from Rhipley and Yazmin.

And had felt red-hot anger and hatred for her parents. Yet, she pushed those emotions down deep. Her encounter with Rhipley had been the most emotion she'd allowed herself to feel in three days. And, once he'd left her alone on that riverbank, she'd forced that anger deep down once more. She knew she'd need to see him again, knew she'd need to work with him to retrieve the Relics, but it didn't mean she had to forgive him.

Now, as dusk was falling, Alexis found herself standing in that same clearing where she'd been speaking with Dimitri in her dream.

Now, she waited for Aurelia.

Like clockwork, the princess emerged from the shadows. Sorrow and regret filled her face, but Alexis wouldn't give in.

"Tell me all of it," Alexis demanded.

Aurelia must have known, then. Must have known, and she, too, had kept the truth from Alexis.

Aurelia didn't speak as she just stared at Alexis, her brows furrowed in a pleading expression.

"No more lies. Tell me all of it, now."

Aurelia let out a deep sigh before speaking.

"D'Roghal had bewitched my sister, Valeria, when he'd visited our castle centuries ago. The queen of the elves had seen the chance for a strong alliance, and proposed D'Roghal wed Valeria, unifying our houses, our people. He was a good male, at first. Charming, charismatic, and he had Valeria wrapped around his finger by the time it all went down. My parents had heard of what D'Roghal had attempted, you see, and they refused the proposal. D'Roghal, however, had already convinced, or rather, spelled Valeria to fall for him, and when he fled to Vendarath, she went with him."

Alexis simply observed Aurelia as she went on.

"The people of Vendarath heard D'Roghal's promise and made him their king. And, in turn, he made Valeria his queen. But, when she chose a Dark Elf as her husband, had accepted him as her mate, and, in doing so, had relinquished her destiny, her duty, Luzhula stripped her of her power. She was Divinely Blooded no longer.

And thus, the world fell out of balance. Many countries have been at war for centuries, many nations have parted. Old allies have become enemies." She paced, her shadows trailing from behind.

"For many years, we didn't receive word from my sister. They erected a large wall to keep outsiders from entering. Only those who searched for sanctuary, or those stupid enough, or brave enough, entered its gates. You see, though they built the wall to keep my- our kind out, for how we'd treated them, they still accepted those who were none the wiser. Though most are aware of the tales of Vendarath, it is a big world. Not everyone cares to heed warnings." Aurelia shook her head, as if recalling such reports of stubborn civilians hoping to find anything other than falling prey to the creatures who lurked there, and finding only that.

"Despite my parents' pleas and wishes, I chose to visit my sister, unbeknownst to them. I had announced that I wished to visit neighbouring villages, offer my charity, and they hadn't questioned it. I found myself on the King of Vendarath's doorstep, and to my surprise, my estranged sister had welcomed me with open arms. She was like my sister, but different. She seemed so unlike the female I'd grown up with, and yet she was still so familiar. It broke my heart when I'd discovered you and your sister." She stopped before a boulder, casting a sorrowful gaze in Alexis' direction.

Alexis held up a hand, pausing the princess. She gestured to her ears, her entire being, as she asked, "Why do we not resemble elves? If our father is an elf — a *dark* elf — should we not also bear some of his features?"

Aurelia clicked her tongue. "Only elves can breed more elves. A fae and elf mating cannot produce a pure-blooded elf, therefore, you took after your birth mother. By all laws of nature, you are fae and fae alone. You may find that your senses resemble an elves', but you will never physically resemble them."

Alexis nodded, having realised she hadn't, apparently, learnt all there was to know about the anatomies of the creatures in this world. How certain offspring came to be. Aurelia continued.

"They hadn't shared news of you, likely because they'd known you were the Divinely Blooded, and knew that if others were to learn of the news, they'd likely come for you, or begin preparing their armies. But I did not wish to see my world further divided, and so I came up with my own solution: I took you and ran. I prayed for forgiveness from Brundhul and Luzhula, and I didn't look back. Eventually, I found myself in the Mortal Realm. Your… *our* home." Aurelia's voice cracked slightly, and she drew in a short breath.

"We'd appeared in a forest, in a world unknown. I'd heard secret tales of another world, but they had been just that: tales.

They weren't factual as far as anyone was concerned. I was exhausted, and as I made my way out of the woods, a mortal man had spotted us. I'd collapsed from exhaustion before he could confront me, and I woke up in his house."

Alexis' heart broke as she realised it was her dad the princess was referring to.

"I woke to you and Amelia giggling away, and though I'd been wary of him at first, unsure what creature he was initially, he'd treated us all with such kindness. He didn't hound me with questions, didn't interrogate me or threaten to turn me in or throw us out. He welcomed us with open arms. Eventually, we fell in love, and I came to be with babe." She laid a hand on her stomach, smiling sadly at the memory.

"Your brother — cousin — was born. He was demi-fae, but I still had enough magic in my veins to alter his appearance. Our kind didn't exist on Earth, you see. At least, I hadn't come across any in my time there. And so, to keep you safe from my sister and D'Roghal, should they come searching, and to keep our general identities a secret, I hid our true features, made you mortal. It took nearly every last ounce of my magic to do so."

Alexis furrowed her brows in confusion. "You lost your magic?"

"Not exactly. Being away from my mother world, where access to magic is infinite, the very source of it, it faded. I had enough in my veins to perform miniscule tasks, but not enough to travel back to Xalentya. Not that I wanted to. I missed my parents, yes, but I had built a family on Earth. You two were safe, and my sister and D'Roghal couldn't fulfil their wishes without you."

"You kidnapped us…" Alexis mumbled, though it wasn't in an accusatory tone, but rather as if she'd come to a realisation.

"I felt guilty for ripping you from your parents. They loved you very much, in their own ways, but for your sakes, for Xalentya's, I made the decision I thought most wise, and I lived with that for the remainder of my life."

Alexis found herself baffled, unsure how to process all this new information.

"Eventually, one of his vampires recognised me while I was out running errands. She warned me that she was sent to hunt us all down to take back to Xalentya, but she took pity on me, recognising why I'd done what I'd done. So, she offered me a choice: I could return to Xalentya with her and pay for my crime, or she could alert my sister of our whereabouts and leave it in their hands."

"Not much of a choice," Alexis scoffed.

"No, but they would have then sent Dimitri and their other vampires had this one come back empty-handed," Aurelia offered. "Despite the outcome, she was nice to me. I had to appreciate that."

Alexis shrugged, shaking her head.

"What I did next will forever be my biggest regret, but I couldn't see you used and abused. I couldn't see Michael and Samuel killed. So, I gave myself up, returned to Xalentya with the vampire, but not before erasing the memory of me from your minds."

She sniffled — the most mortal action Alexis had witnessed her do. It caught her by surprise, and she felt a pang of guilt, of empathy. *No feeling,* she thought to herself. *Feeling gets you hurt.*

"So our deadbeat mother who we can't remember, who dad could never speak of... that was you?" Alexis asked, already knowing the answer.

"I was just trying to save your lives," Aurelia countered softly.

"Yeah, well, a lot of good that did. Dad's dead now, thanks to my birth parents and their evil goons," Alexis spat, forcing back the tears that threatened to emerge.

Aurelia simply dipped her head, a tear falling down her face.

"I am more sorry than you could possibly know, child," Aurelia said, her voice genuine.

Ignoring the apology, Alexis asked, "What did they do to you?"

Aurelia gracefully wiped away a tear. "They beheaded me. My sister didn't once take her eyes from it. She watched me with more hatred and disappointment in her eyes than I'd ever seen. It broke my heart, but even once my soul had left my mortal body, I did not regret my actions."

Alexis could understand that, though she wouldn't say that. Though part of her understood, the other part of her knew that none of the past events would have unfolded had Aurelia just left she and Amelia be. Though, gods only knew what the world would look like now if that had occurred. "I can't fault you for making the decision you did. Anyone would have — it was a lose-lose situation." Alexis briefly met Aurelia's eyes before looking down at her hands. The magic that thrummed there.

"Where have you been? I haven't seen you in my dreams for weeks. You just disappeared."

"I fear Valeria was using what little magic she possesses, and, with the help of D'Roghal, was blocking me from visiting you. I believe she had already erased the memories of my visits to Amelia's dreams since you arrived." She sighed again, clasping her hands together.

"That explains why Amelia thought you deemed her unworthy," Alexis mumbled to herself.

Aurelia simply nodded.

"What do I do now?" Alexis asked hopelessly, stepping to face Aurelia.

"The prophesy must be fulfilled. There is no halting it now," Aurelia replied.

"I don't want any of this!" Alexis retorted, splaying her hands. "I never wanted this. I wanted an ordinary human life." She let out a defeated sigh, taking up one of the boulders.

"Sometimes, we are assigned fates we do not wish for. And for that, I empathise." Aurelia offered, laying a hand on Alexis' shoulder, though she didn't feel it.

"I need to get Sam back," Alexis muttered. That was her priority, what she would focus all her energy towards until they were all free and far from this world and their fates.

Amelia had wanted to see Yazmin, despite everything.

No, she'd *needed* to see Yazmin. Unlike her sister, who was still shunning Yazmin and Rhipley, Amelia didn't wish to shut them out.

She was pissed at first, sure, but then she pondered all the reasons the hunters had withheld that information from them. She'd realised that, should they take on their assigned missions, it would be no help to not be on speaking terms.

And so, Amelia had taken the mature path, decided to be the bigger person. She'd understood why Alexis was treating what had happened the way she was, but that was Alexis' choice.

Amelia made her own choices, and she'd chosen to move past it. They needed to rescue Sam, and that would be her primary focus from this day forward. She knew that would also be Alexis' main focus, and that was all Amelia could ask for. All she *would* ask for.

She heard Yazmin enter the room from behind, approaching on soft feet before pulling Amelia against her. Amelia breathed in deeply and gazed out the window to where she'd been watching Alexis sitting against a tree, Aspen's head in her lap.

Alexis had been sitting there for hours now, content in her own bubble. Amelia wouldn't dare pop that bubble, instead choosing to observe from afar, ready to be there for her sister when and if she asked.

"She's still ignoring Rhipley?" Yazmin questioned.

"She's still ignoring *you both*," Amelia corrected, and she felt Yazmin huff a laugh against where she rested her head upon Amelia's shoulder.

"Well, she's going to need to get over it," Yazmin said nonchalantly, and Amelia warned, "Hey, be gentle."

Yazmin turned Amelia to face her, looking into Amelia's eyes. Gods, she could have sworn the entire ocean lapped in the blues of those eyes, especially in the afternoon sun.

"What comes next needs us all working together," Yazmin said, her tone serious. Amelia knew that, and had been trying not to think of it. Had decided to tackle it, and how it made her feel, when the time came. She supposed that time was now.

"Hey," Yazmin said softly, tilting Amelia's chin between her thumb and forefinger. "We will get Sam back, I promise."

Amelia looked into Yazmin's eyes and smiled sadly. "Whatever it takes."

CONTINUE READING FOR A SNEAK PEAK OF:

RELICS OF XALENTYA

ALEXIS AND AMELIA'S ADVENTURES CONTINUE IN THIS EXHILARATING SEQUEL

CHAPTER 1

Madysen Zephryn's future lay only metres ahead.

She could practically feel the griffin egg within her grasp, could see the golden shell glinting in the sunlight.

"You've got this!" her childhood friend, Charlotte, called from below, where she stood atop a ledge, catching her breath.

Madysen smiled as she reached for another rock, securing her footing as she climbed the steep cliff. The cries of griffins sounded all around her, but she didn't fear them, didn't balk from them.

The griffins of Hyacan Island had a special, centuries old truce with the humans of Lilhan. Every year, new cadets would come to Hyacan Island following their grading, and, as one, final test, would scale the cliffs to retrieve their own griffin egg to raise and nurture as their mount, until the griffin was old enough to ride and train.

Most cadets were unsuccessful, their demise usually caused by exposure to the elements. Or, from falling to their deaths, some only inches from claiming their eggs. But such was the way of the Griffin Riders. Only the best of the best were recruited.

And Madysen would be one of them.

As she neared the giant nest, the mother griffin watching her with narrowed eyes, Madysen secured her footing, hauling herself up to get a good look at what the nest had to offer.

There was only one egg left — not a particularly large egg, especially not compared to Charlotte's, who held hers securely in her arms like a babe, but it didn't matter. Sometimes, the most fearsome griffins hatched from the smallest of eggs.

And Madysen's mount would be as fearsome as the famed war griffins she'd grown up idolising.

As the mother griffin clicked her beak, tilting her head curiously as she observed the newcomer, Madysen hauled herself onto the pillar that the nest sat atop, kneeling before the cluster of branches, feathers, and shiny things. She made sure not to look the griffin in the eye as she bowed her head.

The griffin, deeming the gesture polite enough, didn't make to knock her off, didn't make any threatening movements as she bowed her head in return before turning away to observe the griffins flying around the mountain peaks.

Madysen eyed the egg — the golden shell was enough to pay for a large castle, but thanks to the strict laws of Lilhan, the poaching of griffin eggs was almost entirely non-existent. Some had tried in the past, and few had succeeded, but most who attempted were met with chains and floggings. The worst of the worst were the unlucky few, sentenced to death by Norisk's own personal style of execution: beheading by a griffin. Their beaks were so strong and sharp they could break entire trees in half.

Madysen pitied anyone who met that end, though it was more often than not deserved, a punishment that fit the crime.

As she clasped the egg within her hands, weighing it, she bowed her head once more to the mother griffin, who clicked her beak and rustled her wings. She dared to look down at her friend, who still stood upon that ledge, patiently shifting on her feet.

"How am I going to get down?" Madysen mumbled to herself as she measured the distance between the ledge and the nest. Getting up was hard enough — *this* was the part that got most cadets killed.

"Is everything okay?" Charlotte called. Madysen met her stare, chewing on her lip.

"I might need to stay up here, make this my new home. Unless you can figure out a way for me to get back down," Madysen half-joked.

"Toss me the egg," Charlotte called, placing her own egg safely between a crop of sturdy rocks before holding her hands up, ready to catch the egg.

Madysen considered it for a moment, but deemed it worth a shot — she certainly didn't have any better ideas.

"If you drop it, I'm stealing yours," Madysen called, and Charlotte's answering chuckle was drowned out by the roaring winds.

As Madysen got ready to toss the egg, a crack sounded, and before she could react, the ledge Charlotte stood on began to crumble.

The last thing she saw was Charlotte falling to her death, the golden glint of her egg disappearing into the abyss with her.

Madysen froze. Then she began screaming. But it was useless — Charlotte wouldn't survive that fall, and there was nothing Madysen could have done. She was there and then gone within seconds.

And now, Madysen was all alone.

Alexis had dreaded this day, had tried not to think of it for the past few weeks. The day was made worse when Rampier had announced that she and Rhipley would be travelling to the Mortal Realm together to search for the two Relics it housed, while Amelia and Yazmin would search Xalentya.

Had Alexis been granted the distraction of Amelia and Yazmin's presence, she'd at least have an excuse to ignore Rhipley as much as possible. Now, she'd have no excuse, though she'd still try, anyway.

Rhipley had been respectful these past weeks, hadn't tried to push her boundaries or overstep them. Half of Alexis wished he would, but the other half was grateful.

Amelia had somehow moved past the lies and betrayal, but she'd always been the forgiving type. Alexis, however, didn't have it in her — not right now, anyway.

The only thing she cared about was getting Sam out alive and safe, and getting as far away from this prophecy as she could, duty or no.

As she stood within the courtyard of the Hunter's Guild, wearing her leathers, Alexis shifted uncomfortably on her feet.

Rampier was mumbling something Alexis didn't care to hear. Likely instructions for when they got to Earth. She'd let Rhipley remember them. Let him spearhead this mission.

Yazmin had offered Alexis a hug, and though she'd said it was fine, Yazmin had hugged her, anyway. Then Lukai approached, a sympathetic smile on his gorgeous face.

"Are you going to be okay?" he asked softly, all too aware that Rhipley was likely eavesdropping.

Alexis only nodded, returning Lukai's smile with a tight-lipped one of her own. He sighed before pulling her in for a hug.

She hesitated before throwing her own arms around him.

"I know it's not my place, but just know that he meant well. He always does," Lukai whispered, and Alexis didn't respond.

She'd been forcing her emotions down for weeks now, and she wasn't about to let them slip. She had one goal, and that would be her only focus until it was complete.

Tatiana embraced Rhipley before setting her sights on Alexis. She only dipped her head as she said, "Good luck, and don't get killed."

Alexis allowed herself a small smile. "Thanks for the words of encouragement." As she hugged Aspen, who whimpered, Alexis rose to meet Amelia. Her sister looked like she was five seconds away from bursting into tears, but she wouldn't abandon the mission. No matter how she felt. Alexis pulled her sister in for a tight hug.

"Stay safe. I'll see you again soon, and then we'll rescue Sam, and it'll all be okay," Alexis whispered.

Amelia only nodded, a sniffle escaping her.

When they finally broke apart, Alexis gave Aspen one more pat before stepping to Rhipley's side.

"Good luck," Rampier said, bowing his head to them both.

Alexis smiled, though it didn't meet her eyes, as she accepted Rhipley's hand. Then they vanished, leaving Xalentya, the guild, and their friends behind.

ACKNOWLEDGEMENTS

Working on this first book has been a wild ride, but I did it, and my teenage self, who loved to read and write but could never see it through to the end, would be so proud. I'm excited to continue this series, and, hopefully, many more series in the future.
I want to thank everyone in my life who believed in me and supported me along the way. I'm grateful for everyone who followed me on this journey and constantly reached out to let me know how equally excited they were to read this book.
Thank you to my mother by chance, Tara, who supported me from the very beginning and never failed to express how proud she was of me taking this leap and sticking by it until the end. I love you, and I'm forever grateful for your endless love and support.
Thank you to my beautiful friends, who never failed to message me time and time again, asking when the book will be published, expressing their excitement to read it, and offering their undying love and support every step of the way. Without you, I wouldn't have gotten this far and likely would have given up as I have so many times before.
Thank you to my gorgeous sister-in-law, Kelly, for agreeing to read this long book, despite her busy schedule and newborn baby. Your support and feedback mean the most. Thank you, also, to the rest of my family, who constantly asked about my book, showing their interest and expressing their support.
Thank you to my amazing partner, Royston, for supporting me and loving me through all the doubt and questions and long nights, for seeing how happy writing this book made me, and for constantly showing interest despite never being a big reader yourself. I love you.
And lastly, thank you to Dominique Wall, who, with her very talented mind and hands, painted the cover of this book. Without you, I wouldn't

have gotten this far, truly. Thank you for understanding my vision and bringing it to life.

So, this is for you. The Divinely Blooded book series is for you, my family, my friends, and my loyal audience. I love each and every one of you so very much. The tears, the blood and sweat, the late nights and lunch breaks spent bent over my keyboard, fixing and rewriting countless times. It's all for you.

Here's to many more adventures of Alexis, Amelia, and their friends.

Love, Katriece xo

PRONUNCIATION GUIDE

AGURIS - A-GOO-RISS
ALFLORIAN – AL-FLOOR-EE-EN
ALORA - AH-LAW-RAH
AMARIE - A-MAR-EE
ANSHARA – AH-N-SHA-RAH
ASPAL – ASH-PAUL
AURELIA – OR-EL-IA

BARACARDI – BAR-AH-CAR-DEE
BARDOT - BAR-DOE
BENTHE - BEN-THEE
BRUNDHUL – BROO-N-DOOL
BYAGRAH - BEE-AG-RUH

CALANTHA - CA-LAN-THA
CASHETAN – CAR-SHEH-TAR-N
CHANTI - SHAR-N-TEE
CHRYSANTHI - CHRIS-AN-THEE

D'ROGHAL – DR-ROW-GAL
DAEANIMUS – DAY-AN-I-MUS
DELCE - DELL-SEA
DIVINIUS - DIV-IN-EE-ISS
DONUMAS – DON-OO-MAS
DRAHULL – DRAH-HOO-L
DRESDULL – DRES-DOOL
DUBOIS - DOO-BWAH

ELDOR – EL-DOOR
ELTAPOR – EL-TA-POOR
EQUOIS – EH-KWA
ESKYA – ES-KEE-YA
ESPREN – ESS-PRE-N

FALLANDOR – FAL-EN-DOOR
FENDOR – FE-N-DOOR
FORISTHAVEN – FOR-IST-HAVEN
FUJIN - FOO-JIN

HALDIER – HAL-DEE-AIR
HEDRIL – HEH-DR-EEL
HEREJIA – HEH-REE-JEE-AH
HIRONIA - HERO-KNEE-AH
HYACAN – HIGH-AH-CAN
HYRANDELL – HIGH-REN-DEL

KEIKO - KAY-KO
KOSCHIER – CO-SHE-AIR
KUDRAD – KOO-D-RAD
KUELCADOR – COO-EL-CA-DOOR
KYETA – KEE-YET-AH

LEVETARN – LEE-VE-TARN
LEICHAR - LEECH-ARE
LILHAN – LIL-HAH-N
LUKAI – LOO-KAI
LUZHULA – LOO-ZOO-LA

MAGUS DEPRE – MAH-JIS DEH-PRA
MIKKEL – MICK-ELL
MASHIK – MAH-SH-ICK
MERCERUS - MER-SARE-ESS
MOLLURIE – MOL-OO-REE

NORISK – NOR-ISK

PRONUNCIATION GUIDE

PANJARA – PAH-N-JAR-AH
PELATOR – PEL-AH-TOR
PRESHIA – PR-EH-SHE-AH

QUETHYA – KET-YAH

RAINIER – RAY-KNEE-AH
RAMPIER – RUM-PEE-AYE

SAHATUA – SA-HA-TOO-AH
SANTARA – SAH-N-TARA
SAPHROUGH – SAF-ROW
SHIMA GAI – SHE-MA-GUY
SHURAN – SHOE-RAH-N
SOLARNIA – SOUL-AR-KNEE-AH
SYMANIA – SIM-AH-KNEE-AH

TELASO – TELL-AH-SO
TIETNAM – TYET-NEM
TYEKTAN – TEE-YE-K-TAH-N
TYET - T-YET

URECE – YOU-REH-SEE

VALERIA – VAL-EE-RIA
VELJA – VEL-YA
VENDARATH – VEN-DER-ATH
VUSTOK – VOO-S-TOCK

WYNTERSIER – WINTER-SEER

XALENTYA – ZA-LEN-TEE-AH
XESA – ZEH-SAH
XIOMARA – ZY-OH-MAR-RAH

YU YASHA – YOU-YA-SHA

ZAILAH – ZAY-LUH
ZEPHRYN - ZEFF-RIN
ZEPHYR - ZEFF-EAR

Continue following Alexis and Amelia's story in this thrilling sequel

Available Now

www.ingramcontent.com/pod-product-compliance
Lightning Source LLC
LaVergne TN
LVHW030725250326
834689LV00008B/126